Mark Wanen

OUTBURST

OUTBURST

R.D. Zimmerman

Delacorte Press

Published by
Delacorte Press
Bantam Doubleday Dell Publishing Group, Inc.
1540 Broadway
New York, New York 10036

Library of Congress Cataloging in Publication Data
Zimmerman, R.D. (Robert Dingwall)
    Outburst / by R.D. Zimmerman.
        p. cm.
    ISBN 0-385-32375-1
    I. Title.
    PS3576.I5118O93   1998
    813'.54—dc21   98-18711
                                                        CIP

Manufactured in the United States of America
Published simultaneously in Canada

November 1998
10 9 8 7 6 5 4 3 2 1
BVG

Acknowledgments

Many thanks to those who so generously shared their expertise and encouragement, including investigative reporter Gail Plewacki, producer Cara King, Senior Assistant Hennepin County Attorney Kathryn Quaintance, Sergeant Rob Allen, Dr. Don Houge, Gail and Betsy Leondar-Wright for their insights and wisdom, Ellen Hart, Katie, Lars, Chiara, my wonderful editor Tom Spain, and, of course, the very many transgendered people who've shared their joys, hopes, and triumphs both in a number of books and on the Internet. I tried to get it right, forgive me if I didn't.

OUTBURST

Prologue

Late June

Sex was the last thing on her mind when she'd agreed to help cater the benefit, but it was the first thing she thought of when she saw him.

Dressed in a snug black-and-white uniform, Kris was carrying a tray of canapés—little half-moon pastries filled with smoked duck and a tiny bit of chutney—when she turned from one small group of guests to the next. And there he was, standing in front of the dark-oak bookcase. Tall. Brown hair gone quite silver. Blue suit, blue tie, blue eyes. A strikingly handsome face, perhaps once a bit boyish, now simply and utterly endearing.

She, a born-and-bred Minnesota beauty with short blond hair that she curled to give it height and body, held out the silver-plated tray, found her voice, and said, "Care for an appetizer, sir?"

He turned from a man in a brown suit with whom he was discussing something about the stock market—Up, up, up, isn't it great?—glanced over the platter of beautifully arranged food, then looked at her. And that's what scared Kris, for their eyes met and held on, which in turn sent a rush coursing through Kris's lithe body. She was so quickly aroused that later she would look back on the moment and think that it was as if he'd thrown a switch on in her—no, a circuit breaker, she would silently laugh, because she'd never felt anything so powerful before—but right then and there she concentrated on holding the tray steady. Which proved no easy feat, for he reached for one of the hot canapés and brushed the back of one of his large, warm, hairy hands against her long fingers. Kris tremored as if she were being penetrated—whatever you do, girl, don't drop this fucking tray, 'cause you'll get your ass fired and you need the money, you know you do—then quickly turned.

She was in her early twenties, he had to be in his mid-forties if not early fifties. Surely this guy, whoever he was, was old enough to be her father. Get away, that was all Kris could think of. She looked the innocent sort, but the stark truth was that she'd had trouble enough in her young life, had done more in bed with more guys than most women would do in a lifetime, and so she was wise well beyond her years. She knew what had just happened here, just as she knew it could come to no good.

Escaping from him, Kris continued through the largest home she'd ever been in, a stucco mansion built by some farina heir ninety years ago, a huge butter-cream structure that fancied itself on the hills of Tuscany rather than on the west side of Lake of the Isles in Minneapolis. Kris scurried from the library and into the massive entry hall, a vaulted space with a black-and-white marble floor and now filled with perhaps fifty or sixty guests sipping champagne and munching everything from the smoked-duck pastries to pepper-crusted beef crostini. Only one person, a slim, short man of average looks with what seemed a perpetual frown, had neither food nor drink.

Kris could turn on her manners as easily as she could her coyness, and she extended the tray of hors d'oeuvres to him and said, "Wouldn't you care for something? You've been standing by the front door all evening."

"No," he said, pushing up his glasses with his right index finger and glancing quickly at her. "Not while I'm working."

Such was this law clerk, the host's assistant, who by all accounts was a tad nerdy. Obviously brilliant. Very severe. He'd not only taken it upon himself to welcome each and every guest into the McMartin home—the McMartins, scions of the local newspaper family, were off hiking in Tibet and had loaned out their house for tonight's event—but to oversee virtually every aspect of the event. And back in the kitchen Kris had been forewarned that this guy, not his boss the judge, would be the difficult one to please. In other words, beware the hired pain in the ass.

"Of course," Kris replied, her lips parting into a gentle smile, for she was first and foremost a temptress. "But how will you know if our food is up to your expectations if you don't try anything?"

"Oh, right," he said, focusing on the canapés with workman-like concentration.

Offering him a napkin, Kris added, "The duck ones are my favorite. They're luscious."

After examining them all he chose one and shoved the entire thing into his mouth. When fresh guests suddenly appeared at the door, however, he all but jumped and all but swallowed his food whole. He then quickly, carefully, nervously wiped his right hand and held it out.

"Thank you for coming to the fund-raiser. I'm the judge's law clerk, Douglas Simms."

Turning back to the guests, Kris foisted the rest of her food on several clumps of people, then headed toward the living room. But first she glanced back. No, he hadn't emerged from the book-lined room, wasn't lingering in the doorway, as she had both half hoped and feared. Nothing. That was nothing back there, she told herself. And you should be glad.

Carrying her empty tray, Kris descended two steps into the living room, a huge space that alone was bigger and taller than most houses. There were supposed to be some three hundred people here, which it most definitely seemed there were, to raise money for the Poverty Law Foundation. Kris even recognized some, including the Milquetoast mayor of Minneapolis and a clump of media personalities. Turning, she even saw that gay guy from TV, Todd Mills, who was now trying to bear up as Babs Curtis, the larger-than-life radio personality with the large voice and pearls, was assaulting him with her large banter. Kris even scored a scowl from Ms. Curtis, who, unseen by virtually anyone else, puffed out her chest as if to say, Young lady, you may have gorgeously slim legs, lips like an overripe plum, a nice flat tummy, and the most lascivious of faces, but, girlfriend, those titties of yours are nothing compared to these bazooms. And thank God for that, thought Kris, hurrying along. Sure, she could use a little more chest, but not jugs like those.

She proceeded along the back wall of the living room and past the grand piano, where some bald guy in a tux was playing light classical music that was all but drowned out by the buzz of the crowd.

As she slipped past the Steinway, the musician, who was certainly old enough to be her grandfather, swooned toward her and mouthed, "I love you!"

Shit, she thought with a sour smile, too much makeup. Kris had waitressed before, but she'd never worked a catered party, and she was here only because her neighbor and pal Burt had begged her just three hours ago. Two of our waiters have this summer flu thing, he'd pleaded, I'm beyond desperate!

"This is the biggest contract Travis has ever got," Burt said, referring to his boyfriend, Travis, with whom he owned Peacock Catering. "And every rich person in town is going to be there, because the buzz is that this really isn't about raising money for some stupid foundation. No, they're saying this is really Judge Stuart Hawkins's debutante ball—supposedly he's just a few weeks away from resigning so he can run for governor. We blow this and Travis might as well flush his business down the toilet. We succeed and we'll be catering banquets for the future governor, because if Hawkins does in fact run he's sure as hell going to get elected."

Okay, Kris had said, but how was she supposed to know that you weren't supposed to outshine these matrons, that six o'clock in the evening was much too early for the depth of her eyeliner and the richness of her lipstick? She was only just learning how to tone down her beauty, that only a hint of makeup made her blue eyes and high cheekbones look more classic than cheap. Yes, she with her short blond hair and her slim but regal stature was a real Scandinavian beauty. She knew that for a fact, couldn't help but pass as such.

On the far side of the room Kris climbed two steps and passed through an arch into the dining room. And there he was, so utterly handsome and so obviously waiting in ambush. An empty glass of champagne in one hand, a crumpled napkin in the other, the silver-haired man fixed his eyes on her as steady as headlights on a doe. More than several people noticed, Kris was sure, and this time her pale skin flushed not with desire but with embarrassment.

He took a half-step toward her. His thin lips parted. And Kris ducked to the right, whooshing through a swinging door, passing through a pantry that was lined with fine dishes and crystal glasses, then entering the huge kitchen. Kris swung her doily-covered platter onto the center island and stood there. Oh, shit, why had she agreed to this?

"Whatsamatta, doll face?" asked Travis, dressed fully in chef drag, replete with the tall hat, as he used a pastry bag to squirt a dollop of artichoke mousse on a line of five-dozen toast points. "You look all red. Listen, there's no way in hell you can get sick, too, but if you are, you go down through that door over there. You go into the basement where we got all our extra dishes and you puke down there. Am I clear?"

Kris nodded. "I'm fine."

"Good. Then don't just stand there, get these frigging toast points out of here."

She reached for them.

"No!" screamed Travis. "Get yourself a new doily, Kris! That one's all greasy! And put some parsley in the middle, for Christ's sake!"

Jan, red-haired and voluptuously plump, whooshed in with her empty tray, saying, "Travis, Judge Hawkins loves the phyllo triangles. Got any more?"

"Oh, fuck!" Travis raced to the stove, threw open the door, and pulled out two cookie sheets of spinach-and-feta appetizers, the phyllo darkly browned but not burnt. "Thank God!"

There was no space let alone time to linger in here, so Kris loaded up her tray again, then headed out. Entering the dining room, she scanned the chamber. Flowers, tall and lush and colorful, stood in a vase on the long dinner table. Scattered about on mirrored trays were blanched asparagus spears wrapped in prosciutto, imported cheeses, delicate crackers, and turkey tartlets.

And on a sideboard sat huge silver coffee servers, rotund and steaming.

But he was not about.

Relieved, Kris continued with the job at hand, passing the artichoke mousse on toast points, which—considering this moneyed crowd—were seized with unsophisticated glee. Kris made it only midway into the living room before her fare was gone. She glanced through a group of people, saw the piano player lifting both hands from the keyboard and blowing her a schmaltzy kiss. No one, though, seemed to notice his broadcasted affection or, for that matter, the pause in music, since you could barely hear anything above the din of conversation. Only another hour and a half, thought Kris, and this would be over. These fancy folk would go back to their world, and she would retreat to hers.

When she turned to head back to the kitchen, however, there he was. Kris's heart skipped along like a rock on water, then sank into heavy pounding. He stood in what could only be superficial conversation with a much older man in a double-breasted navy-blue blazer and a gray-haired woman dripping with gold bangles and rock-sized jewels. Oh, shit, thought Kris. She'd always been attracted to older guys, but that had never meant someone over thirty. Yet here was this guy and he was, she swore, the most attractive man she'd ever seen. And when their eyes locked again, this time so briefly, she knew in a flash that they'd both been transported to the same lustful fantasy. Nearly paralyzed, Kris watched as he broke away from his conversation and started toward her, her flushed body telling her mind exactly what she didn't want to hear: Yes, he really wants you.

Forget it, she told herself. Stop it. Not long ago she'd sought her future in California, but instead had discovered trouble, the big kind, when she'd spread her legs for a hot guy. And this, she sensed, was no good, too much the same. She spun the other way, heading not toward the kitchen and another load of canapés, but away from him and out the other end of the packed living room. As she made her way up the two steps, she saw him following. Oh, no. Please. The cumbersome tray in hand, she darted past the judgmental eyes of Mr. Major-Domo by the front door, past the library, down a narrow hall, and to a staircase that curled downward. She glanced back, thought she'd lost him. Just to make sure, though, she descended, following the wooden steps down and into an old entertainment room, which in this grand house had a huge fireplace, wrought-iron light fixtures, dark-oak woodwork, and a billiard table in the middle. Perhaps, thought Kris, she'd be able to hide here until the party was over.

But, no. Footsteps, heavy and sure, on the stairs sounded the alarm. Tossing her silver tray like a Frisbee onto the billiard table, she darted toward a door, pulled it open, and entered a dark, unfinished basement. Kris passed beneath old pipes, dangling wires, while overhead, just atop those heavy beams, the party continued, footsteps clomping, voices laughing, and somewhere— broadcast better down here via vibration—the piano. She came around a corner, entered a workroom filled with old screen windows, a dusty air conditioner, and proceeded to a long workbench covered with a mound of tools and household supplies. She, Kris told herself as she leaned against the bench, was going to get her life in order. That was why she'd fled Los Angeles and returned home. It was about getting away from the dark shadow of that cop and his toxic brother, about healing, about getting her life in order. She deserved to be happy, damn it all. And she deserved a good man.

She froze when she heard his steps glide across the concrete floor.

With a husky tone, he called across the dank room, saying, "You're the most beautiful young woman I've ever seen."

She wanted to cry right then and there, unable to believe that he was seeing her as such. Oh, God, you're not supposed to believe in this kind of guy. The perfect kind, the Prince Charming stud. But he was just that, wasn't he, or shouldn't she at least find out? No, she should bolt away. He had to be like the one back in L.A., nothing but a hurricane of problems. There was another way out of here, wasn't there? A staircase that would lead up to the kitchen?

Yet Kris didn't move. Her back to him, she clutched the edge of the grimy bench and stood there in her tight black waitress uniform, her blond hair flopping into her eyes. As his feet shuffled closer, Kris closed her eyes, bit her bottom lip. She wasn't a whore. She just wanted love. Someone who'd wrap his arms around her and tell her that all the pain she'd already experienced in this short life of hers was done. Over. No more.

And he did just that. He came up behind her—she counted the steps. Five. Kris tensed as if she were about to be attacked, then felt his arms slip around her trim waist and pull her against his strong, warm body.

She started trembling, shaking all over. What was happening here? Couldn't he read her? Didn't he realize that it was she who was the black hole of chaos?

He said, "It's okay."

And by the way he said it she understood that he didn't mean, It's okay, I won't hurt you. No, he meant, From now on everything's going to be fine.

Kris swooned, yet he held her steady. She wanted to stand like this forever, facing a sea of chaos with this mountain of security embracing her from behind. But of course that was impossible, because through their layers of clothing she felt the strength of his erection rise and press up against her ass. In one swift whirl, she spun around, lifted her mouth to him, and they were kissing, her full lips pressing hard against his thin ones. Their tongues exploded and intertwined, and Kris reached beneath his suit coat and clawed at his back, used all the strength her thin arms could muster to pull him closer, closer, closer. She let herself be gobbled up, ran her moist lips over his clean-shaven cheek, drank in his cologne, felt his mouth on her ear. Above the flagrant lust it flashed in Kris's mind: This is it, this is him, this is what I want. He reached down, caressed her tomboyish chest, then leaned over, kissed her neck. And of course, then he reached down, ran his meaty hand down her flat stomach, lower, lower, lower.

She grabbed his hand, said, "No."

"Oh, my God, you're so beautiful." A moment of sanity prodded him. "How old are you?"

"Old enough."

With that his fingers crept down an inch. She clutched his hand more tightly.

"I'm having my period," she pleaded, hoping she wouldn't have to tell him something like she bled a lot. "Please."

His hand was firm and unflinching, but Kris was experienced in these matters, she knew how to do this, knew how to handle the situation, send it careening off in another direction. And so she reached down, felt the hard metal of his belt buckle, felt the fine, thin wool of his pants, felt him rigid and determined. She stroked him once lightly, and he moaned from his gut, shook as if he'd never been touched. Cornered against the bench, Kris slid down. With one hand she rubbed his crotch as lightly as she could, then with the other reached up and popped open his buckle. With one quick tug she ripped out his blue shirt, shoved up his white undershirt, then lunged forward, rubbing her buttery soft cheek against the fur of his stomach.

"Oh, Jesus," he moaned, his hands clawing through her hair.

With one definitive strike, she ripped down his zipper, shoved down his pants, then grabbed at his red plaid boxers and nearly tore them away. He sprang out, and at first she knelt there in awe. Recalling something she'd glimpsed atop the workbench, she reached with her left hand for a jar of petroleum jelly. Yes, she thought as she awkwardly popped open the container and smeared one of her fingers. She was going to take him somewhere he'd probably never been before, somewhere he'd certainly never forget.

"Oh, God," he begged, his voice barely audible, "suck me."

She opened her mouth and drank him up as slowly, as luxuriantly as if she were partaking of the finest Armagnac. Her right hand embraced the base of his shaft, while the other reached down between his legs and crept toward his ass, and all at once he fell forward, bracing himself with both hands on the workbench. He groaned and cried, but then stiffened as he realized the direction of her wayward finger.

"Wh-what are you . . ."

Pulling him out of her mouth, she said, "Do you want to ride the naughty pony?" When it was clear he didn't understand, she added, "I just want to tickle your walnut."

He laughed nervously. "My . . . my what?"

"Your prostate."

"What? How do—"

Her voice all velvet, Kris asked, "Come on, you saw *Last Tango in Paris,* didn't you?"

She glanced up, saw the look of fear, even disgust, but went ahead before he could protest. First she sucked him back up. Next she just did it, she penetrated him. At first he tensed, horribly so, but when she reached her nut-size target it was as if he'd been struck by some erotic lightning bolt. Of course he'd never been taken like this, touched in this hidden corner of delight, that much was clear by the veins bursting in his neck, the deep scarlet color of his face, and his groans, which grew more animallike with each thrust.

And when she was through with him just a few minutes later, after she'd blown him to the moon and sucked him back again, she pulled herself up. The party was still going full force overhead, and he lifted his shorts and pants, then pulled a handkerchief from his breast pocket and handed it to her.

Watching as he made a feeble attempt at tucking in his shirt, Kris wiped her hands and wondered if she'd ever see him again, this dream. Or had that been it, a shot in the dark, so to speak?

"My name's Kris," she volunteered. "What's yours?"

Suddenly the very boyish side of him spread over his face. "You don't know?"

"No. Why should I?"

"Because I'm hosting this party. My name's Stuart. Stuart Hawkins."

Kris tried to speak but couldn't, for there was no way she could tell him. She stared at him, the lust and love and fantasy she'd felt for this most manly man now totally zapped. And then she burst into tears. This dream of a guy was Judge Stuart Hawkins?

She darted to the side, outran his reach.

"Hey!" he shouted.

Kris wouldn't be stopped. She ran out of that dank workroom, charged into the hall where Douglas Simms was now searching for his boss. He spied her through his thick glasses, and his serious face turned all the graver, for he was no dummy, he knew at once what was going on down here.

"Come back!" snapped the aide.

Kris spun around, darted the other way, tore through another door, into another room where Jan and several other servers were down getting more glassware.

"Kris, you okay?" gasped Jan.

Dan, one of the guys, asked, "What happened?"

She saw the bathroom, a little yellow room with a ratty old toilet and sink. She ran in there, slammed and locked the door behind her. Oh, Jesus Christ! She turned and bent over the sink, sobbing as she never had done before.

Dear God in heaven, the most prominent judge in the state, the man who very well might be the next governor of Minnesota, would kill her if he ever found out her deepest secrets, not simply that she'd been castrated in a freak accident, but that her real name wasn't Kris, but Chris. As in Christopher.

Chapter 1

Mid-July

In the following days the headlines would brag how the savage summer storm had descended upon the murder, the city's fortieth of the year, and wreaked havoc upon brutality. But, of course, beyond the chance of a thunderstorm, Todd knew none of what was to come.

It did occur to him that for once the weather guys weren't going to screw up, that the midsummer heat and humidity were about to be doused with rain. As he parked his Jeep Grand Cherokee on the edge of the Mississippi River in downtown Minneapolis, Todd, wearing black jeans and a freshly pressed blue shirt, glanced out the windshield at the skies now looming so dark over the river and to the northwest. It was going to pour, there was no doubt about that. On a hot July night like this it was usually light until nine-thirty or ten—the long days one of the few payoffs these northern parts offered after the long winters—but not tonight. As predicted, something was blowing in from the westerly plains, clouds so black and virulent that they not only blotted out the setting sun, but sucked up whatever light was left of the day. Even as Todd sat there, the streetlights flashed on, and he glanced at the clock on the dashboard, saw that it was seven twenty-five. He just hoped that this guy would be on time, that whatever he had to say would be quick, that this furtive meeting would be over before the skies slit open.

He was just reaching for the door handle when a muffled sound started ringing in his briefcase. Leaning over to the floor in front of the passenger seat, he stuck his hand in his leather case, groped about, then pulled out his cellular phone.

Flipping it open, he said, "Todd Mills."

"Hey, it's me."

"Hey, you. What's up?"

"Just driving around," replied Steve Rawlins, Todd's boyfriend, who was a homicide investigator on the Minneapolis police force.

"Burning up taxpayers' money, are you?"

"Right," laughed Rawlins. "I'm on middle watch until tenthirty," he said, referring to his shift on Car 1110, which was manned twenty-four hours a day, seven days a week by investigators. "Want to get a late bite to eat when I'm done?"

"Sure. I'm meeting this guy—the one I told you about—down at the Stone Arch Bridge. I just parked in the lot in front of the Whitney Hotel, but this shouldn't take too long. In fact, I should get going. I want to get this over with as quickly as I can before it rains."

"Don't forget your phone. I mean, you don't know this guy, do you?"

"Don't worry, Sergeant," joked Todd. "In fact, I bet he doesn't even show—it looks like it's about to pour."

"Well, be careful. Actually, we're having a pretty quiet night, so I'll give you a call in a bit. Hey, and think about where you want to eat."

"You bet."

Todd hung up, slipped his phone into his shirt pocket. He sat there for a moment, told himself he had to stop obsessing about it—Rawlins's health. Everything was going to be okay. Only a few months ago Rawlins had been shot at the Megamall, but he'd recovered just fine. In fact, perfectly. Now the only question was would he survive HIV infection.

Trying to escape the worry, Todd climbed out of the Cherokee into the thick, humid air, which immediately closed in all around him. Breathing with gills would have been easier, he thought, and then wished that he was already in some air-conditioned restaurant having a nice meal and a glass of wine. Looking at the darkening clouds, he started toward the Stone Arch Bridge, a serpentine structure of granite and limestone built over a century ago to carry the trains of the Great Burlington Northern across the Mississippi. According to the various historical markers along the way, the nearly hundred-per-day passenger trains on this route were long gone, and the bridge had recently been converted to pedestrian and bike use. Todd proceeded onto the bridge, his eyes scanning past the massive lock, past the harnessed falls of St. Anthony, and to the purple-black billows of clouds now shimmering and popping with lightning.

He hated this kind of meeting. As Channel 10's investigative reporter he got calls like this every week, each one more odd than the next, first someone going on about a conspiracy to rob the Federal Reserve bank, the next claiming her next-door neighbor had stuffed her poodle down the garbage disposal—never mind the alien sightings, there were so many of those. So when Todd got the call this afternoon, at first he was skeptical. The man on the other end, however, was insistent.

"What do you mean," Todd had interrupted, "someone's blackmailing you?"

"I'll tell you when I see you, but it's very serious. And there's nothing someone like me can do."

Todd made a snap decision and said, "Give me your number. I'll call you right back."

Todd had mumbled something about wanting to go to his office, but the truth of the matter was that Todd wanted to make sure this guy was legit. He'd had something like that before, a guy who claimed he was a doctor when in fact he was nothing more than a patient with a gripe and a thirst for revenge. Todd was going to make that kind of mistake only once.

"No!" the man had replied, his voice all hushed. "Listen, I can't talk anymore. I . . . I just can't. But I swear, this is for real. Meet me tonight in the middle of the Stone Arch Bridge. Seven-thirty."

"But—"

"I need your help. Please . . . just be there tonight."

The line had clicked dead.

And now Todd was here, walking along the broad bridge, wondering if this guy was going to show and what all the drama was really about. Or was this nothing, was Todd merely a fool for being here? No, his job was all about hot stories and great ratings, so he had no choice but to come tonight. WLAK management expected something sharp from Todd at least every six weeks, and he'd passed that milestone last Friday.

He looked beyond St. Anthony Falls and to the north. No thunder, at least not yet, but the black clouds were throbbing, a near continuous pulse of white light. The air was oddly still, too, just the way things got before the shit hit the fan. There hadn't been any mention of severe weather, but when a cold front dropped from Canada and collided over the plains with a warm front from the Gulf of Mexico, anything could happen. A few years back the sirens in Todd's neighborhood hadn't gone off until five minutes after a tornado had Hoovered the better part of a strip mall into the heavens.

Todd didn't like this.

And apparently no one else did, for he looked up and down the bridge and didn't see another soul. Something was going to hit—and soon—and everybody but Todd had the brains not to venture out onto a high bridge over an endless wash of water. A human weather vane Todd did not aspire to be.

He glanced at his watch. Seven twenty-eight. He would give this guy seven minutes and then Todd was out of there.

As he continued to the middle of the bridge, Todd wondered why the hell he'd gotten the call in the first place. Was it his notoriety and his relatively new position as investigative reporter at Channel 10? Or the fact that he was queer?

Because some part of Todd would always be paranoid, he suspected the latter, that this might be some kind of bizarre setup. In his early forties and in great shape—"If you're gonna work in broadcast you gotta keep that chest bigger than your gut," his agent, Stella, continually prodded—Todd had thick brown hair, a handsome face that was a tad broad and a tad rugged except for the eyes, which were soft, too soft for his face. Whereas he used to be extraordinarily closeted, the events of his life had now made him the most visible gay person in Minneapolis, and from time to time he got calls at the station asking him out to dinner. From time to time, too, he got threatening messages on his Voice Mail. Hate mail too. Which is what he feared out here tonight, an attack of some sort. But, no, thought Todd, the tension and worry in the caller's voice had been real, hadn't it?

Reaching the midway point of the bridge, Todd stopped and looked around. Virtually no sign of anyone, male or female. He stared at the falls as they roared over a broad concrete apron the milling giants had built so long ago. Looking straight down more than a hundred feet, the dark, muddy waters of the Mississippi swirled and churned. Next, raising his head, Todd gazed at the glass towers of downtown Minneapolis, huge modern boxes that sprouted like Oz on the plains. Oz, Todd mused, about to be slapped by an evil storm, for the thunder was starting now, not just an occasional burst, but long and steady rumbles. This was going to be a biggie.

Something grasped his right shoulder, and Todd jerked away and spun around. "Jesus!"

Before him stood a young man, twenty-five, maybe thirty, short brown hair poking out from beneath a blue baseball cap. His face was pure, simple, with a lot of color in the cheeks, and there was no doubt about it, he was gorgeous. A plaid shirt concealed his upper body, but even so his strength was more than apparent.

"You're Todd Mills. I recognize you from TV," he said, with a broad smile that showed off bright, white teeth.

He was awfully pretty, this guy, and Todd couldn't help it, couldn't help but wonder: gay? Their eyes caught and held for a millisecond too long, and before Todd had a chance to consciously contemplate the other man's sexuality, his instincts flashed: yes. So what, wondered Todd as he noted that the other man's eyes perfectly matched the blue plaid of his shirt, is this all about?

Todd said, "And you're . . ."

"I'm Mark." He saw the confusion on Todd's face, and added, "Mark Forrest."

A few drops of rain started to fall, and Todd looked at this man, who on the phone this morning had sounded so secretive and confused, yet now appeared so animated, even jovial. Tread carefully, Todd told himself, determined not to be duped either by this guy's good looks or his story, whatever that might prove to be. Who even knew, thought Todd as he double-checked and noted that the other man wasn't wearing a wedding band, if Mark Forrest was his real name.

"So what's up?" asked Todd, glancing over at the clouds and thinking they had but a few minutes before it started pouring.

"Huh?"

"What do you want? Why did you call me?"

Forrest looked at Todd as if he were nuts. "I didn't call you. You called me."

"What?"

"You called and asked to meet secretly with me. Said it was something about a blackmail story."

"No, I didn't. I never called you." Wondering what the hell this was all about, Todd said, "I got a call this morning from a guy who said someone was blackmailing him. I'm presuming that was you."

"What?" Forrest said with a confused grin. "Fuck, no. I got no secrets."

He studied this Mark Forrest, saw the wholesomeness leaking out his pores, and Todd's instincts told him that Forrest was telling the truth. Yes, he was part of the younger generation, the young gay guys who'd never considered the closet and had always been out, easily and naturally so. Which meant only one thing. Then again, this wasn't the first time something like this had happened, nor would it be the last.

"Come on," said Todd as the rain started coming down in large pellets. "Someone set us up."

"But—"

"Let's just get out of here. My car's over there. We'll figure it out."

Out of nowhere a huge gust of wind exploded over them, and in an instant the rain was hitting as hard as if it were being sprayed from a fire hose. A burst of lightning struck just up the river, followed almost immediately by a deafening explosion of thunder.

Todd lifted his arm up to shield his face from the pelting water, opened his mouth to speak, but suddenly an enormous sound drowned him out, a wail that rose and continued in desperate warning. Shit, you didn't grow up in the Midwest without knowing what that meant, without knowing that the only time it was safe to hear sirens like those was the first Wednesday of the month at 1:00 P.M.

Scanning the skies for a funnel cloud, Todd grabbed Mark Forrest by the arm and, above the ever-increasing wind, shouted, "We gotta get out of here!"

Forrest hesitated just a moment, that was all. Then the two of them turned, started toward the downtown side of the river. Todd was already soaked, but with any luck they could make it safely to his car. As he took a step forward, however, a huge blast of wind blew him off-balance. Oh, my God, thought Todd, is this really a tornado? A dazzling and deadly lightning bolt struck a lamppost not fifty feet in front of them, followed instantly by thunder so loud that Todd could feel the force of the sound reverberate in his chest. Shielding his eyes with his right hand, Todd looked up, saw the blackened lamppost tip off the bridge and blow to the turbulent waters below. The wind, Todd realized as the two of them struggled along, was coming from the right, whooshing down the river from the northwest and growing stronger by the second.

Glancing toward downtown, Todd saw nothing, not a single light. All of the buildings were gobbled up by the darkness, swallowed by the rain and clouds and wind. Jesus, just how bad was this going to be?

Suddenly a figure in a hooded yellow slicker emerged out of nowhere, someone small, someone running desperately along the Stone Arch Bridge. Another fool, thought Todd, as Mark and he charged on, their heads bowed against the torrent. Someone else looking to get killed.

A huge gust came up, Mark lost his footing, and with a wide grin, this cowboy of a guy screamed, "Holy shit!"

The approaching man was struck by the same gust, and he swerved and caught himself on the railing. Clasping the hood over his head with his left hand, he rushed on, nearing Todd and Mark.

Another burst of wind blew back the guy's jacket, and it was then that Todd saw it, the glint of metal. An umbrella, thought Todd, useless in such a storm and folded up for safekeeping. The rain pelted Todd's face, and he closed his eyes, opened them, struggled to see.

White light burst all around them and the skies exploded like a bomb. Suddenly that other person was swerving right at them. Stumbling toward them like a drunk as he reached into his jacket. Dear God, thought Todd, wiping at his eyes. That was no umbrella, that was a gun.

"Look out!" screamed Todd into the roar of the storm.

Forrest, still grinning, glanced at Todd, wiped the water from his face, and shouted back, "What?"

Todd pointed at the assailant, but Mark Forrest never really saw what was happening, never understood. There was another explosion, this one from the gun, and in a split second a bullet slammed into Forrest's deep chest. It threw him back and he stumbled across the bridge. Clutching the railing for support, Mark Forrest looked down at himself, saw the watery blood washing down his chest, next looked up at his killer, and only then perhaps realized what this was all about.

As Todd started to rush to Forrest, he froze. The small man was whipping around, his yellow slicker a blur as he trained his pistol on Todd. Reflexively, Todd threw himself to the side, fell as he scrambled to escape, and behind him heard the single burst of a gun.

And then the heart of the storm struck them all.

Todd tried to stand up, to rush farther away, but was blown on his side like a twig. As he landed in a puddle, he glanced back, saw the assailant hurled aside by the wind. A wall of water seemed to crash over Todd, rain that bit and pelted so hard that he could barely see two or even three feet. He looked to the side, thought he saw Mark Forrest somehow hanging on to the railing. And still the wind gained in strength, barreling down the river, blasting everything in its path. Todd crawled to his knees, tried to stand, and thought for sure this was it, he was going to be sucked into the skies. He threw himself to the side, grabbed at the base of a lamppost, and hung on, hoping to hell that just this once he was stronger than Mother Nature. Above it all, he heard a rattling and ripping and raised his head to see a sign, one of the historical markers, blown from its stand. As it came hurtling at him, Todd clutched his head, but it wasn't enough, for the sign struck him with such force that Todd's head seemed to explode. He tried to open his eyes but couldn't, and the massive summer storm went from dark and overpowering to totally black and quiet.

Chapter 2

As soon as the elevator chimed and the doors eased open, the man rushed out of the lift and down the hotel hall, his wet head bowed, his chest heaving. He reached into the pocket of his jacket, felt for the plastic room key, pulled it out, then slipped it into the lock of his room and opened his door.

Shit, he was wet, for nothing had prepared him for the ferocity of the storm. In fact, he thought, carefully locking and bolting the door behind him, he was as wet as if he'd just jumped into a swimming pool. They rarely had storms like that where he came from, and certainly not with that kind of thunder and lightning.

Water dripped onto the maroon carpet from his raincoat as he hurried past the sleek bathroom, past the sliding mirrored doors of the closet, and into the spacious room that was lined on one side with a single huge window. His hands shaking, he pulled off his coat and dropped it on the edge of the messy bed, then made directly for the dark-wooden desk, where he pulled open a center drawer. He grabbed a piece of the Hotel Redmont's tasteful stationery, reached to the top of the desk for one of the hotel's ballpoint pens, then hesitated one single moment. Yes, he thought, his heart thumping, his head pounding. There'd been no other choice. He had to be enterprising. Yes, *enterprising,* and so with trembling hands he scribbled it down: *GMF.* Absolutely. No doubt about it. And he wrote it down again and again. *GMF. GMF. GMF. GMF.*

Satisfied that he'd done everything right, he dropped the pen and turned to the window, which was sealed as tight as a fish tank.

Lifting aside the thin white curtain in front of the glass, he looked out at the clearing skies, at the strong light bursting through the clouds. No one had seen him down there by the river, had they? No, he was positive. The dark energy of the storm had blotted everything out, provided the perfect shield. Still . . .

He had medium-brown hair, skin that tanned easily, and a thick shadow of a beard, which he'd shaved once in the morning and trimmed up again with an electric razor before dinner. His broad shoulders made him look bigger than he really was, but he wasn't overweight, not by any means. With a tight waist and trim but strong legs, he was still in great shape, particularly for his mid-thirties, which was the primary reason he'd been able to make it back here so quickly. He'd all but run the entire way from the Mississippi.

Letting the curtain fall, he turned to the king-size bed, started toward it, then froze, staring at the sheets and blankets that were kicked and pushed and shoved this way and that. Jesus Christ, just a mere hour or two ago the two of them had been in this bed, kissing and groping and sucking, two sex-starved men feasting on flesh and seed. Only now did he see how horrible it was, how stupid, the meeting, the act, the fuck. If only he'd been able to resist. If only he'd been able to bottle up the temptation and stuff it away. To abstain once and for all and forever. But, no, he hadn't been able to stop himself, nor the sin.

Shaking his head, he thought it again, chanted silently: *GMF*.

And then it happened—the phone rang. Glancing at his watch, he knew exactly who it was, knew that she'd be calling to check on him. Yes, he'd made it back just in time.

As he reached for the phone—hesitant yet knowing he had no choice but to answer the damn thing—he couldn't help but think: Dear God in heaven, why had he ever fallen in love with a beautiful young man by the name of Mark Forrest?

Chapter 3

Todd had no idea how long he lay there, ten, maybe fifteen minutes, but when he began to stir, the thing that surprised him the most was the light. It was so bright. Lying in a shallow puddle, Todd stared through the railings of the bridge at the gap in the billowing clouds, where he saw the setting sun, brilliant and gorgeous and red. He rolled on his side, looked around. What the hell had that been? A tornado?

He pushed himself up, sat back, and leaned against the railing. Right next to him, lying in a shallow puddle, was the sign, the historical marker that had walloped him. Rubbing his head, he started to read the text, which went on about hard winter wheat that was shipped from all over the Upper Midwest to the mills located alongside St. Anthony Falls.

Above the roar of the river, Todd heard it, the steps. Someone was running this way. He clenched his eyes shut, pressed the heel of his hand against his brow, tried desperately to make sense of this. Hearing someone close in on him, he opened his eyes, looked to his right, saw a huge sign towering in the distance that read PILLSBURY'S BEST FLOUR.

Something horrible had happened, he knew that much. But what? In the back of his mind he heard the warning: Be careful. Right. And recalling that, Todd reached up, felt his breast pocket. The phone. He fumbled around for it, pulled it out, and flipped it open. But what was the number? Who was he supposed to call?

The running steps were zeroing in on him, and Todd pressed

himself back against the railing. Phone in hand, he glanced to his left, saw the figure charging this way.

Wait, he knew that person, that man. And Todd knew what this meant, didn't he? Hadn't he told him where he'd be? Sure, and Todd was glad to see him, this guy with the dark brown hair and mustache, who was stocky and muscular, none too tall.

He knelt down to Todd and reached out, saying, "Are you all right?"

Todd clutched his hand. "Rawlins."

"Are you hurt?"

"I don't think so." Todd touched his head. "Something hit me." He lowered his hand into the cool puddle and touched the plaque. "This sign—it blew from the other side."

"There was a big storm."

Todd stared at the break in the sky and squinted into the bright sunlight. Huge, puffy clouds towered one atop another. Neither white nor black, but now a sunset-infused red, the clouds filled the entire sky. Beautiful.

Todd said, "A tornado."

"Actually, the radio's already calling it straight-line winds."

"Oh," mumbled Todd, realizing that would explain the hurricane force of the storm.

"Come on," said Rawlins, taking Todd by the arm. "Are you sure you're okay?"

Todd nodded as he started to get up.

"What about the guy you were supposed to meet? He didn't show, did he?"

Todd's heart squeezed into a tight fist. He pulled himself all the way up, hung on to the railing, and looked down the bridge to the east. There was no one else sprawled about, and as the memory came flooding back, he turned and looked out over the surging Mississippi.

"Oh, shit," muttered Todd.

"Are you all right? Do you want to sit down again?"

"Someone was shot."

"What?" snapped Rawlins, quickly scanning the bridge. "What the hell are you talking about?"

"I . . . I . . ." He shook his head. "I met some guy and . . . and someone else came and . . ."

Dear God, he thought, realizing the most amazing thing of this most unusual evening: Not only had the short man with the gun vanished, so had the body of Mark Forrest.

Chapter 4

For years—really ever since the accident that had maimed her genitals—Kris had been made to feel that there was no place for her in this world. Laughed at and mocked as if some kind of freak, rejected and shunned as if some kind of leper, there had been times when suicide seemed not only like a good idea, but the only isle of safety. But, no, the truth was that while she'd been depressed, at times severely so, she possessed no real thirst for her own death. And, no, she wouldn't be defeated by the judgment of others, of that she was more determined with each passing day.

Still, she couldn't deny that things were a fucking mess. And when she turned her boat of a car off Lyndale Avenue, then finally brought the thirty-year-old Oldsmobile Ninety-Eight to a clunk of a stop, she couldn't help but bow her head on the steering wheel and sob. When in the name of God would things start getting easier?

It was nearly ten o'clock and dark. And wet, of course. That huge storm, the likes of which Kris had never seen, had doused everything, including her. Hours later, her white blouse still clung damply to her back, and her black jeans were still bunched with moisture. On her car radio she'd heard the disc jockey call the storm something like straight-line winds, but what the hell did that mean?

Through her tears she looked up at the little ticky-tacky white house, a mere box of a thing stamped out in this postwar neighborhood on the southernmost edge of Minneapolis. Replicated in mind-boggling numbers, there was nothing but the same house for blocks, this one white, that one blue, that one mustard, and Kris thought, Shit, what am I doing here? She'd come back to Minnesota, hoping everything would be different, that she could pack her trusty Olds with her few belongings, leave California and her woes behind, and find not only safety back in the Heartland, but answers. And solutions. What a fool. Instead, here she was in the blandest, most boring corner of the world, and her troubles had merely hitched a ride along. Oh, Christ, she thought. Of all places, why here?

She wiped her eyes with the back of one of her long hands, blotted at her nose, and glanced at herself in the rearview mirror. Girlfriend, she thought, you look like shit warmed over. But who cared? No one. And that was exactly the point, for at best everyone found her a beautiful freak.

Kris heaved open the big old door of the car, stepped out, and her shoe immediately sank into a puddle. She cursed and cussed, skipped to the curb, and forgot about her stuff in the trunk, which was latched shut with a twisted coat hanger stuck through a couple of rust holes. As she climbed the walk and approached the front door, she heard a television and voices, little ones, all of them blaring away. Crap. She'd hoped they'd all be in bed by now, God only knew they should be. Much too late for young things like that to be up. Had her cousin lost her mind?

There was no way Kris could face anyone, especially them, and she turned, quietly slunk past the two living room windows and around to the side door. With her key she unlocked the door, carefully opened it, and stepped inside and onto the landing. The kitchen was to her right, up just two steps, and while the light was on over the range, no one was in there. Flicking on the basement light, Kris hoped she could simply disappear unnoticed into her room downstairs. She grabbed the handrail, took one step, another.

"Kris?" called a voice. "Kris, is that you?"

"Krissy! Krissy!" cried a couple of little voices.

From the other room her cousin continued, demanding, "What are you doing sneaking in the back?"

Kris froze on the fourth step and muttered, "Oh, fuck."

There was a stampede of feet, and they were there within seconds, Maureen and her four-year-old twins, Ricky and Rachel. Kris quickly ran a hand through her hair and tried to make herself presentable, which, however, was hopeless.

"Yeah, it's me," replied Kris, her voice deep.

"Where have you been? I thought you were coming straight home from your therapy appointment," said Maureen, appearing on the landing. "You saw Dr. Dorsey, didn't you? You didn't skip again, did you? You've already missed one out of your first three sessions, and I'll bet he'll drop you if—"

"Don't worry, I was there."

"Well, then, where have you been since? Do you realize how worried I've been about you? I mean, that storm—there're trees down everywhere!"

"The 'lectricity went out!" exclaimed Rachel.

"We lit candles!" added Ricky.

Kris turned and glanced up at her cousin, who was a good ten years older than her, a good deal heavier, and simply not as pretty. Maureen had similar blond hair, but somehow it wasn't as pure, as soft, not as bright, and her eyes weren't nearly as blue or sparkly as Kris's either.

Maureen took an equally judgmental assessment of Kris, then grabbed the children by their shoulders and shooed them out. "You two go back and watch the end of your movie!"

"But—" they whined in unison.

"Now!" ordered Maureen, who scooted them out, then turned on Kris. "Your appointment with Dr. Dorsey was supposed to end at six. What the hell have you been doing since?"

An interrogation was not what she wanted, and Kris said, "Not much."

"You look like hell. What happened?"

"Nothing."

"Right, you expect me to believe that?" Maureen started down the steps. "No one hurt you, did they? You're all right, aren't you?"

"I'm fine. I just had a bad night, that's all."

"I was expecting you hours ago. You're soaking. Where have you been?"

"Just out. Out walking."

Maureen shook her head in disapproval. "Where?"

"Shit!" snapped Kris, her voice losing its femininity and becoming deep and harsh. "You're worse than my own mother! I didn't move all the way to this stupid place to be interrogated by some stupid cow like you!"

Maureen's eyes flared in anger. "And I didn't agree to open my house to some ingrate like you!"

Tears instantly blossomed in Kris's eyes. "Just fuck off! And don't worry, I'll be out of here soon enough!"

With Maureen screaming a string of unpleasantries behind her, Kris turned and bolted down the stairs as fast as she could. She rushed across the red linoleum floor, reached the dark-pine door to her bedroom, opened it, then slammed it shut as hard as she could. There was no doubt about it, everyone—men and women, straights and gays—found her too "different" and because of that somehow threatening. She felt as if she was walking on a tightrope with no safety net beneath her, and everyone down below, including all her family—her brothers and sister, her mother and father—were looking up at her and chanting: "Fall!"

So could they be right? Was she really that bizarre, that atrocious?

No, girl, came her internal reply, you're not. You're not at all. Just don't, don't, don't give in. Just remember all of your sisters out there in this great big universe.

Right. When she was in California Kris had used a friend's computer, surfing the Internet day after day, week after week. Discovering a worldwide community, she realized for the first time that she wasn't alone, that there were hundreds of thousands if not millions of transgendered people just like her. She'd made friends on the Net, shared stories, laughed, cried, and confessed, all the while learning what estrogens were the best, where to buy shoes for her long feet, and exactly how doctors used the skin from the penis to construct a vulva and a vagina.

Yet now she was here in this Minnesota, without a computer

and cut off from that new world. Consequently, she felt more isolated and alone than ever before.

It was a tiny room with dark-pine paneling and a single bed, on which Kris now dropped herself. She bowed her face into her hands and tried to hold back the tears. She was such a fool, such an idiot. She never fell in love with anyone her own age, only guys a lot older than she. Oh, and straight. Often married to boot. It was just like her shrink had told her: She went for the guys she could never have, the ones that were perpetually and eternally unavailable. But did she listen to that? Learn anything? Hell, no, for here she'd done it again, fallen crazy in love with a guy she could never have. What was even more stupid was that late this afternoon she'd gone and blurted it out to her shrink.

Seated in his small office downtown, Kris had said, "You're never going to believe who I have a crush on."

"Try me," replied Dorsey, a small man with thick gray hair and heavy glasses that did little to mask his intense eyes.

"Stuart Hawkins. You know, the judge, the one who's in the paper all the time. He's just so . . . I don't know . . . so sexy. I can't stop thinking about him."

Dorsey had sat in his hard wooden chair for a long time, those beady eyes not blinking, his thin lips not moving. Or had he been trying to stuff his amusement? Had that been it? The very possibility had made Kris so pissed that she'd almost blurted it out, told him that just a couple of weeks ago she'd finger-fucked the good judge.

But then Dorsey had muttered his usual nonjudgmental, nonindicative grunt, saying only, "Oh."

And Kris had tapped every bit of her considerable will to be silent, because, no, she guessed Dorsey wouldn't have believed her. At best, he'd just chalk it up as another of her fantasies, all too many of which focused on so-called straight-acting, straight-appearing fatherly types. Could she help it if she just wanted a good lay from a solid hunk?

Blotting her eyes, Kris pushed herself to her feet, then crossed to the small half-bath, a tiny room packed into one corner of her bedroom. Kris stepped in, flicked on the light, and looked at herself in the mirror of the minute medicine cabinet. Ew. Nasty. She saw hair that was wet and tousled, puffy red eyes, and a face that was definitely not male, one that was in fact becoming less so by the day. While she'd always have her small Adam's apple—which neither surgery nor drugs could ever eliminate— the months of hormone therapy had already had an amazing over- all effect. In that way she was lucky: Because her testicles had long ago been removed, she wasn't having to take large doses of es- trogen to suppress testosterone production. And as soon as she'd started taking it orally, she had been quick to see breast develop- ment, a softening of her skin and body, not to mention the im- provement in her complexion, which had cleared so beautifully. The estrogen had even aided in the effectiveness of the facial electrolysis she'd had out in California. Now rubbing her smooth chin and cheeks, she recalled the Cadillac of treatments she'd endured, which had cost a whopping four thousand bucks and had been paid for entirely by her transgender mentor, a wealthy heir- ess and sometime lawyer who'd already done likewise. Kris had been unsure at the time, but the procedure, which had lasted seventy-one and a half horribly painful hours, had been definitely worth it.

She reached for her makeup bag, rumbled through her cos- metics, and the first thing that came to hand was, oddly, her old double-headed razor, now crusted with rust and so dull the blade would barely cut butter. Holding it between her long painted fin- gernails—fake fingernails, naturally, because the night of the infa- mous accident she'd also lost the tips of three fingers—she wondered why she'd never thrown it away, at the same time real- izing she never would. It was true: Once she'd been so desperate to escape her problems and this world that she'd considered sui- cide. A few years back she'd held this very same razor much as she did now. Back then, however, she'd popped out the blade and pressed it against her left wrist. All she'd had to do was apply a little pressure, cut through her skin, and bleed out. After all, she'd thought that night, wasn't a miserable fate like that the destiny of every weirdo like her?

But then she'd stopped, suddenly realizing what it all meant.

And suddenly angry for the first time in her young life, furious that she'd been pushed that far, to the very brink.

It was true: The only image she'd ever seen of someone like herself was, over and over again, the one straight society had presented, that of the sick, psycho killer who had no place in this world. But did she really hate herself that much, was she really so evil, so horrible? Absolutely not! And so the very next instant she'd taken back her life, calmly lifting the blade from her wrist and putting it back in the razor, if only to say one thing and one thing alone: Fuck 'em.

"Krissy!" now called a tiny voice.

Shocked back into the present, Kris spun around.

"Mom says she's sorry," said Rachel, standing in the middle of the bedroom in an oversize T-shirt. "Will you read me the story?"

"Oh, honey, I don't know, I—"

"Come on, please!"

"But I had such a long day."

"Krissy, you didn't finish the story last night, the one about the owl."

Kris stared down at the girl, saw her straight hair curling just at the ends, the face all round and hopelessly angelic. Wasn't that the kid she was supposed to have been?

"Okay, okay . . ." said Kris with a smile. "I'll be right there."

"No, come on. Come with me now," begged Rachel, stepping into the bathroom and wrapping both of her tiny hands around the wrist Kris had once wanted to slit.

"Sure, sweet thing."

Setting the rusty razor down on the edge of the sink, Kris looked quickly at her image in the mirror. Screw the system, she thought as she was led away. Screw the programmed system that says you have to be one or the other, *M* or *F*.

Chapter 5

"I'm not crazy," said Todd. "I saw someone get shot."

The day after the storm, the day after Mark Forrest—if indeed that was his real name—had vanished, Todd stood on the Stone Arch Bridge, staring through the haze at the roaring falls of St. Anthony. The mighty Mississippi was all the mightier from last night's torrential rains, and a continuous wall of water burst over the concrete apron, rushed and swirled its way toward the inevitable gulf.

Todd felt a hand on his back, and then heard Steve Rawlins say, "I'm sure you did." Nodding to the sheriff's boats anchored down below and the handful of divers, Rawlins added, "And I'm sure they'll find the body soon."

The air was close and hot, a slight rain was falling, and Todd pulled up the collar of his shirt. "This just doesn't make any sense."

Last night Rawlins had taken charge because, of course, he and his partner, Neal Foster, were in Car 1110, meaning that as the homicide investigators on duty the case was automatically theirs. The trouble was that at first there'd been no indication of any crime—no gun, no bullet casing, not to mention any sign of a body. Thanks to the heavy rains, there hadn't even been any visible traces of blood. Insisting, however, that this be thoroughly handled, Rawlins had called Car 21, the Bureau of Investigation team, and the guys on duty in that division had gotten out their pump bottle of luminol and sprayed the chemical on part of the bridge. As the summer light had faded, they'd then shone a black light on the spot and certain proteins had fluoresced, indicating blood and plenty of it. A full investigation had been immediately set in motion.

And now a bunch of divers were down there bobbing for a body.

"I was standing right here," began Todd, hanging on to the railing, "wondering if anyone would show."

"Okay." Rawlins was a rugged kind of guy, who was nevertheless naturally patient, thorough. "Go on. Just take it slow."

"And then someone came up behind and touched me. It was him, this guy, this Mark Forrest."

"The mysterious Mr. X. We're still searching, but no one by that name has been reported as missing."

"Well, this guy, whatever his name was, was no bum. I got the sense that he was gay, but I could be wrong. Anyway, he was gorgeous, and someone's going to want him back, someone's going to come looking for him. You can trust me on that one."

"He said he was here because you called him?"

"Right. And I was here because I got a call from someone, a guy, who said something about blackmail." Todd shook his head. "So obviously there was some sort of setup going on."

"I guess so." Rawlins scratched his neck and asked, "Do you think the whole shooting could have been staged somehow?"

"What do you mean?"

"You know, fake bullet, an old bag of blood. A scam of sorts for a television reporter."

"Maybe, but why? I can't think how it would connect to any of the stories I'm working on. Not even the one about the drug dealers in the suburbs." Recalling the look on Mark Forrest's face, he added, "I haven't seen that many people shot, but it sure as hell looked real to me. And Forrest certainly didn't look like some kind of shyster. If anything, he seemed very genuine."

For the third or fourth time they walked through exactly what had happened. And where. Todd was sure of the exact spot he'd been standing when Forrest had approached him. He was able to recall what they'd done as soon as the rain had started pelting down. He remembered, too, when he'd first seen the approaching figure.

"Then the wind hit," said Todd. "It just came roaring down the river with nothing to block it. I thought it was a tornado."

But it hadn't been. There hadn't been any great vortex, no massive twirling wind sucking everything upward. Rather, it had been the nearly as destructive straight-line winds, which were brought by derechos, a phenomenon of squall-line thunderstorms that sent blasts of cold air hurling downward in a straight, broad, destructive swath. And yesterday's sheer wall of force had bowled over the plains at, according to weather experts—which every other person in Minnesota considered himself to be—nearly one hundred miles per hour and dumped over two inches of rain in ten minutes.

"So the last time you saw Mark Forrest," Rawlins said as he moved to the railing on the other side of the bridge, "he was standing here."

"Clutching the bullet wound." Todd ran over the sequence in his mind. "Then that sign hit me and I blacked out for a few minutes."

So as best they could figure, one of three things had taken place. Mark Forrest had been blown into the river. The person who shot him had dragged away his body. Or it had been a total ruse and no one had been killed.

Todd crossed to the metal railing, which was tall, nearly chest high, and said, "But I don't get how anyone could have been blown over this. I mean, maybe if that had been a tornado he could have been sucked up and dumped into the river. But the wind just came hard from one side, so if anything it would have just pinned him against the railing, not thrown him up and over. And the guy with the gun wasn't very big, I'm sure of that, so if he'd dragged Forrest away there would have been bloodstains or drag marks or . . . or something."

"Yeah, the B of I guys did a pretty good job of going over the entire bridge," said Rawlins, for they had combed everything, including the parking areas on either side of the river. "Here's another possibility: The assailant dumped the body over the railing while you were blacked out."

"Perhaps."

Peering down at the small fleet of boats and the turgid water, Todd considered that possibility, thinking how it was the one scenario that made the most sense. But if that were really the case, if Forrest had been heaved into the Mississippi, where was the body and when would this vast river give it up? The current was swift here, with swirls of root-beerlike foam curling and turning, and Todd gazed from one bank to the other. On his right the ruins of the Gold Medal flour mill towered in the haze like an abandoned castle, on the left stood an amalgamation of dark brick buildings, while straight ahead, maybe a half mile downstream, the murky waters churned over another dam and through another lock. If the body of Mark Forrest were really in the Mississippi, would the divers be able to find it, or had it disappeared permanently into the mucky bottom?

Todd stared down at one of the columns of the bridge and said, "If he'd been tossed over, it would have been somewhere around here. Maybe he would have struck the side of the bridge, but I don't see any blood."

"Neither do I," seconded Rawlins, who stared through the haze at a small group of cops combing the far bank. "We should probably check out the next lock, see if there's anything hung up down there."

"That's a pretty thought."

Rawlins walked down the bridge about fifty feet to the spot where his partner, Neal Foster, stood leaning on the railing and watching the sheriff's divers far below. Nearing sixty, bald, and paunchy, Foster had been on the force forever and was one of the more respected investigators around. Three years ago when his partner had retired, he'd brought Rawlins from the juvenile division into homicide when they'd been working on a bridge case, a juvenile homicide. Rawlins now spoke briefly with him, Foster shrugged, and Rawlins headed back to Todd.

"Foster's going to stick it out here," said Rawlins. "Come on."

As the rain misted them, they walked briskly toward the downtown bank of the river.

"Thanks for taking this so seriously," said Todd, gently squeezing Rawlins on the arm.

"Thank God you weren't hurt."

"No shit. Do you think the police would have been so thorough about this if you weren't involved?"

"I sure as hell hope so. After all, the luminol did show blood—and a lot of it too," said Rawlins. "But don't forget, they know you. You're Mr. TV. Actually, one of the guys wondered if this wasn't a drill, a test to see if they were really doing their job."

"You mean they were worried it was part of some exposé or something?"

"Exactly."

Todd shook his head, said, "Everyone's jaded, aren't they?"

Rawlins shrugged. "Especially me."

"Enough of that."

"Oh, that's right. I'm supposed to be happy and hopeful."

"Just positive," said Todd, instantly regretting his choice of words.

With a dark laugh, Rawlins looked over his shoulder to make sure no one could overhear—on the force and everywhere else he was out about his sexuality, but most definitely not about his health—then said, "That's the one thing I wish I could forget."

Back in the parking lot, they left Rawlins's Taurus and proceeded in Todd's dark-green Grand Cherokee. This next stretch of the Great River Road, a riverside parkway with a road, bike path, and pedestrian path, had yet to be completed, and so he turned just past the renovated mill that housed the Whitney Hotel. Heading by another mill, a now-desolate building where sluices had once powered looms that had woven blankets by the thousands, he came to Washington Avenue and turned left. Neither one of them had ever been down to the next lock and dam, so neither one of them knew how to get down there. With the windshield wipers swiping slowly back and forth and the air conditioner on high just to thin the thick air, Todd took one turn, which ended in a dead end. Struggling to see through the slow rain, Rawlins suggested another road, which led past a liquor store and ended at some railroad tracks. In the end, Todd decided to drive to the west bank of the University of Minnesota.

"The parkway starts again down there," he said. "I think we can park down on the flats and walk up toward the next lock."

"Great. That'll give us a good look at the river too."

Where once had stood a shantytown inhabited by dirt-poor Scandinavian immigrants, where later had been piled an enormous mountain of coal used by the U, now stretched a new portion of the river parkway. Todd drove down a steep road that led to the river, turned left, and entered one end of a long public lot that had recently been constructed. He drove toward the end, parked, and he and Rawlins got out and plugged the meter with a couple of quarters.

The rain fell in an annoying tempo between a mist and a light drizzle, not something that called for an umbrella, but enough to dampen everything. Todd glanced across the river, which was none too wide at this point, and looked up the tall, ragged limestone cliff at the university buildings on the east bank. This definitely felt like an old river, one that had been cutting itself deeper and deeper into the earth for thousands of years. And this area definitely felt like a lost part of the city, something hidden away like a scruffy, shameful child. The city in its own sluggish way was trying to reclaim the Mississippi, turn it from a workhorse of water power and barge traffic into a recreational treasure. When the parkway was completed, when the road and paths were extended upriver another mile or two to the Stone Arch Bridge, that just might happen too. In the meantime, though, this was an obscure place, unknown to most, used by an anonymous few. Todd heard a car, looked over his shoulder, and saw a rusty white Honda Civic station wagon pulling into a far corner. So what was their story, that man and woman in the front seat, what were they doing down here on such a dreary day?

The parkway simply stopped, a band of pavement that ended and immediately turned into dirt. Random young trees sprouted every which way, and Todd and Rawlins cut through them and made their way to a hidden beach. Todd pushed aside some branches, came upon some sand, and walked right up the quickly moving water.

"You know," he said, staring at the water, "we drink the water from this river every day, but I don't think I've ever been this close to the river itself. I don't think I've ever been to a place where I could just stick my foot in it." He looked straight up, saw an abandoned steel train trestle towering way overhead and covered with graffiti. "Many jumpers?"

Rawlins shrugged. "A couple or three every year, usually in winter when they're guaranteed a quick death. Some guy jumped off this one, what was it, last March. Smashed right through some ice floes."

"How long did it take to find his body?"

"Almost two weeks."

"Where?"

"Downtown St. Paul. Got hung up on one of the houseboats."

"So it could take that long or longer," suggested Todd, "for Mark Forrest's body to turn up."

"If in fact it does surface."

Right, thought Todd, because certainly not everything that tumbled into the Mississippi actually rose to the top. Mark Forrest's body, after all, could be pinned anywhere down there, including against the base of the lock and dam where it could remain . . . well, until there were no remains.

They continued up a dirt path and into some heavier growth. The river bent, and up ahead Todd could make out the Tenth Avenue bridge as well as that of Interstate 35W. If there was no body, if no one had been killed, Todd tried to conjure what this might be all about. The biggest story he was working on, of course, was about the suburban drug scene. After repeated attempts, he'd finally gotten a couple of dealers to talk to him; as long as their faces were concealed they agreed to have the conversation taped.

"Shit, man," said one dealer, who'd recently moved up from Gary. "These people up here are shit crazy for drugs. I'm selling ten times more than I was back home."

"Fuck the inner city," said another, seated in the front seat of a Channel 10 van, his face concealed by the headrest as he was

taped from behind. "Those folk can't afford squat. The only business worth doing is in the suburbs, because that's where the white
folk with money live. That's why I set up shop out there. You gotta
go where the money is, man, and that's the suburbs."

But how, Todd now wondered, could a faked death tie into
that? Was someone trying to frame Todd for a murder? But why?
The paranoid side of Todd, which for so long had worked at con-
cealing his sexuality, searched for some scheme but could find
none. Or could this be one of Channel 7's elaborate schemes? No,
even they, his former employers, weren't that warped.

Rawlins veered to the left, Todd glanced after him, and a part
of Todd wanted both of them to chuck all this. His career in
television. Rawlins's as a homicide investigator on the Minneapolis
police force. All their friends, everything they had here. Instead,
he envisioned the two of them escaping. Running off to France
and biking through Provence, pushing on and on so that nothing
could catch up with them. Hiding out in sunny Mexico where no
one could find them. Dear God, thought Todd, staring after the
perfectly handsome and healthy man. What will I do if I lose him?

So was it here, the miracle everyone had been waiting for?
Was there really a chance of saving Steve Rawlins from AIDS?

Slipping into a downward spiral of fear—If he gets sick, will I
know what to do? Will I be strong enough?—Todd followed a
narrow trail onto a low ridge. He gazed up through the mist at the
freeway bridge in the distance. He glanced over at the swift waters
of the river. Along the bank he saw some pop cans, a tire. And
some material lurking and waving just beneath the surface.

He recognized it, really, before he knew what it was. He'd
seen that plaid, of course. Seen it quite recently.

"Rawlins!"

He cut swiftly through the undergrowth. And the closer he
came, the more he saw. Jeans. A brown leather shoe. One bloated,
semifloating hand. Todd rushed down to the water's edge and
stared at the half-submerged figure.

"What?" called Rawlins, cutting through the shrub.

"It's him."

The corpse of Mark Forrest was caught up on the tire, one leg poking through the center, the rest of his body tugged downstream by the current. He was facedown in not quite a foot of water, but Todd knew it was him, the same guy he'd met on the bridge.

Rawlins, of course, stepped into his training as quickly and automatically as if he were putting on an old shoe. He moved right to the water's edge, took a mental note of the scene.

"Do you have your cell phone?" asked Rawlins.

"It's in the car."

"Go call nine-one-one."

Ready to tear back to his car, Todd took a half-step. Then stopped. Rawlins was stepping into the water. The possibilities flashed through Todd's head, and he wanted to scream: Don't! That water's filthy. You might have a cut on your foot. You might get an infection. But nagging, as Todd had learned the hard way, had done zip for their relationship, so he forced himself to turn and dash through the brush. Right. As Rawlins had said more than once, if HIV didn't kill him, then the worry was going to kill Todd. Trying not to imagine the world as one gigantic infection, Todd reached the dirt path seconds later, then finally the pavement and the end of the parkway. As fast as he could, he tore into the parking lot and up to his truck, where he dialed 911 and reported what Sergeant Steve Rawlins and he had found. And where. He hung up and was about to take off when he dialed a second number. Rawlins probably wouldn't like this, but after all Todd had a job to do as well.

"Good morning, Channel Ten. How may I direct your call?"

"Hi, this is Todd Mills. Who's this?" he said, never able to remember the receptionist's name.

"Renee."

Right. "Listen, Renee, would you get me the assignment desk right away? It's an emergency."

"Of course."

When the editor on duty picked up, Todd relayed the situation and demanded that a photographer be rushed to the scene. Even more quickly, Todd hung up, then slammed shut his car door, and charged out of the parking lot. As he did so, he glanced over at the small Honda station wagon, and through a veil of steam on the car windows saw a half-naked ass rising up and down, up and down. It flashed through Todd's mind: Boy, the sirens are going to scare the shit out of them.

By the time Todd had run back down the path, over the ridge, and to the spot, Rawlins was standing knee-deep in the water. He wore a thin pair of latex gloves, and while he hadn't moved or flipped the body, he had retrieved a black nylon wallet, which he was now thumbing through.

Todd stared at the body, saw the blue plaid shirt. And the head, which looked severely mangled.

Todd asked, "What happened to him? Was he shot in the head too?"

"I don't think so. It looks more like he did in fact get caught up in the lock. His face is almost ripped off." Rawlins studied a plastic credit card. "But it's him. It's Mark Forrest. His driver's license says he lives at 4895 Young Avenue South." He came to another piece of ID, stared at it, and gasped, "Jesus Christ."

"What? What is it?"

"He's a cop. A cop with the Minneapolis park police."

Chapter 6

High in the court tower of the Hennepin County Government Center, Douglas Simms sat in his small office, a tiny space he'd occupied for almost five years as law clerk to Judge Stuart Hawkins. Beige carpeting, teak bookcases, and a teak desk heaped with books and files and documents filled the small room, but Simms's mind was not on the legal briefs he needed to write, nor on the murderers, rapists, and swindlers who awaited trial just down the hall. No, he turned and stared out the long, narrow window and recalled the gorgeous young blond girl from the benefit party last night. She was trouble, that much was more than clear the moment he'd discovered Hawkins and her in the basement. And now it was obvious she was trouble that wasn't going to go away.

Damn Hawkins to hell, silently cursed Simms.

Not more than five minutes ago the judge, dressed in his usual tasteful suit, had come in here supposedly to inquire about a legal brief he needed this afternoon, then told Simms he was meeting an old law-school pal for an impromptu lunch. He'd be back in an hour, hour and a half tops. "There's this great little Thai place up on Nicollet," he'd explained with a small laugh. "Wonderful noodles, dyno curry. But don't worry. No beers. None of that." With the upcoming events, he'd said with a wink, he had to play it straight and narrow.

No shit, Simms now thought as the little Nazi in him raised its ugly head. After all, Hawkins had nearly gotten a DWI last month—and would have had the police officer who'd stopped his swerving car not given the good judge a break. Dear Lord, wouldn't the media have gobbled that one up, a drunk judge about to announce his bid? Shit, Hawkins's plans for the governorship would have been sunk even before they were launched.

The small man turned back to his desk, rubbed his brow. Oh, God. Simms was so very, very close to finally getting his ticket out of this rat ass of a career and this shitty little office. Hawkins was talking about making him his campaign manager, but Simms was beginning to think it would be a miracle if that really came to pass. Hawkins, it seemed, was doing just about anything possible to screw things up.

And now this.

Simms didn't get it, not one damn bit. That girl, that blonde, was nothing but a disaster waiting to happen, even he could see that. Whether in that dingy basement Hawkins had kissed her or groped her, fucked her or whatever—after all, he'd caught Hawkins zipping his pants—Simms knew nothing good was going to come of it. But rather than leave the incident in the past, Hawkins himself was obviously going for a carnal repeat.

"Call Peacock Catering," he'd just ordered Simms. "Get them to cater a very special dinner for two at my condo. Make it for later this week. And tell them I don't want anyone but Kris to serve that meal. Clear? I only want her!"

Christ, thought Simms, who the hell was he, the judge's personal pimp?

Dear God, why couldn't she be older? Better yet, an heiress. Someone prominent. From a rich family. At least then she'd be of value. Instead, every alarm in Simms was going off. Sure, this Kris was young and gorgeous, as striking as she was tantalizing, but there was something else about her, something odd that Simms had taken note of from the very moment he'd set eyes on her. But what was it? He couldn't help, of course, but see her from a different angle than Hawkins did, and from his vantage he didn't trust what he saw.

So how was he going to handle this? Of course he had to contact Peacock Catering, of course he had to get things set up, but in the meantime how the hell was he going to keep this young woman from literally fucking everything up?

Chapter 7

The voice was deep and slow, difficult and pained. "Come . . . get . . . get me."

"I can't, Mom."

"Come . . . come . . ."

Trying to stem the frustration, Ron Ravell slumped against one of the airport's ubiquitous pay phones and rubbed his forehead. You can't afford home care, he told himself. She needs someone all the time, and around-the-clock care at home would be just too damn expensive. Besides, it's a fantastic nursing home. One of the very, very best in Los Angeles. She has a lot of her own furniture in the room—lots of pictures and photographs on the walls too—and they're taking good care of her, they really are.

"Ro- . . . Ronny?"

"Mom, I'll be there tomorrow, I promise."

Always the dutiful son, he was calling his mother just as he did every day when he was working and couldn't come to see her. As a flight attendant based out of LAX—the Los Angeles airport—he tried his very best to work only the western cities and not be gone very long. He had a reasonable amount of seniority—eight years— and so he always tried to finagle his schedule to be back in town at night, simply because now there was no one else, not since his brother's murder a year and a half ago.

"Listen, Mom, I won't get home until late tonight, so I can't come see you today. I'm working. But I'll be there tomorrow, I promise." He took a deep breath. "How's everything? What did you have for lunch?"

"Ronny, plea- . . . please. I . . ."

Even he couldn't make out what she said, so garbled were her words. But surely she understood the kind of care she needed, didn't she? Couldn't she? Maybe she'd had another stroke, a mini one or something, one so small that neither he nor the aides nor the doctors had noticed. She did seem to be getting worse, there was no doubt about it. Over the last month or so her speech had gotten more slurred, her thoughts less coherent.

He wanted to cry. Every single fucking day he wanted to sit down and cry. He used to be a happy enough guy. Reasonably popular too. With nice eyes, dark eyebrows, and a slim jaw, he'd had no shortage of dates. In fact, he'd been dating one guy for almost two years.

But then Dave had been killed and everything had changed.

Now there was no big brother taking care of everything, telling Ron to do this, make sure of that. And either Ron had forgotten all about the boyfriend or the boyfriend had gotten sick of waiting around, so he was gone too. And Ron was all alone. What a mess. He didn't want his mom to die, not ever, for she'd always been there for him, never wavered in her support or love even when he came out, but how long could he go on like this? Better yet, how much longer could he keep her in such an expensive place? Perhaps he was going to have to follow his lawyer's recommendation and move his mother to a nursing home that accepted MediCal, the state insurance plan.

She mumbled, "Wh- . . . wh- . . ."

Ron couldn't help but smile, for he understood exactly what she wanted to ask. Which meant that some part of her was still there, that his real mom was still inside the tired, withered body, hidden but there. She'd always been so fretful about her boys, one a cop, the other a flight attendant. A case of the nerves it gave her, she said, worrying one second if Dave would get shot, the next moment if Ron would crash. So she always wanted to make sure she had it—his work schedule—and she was always asking, "Where are you going next, Ronny?"

Wanting her to think that he wouldn't be far away, Ron now

said, "Where am I going? Just down to San Diego. In fact, I need to go right now."

"L-l-love you."

"I love you, too, Mom."

Reticent to break the connection, he held the receiver to his ear a moment longer, then hung up. Not moving, he stood there, staring at the phone, a pathetic smile on his lips. This was too much. Way too much. And the truth was that he himself wasn't doing so well, no, not at all. But, then again, why should he?

Damn the Los Angeles police. And damn the medical examiner. They'd both completely fucked up the case. There was no doubt that thanks to their incompetence and theirs alone, his brother's killer had been allowed to go free.

Shaking his head, Ron shuffled down the concourse, wondering how many more cops would have to be killed before Christopher Louis Kenney was finally caught. And convicted.

Chapter 8

It was well after three, hours since Todd had retreated from the waters of the Mississippi to his office, a tiny space with a glass wall and door overlooking the hum and confusion of the Channel 10 newsroom. Not at all sure how he should write the script for tonight's story, he sat there staring at the large color monitor of his computer, an eerie thought overcoming him: If I write this the way it happened, fact for fact, am I merely playing into the killer's hands?

Despite the recent doubling in the Minneapolis murder rate, a cop-killing still garnered a lot of attention in the metropolitan area, and the murder of Park Police Officer Mark Forrest was going to get top billing on the 5:00 P.M. news. Even yesterday's straight-line winds, estimated to have caused almost ten million dollars in shingle damage alone, weren't going to be the lead story in weather-obsessed Minnesota.

Todd glanced at his watch and realized he was running out of time, for he himself was scheduled to be right there at the top of the news. All afternoon, promos had been running featuring dazzling graphics with lightning bolts, the tumultuous waters of the Mississippi, a gunshot, and a voice-over stating: "WLAK's own investigative reporter, Todd Mills, witnesses the cold-blooded slaying of a park police officer. Details at five." It was, after all, real TV at its best and most macabre, and the station, no fool, was playing the card to the hilt.

But should Todd deliver it straight and simple—dishing out just what he'd seen, what had happened, who had fallen—or should he resist possibly being someone else's pawn, because, after all, this whole thing was too strange, wasn't it? If he pushed things to the limit, as he was increasingly tempted, that might help things develop in some bizarre way, thereby keeping Todd at the forefront of the story. He had to be careful, however, not to overstep that distinct but very fine line separating journalism and investigation; the police, for example, could give out misinformation to lure the killer—say, the number of times the gun was fired—but ethically Todd couldn't. On the other hand, Todd didn't have much choice but to do something, anything. He'd been getting pressure over the last six weeks—i.e., you gotta earn your keep, pal, what with the upcoming ratings and all—to come up with some big story. Could this be it, dropped out of a heinous storm and into his lap?

Todd and Rawlins had proceeded down their separate and not very compatible paths as soon as Todd's favorite WLAK photographer, Bradley, had arrived at the river. After Bradley had footage of the coroner loading the body and shots of the detectives cordoning off the area and searching it, Todd and he had headed to the Stone Arch Bridge. Leading the way onto the structure, Todd had walked through it all, explaining to the photographer the details of the storm and the killing.

"Okay," the black man had said, carrying his Betacam camera and scrutinizing the area for the best angles, the best light, the most-dramatic shots. "We have some footage of yesterday's storm I can splice in too. That should work real well."

Once they'd finished up there, Todd had returned to the station, retreating to this small glass-walled office and spending the better part of two hours figuring out just how the hell he was going to come at this thing. As he now sat in front of his computer, the big question, of course, was just how much he should or shouldn't say. It just kept hitting him: This was too easy. The darkest of storms. The most violent of winds. A handsome young cop. A strange meeting. A mysterious figure with a gun. And finally a gruesome end in the mightiest of American rivers.

Oh, brother. Seldom did the sizzle get much better, he thought, gazing around the small chamber, which was replete with

various tape players, another desk, another computer, and video-
tapes scattered about like used Kleenex. This should be a snap;
the shock value was all right there, as obvious, as glaring, as a
bomb in the middle of a shopping mall. So why was he so hesitant
to exploit this, what was making him so uncomfortable?

Once he'd hidden the truth of himself beneath layers of half-
truths. Married? No. Divorced? Yes. Dating anyone? Sometimes.
Without realizing it, over time and out of fear, the Emmy award–
winning Todd Mills had become quite a competent liar, saying
almost anything but the truth just to keep people from peeking in
that closet, which in his case held as much as a walk-in. A large
one.

Getting to know Todd back then had been like taking an onion
and peeling back one layer after another after another, each stra-
tum supposedly revealing something new. At the same time, however, each piece of information had been both inconclusive and
incomplete, for that was how compartmentalized he'd kept his
life. And no doubt about it, Todd had worked his hardest to make
sure the parts never equaled the whole and that no one could put
them all together to form a complete picture of him. In a desperate attempt to keep anyone from guessing the truth, he'd bandied
about the word *divorced* for all it was worth, sidetracking countless employers and coworkers, not to mention friends and family,
when in fact he'd been divorced more than twice as long as he'd
been married. But no one ever figured that one out either. Of that
he made sure.

So what was going on here, now, today? How many layers
were there to Mark Forrest's murder, and how difficult would it
be to peel them away and expose the real truth? And was Forrest,
as Todd suspected, actually gay?

Obviously his meeting with the young policeman had been a
setup. Yes, the blackmail crap on the phone had been a ruse to get
Todd there, just as it had been to get Mark Forrest to show up.
But why? The simple, most transparent explanation, thought
Todd, running his hand through his hair, was so he would witness
something. And that something undoubtedly was Mark Forrest's
murder. But why? Why would anyone want someone—particu-

larly Todd Mills, a television reporter—to witness a murder?
There had to be, Tood was certain, a very specific reason—definite, credible coverage?—and if Todd could unveil that reason,
then he'd certainly discover what this was all about and quite
possibly who had shot Forrest last night.

Could it, he again wondered, scratching about for possibilities,
have anything to do with Todd's own sexuality?

To be sure, Todd was obsessed with the issue, but if he was
chosen as the witness because he was gay, that suggested that
Mark Forrest of 4895 Young Avenue South was also gay. What
then? Was this some sicko's plea for help, a closet case screaming,
begging, to be caught? Making a mental note of that, Todd resolved to check deeper into Mark Forrest's sex life. So far he
hadn't been able to turn up anything; the park police—completely
independent from the Minneapolis police—had revealed precious
little. Something else to check into: another murder, that of a gay
man, who'd been killed last month with a bullet in the chest.
Could this, Todd wondered, be the start of a serial killer's morose
career? Todd's ambition, which tended to come in oversize
clumps, caused his heart to rush because, yes, he'd been called an
ambulance chaser time and again, but if there was a gay serial
killer in Minneapolis, he wanted to be the first one to post the
alarm.

Someone rapped on the glass door, and Todd sat up.

Nan, one of the producers for the evening news, a short
woman with short dark hair and a wide face, shoved open the glass
door. Perhaps she was just trying to be hip, perhaps *très* New
York, but she always wore black. Even in steamy July.

"So what's taking so long?" she demanded with a forced smile
that belied her frustration. "What are you writing, the great American novel? Step on it, pal, 'cause I want to go over this with you
and Bradley."

"Give me twenty minutes."

"Nope, ten, not a second more," she quipped as she turned
and walked briskly away.

Stretching over and shoving the door shut, Todd shouted,
"Next time close the door!"

He turned back to the computer, looked at the color monitor. There was just something here he didn't like, but what? Never willing to be anyone's dupe, he realized there was only one way to find out. He had to force this thing along by whatever means, and he had an idea, a rather conniving one. Yes, experience had taught him exactly how to irritate a murderer.

Wanting to run the idea past Rawlins, Todd reached for the phone, punched in Rawlins's number, but then just as quickly slammed down the receiver. No, the media and the police can eat, drink, and sleep together, but they can't transgress that invisible boundary, the one that divides the media's freedoms from the securities of the police. It just didn't make for good pillow talk, and if Todd probed Rawlins for any further thoughts on the case, then Rawlins would probe Todd, and, no, he didn't want to tell him what he intended to do. Right. He would, however, run it by both Nan and Bradley. Quickly rolling back his chair and standing up, he thought how maybe it wasn't such an asinine idea after all.

Not quite two hours later, Todd found himself back on the Stone Arch Bridge with a stick microphone in hand and Bradley's Betacam trained on him. From the camera a thick cable stretched down the bridge and all the way to the riverbank, where one of the station's ENG—electronic news gathering—trucks broadcast the microwave signal back to the station. From the station the complete show would be broadcast locally and much farther, actually, for as of recently all of WLAK's programming was fed to a Canadian company via satellite for cable distribution across that country.

Pressing the earpiece into his right ear, Todd heard a godlike voice beckoning from the studio in the suburbs.

"We're two minutes away, Todd," called Phil, the 5:00 P.M. line producer.

"Okay."

The news director's voice then chimed in, saying, "Voice check, please."

Todd cleared his throat. "Good evening. This is Todd Mills, and I'm reporting live from the Stone Arch Bridge."

"Got it."

Todd looked over at Bradley and said, "How's my tie?"

"Perfect," replied the photographer.

Todd then looked down at the small monitor that was tilted up to him from between the legs of Bradley's tripod. Yes, he'd have a perfect view of the package, the segment they'd earlier taped and edited and that would run after Todd's intro.

A few seconds later the line producer came back on. "We're thirty seconds from the top."

Todd rolled his head from left to right, cracked his neck, and then stared at the monitor on the ground as the evening news began.

With a small crowd gathered behind him on the bridge, Bradley peered into the camera and said, "Looking good, Todd."

And then Todd saw the image of the news anchor on the monitor and heard his voice via the IFB transmission and the earpiece.

Sounding—as always—smooth, deep, and confident, the man said, "Good evening. This is the WLAK evening news, and I'm Tom Rivers. Tonight's top story is the tragic news of a cop-killing in downtown Minneapolis. Last night, just as severe weather was overtaking the city, Minneapolis Park Police Officer Mark Forrest was gunned down on the Stone Arch Bridge. There was only one witness to the murder: WLAK's investigative reporter, Todd Mills. We now join Todd live from the Mississippi River." Tossing it to him, Rivers simply said, "Todd?"

Todd stared at the lens and said, "Tom, it's been a very sad twenty-four hours. It started about four o'clock yesterday afternoon when I received a call at the WLAK station in Golden Valley. The caller didn't identify himself but pleaded to meet with me, claiming that someone was blackmailing him." Todd took a deep breath, realized he was tense, and tried to lower his shoulders. "After consideration, I agreed to meet with him right here on the Stone Arch Bridge, which spans the Mississippi in downtown Minneapolis." Todd then spoke his role cue, the predetermined line that would trigger the package, saying, "But, unfortunately, all that followed was a violent storm and a violent murder."

Bradley swung his camera over the water, and the piece dissolved into the taped segment with Todd's voice-over. He went through it all, meeting a man dressed in plainclothes, the storm, the gun. The missing body. Bradley had spliced in different shots of last night's storm, the lightning and the thunder punctuating the entire story and of course casting a spooky, deathly tone over the whole piece. Next came the all-important shot—virtually a requirement of any television reporter's murder story—of Mark Forrest's body being carted away. Todd concluded by saying that until he found Forrest's body he had no idea that Forrest was a cop. And not a cop on the thousand-member Minneapolis police force, but one of the forty officers with the equally trained Minneapolis park police, a totally independent and separately chartered force that was actually older than the city police and whose only duties were to protect the city's vast park system.

With the audio coming through Todd's earpiece and the visual on the monitor tucked beneath Bradley's tripod, Todd paid close attention. As soon as the segment ended, he picked up.

"Tom, it was quite a horrible and shocking evening, as you can well imagine," he said into the stick microphone, keeping his conclusion tight and tossing it back to Rivers.

"Were you threatened as well? Did you sense any danger to yourself?"

"I'm never comfortable, Tom, when a loaded gun is present." Okay, thought Todd, time to make himself look great. "A total of two shots were fired, one of them directly at me."

"And what did you do?"

"I dove to the side. Fortunately, the strength of the storm was just hitting, which made it very difficult for the perpetrator to take careful aim."

"My word, how terrible."

Out of nowhere, Nan, the evening producer, broke in, shouting into Todd's earpiece, "Love it, love it! Your fans are gonna be weeping, Todd!"

"Thank God," said Tom, "you weren't injured as well."

And now, Todd thought, time to set the bait. "I can say only one thing: The killer of Officer Forrest must have a distinct and definite death wish. To gun down a cop is an inordinately stupid thing to do, simply because it means that the perpetrator will always be hunted, and be hunted by professionals with guns."

"Absolutely."

"And that, of course, implies that the perpetrator values his own life least of all." Aware that anchor Tom Rivers never made anyone but Tom Rivers look good, Todd felt it necessary to toot his own horn, saying, "To conclude, tonight the police are following several leads in the case. Given what I was able to tell them, the authorities are looking for white male, trim, and not too tall. At the time of the shooting he was wearing a yellow rain slicker."

"What about Mark Forrest? Did he have any idea what this was about before he was shot? Did he say anything to you that indicated he was in danger?"

"No, actually, he didn't."

"Todd, thank you very much, and all of us here at WLAK Channel Ten are relieved that you were not injured in this as well."

"Thank you." Todd smiled and said, "For WLAK TV, this is investigative reporter Todd Mills reporting live from the Mississippi River in downtown Minneapolis."

Todd stood still until Bradley looked up from his camera, giving Todd a big thumbs-up. Okay, the hook was baited and set. Now all he had to do was wait and see if there were any bites.

After all, there was nothing that made a killer more angry than a reporter who made him look like an unsophisticated fool doomed for failure.

Chapter 9

It was borderline hot, and the man in the parked white car had both the front and rear windows completely open in hopes of catching that hint of a breeze, the one that had just started flitting about the city as day faded into evening. He wanted to run the air-conditioning—the humidity was so damn high that his shirt was sticking to the back of the seat, which drove him nuts—but he didn't dare. No, he didn't want to turn on the engine, for a parked car with a running engine might attract attention, and the last thing he wanted was for someone to notice him.

It was a quiet street, half of it still lined with tall, graceful elms, the other half replanted with spindly little things—maples, he thought. No, wait a minute, he thought, peering at the pathetic branches. Those were ash.

Whatever.

But it was a quiet neighborhood, of that he was most definitely sure. In the sixty minutes he'd been sitting out here, there'd been no kids about, which relieved him, for the last thing he wanted was a group of kids racing up and down the sidewalks, taking note of the stranger on the block. He was pleased as well that even on such a warm night there wasn't anyone lingering on any of the front porches of these solid, wood-framed houses. Couldn't he therefore infer that empty-nesters and single people lived here?

Well, there was at least one single person, of that he was sure: a gay man who lived on the second floor of that duplex just up on the left.

Behind him he heard the gentle hum of an engine, and he glanced in his rearview mirror. The street itself was straight and in decent repair, the curbs looking no more than two or three years old, and down it now came a small red car. Behind the wheel was a woman with long blond hair, that much he could tell, and when she passed him she seemed not to notice anything out of the ordinary, that his car didn't belong here. Focused on her, he watched as she drove three houses past the duplex, pulled to the right, and parked. Reaching for a pen and the yellow legal pad on the seat next to him, the man jotted it all down: the red car, the blond woman, the return home at—he noted, checking his watch—six thirty-three.

Very good.

He now had almost this entire midsection of the block accounted for, and in turn a reasonably good idea of the pattern of the lives of the people who lived here. The only house that he really couldn't tell anything about was the white clapboard one just next door to the duplex. With peeling white paint and the curtains drawn, it didn't look as if anyone was living in the structure. Then again, it didn't look completely abandoned, for there were no newspapers or flyers lying about on the front steps or tucked in the front door, there were no envelopes bulging out of the mailbox. As far as a car, perhaps it was stashed in the garage off the alley. So someone could be living there, easily so. An old person. Right, he surmised. Someone frail. Someone who didn't get out much. Someone who didn't have anything better to do all day than peer out the windows and see who and what was lurking on the block.

So be careful of that one, he admonished. Absolutely.

Suddenly the door of the duplex opened and his next target stepped out. Wasting not a moment, the man in the car calmly pulled a newspaper from his lap and looked at it as if he were reading. With his face concealed, he watched just over the top of the pages as the other descended from the front porch to the street. Noting the fresh shirt, pressed pants, and slicked-down dark hair, he gathered that this guy was going to meet someone, undoubtedly for dinner. And the man in the car easily guessed just who that might be.

This was good. Very good. He needed to find out which door this guy primarily used. And now it was clear: the front one. Which meant he'd lay his trap in the rear.

Yes, thought the man in the car as he watched Sergeant Steve Rawlins climb into his silver Taurus. This one's going to be easy, very easy.

Chapter 10

After he did it at five, he did it at six.

And in a few hours—at ten, to be precise—he'd do it again on WLAK's 10@10. A live intro to the story, followed by the package recounting the murder of Mark Forrest.

If there wasn't anything new from the police by then, Todd schemed as he drove into town for dinner, he'd try his best to put a fresh spin on it, add a few things of his own, kind of spice it up a bit. Viewers, after all, always had to feel as if they were getting the latest, that there was some payoff for tuning in. And Todd was determined to give it to them.

The great stories, the ones every reporter dreamed of, were the ones that grabbed you by the throat. The ones you couldn't get out of your head. The ones that made you hunt obsessively for the truth. Although he'd never voiced it, the things that made Todd realize how thoroughly he loved his job were the kidnappings, the beatings, the murders—the more bizarre the better. If that body is really him, that Russian stockbroker, then where's the head? The hands? Or how could that young, attractive mother really have done that to her kids, set the house on fire with them in it? Was it in fact the stepfather? Or how could a son have done that to his mother, drugged her up on pain medication and then buried her alive in the tomato patch?

He'd never admit it, but the extremes of the human condition were what Todd feasted on, and this, a strange cop-killing, was a hell of a story, no doubt about it. Intuitively he sensed that there was enough meat here to keep him going for weeks, if not more.

That he had been at the murder scene—been not simply a witness, but nearly a victim as well—was spectacular. Virtually no other station in town could even begin to touch it. In television's perpetual race to be first, he'd stolen the show. The best that any other reporter could do was stand on the sidelines and report what Todd Mills was doing. Shit, he thought, a smile shining through his exhaustion. No way could anyone take this away from him. He was at the top of the pack right now. That much was already clear, for Nan, the producer, had watched the broadcasts of both WTCN and KNOR—it was regular practice to tape the competition just to keep apprised of the enemy—and both of them had led off not with the cop-killing, but the severe weather. The murder came second, each station stating that a suburban cop had been murdered in the city and that the police were pursuing the matter with the help of a firsthand witness. No mention was made, of course, that that witness had in fact been the competition's own Todd Mills. Uh-uh. That just wouldn't happen in today's broadcast world. They'd reported with great speculation and near glee when Todd had been outed and questioned for murder; they'd covered the darkest, most difficult days of his life, but no mention was or ever would be made of this success.

He glanced at the dash, saw that it was five after seven. He was a tad late for their dinner reservation but not terribly so. Rawlins, the born-and-bred Minnesotan, was always either exactly on time or a few minutes early. Janice Gray, a defense attorney whose life was stretched in every direction either by a court case or a charitable board she volunteered for, was always a few minutes tardy. With any luck Todd would fall between the two.

Entering downtown, he turned left, heading north on Hennepin Avenue. Both Minneapolis and St. Paul, he thought, noticing a group of vacant lots where once had stood several buildings, were teetering. Once a region of progressive planning, The Cities had taken a huge tumble in the last ten years—the leadership and the public interest both had waned just as things like the stupid Megamall had selfishly waxed—and they were taking steps toward becoming the Detroit or Los Angeles of the tundra. It drove Todd nuts.

As he crossed onto the Hennepin Avenue bridge and over the Mississippi, he glanced downstream, saw the Third Avenue bridge and caught a glimpse of the Stone Arch Bridge way down there. Should he do a live broadcast from there again tomorrow, or would that be too repetitive?

Crossing to the other side, he passed Riverplace and Nye's, that venerable old Polish restaurant and piano bar, and parked. He picked up his cell phone, switched it from ring to vibrate, and slipped it into his front shirt pocket.

"Go out for dinner, yeah, sure, Todd," Craig, the late-night news producer, had blessed. "Do that. Get something to eat. But don't go anywhere without your phone in case I gotta get ahold of you. And be back here by nine-thirty, not a split second later. Read me? You're on at the top of the ten o'clock."

Café Bobino was just a half-block ahead, and as Todd walked toward it, he realized just how exhausted he was. And no wonder. His adrenaline had been stuck on high ever since late this morning when Rawlins and he had discovered the body of Mark Forrest. Hopefully a good meal would restore him.

What used to be a funeral home, then a cabaret, was now a hip restaurant and wine bar, proving that you could bring things back from the dead, and as Todd walked in several heads turned his way. Gay men, four of them seated at the bar, scanned him up and down in that queeny kind of way, then almost in unison returned to their glasses of cabernet. So what was the once-closeted-and-now-very-out Todd Mills, the television personality, to them? Hero or pariah? Or merely a lightning rod of gossip? He still didn't have a handle on it, how he fit—or if he did at all—into the gay community.

The host, a short man with short bleached white hair and wearing a white T-shirt and a pale green cotton vest, eagerly rushed up.

Addressing Todd before he could even get a word out, the host said, "Good evening, Mr. Mills. Right this way, please. The other two in your party are already here."

The price of fame or notoriety—or both—was the lack of anonymity, a dear price that Todd had always been more than willing to pay. He followed the host along the side hall of the café, glanced through an archway, and saw both Rawlins and Todd's longtime and dear friend, Janice, seated at a corner table, a glass of white wine before each of them. This wasn't good, his being the last to arrive.

The dining room was small, with muted yellow walls, dim lights, and a bustling kitchen at the rear. As Todd crossed to his table, several more heads turned his way, but he didn't let on that he noticed them noticing him. Keeping focused, he made a direct line to these two, his pals and family of choice—the hunky gay cop and the beautiful dyke lawyer, as he called them. They all spoke, all three of them, at least once a day, checking in with the slightest detail of life—who watched what on TV, who was out of cereal, etc.—and, of course, discussing ad nauseam just what course of medical action Rawlins should take in his battle against HIV and when, even if, he should tell Foster, his partner, or Lieutenant Holbrook, his superior, or anyone else at the police department about his health status.

Janice, whom Todd had dated way back in college at Northwestern University, was tall and thin with short dark hair and a quick smile. She had pale skin that was very soft, very lovely, and a small mouth that looked for any opportunity to burst into a wide grin. Now dressed in slim blue jeans and a cream-color cotton knit top, she looked the very image of summer informality; by day, however, there was no doubt about it, she was one hell of a defense attorney. Upon seeing Todd, Janice's smile bloomed, and he realized what a change had come over her in the last year. He saw how much more real her happiness was, for not long ago she'd solved the greatest mystery of her life, which in turn had lifted some kind of awful cloud from her and actually had bound the two of them together with true familial ties. Yes, she was noticeably brighter. Much more at peace, no doubt about it.

"Hi," he said, bending over and kissing Janice.

"Hello, doll," she countered, proffering him a generous smack of her lips on his cheek.

Rawlins sat in the corner, and Todd was going to reach out and squeeze his hand or kiss him—with any luck they had decades and decades left, but who knew, certainly not the doctors; and Todd didn't care if anyone saw him kissing another man, because the threat hovering over Rawlins had taught Todd once and for all what was truly important in life—but Rawlins was checking his watch and not moving. Instead, Todd sat down in the seat they always left him in any restaurant, the one that positioned him so his back was to the main part of the room, the one that left his face the least visible to the public.

"Come on, Rawlins," begged Todd, the tone of his voice trying to make light of things. "On a scale of one to ten, I'm not that late."

"What?" said Rawlins, looking up. "Late? No, not too bad, not tonight."

Todd glanced at Janice, who rolled her eyes as she took a sip of her wine. Okay, thought Todd. What's going on? What have I done?

A gorgeous young waitress appeared at the side of the table, her body trim, her skin a midnight black, her hair as short as could be. Huge gold hoops dangled from her ears.

"Would you care for anything to drink, sir?" she asked. "A glass of wine perhaps?"

Todd had it in the genes, the booze thing, and he was always cautious, always fearful that his father's curse would be his, and he said, "You know what, I've got to go back to work, so I'll just have a glass of iced tea."

"Of course."

As the waitress disappeared, Janice's eyes followed her and she said, "Todd, will you lie to me and tell me I was once that young and beautiful?"

"You were once that young and beautiful—and you still are. But it's not a lie, it's the harsh truth."

She took a deep breath and closed her eyes. "Hey, I have a question. Can a dyke be a fag hag?"

With a grin, Todd said, "The politically correct answer is that a dyke can be anything she damn well wants to be."

He picked up the menu and pretended to look at it, meanwhile glancing across the table at Rawlins, who was just sitting there. Smoldering. Todd didn't dare ask how Rawlins felt, which had become a taboo question—I'll let you know if I feel anything but great, Rawlins always snapped—but he looked at him closely, studied his eyes. His color is good, the eyes clear. Yes, he's fine, concluded Todd. Just pissed. So, he wondered as he eyed Rawlins, then Janice, what's going on here?

"I give," confessed Todd. "What did I do wrong? Will one of you please tell me?"

Rawlins perused his menu. "Nothing. Nothing that we're supposed to talk about anyway."

"What the hell does that mean?"

Making light, Janice shrugged. "It means, he's a cop. You're a reporter."

At first Todd didn't get it, but then it hit him, and he thought, shit, he should have seen this coming a mile away. "Ohhhh, thank God, we've finally got that straight."

Rawlins kept his nose in the menu, uttered not a single word, and shook his head.

"Listen, I'm not adverse to playing telephone," began Janice. "So I don't mind saying that about two minutes before you came in, Todd, Rawlins expressed his, well, frustration with you for—"

"Knock it off, Janice," snapped Rawlins.

"No. I want to enjoy dinner, not suffer through it, so the two of you better get this out of the way."

"All right, then." Rawlins slammed down the menu and leaned across the table. "What the hell was that all about?"

Todd didn't flinch. What could he say?

"I saw you at five," said Rawlins. "And at six too."

"Rawlins," began Todd, his tone more defensive than anything else. "I've got a job to do. Besides, I didn't give out any false information."

"Fuck the media. You shouldn't talk about a killer like that. You're supposed to report the news, not make it."

"You don't understand. I'm sure that guy's playing with me, I'm sure he's using me, so I—"

"You should have called me. You should have cleared it with us."

"Rawlins, I don't need your fucking permission to say what I want on television," said Todd, bristling. "We've been through this, goddamn it all. You're a cop."

"No shit."

"I'm sorry, but it's something WLAK really wanted to do. And I think it was a smart move."

Rawlins shook his head, then turned and stared blankly across the room. "Playing with a killer is stupid. Whose dumb-ass idea was this?"

Todd shrugged and replied, "Mine."

"Figures."

Janice took a brief sip of wine, then pushed back her chair. "Now that you guys are on a roll, I think I'll go powder my nose . . . or . . . or go chop wood or whatever it is lesbians do when they want to get away from men."

Leaning forward as Janice left, Todd kept his voice low and tried to explain. "I thought about calling you, Rawlins. I wanted to. I really did. But it comes down to the ethics thing again. You know, just what the media is supposed to say—or is obligated to say—to the cops."

"And vice versa." Rawlins shook his head. "Listen, I thought you and I, Todd Mills and Steve Rawlins, had a personal agreement: I don't hold out on you, and you don't hold out on me. As it is right now, you know virtually everything the police do, absolutely everything that's going on in this case. I haven't cut you out of anything, Todd, and—"

"But—"

"You fucked up, no two ways about it."

Okay, so maybe he had. And in the back of his mind he'd known it when he was doing it, too, just as he'd known it would come to something like this. Right. Taking his spoon and twiddling it between his thumb and forefinger, Todd had known Rawlins would have a shit fit. The trouble was, Todd had been willing to face the consequences, absolutely so.

"I didn't call you," said Todd, putting it all out on the table, "because I didn't want you to say no."

"Which I would have."

"Rawlins, something's rotten in Denmark."

"No shit, Sherlock. A cop was killed." Rawlins looked right at Todd with those big, deep, disarming eyes. "Listen, a couple of things happened this afternoon that you don't know about yet."

"Like what?"

"First, my partner's mom died."

"Neal Foster's? Wow, I'm sorry."

"Well, it wasn't unexpected. She'd been sick for a long time. What that means, though, is that Foster's gone for the next week or so." Rawlins shrugged. "Consequently, I spent the better part of the afternoon arguing with Lieutenant Holbrook."

Todd had wondered if it would come to this, an official conflict of interests, and he bent forward and rubbed his eyes. "He wanted to pull you from this because of me, right?"

"Exactly."

Holbrook knew all about them, of course. Hell, it was only last month that he and his wife had had Rawlins and Todd over for dinner. So how, wondered Todd, had Rawlins stopped Holbrook from assigning this case to someone else?

"Presuming the case is still yours, what did you have to do? What kind of price did Holbrook make you pay?" asked Todd.

Rawlins shrugged. "I have to sleep at my house, you have to sleep at yours."

"What?"

"A separation of sorts. After dinner tonight we're supposed to talk only in a formal setting."

"Oh, great."

This, he knew, wasn't going to be easy. Or fun. Except when one of them was working through the night on either a story or a case, they'd hardly been apart since they first met.

"Shit." Trying to make light of it, with a shrug Todd said, "Well, then we're just going to have to figure out real quick who killed Forrest."

"No kidding." Rawlins took a deep breath. "There's one more thing, which is actually the main reason Holbrook is letting me keep the case. As it turns out, he thinks I might have some connections or insights into this that the other guys wouldn't. Which is to say, you were right—Mark Forrest was gay."

"What? You're kidding?"

"Nope. And that info's for public consumption too—we got it from the park police late this afternoon. Apparently Mark Forrest was out as a gay cop and had been since the first day he was hired."

"Do you realize what that means, Rawlins?" said Todd, leaning forward, unable to squash his excitement. "It means that there could in fact be a gay serial killer out there—after all, that guy who was killed last month was also shot in the chest. It also means I was almost certainly set up. I don't know why, but it's pretty damn clear that I was. And we both know that whoever killed Mark Forrest is going to be watching everything I say. Actually, there's no doubt in my mind that I'm going to get some kind of reaction from the killer."

"Shit, you're trying to get yourself hurt, aren't you?" Rawlins put his elbow on the table and bowed his forehead into the palm of his left hand. "Todd, don't you see you're being used to get as much media exposure as possible?"

"That's my point—I don't want to give him exactly what he wants."

"Do you know how pissed off that's going to make him?"

"Yes, but—"

"Todd, what are you trying to do? Turn this into something bigger than it is? Are you going for another Emmy?"

The anger whooshed through him, but he sat quite still. No, he wouldn't deny it. Not at all.

"Rawlins, in case you didn't realize it, I'm always going for another Emmy."

"Yeah," he replied, defeated. "I know."

At first he didn't know what it was, the quivering against his chest. Todd sat back, touched the shaking thing in the breast pocket of his shirt, and felt a hard plastic case. The phone. That was probably Craig. Probably calling to bug him about something. Or to tell him he needed to get his butt back to the station. Of all the times he didn't want to talk to anyone at Channel 10, this was probably right up there at the pinnacle. Perhaps he shouldn't even answer it.

"What is it?" asked Rawlins.

"A call."

"Oh, Christ. You and that job of yours."

Todd hesitated, glanced at Rawlins, who was glaring at him, and then decided to answer it, if only to show Rawlins who was in charge of what. But how? Todd pulled the phone from his pocket and stared at it, for he still didn't get this, the private-phone-in-a-public-space deal.

"Excuse me," said Todd, pushing back his chair.

As the small phone vibrated with its silent rings, Todd exited the main part of the restaurant and stepped into the side hallway. He moved up against a window, flipped open the phone, and lifted it to his ear.

"This is Todd Mills."

"Whatsamatta with you?"

He didn't know the voice, nor could he even tell if it was a man or a woman, for if it was a guy he had no resonance to his voice, while if it was a woman she'd been smoking way too long.

He asked, "Who is this?"

"I mean, what kind of reporter are you anyway?"

Suddenly he realized who it might be, and fearing and hoping he was right, Todd's heart tripped, then started pounding. Yes, he realized. The voice indeed was that of a man, the voice perhaps purposely hoarse or faint. But was it him?

The voice demanded, "That was pathetic. I thought you were supposed to be good. That's why I picked you, asshole."

Todd saw their waitress coming down the hall from the bar. The desperation all too apparent on his face, he raised his hand and flagged her. When she came over, Todd reached to her tray and grabbed her pen and a handful of cocktail napkins. On one of them he wrote: It's him—the killer! And then Todd frantically pointed to their table and Rawlins. The waitress, understanding only that this was most urgent, hurried off.

"I'm sorry," said Todd. "Who is this? Do I know you?"

"Of course you do, you moron. We met on the bridge over, I guess you could say, troubled waters."

"I see," said Todd, unfolding the napkin and frantically jotting down what was being said. "But how did you get this number?"

"I called the station and told them I was a cop and that we had an emergency."

Todd hesitated, glanced over his shoulder, saw Rawlins rushing over. "But . . . but how do I know it's really you?"

"Oh, fuck off. Of course it's me."

"I get crank calls all the time."

"Yeah, well, if you fuck up all the time, I'm not surprised. I mean, I know you're a homo, but why did you make that stuff up about me? None of it's true, you know. None of it."

Rawlins was at Todd's side, and Todd jotted on the napkin: Yes, it's him!

"Tell me something," said Todd, his mind working frantically. "Prove it."

"You're playing with me, aren't you?"

"No, I—"

"Don't make a fool of me. I don't like it when people do that. And don't say that crap about me either."

Rawlins ripped the pen from Todd's hand and frantically started writing.

"Okay . . . okay . . ." began Todd, reading Rawlins's words. "So you're the guy who killed Mark Forrest on the bridge?"

"Yes, asshole."

"Why did you do it?"

"Because . . . because I like killing cops," he replied with a laugh.

"So you've done this before?"

"Duh."

"When?"

"A while ago." The voice shifted, got more bossy again. "Listen, I just called because I wanted to warn you: Don't do that again, don't talk about me like that. You don't know me—I'm not an idiot. I know perfectly well what I'm doing."

"Who are you?"

"That's for you to figure out."

Todd said, "But—"

"Here, try to guess this one, you moron: Either brother or sister, I am neither." He laughed. "Or am I either?" He laughed again. "Ta-ta."

Desperate not to lose him, Todd blurted out, "I think this is a crank call."

There was nothing, and then an irritated "What?"

"You've got to prove it."

"Oh, Jesus." A moment passed, and then the caller said, "I fired at you as you dove to the ground. And I missed on purpose, asshole." The wispy voice laughed, said one last thing, and hung up.

Stunned, Todd was silent, then quickly said, "Hello? Hello?" He shook his head, then pushed the OFF button and folded up the phone. "Crap, he hung up on me."

Right by Todd's side, Rawlins looked at the scribbles on the napkins and said, "Are you sure it was really him, the guy who killed Forrest?"

Todd nodded as he jotted down the last of the conversation. "It was him, all right." Not really sure who had snared who, he shrugged and pointed down to his writing. "This is pretty much everything he said, plus . . ."

"Plus what?"

"The last thing he said was that if I didn't stick just to the facts, he was going to make me suffer, really suffer."

Rawlins stared at Todd, his brow furrowed with confusion. "What's that mean?"

"Hell if I know," said Todd, wanting to shrug it off but knowing he didn't dare.

Chapter 11

Examining the black cotton jacket, Kris stood in front of one of the mirrors at Dayton's, the grand department store that had done its best to keep The Cities more or less in style since before the turn of the century. Wearing tall black boots that she'd bought from a transgender store she'd found on the Net, tight black jeans, and a skimpy white top, Kris was the very picture of youth. And, of course, lust. A hip Lolita, she mused with a grin, that was her goal. Yep. She kind of liked the way the jacket brought everything together. It had a kind of sixties, kind of Beatles cut to it. Very mod. Straight arms. Broad at the shoulders. Cut in at the waist. Then flared, which was good because it made her narrow hips, the weakest of her attributes, look broader and more feminine than they actually were. She could, she supposed, one day have hip augmentation if she wanted, but for now . . .

Yes, it was only eight, the store would be open another hour and a half, she could keep looking, but this might do just fine. With it on, she looked cute and perky. A little waifish, perhaps, which never hurt 'cause the guys always liked that about her. But then she could just drop the coat—as she now did—and there she was, in the tall boots, tight jeans, and sexy top. No bra. Her hormone-induced tits poking out as best they could. And her blond hair all perked up.

Yes, she thought. Stuart Hawkins would like it very much. He'd appreciate that she would come to his place all wrapped in a summer jacket that she could drop in an instant and then display everything great about her body. Oh, yes. She'd seen him only that one time, but she knew his taste. And she was it. He didn't like women. Nope. He wanted girls, the younger the better. She'd sensed that as soon as their eyes had met over the canapés, was sure of it as he pursued her throughout that great house and into the tool room, where they'd disappeared into a vortex of desire.

She turned to the side, smoothed a wrinkle with her left palm, and smiled, still unable to believe that she'd actually passed, that Hawkins had been totally convinced. Okay, okay, so her hands weren't so great—they were a little too broad, the fingers a shade too long—but there wasn't a thing to be done there, and, besides, he hadn't picked up on them.

Funny, she thought, now clasping her hands together, she hadn't expected to hear from Travis so soon. And when asked if she could help cater a private dinner party, she'd replied without too much thought.

"Yeah, sure."

Only then, only after she'd agreed to the work, did she learn the specifics. Her heart flinched when she heard the name. Stuart Hawkins? Of course she knew what this was all about. It had nothing to do with Travis's beautiful food. No, it had everything to do with her. With Kris. And lust.

She hadn't been able to get that adorable, boyish face out of her mind. That tall, manly figure. Those broad shoulders. The pinstripe navy-blue suit. His hot, moist mouth. The strong tongue. And as much as she'd hoped he'd forgotten her, that he'd dismissed their encounter as some stupid indiscretion, now she knew the truth: He'd been thinking of her all this time too. So did this mean this was it, the big romance she'd been wanting, searching for? Was he the one? No, of course she didn't want to have anything to do with a judge and slipping in and out the back door after midnight, for an important man like Hawkins could never be open about his relationship with a woman like Kris. Never. Some reporter would go digging and expose the pathetic muck of Kris's life. But if Stuart Hawkins really did love Kris, might he give it all up to pursue quite another dream, that of the two of them blissfully happy?

So should she go? Should she really show up at his place for what could only prove to be a night of want, of unbridled passion?

The very thought made her penis, packed so tightly in her crotch, stir with desire.

Horrified by so brutal a reminder of just who was who and what was what, Kris froze. She closed her eyes. Took a deep breath. Bit her lower lip. And forced herself to think of cold water and mocking, laughing voices and . . . and . . . and it worked. The penis was just an inflatable thing, and, tucked beneath her spandex undies, which of course had been strategically reinforced, it thankfully began to shrink, rapidly so in fact. Glancing down ever so carefully, she saw that she hadn't lost her feminine profile. Excellent. At least, she thought, she didn't have to deal with testicles too. That was the one good thing about not having any, that she didn't have to push them up inside herself.

But what the hell was she thinking? What kind of fantasy was she lost in? Of course she couldn't go. They'd kissed down there in that tool room. They'd embraced. And when things had gotten gloriously overheated, the only way she'd been able to keep him from reaching between her legs and discovering her secret was by going down on him. But no, that wouldn't work again. Just as she dreamed of peeling every bit of clothing from that hunky body, so did he surely envision her naked and in his arms. And she knew that could never come to pass. The last time someone had discovered that, no, she really didn't have a vagina down there had proved nothing less than disastrous. Never would she forget the look on that policeman's face. Nor would she forget how he had struck her, his fist cracking her jaw with such force that she was hurled back. Oh, God. She recalled that night. Recalled scrambling for that gun.

And him bellowing, "I'm going to kill you, you fucking freak!"

But of course that wasn't how things had turned out. No, not at all.

Kris started to cry. Her eyes swelled with sadness, for she knew that her secret dream—that of a man falling in love with her and the two of them tumbling into a wonderful, healthy relationship—was nothing more than a fantasy, a totally impossible one at that.

A voice behind her exclaimed, "My God, that jacket fits you perfectly."

With the forefinger of her right hand, Kris quickly wiped away her tears, then turned around and said, "Oh . . . oh, thank you."

"You've got to buy that," said the salesclerk, a young woman with straight brown hair and a big smile outlined with bold red lipstick. "You look great in it."

"Thanks," said Kris, slipping off the jacket. "But I can't get it, not tonight anyway."

"Oh, come on."

"No. No, really, I can't."

"You've got to." The clerk giggled. "At least let me put it on hold for you. I can do it for, like, seventy-two hours."

Kris shrugged. "I don't know. Maybe."

"Great. I mean, you have nothing to lose. You've got three days to decide if you want it. If you come back before then, it'll be here. If you don't, then it'll just go back out on the rack."

"Well . . ."

Well, why not, decided Kris. And so she followed the salesclerk to the checkout counter and wrote down her name and number. A few minutes later Kris tucked a claim check in her pocket.

"Thanks," said Kris, her voice hushed as she turned to go.

"Oh, no prob. I'm sure you're going to come back. It's just too perfect on you."

And I'm sure I won't, thought Kris. No. She'd buy it only if she was going to go to Stuart Hawkins's, but there was no way that she could do that. Nope. Thank God she'd come to her senses. As she made her way toward the main ground-floor doors, she saw his face again. Not Stuart Hawkins's warm, charming face. But that of the cop and his look of horror just before the gun went off.

Oh, God. He was dead and buried all because of her.

Chapter 12

The rest of their dinner was kind of a disaster. In fact, Todd stayed barely another five minutes at Café Bobino.

"I've got to get back to work," he said, excusing himself.

"Like I don't? It's probably impossible, but among a hundred other things I've got to see if I can get a trace on that call," said Rawlins. "Come on, Todd, sit back down. We can eat and be out of here in ten minutes."

"No, I'll just grab a sandwich from the machine at the station."

Janice took a sip of wine, then quipped, "Frankly, I prefer risotto to plastic."

"I'm sorry," continued Todd, "I've just got to get back and figure out what I'm going to do for the ten o'clock."

Janice put down her glass. "So what *are* you going to do?"

"I don't know," said Todd, shifting in his seat because, after all, he didn't like lying, particularly not to the two most important people in his life. "A phone call like that kind of changes everything we had planned."

"No shit." Rawlins shook his head. "I don't like this."

"Neither do I," seconded Janice. "There are a lot of nuts out there, most of whom I come across on a daily basis in court. This guy's obviously really dangerous—he's already killed a cop, you know."

Todd looked at Janice, then Rawlins. The two of them were staring at him, pressing him to reveal how he might handle this. He had an inkling—more than one, actually—but he couldn't tell them, or at least not Rawlins. At first, just after the call, he was frightened, even shaken. Then, however, it started kicking in, that old sense, the one that pushed him to ask question after question and that caused him to hound a victim, to follow a drug dealer, to tail a judge, until he had the complete answer to a complex question. And this time he'd succeeded, at least so far, for he'd brought things more or less into the open. He'd poked at the story of the murder of Mark Forrest, and the killer had bitten back. Yes, the man who'd shot Forrest had peeped out of his hole.

So what would Todd's next move in fact be? He looked directly into Rawlins's dark eyes, which were staring right back at his. But it wasn't Rawlins, his lover, studying him with worry. No, it was Rawlins, the homicide investigator. And this, once again, boiled down to freedom of the media. No, Todd couldn't reveal his thoughts, because, of course, what Todd was thinking of doing would piss off Rawlins every bit as much as it would the killer.

Todd pushed back his chair, rose, then leaned over and kissed Janice on the cheek and said, "I'll talk to you tomorrow."

"Take care, sweetheart."

"Rawlins," began Todd, wanting to at least hug the other man, "I guess I won't see you tonight, so—"

"Just don't do anything stupid."

"I won't."

"I wish I could count on that." Rawlins shook his head as he fiddled with his napkin. "Have I ever told you how often people like you fuck up a case by reporting the wrong things at the wrong time?"

"Repeatedly." Todd glared at him. "Have I ever told you it's best if you do your job and I do mine?"

"Yeah, yeah, yeah," mumbled Rawlins, now staring at his glass of wine. "I'll be watching at ten."

"That sounds like a threat."

Rawlins shrugged but said nothing.

Well, screw you, thought Todd, forgetting about the hug as he stormed away. He didn't have time for this, not now, not tonight. The police hadn't succeeded in establishing some sort of contact with Mark Forrest's murderer, he had. And that murderer hadn't contacted Rawlins or anyone else at the Minneapolis police department. No, he'd called Todd directly. So this was his baby, Todd's, and his alone. He had to keep at it too. Not let it go. This was going to make for news. Big news. Hot news. Of that Todd would make sure.

The frustration clearly smoldering on his face, Todd made his way through the tables and chairs, down the side hallway, and past the bleach-haired host, who stood next to his stand, clutching a stack of menus.

"Leaving so soon, Mr. Mills?"

"Unfortunately," Todd managed to reply.

He pushed out the door and burst into the hot, thick summer air. Where the hell, he thought, looking up and down the street, was his car? Down toward the river a huge swarm of bugs swirled in the orangish glow of a streetlight, and there, beneath all that, stood his dark-green Cherokee.

He knew all too well that no relationship was easy, not by any means. Up to this point, he had in fact screwed up—no, ruined—virtually every one he'd been in. Starting with Janice so long ago, then moving to Trish, his ex-wife, and next Michael, Todd had managed not only to make every mistake possible but to hurt every person he'd been involved with. Okay, so with Janice it had been more or less a mutual error, for they'd both been mired in the muck of sexual orientation and flailing about for answers. He'd married Trish, however, out of desperation, not only hoping he loved her but determined to prove something, specifically that he wasn't gay after all. As if using her hadn't been bad enough, Todd then went on to Michael, giving himself sexually to him yet never fully emotionally, which in its own way had killed that relationship as well. And now Rawlins . . .

"Damn it!" he cursed aloud.

Todd stopped, grabbed onto a parking meter with one hand, put the other to his forehead, and took a deep breath. More than one person had called him selfish. A great many had labeled him self-centered. So what was he supposed to do here? Do a job that he was not only paid handsomely for but that he was great at, a job that came to him as naturally as breathing—and that he craved just as dearly? Or was he supposed to succumb to the wishes of the person he loved more than anyone or anything else?

Wait, it was Rawlins the cop, not Rawlins the lover, who wanted Todd to step back and turn this whole thing over to the police, right?

Notwithstanding that there had been no visible homosexual role models when he was young, Todd just didn't know how you did this, this same-sex relationship thing. Two guys most often meant two careers as well as two healthy egos, which was quite clearly the case with Rawlins and him. In a straight relationship it started unfortunately with sexual definition—who was the man and who was the woman—while in a gay relationship it was often defined in sexual parlance, who was top and who was bottom. And that highlighted the lack of difference between a straight and a gay relationship, because in the end it all came down to dominance. Which in fact was the major struggle between Todd and Rawlins. The career stuff was an especially huge issue, one that they'd never discussed but that played itself out almost daily as the detective who sought justice and the reporter who sought truth struggled to establish who and which was more important.

Somewhat surprisingly, Todd was only just coming to the realization that the world didn't spin according to him. For so long he'd fought his sexuality, did everything he could to deny it, to prove he wasn't a fag and therefore a despicable deviant, an incompetent ninny unworthy of love, a fairy who couldn't do anything but swish about. Ever since he could remember, he battled all this self-hatred by becoming the best goddamn investigative reporter there was, fighting to prove his worth to others as if his life depended on it, which he believed it had, and going at it so obsessively that he now had trouble stepping back. To further complicate things, Todd had learned by example—that of his father, the Polish immigrant, who demanded support and nurturing but never returned it to his partner, his unwavering wife, Todd's mother. Yes, rightly or wrongly, Todd had adopted this most "guy" of characteristics, following in his father's footsteps, always taking more than giving. And never had Todd been so fully and absolutely challenged as he had been not only by Rawlins but, in particular, by Rawlins's health status. Which meant that for the first time in his life Todd found himself in the position of wanting to give more than get.

Todd heard steps behind him and quickly turned, hoping more than anything that it was him, Rawlins. It took but a mere second for Todd to fantasize Rawlins rushing out, the two of them embracing, Todd pulling the shorter but thicker and stronger man into his arms. Instead of the chance to take this all back to square one, however, Todd saw not Rawlins but some other man, a tall skinny guy with a cigarette perched between his lips, hurrying down the sidewalk.

So what should Todd do?

Go back, he told himself. He should just return to the restaurant, apologize. Tell Rawlins how much he loved him, that this was a blip, nothing more. That Todd was just trying to do his job. That he'd do just as Rawlins wanted, whatever that might be. That . . .

He took a step back toward Bobino's, at the same instant glancing at his watch.

"Shit," he muttered to himself, stopping just as quickly.

He had a job to do, and all of this was, first and foremost, about work. And if, in light of the mysterious call from the killer, Todd was now going to change what he was going to say on the 10:00 P.M. news, if he was going to come at this thing from a different angle, then he'd better hightail it out to WLAK right this second. Time was of the essence. Absolutely, he thought, turning around and again heading for his vehicle.

After all, later on there'd be plenty of time to sort through all this with Rawlins, right?

Everyone at WLAK received the news of the threat against Todd as if it were the best of Christmas presents.

"This is too great," exclaimed Craig, the late-news producer, a young guy with light hair, big glasses, and a permanent smile affixed to his face, as he paced back and forth in Todd's small office. "I mean, not only are you and WLAK in all the newspapers, but now you're part of the story. This is so cool!"

"Glad you think so," Todd muttered, seated in front of his computer and seeing the perversity of all this more clearly than ever.

"I mean, the killer really called you?"

"Scout's honor."

"This is just going to keep the whole thing right on the front burner. The viewers are going to love this. I mean, you're a potential victim, you realize that, don't you, Todd?"

"Yes, thank you very much." Todd was reluctant to add, "There's one more thing—Mark Forrest was gay."

It was like throwing gas on an open fire, and Craig said, "Oh, this is so unbelievably hot! This is so perfect! Man, oh, man, what a story!"

Todd's journalistic instincts—which ran so completely opposite to Rawlins's procedures—were precisely the ones Craig wanted to go with. And for good reasons. Todd's broadcast tonight at ten o'clock would not only keep viewers glued to WLAK but would undoubtedly be reported in tomorrow's papers. What great publicity. Channel 10 right there at the front.

But how actually to do it?

A year ago, perhaps even a mere six months back, Todd would have played it all for the sizzle, for the paramount effect—namely, for the ratings and what impact they would bear upon Investigative Reporter Todd Mills and his career. But now . . . now perhaps he wasn't so much smarter as he was a tad bit wiser. Yes, he had to report on this latest development, but he had to do it just right. Instead of a cotton-candylike buzz, he was determined to provide something of lasting value.

Todd wrote the script as he saw fit. Craig read it, grimaced, and wanted more jazz, more sparks. Todd refused.

"Listen, if I can't do it the way I see fit," he calmly said, "then I'll have to skip the ten P.M. and—"

"What?" Craig shrieked without losing his ubiquitous smile. "You can't do that!"

"Of course I can. I'll just leave now, think about it overnight, and then perhaps do the story tomorrow."

"No fucking way! Management will have a shit fit, you know."

Craig pulled at his hair, paced one step, then froze. "Wait a minute, you're blackmailing me, aren't you?"

"What kind of person do you think I am?"

"Sick, very sick. I'll get someone else to do it."

"It won't work—I was the one who spoke to the killer. Nobody can do this report but me."

"Jesus Christ, Todd!"

Of course Todd was blackmailing him. Refusing to go on at ten and declining to do the report until tomorrow would give all the credit not to Craig, the night producer, but to tomorrow morning's producer.

"Okay, okay, I give," said Craig, surrendering and rubbing his sinuses at the top of his nose. "You'd just better be great."

"Aren't I always?"

The next decision was to not send Todd back to the Stone Arch Bridge, where they had planned for him to do a live report in the darkness of the night. Rather, the decision was made for Todd to broadcast right there from Studio A at WLAK. A minute before the top of the hour, Todd seated himself at the newsdesk adjoining Channel 10's latest discovery, the late-night anchor, Martin Steward, a tall, slender Native American with silky black hair and a chiseled face. Todd fitted the clear earpiece into his ear, then nodded a greeting to Martin, who returned it with a savvy smile. Yes, they both knew what was up, that in large part they had their jobs because they were the perfect tokens: the Indian who could dress like a white man, and the fag who could carry himself like a straight guy.

"Okay," came the line producer's voice via IFB transmission into both Todd's and Martin's earpieces. "We're thirty seconds in front."

A few moments later the distant news director, seated somewhere out there at his computerized panel, began the countdown, his godly voice cooing into Todd's earpiece and head, "Ten, nine, eight, seven . . ."

Precisely on cue, the anchor looked directly into the robotic camera that floated just a few feet in front of him and said, "Welcome to WLAK's Ten at Ten Report. I'm Martin Steward.

"Our top story tonight continues to be that of the murder of Minneapolis Park Police Officer Mark Forrest, which has unfolded this evening with a shocking new development. The story began last night at approximately seven-thirty just as torrential rains and hundred-mile-an-hour straight-line winds were striking the Twin Cities area. WLAK's investigative reporter, Todd Mills, was following up on a lead, which had taken him to the Stone Arch Bridge in downtown Minneapolis, when he witnessed the shooting of Forrest. The body apparently tumbled from the bridge and was not located until late this morning, when Mills and a homicide investigator discovered the body downstream in the Mississippi River.

"In what could be the strangest twist to this story, however, now comes the report that Todd Mills has received a phone call from a man who claims to have pulled the trigger of the gun that killed Sergeant Forrest." Tossing it to Todd, he said, "Here to report is Todd Mills."

Like the naggiest of moms, Craig's voice cut into Todd's earpiece. "Okay, Todd, milk it! Be real sincere! I want viewers crying!"

The second camera, controlled by the news director via computer, zeroed in on Todd and the light atop it flashed red. Just at that moment the floor director pointed directly at Todd, indicating he was live. Oh, brother, thought Todd, realizing what he was about to do. This was like reaching into a hornet's nest and smacking about. No doubt about it, this was going to turn things into a hell of a brew.

"The murder of Officer Mark Forrest has been both odd and mysterious," began Todd, his voice deep and even. "No motive for the shooting has yet to be identified, nor has any suspect. However, park-police officials this afternoon stated that Officer Forrest was gay and completely open about this aspect of his life with his family, friends, and coworkers. Just what bearing this might or might not have on the case is not yet known, but police will be studying this information to see if there's any kind of link to the murder of a gay man just last month.

"Additionally, several hours ago I received an anonymous telephone call from a man who claimed to have shot Officer Forrest. In no uncertain terms he stated his frustration and anger at me for speaking earlier of his personality." Go ahead, thought Todd, his eyes following the TelePrompTer, just read it. "In the course of the brief conversation, I was not able to give my reply, which I will do in just a moment."

Craig's voice chirped, "Beautiful, Todd. Beautiful."

Struggling not to trip up while someone was babbling away in his ear, Todd kept his eyes on the text and continued to read. "First, however, let me go back over the story step by step."

They cut once again to the package, only slightly modified for the late news. With Todd doing a voice-over, the tape proceeded, first showing scenes from the storm, then the spot where the shooting had taken place, and next the police and Bureau of Investigation guys scouring the area late last night. The footage continued, showing the police earlier today pulling the mutilated body out of the river and the medical examiner carting it away. Because, of course, it was important to the station as well as to the security of his own job, Todd didn't just toot his own horn, he blew it like any other reporter would, without hesitation describing how frustrated the police had been both late last night and again this morning. Todd, however, hadn't acquiesced, for he was certain of what he'd witnessed. Rather, with the help of one particularly dutiful investigator—whom Todd didn't mention by name because he wasn't certain what Rawlins would want—Todd had continued the hunt for the truth, eventually locating the body of Officer Forrest nearly a mile downstream from the Stone Arch Bridge.

When the taped footage concluded, the camera in front of him again went live, and Todd, staring directly into the lens, continued reading the TelePrompTer, saying, "As of this moment, the authorities have no suspects in custody, nor do they know of any motive for this heinous act.

"But as I mentioned earlier, several hours ago I received an anonymous and mysterious phone call from a man who identified himself as the killer of young Officer Forrest. I was rather doubtful at first, wondering if it wasn't some sort of crank call, but eventually I was convinced of the veracity of his identity. The caller then lambasted me for not just sticking to the facts, threatened me personally, and hung up.

"Let me now say that I, as well as the police, have every reason to believe that you, the killer, lured me to the scene of the crime in an attempt to get maximum television exposure. And since I also have every reason to believe that you, the person who so cowardly gunned down a young, off-duty policeman, are now watching this broadcast, here is my reply."

Out of nowhere came Craig's voice. "Bravo!"

His brow creased with anger as if he were staring not into a camera but into the eyes of a killer, Todd said, "Neither I nor WLAK will be used. You have committed a terrible crime, and I will not, I repeat, will not glorify your disgusting act of murder. In other words, this is not a game and I will not play along." At least, thought Todd, not according to your rules. "At this time I urge you to turn yourself in to the authorities."

Todd then turned to the late-night anchor and tossed it to him, saying, "Martin, at this point I have nothing further to add."

Martin stammered ever so slightly, then said, "Todd, thank you very much for that most interesting report."

The light atop the camera aimed at Todd flashed off, and then Todd took off his earpiece and slipped away from the newsdesk.

As 10@10 continued and Todd made his way through the dark studio, he couldn't help but smile. That, he knew with blustery and smug confidence, was TV at its best—both sizzle *and* substance.

Chapter 13

Jesus Christ!

What kind of idiot was that guy? And what the hell did he mean by that, a game? *Game?* Shit, Todd Mills was a fool. A complete and utter fool who understood nothing. Well, fuck him! It was completely obvious he was the one turning this into a game, he was the one exploiting this for his own purposes! Well, screw him and screw the media!

In his room at the Redmont Hotel, the man jumped from his hotel bed, where he'd been sitting and watching the late news, then stormed across the small room and hit the OFF button on his TV. He clenched his fists and his jaw, wanted to scream out, to smash the TV, to break everything in sight.

Instead, he went over to the desk and dropped himself in the chair. Fuck, this wasn't the way it was supposed to have happened, no, not at all. And he grabbed a hotel pen and another sheet of paper from the drawer and started writing, scribbling it not once or twice, but over and over and over, going all the way down the page, filling line after line, being enterprising and furiously jotting: *GMF.*

The phone started ringing, and he stopped and stared at it. Of course it was her. Like some sort of threat, she'd said she'd call every night. Only tonight he couldn't do it. Couldn't pick up the receiver and pretend. He was too upset. Too scared. If he spoke to her tonight he'd tell her off, tell her to go straight to hell.

You just gotta pull it together, he told himself. Gotta be tough. Gotta stuff it all back in the closet where it belongs. After all,

Mark Forrest is finally gone, this time for good, and isn't that just what you wanted? Yes, absolutely, and you know what you have to do now, don't you? Just keep quiet, that's all, and no one will ever find out.

After six rings the phone finally shut up, and he started writing again, continuing down the page, scribbling *GMF* and this time chanting along like a mantra, saying, "Gay Mother Fucker."

Chapter 14

It had been a shit day at the office. And now it was a shit night. Oh, God, moaned Douglas Simms to himself, at this rate he wasn't going to get out of his cramped office in Government Center until after midnight. It didn't help that since late this afternoon he'd had trouble concentrating. Or rather, he'd been able to think about little else than that blonde, Kris Kenney. More so than ever, he sensed she was a disaster waiting to happen.

Well over twelve hours ago he started working on a legal brief for Judge Hawkins, a brief that was needed first thing tomorrow but which Simms was beginning to think would take another full day of research. Sitting at his chaotic desk and sipping something like his tenth can of Coke, he started trembling. He stared at the mountain of books and papers and knew there was so much work, plus so much other crap, that he could stay virtually all night and still barely make a dent.

So what about Kris Kenney? Just who the hell was she?

That was what really scared him—he couldn't find out anything about her. Not a thing. When he'd booked Peacock Catering—insisting, as instructed, that Kris be on hand for the good judge's carnal meal—he'd been able to weasel out only her last name and that she did in fact live in Minneapolis. Nothing more. He'd then searched the phone books, finding a single "Kenney, K." Wanting to ascertain that it was in fact she, he'd called and discovered that, no, there was no Kris at that number. Simms had then called directory information, asked the operator for the number, and been told there was an unlisted number for a Christopher Kenney and that was it.

Wait a minute, now thought Simms. It hadn't occurred to him, but perhaps she lived at home with her parents, perhaps the answer was that simple. Be that the case, however, shouldn't there still be some record of her somewhere, somehow? Absolutely. There should be a social-security number, a driver's license, a vehicle registration. Something at least. Yet this afternoon he'd called a buddy of his over in City Hall and asked him to dig up what he could using the computers over there. And the answer had come back almost immediately: nothing. As far as the city of Minneapolis was concerned, a young blond girl by the name of Kris Kenney simply didn't exist.

Leaning back in his chair and rubbing his eyes, Douglas Simms was beginning to understand what he had to do. He'd worked much too hard to get this far. His plans were proceeding perfectly, and, yes, things were just about to fall into place. And there was no way in hell he was going to let some young bitch ruin it.

Right. The sooner he got Kris Kenney out of the picture, the better.

Chapter 15

After spending several hours at the downtown police station, Rawlins went directly home and watched 10@10 from beginning to end. In the rather tattered living room of his second-floor apartment, he sat quite still in an old red leather chair that had once belonged to his grandfather. Right at the top of the show came Todd, of course, then a few more comments by the anchor, followed by the general news, weather—a Minnesota obsession, and rightly so—and finally sports. As he sat there in the low and worn chair, his fingers rubbing on the cracked leather of the arms, as the news concluded and moved into another episode of $M^*A^*S^*H$, which seemed stuck on eternal repeat, Rawlins thought how pissed he was. How totally pissed. He picked up the remote, clicked off the TV, and walked over to the phone. He glanced at his watch, knew of course that it was too soon for Todd to have made it home—which was exactly what he wanted, because after all they weren't supposed to be talking—and then, unable to stop himself, dialed the number he knew better than his own. After four rings Todd's Voice Mail picked up.

When prompted for a message, Rawlins took a deep breath. And then slammed down the receiver.

"Fuck," he cursed to himself.

He wanted to yell at Todd. He wanted to tell him he was a fool. And he wanted to tell him how much he loved him. Instead, he said none of it.

It kind of scared him. Rawlins had had too many boyfriends in his life, too many dates, too much casual sex in his search for something, or rather someone, that Mr. Right. Not long ago he'd given up, come to the realization that there was no singular perfect guy out there who'd fit the bill completely and totally. And he believed that now, today, more than ever. Todd was by no means perfect—like tonight, he could be a stubborn, self-centered pain in the ass—but for some inexplicable reason Rawlins knew that that didn't matter in the greater picture of things. And Rawlins had never felt like that before, he'd never been blinded, let alone knowingly so. Maybe that was love, meeting someone and being instantly able to forgive them so much—almost anything, really. Yes, pondered Rawlins. Right from the start he knew that there was nothing he wanted more than Todd Mills, that there was lust of course, buckets of it, but so much more. The very moment he'd met Todd was what Rawlins still called "the day the earth shook." Now thinking back on it, Rawlins recalled how awful that day had been for Todd, how exposed and naked he'd been to the judgment of the world. And perhaps that was why Rawlins had fallen so fast and so hard for him, because for the first time Rawlins had been able to see someone without a trace of pretense. Rawlins had been able to look at Todd and in a split second see and understand who Todd really was, and then fall in love with that very same person.

Rawlins crossed the living room and turned off a standing lamp. There had never been, nor was there now, a question or doubt in his mind. Rawlins wanted to spend the rest of his life with Todd, whether given his health status that be five days or, with any luck and by the grace of God, fifty years. He was in love, wasn't he? Yes, absolutely and totally. So for now it was kind of good that Lieutenant Holbrook had ordered the two of them to stay apart until this case was resolved. An enforced separation until things cooled off wouldn't hurt either of them.

He didn't know diddly, Rawlins realized, about how you made a relationship good, let alone how you kept it alive and well. He was confident, though, that what Todd and he had going was great, and the last thing he wanted was to blow it. Right. He feared that if he went to Todd's tonight, as he was so tempted, he wouldn't be able to hold his temper, that he would get mad at Todd and things would escalate from there. All too easily he could picture this erupting into a huge fight, and the last thing Rawlins wanted was to blow this out of proportion. Maybe Rawlins was being just a tad paranoid, but he didn't think it was worth it, arguing over the murder of a cop who was already dead and gone, when what mattered most to Rawlins was their future, his and Todd's. Far better, Rawlins mused as he passed through the dining room and pushed the old OFF button of the small chandelier, to stay here and let things cool off.

Entering the kitchen, he glanced at the wall clock, saw that it was approaching eleven. Almost the end of another day, he thought thankfully. The sinus infection that had alerted him and his doctor to his HIV status had long ago faded after a third course of antibiotics. When neither amoxicillin nor Augmentin had worked, he'd switched to a third, clarithromycin, which had done the trick, and he'd felt nothing short of perfect since. Even the gunshot wound in his shoulder had healed beautifully. But there were going to be plenty more challenges in the near future, per- haps tomorrow, perhaps in a year or two or three. Sure, now he had a viral load just under five thousand, a T-cell count of about 450—a tad below normal, it indicated moderate immunosystem suppression—but sooner or later he'd be on some protease inhibi- tor, taking this cocktail and that. For the time being, his doctor, choosing a somewhat radical and risky position, had advised against any of the current meds.

"We don't want you building up resistance to anything," his doctor had said. "There are three new drugs coming down the pike, and I think they'll work best if you're a treatment virgin."

And even though that approach made Rawlins rather ner- vous—he liked to tackle things and deal with them right away—he also didn't mind, for entirely the wrong reasons. Going on a strong course of medication would mean medical-insurance claims. Med- ical claims would eventually mean coming out as an HIV-positive cop on the Minneapolis police force. And who knew what that meant, whether they'd fire him, demote him, or just assign him nothing but desk work, for no one had yet come out of that closet.

Rawlins had gone to the U—the University of Minnesota— and received his B.A. in English. He couldn't quite remember

what had prompted him—trying to make order out of chaos?—
but the following year he'd enrolled in the police academy and
gone through seven months of classroom and skills training. And,
no, he hadn't been out back then. Anything but. During all his
years as a patrol officer, later as a sergeant working juvenile, he'd
been terrified that someone would find out he was queer. After all,
he hadn't been able to escape his own homophobia, nor for that
matter other threats, like the one made during FTO—the field-
training program—when the guys bragged how they felt sorry for
the first faggot to come out, because they were going to beat the
shit out of him.

But then a dyke had done just that.

Bravely leading the way, the first Minneapolis police officer to
come out of the closet was a lesbian, who did so back in 1992. The
first gay man to come out wasn't until a full year or two later.
Rawlins was the fourth, and it had been a horrible, awful hump for
him to go over. But it had gone without a hitch. Contrary to his
fear, Rawlins didn't have then—nor had he since—any problems
as a result of his sexuality.

But would he as an HIV-positive man? Would any of the cops
want to work with him again? There was no way of telling, of
course. Not until he got there.

Heading to the bathroom at the end of the hall, Rawlins
splashed his face and brushed his teeth. Out of habit, he then
checked the lock on the back door, glancing out the window as he
did so.

His bedroom wasn't anything special, a small box of a room
with a futon on a low platform, a long bookcase made up of bricks
and boards beneath the windows, a single small closet, and his old
desk. Even to Rawlins, who'd never been much attuned to these
things, his place was beginning to look shabby and in need of
much more than just a coat of paint. It was unbearably stuffy too.
And hot. He took off his shirt, ran his fingers over the thick, still-
red scar on his left shoulder, then slipped off the rest of his clothing. He lifted open both windows and climbed naked into bed.
Yes, he thought, glancing about the pathetic room, they'd ended

up spending their nights at Todd's condo for much more than just the central air.

Picking up a copy of a thriller set in Berlin, he read until his eyes began to close almost thirty minutes later. He put down the book, turned off the light, but no sooner was his head settled on his pillow than he was suddenly awake all over again.

Why hadn't that bastard called?

In the back of his mind Rawlins had thought Todd would at least try. He'd envisioned staring at the phone, smugly letting it ring, though now he rolled on his side, saw the old dial phone on the floor next to his bed, and knew that if it rang this moment he'd jump on it. But nothing happened. That's right, Rawlins thought. And nothing's going to, for Todd's nothing if not resolute. Or, more accurately, a stubborn son of a bitch. Rawlins had told Todd they were supposed to talk only in a formal setting, so Todd sure as hell wouldn't call. No, Mr. Control himself wouldn't be the first one to crack. So would Rawlins?

Oh, shit. Was this stupid or what?

Rawlins tossed from one side to the other, kicked off the top sheet, pounded a fist into his pillow. Why the hell was he here alone and boiling hot when he could be there with him in air-conditioned splendor? Damn it, they should just forget Holbrook's stupid orders. They were grown men; they could observe a boundary.

Shit. At the very beginning of their relationship Rawlins hadn't been able to sleep all that well with someone else in the bed—Rawlins couldn't stretch out as much, Todd hogged the blankets, Todd breathed too loudly. Now, Rawlins realized to his frustration, just the opposite was true. This was lonely, being here by himself. No one to kiss, to touch, to grope. Was he going to be able to sleep at all tonight? Probably not.

Which was why he heard it, that first sound, a rattle of sorts.

Rawlins was lying in bed, staring up at the dark ceiling, when it came. For a moment he was quite still. Were those his downstairs neighbors, Mike and Amy, stirring about? No, it was from outside. Jesus, he realized. Someone was out there.

And suddenly he couldn't have been more awake.

Chapter 16

Opening the refrigerator, Todd pulled out an old, half-drunk bottle of white wine and poured himself a glass. Oh, brother, he thought, taking a sip. His mind was still racing—he'd been on the air barely an hour ago—and at this point he felt as if he was going to be up half the night.

Leaving the sleek, all-white kitchen, he moved into the hallway and called, "Girlfriend? Girlfriend, where are you?"

When the black cat, which defined the word *fickle*, failed to appear, Todd took his wine into the living room, grabbed a legal pad and pen, then slid open the balcony door. Stepping outside, he stared at Lake Calhoun, the oval body of water just across the street. Transfixed by the moon and its light shimmering on the still waters, he took several sips of wine and sat down on one of two metal chairs.

So how was he going to do this and what exactly was he going to pursue tomorrow?

Though Todd would have been surprised if Forrest had been anything but queer, it was now confirmed. Their eyes had caught in that way, hitting and holding a mere fraction of a second too long, each of them thinking, I'm one, are you one too? And Todd was sure of it, certain that someone like Mark Forrest—young, handsome, and out—had a Mr. Wonderful, someone who wasn't going to let him go. But if so, who was he, where was he, and why hadn't he come forward, either reporting Forrest as missing or now wanting to identify the body or some such? Or was Todd all wrong, was Forrest in the middle of his fuckathon days, going through guys on a daily or weekly basis? Perhaps.

In the glow of the light from the living room, Todd started jotting it all down on the yellow pad. He began where it all began, with that phone call, the very first one Todd had received, the one begging Todd to meet down on the Stone Arch Bridge. He recorded the approximate time, paused, and then added a note. Yes, that caller and the killer were surely one and the same, just as the killer and the man who had called Todd this evening were undoubtedly one and the same. If he would only call again, mused Todd, then he'd be ready, he'd be certain to get a recording of the voice. He kicked himself for not having been so prepared earlier, but who would have thought the killer would call out of the blue?

Moving on, Todd went through it all, every event, every time, from the meeting on the bridge to the shooting to finding the body to tonight's phone call. He was going to have to be methodical about this. Obsessive too. Over the next few days he knew he'd write this over and over again, adding a bit more each time, always looking for a connection or a hole or something. Everything had to tie together, there had to be some link. So what was it, who was it? Exactly, which led Todd back to his first thoughts—who was Forrest doing?

Fixated on Forrest's sex life, Todd took another sip of wine, then slipped back inside and grabbed his cordless phone from the coffee table. Dropping himself on his leather couch, he thought for a moment, recalled the number, and dialed.

On the second ring a voice said loudly, "Hello, hello?"

"Jeff?"

"That's *moi.*"

"It's me, Todd."

"Hey, you old closet queen, how are you? Long time no gab," he said over the blare of Barbra Streisand.

"I take it I didn't wake you up?"

"Oh, heavens no," said the bank teller by day and drag queen by night.

"So what are you doing home tonight? I thought I'd get your machine."

"I'm taking the night off. You know why? I'm getting sick of the straight people down there," he said, referring to the mega-gay complex, the Gay Times, where he often performed. "I mean, what's going on? Have we, the oppressed, made too much progress, or what? I mean, we're talking about a drag show. We're talking about big old homos in beautiful gowns and tons of makeup. I mean, do you realize that eighty percent of the audience last night was straight, and—"

"Jeff," interrupted Todd, knowing that he'd have to cut in at some point. "I need your help."

"Sure, doll."

"You told me once that all the bartenders know when Rawlins comes in to the Gay Times. Is that right?"

"Of course they do, and it's not because he's dreamy, it's because he's a cop. Trust me, the bartenders always try to know the cops and know when they come in."

"Okay, then I have a favor to ask. Will you check on another cop for me, a guy by the name of Mark Forrest? Will you find out if he was in there recently? And with whom?"

"Why? Don't tell me you got trouble in paradise and you're looking for another hunk in blue?"

"I guess you haven't seen the news in the last couple of days. Mark Forrest was a park police officer, and he was murdered. He was also gay, and I'm trying to find out if he was dating anyone."

"Oh, my God, I should start reading the papers again, shouldn't I? Listen, I'll do what I can. I'll get as much four-one-one as possible. Tomorrow soon enough?"

"Perfect."

Todd gave him a few more details and then hung up. Still clutching the phone, he knew what he wanted to do next, whom he wanted to call, very much so. But should he? Dare he? And then, without another thought, he started dialing. Then stopped halfway through.

No, he wasn't going to give in. He wasn't going to call and check on Rawlins. He couldn't. Nope, he wasn't going to be the first one to break.

Averting that number, he dialed another.

A groggy voice answered on the fourth ring. "H-hello?"

"Oh, shit, Janice," said Todd, for he'd completely forgotten the time. "I woke you up."

"Oh, shit, Todd, you did."

"I'm sorry." Realizing how self-absorbed he'd been, he quickly added, "Listen, it can wait. I'll call you back tomorrow."

"Forget it, Todd," she said with a yawn. "I'm awake. What's . . . what's up?"

"Nothing, I . . ." Now it sounded stupid, sophomoric. "Oh, brother."

"Oh, brother, what?"

"At dinner tonight was I . . . well, was I a jerk to Rawlins?"

"Why aren't you asking him?"

"Because I can't. We're not supposed to talk in anything but an official setting, remember?"

"Oh, right—police orders," she said, stifling another yawn. "Well . . ."

She'd tell him, give it to him straight, of that he was sure, and Todd felt himself flinching, for of all the people in the world, Janice and her opinions mattered the most to him. It wasn't simply that they had dated back in college and that they now had a unique family bond that would forever unite them. And it wasn't simply that she was always honest. No, it was more the way she always delivered the truth, frankly but softly. Or rather she was always direct but encouraging. He relied on her for this—relied on her perhaps way too much. But she had a way of helping him through the muckier corners of his life, nurturing the better parts of him in a way no one else could. When he'd been deep in the closet, she'd been one of the few to know that he was gay and virtually the only queer person not to cast judgment.

"You know what I hate about gay men?" she said, the sound of her sheets crumpling in the background as she rolled over. "You think the words *gay* and *sex* mean one and the same thing."

"Oh, we do, do we?" said Todd with a smile, for this was vintage Janice, wise and irreverent.

"Yes, you do. I mean, the whole world knows the power of testosterone, and I'm not knocking it, I'm really not. I mean, there'd be a whole lot less Lesbian Bed Death if dykes could get a hit or two of it. But you guys think with your dicks, you know? Yet what does sex take up on a good day, fifteen minutes? On a great day, thirty?"

"Something like that."

"But . . ." She yawned again. "But you're still gay the other twenty-three and a half hours, right?"

He'd often told her that she should have been a shrink instead of a lawyer, and he now ran his hand through his hair and said, "Yeah, of course, but, Janice—"

"That's my point—you're not gay simply because you have an orgasm with someone of the same sex. You and I and Rawlins and every other queer person are gay because our primary emotional relationships are with someone of the same sex. And let's face it, the best part of being in a relationship isn't just the sex, it's having someone to have breakfast with, go walking with, do the gardening with, and—"

"Janice, listen, I'm sorry I woke you up," he interrupted, wondering where this late-night conversation was going. "Maybe we should talk tomorrow."

"No, you asked a question and I'm going to tell you. You see, sometimes . . . sometimes you just have to stop thinking about yourself and whether you should've done this or that, whether you looked good or stupid. Or who was right or wrong. You gotta forget all that crap and just give and give and give. That's how you keep a relationship alive and healthy and happy, Todd. Sometimes you just have to forget all about being the top dog and you gotta bow to your partner and give with every bit of your heart. And then still keep giving."

Staring out the balcony doors and finally seeing it all, he said, "I guess that means I was a jerk."

"See, you're not so dense."

Chapter 17

A moment later it was completely quiet, and Rawlins turned toward the open windows, stared into the dark, and tried to hear something, anything. There was the low, nearly continual hum of insects, a dog barking in the distance, and then . . . yes, there it was again. The sound of something moving ever so carefully, perhaps that of a shoe sliding through grass. Or was it just some sort of animal?

A couple of years ago Rawlins had come home quite late—he and another cop had been staking out a suspected crack house, to no avail—and he'd parked in the back, just as he'd done tonight, in the space alongside the garage. Exhausted and stiff, he'd climbed out of his car, clutching the jumbo cup of cold coffee he'd bought four hours earlier at a SuperAmerica gas station. Heading toward the vinyl city-issued garbage can, he saw that the lid was flipped open. Not thinking much about it, he threw in the entire cup, coffee and all. Immediately there was a childlike shriek, a scream so shrill that Rawlins had jumped a good six feet. So was this happening again, had the street-smart and pervasive raccoons of Minneapolis invaded the garbage?

In an instant Rawlins was on his feet, padding naked through the apartment, past the bathroom and to the back door. Scratching the dark hair of his chest, he looked down from the second floor and his eyes fell immediately to the garage, a sagging wood-frame structure surrounded by an out-of-control raspberry patch. Off to the side, visible in the light from a lamp in the alley, sat his car, a silver Ford Taurus. And between his vehicle and the garage stood the large black garbage container, now completely undisturbed. Rawlins looked about, searching the bushes that were thick with the junglelike leaves of a hot, humid midwestern summer. He then moved to the side and checked the wooden staircase that doubled back and forth down the rear of the old house to the backyard. Nothing.

Something off to the side caught his eye. Rawlins pulled back from the glass, but, yes, someone was out there—a man, none too big, slipping through his backyard. So was it just someone cutting through his yard, a neighbor taking a shortcut? No. Rawlins noted how the man was moving, slowly, carefully, and knew this wasn't right. Either this guy was scoping out his house, trying to discern an easy way to break in to the downstairs apartment, or . . . or . . . Wait, he was moving back toward the garage. What was he going for? Rawlins's car? There had been a rash of car robberies, where the windows were smashed in and radios ripped off. Or could the guy be going for the garage? In the past year there'd been a handful of garages torched, the work of some warped punk.

Whatever this guy was about to do wasn't good, that much was more than obvious, and Rawlins rushed back to his bedroom, pulled on his jeans, then went to his closet, where his shoulder holster hung. He took his gun, flipped open the barrel. Yes, fully loaded. Barefoot, he turned, started across the room, then froze. There was a different noise, this one more distinct, much closer . . . and definitely not from outside. Holy shit, thought Rawlins, with a shock of realization. Someone was in his apartment. What the hell was going on here; was he about to be hit from front and back?

It was all instinct. His years on the force clicked in, and he raised his gun, clasping it between both hands in a prayerlike grasp, and swept across the room as silently and effortlessly as a ballet dancer. He paused at his doorway, pressed himself against the door trim, and listened but could sense nothing. Holding himself perfectly still for what seemed like minutes but was only seconds, his breathing slowed to next to nothing even as his heart throbbed. Okay, you bastard, what the fuck are you doing in here and where the hell are you?

Rawlins moved his shoeless right foot an inch or two ahead, slipped forward, and peered around the doorjamb. There. Down the hall, through the kitchen and dining room, Rawlins saw a figure move. Rawlins couldn't tell if the guy was armed, but he was definitely coming this way, there was no doubt about that. Yes, and one of the maple floorboards creaked as the intruder boldly maneuvered from the living room, around the dining-room table, and toward the kitchen.

That's right, thought Rawlins, his finger tightening on the trigger. I don't know how the fuck you got in here, but come on. Come all the way. I'm waiting.

Rawlins slunk back in the doorway, surprised that the guy wasn't hesitating, wasn't checking out his color TV or CD player. And that fact alone sent a shiver of fear up Rawlins's spine. What the hell was this all about? Why would one guy be lurking in the backyard while another was brazenly moving through his apartment? Rawlins's mind whipped back through the cases he was working on, tried to think who might have put out a hit on him. And why.

The soft sound of rubber-soled shoes moving over linoleum reached Rawlins. The kitchen. Jesus, he thought. The guy obviously thought Rawlins was asleep, and he was making straight toward the bedroom.

Rawlins slunk away, pressing his naked back against the cool plaster wall. It was only a matter of seconds, a matter of moments, before the guy would round the corner and enter the room. But would he just slip in? Or would his entry be more dynamic? His heart pounding thick and hard, Rawlins raised his pistol, ready to fire away. And then it happened: Without hesitation the mysterious figure turned from the hallway and proceeded into the bedroom. In the spark of a second, Rawlins bolted out of the darkness.

"Freeze!" he shouted as he flew forward.

Using all his weight and strength, Rawlins hurled himself against the other man, catching him totally unsuspecting. The intruder yelped and fell back with surprising ease, and Rawlins plowed forward, smashing the guy against the other wall and jabbing his pistol against the guy's temple.

"Jesus Christ!" cried the man.

Rawlins had lusted after that voice, had caressed that body, and in horror he demanded, "Todd?"

"Rawlins . . . what the hell are . . . are . . ."

"Oh, shit!" Rawlins jerked away nearly as quickly as he had first seized Todd. "What the fuck are you doing sneaking in here? I could've killed you!"

Todd's eyes were large and shocked, and he started to say something, stopped, then said, "I wanted to apologize and . . . and I was afraid if . . . if I called you wouldn't answer. So I just came over. I know I'm not supposed to see you, but I have a key, you know."

Of course. More than once Todd had come home late from work, entering not this apartment but his condo, slipping quietly about, undressing, and then crawling in bed with Rawlins, who was already asleep. And that apparently was exactly what he'd been planning and hoping to do here.

But, thought Rawlins. "Who's that other guy?"

"What other guy?"

"The one in the backyard."

"The hell you talking about?"

This wasn't adding up, not by any means. Not wasting a moment, Rawlins, still clutching his gun, abandoned Todd and rushed out of the bedroom and down the short hall. He hurried up to the window in the back door and looked down. The figure obviously hadn't heard Rawlins shout and was now disappearing around the side of the garage. Clutching his gun and still wearing only his jeans, Rawlins ripped open the door and burst out. Taking the old wooden steps two at a time, he raced downward, leapt onto the grass, and tore across the yard.

From the top of the stairs, Todd screamed, "Behind you!"

The danger registered in a single instant, and Rawlins threw himself forward and hit the ground, his chest skidding on the grass. The very next moment a blast exploded behind him. Rawlins rolled over, twisted around, in those seconds already thinking, realizing, thanking God that he'd missed, that whoever had fired had failed to hit him, his target. Flattening himself, Rawlins stretched his arms before him, trained his gun on the dark figure lurking in the bushes. Squinting, he took aim.

And then his target was gone. Vanished.

Rawlins sprang to his feet, his bare feet digging into the ground. As fast as he could, he tore across the small yard, jumped through the bushes. He saw him, saw the last of the guy racing into the alley, and Rawlins wasted no time. Clutching his gun in both hands in front of him, he rushed after him, pausing at the edge of his neighbor's garage. Peering around the corner, he ascertained the guy wasn't right there, then charged into the alley. In the faint light Rawlins scanned the old garages, the cars, the garbage bins. But there was nothing. No one. Hearing something up to the left, he tore back into a run. Then slowed to a defeated halt.

Now sensing distinct steps behind him, Rawlins turned, saw Todd running out from behind the Taurus.

"Holy shit, are you all right?" Todd demanded, his face much too pale.

"Yeah."

"That asshole took a shot at you!"

"I know . . . and he missed."

"Yeah, but—"

"Todd, don't worry. I'm okay. He fired at me and he missed."

"But who the hell would do something like that? Who'd—"

"I don't know," said Rawlins, his chest heaving and sweat blistering on his forehead. "Maybe . . . maybe he wanted to steal my car."

After a long moment Todd said, "We both know that's bullshit."

"Yeah, I suppose we do."

Chapter 18

Should she really tell him?

"I . . . I . . ." Kris began.

Ten minutes into her early-morning session, Kris sat in her shrink's office as Dr. Dorsey ran one of his hands through his shock of thick hair and stared at her. Buckling under his intense eyes, Kris turned and gazed out the window, noting the morning pedestrian traffic on Nicollet Mall in downtown Minneapolis. Well, what the hell was she supposed to say? Should she really tell Dr. Dorsey about Stuart Hawkins, that a soiree of sorts had evidently been set up for this evening? And that Kris wanted nothing more than to run right into the arms of that gorgeous man?

"Go ahead," urged Dorsey in his soft voice as he sat in the hard wooden chair opposite her.

Even though this was only something like her fourth session, she knew his game, his ways, she thought, staring out at the bright sun. The voice might be easy and gentle, but it didn't belie the truth. No, shrinks were so uptight. So reserved. And while pretending not to be, so judgmental. They always prided themselves, she was absolutely sure, on having heard everything. But would Dr. Dorsey have heard anything like this, that she'd finger-fucked the most widely known judge in the state?

"Is there something you'd like to tell me?" asked the good doctor, crossing one leg over the other.

Kris couldn't help but grin. In fact, she had to stuff it, an urge to burst into a huge laugh. Unbelievable—Hawkins hadn't read her as a guy, she'd passed as a woman, and she'd actually penetrated him!

"What is it?"

Kris averted Dr. Dorsey's dark, intense eyes. She wanted to tell him, this diminutive man in his tweed coat, blue shirt, and khakis, she really did. Kris knew precious little about him, only that he was married, and secretly she wanted to make him jealous. She wanted to tell him not simply about her crush on Hawkins, but how she'd actually been with him, just what they'd done and where, every little sordid detail, hoping for a reaction of some kind from Dorsey, hoping that once and for all she'd find out what Dr. Dorsey really thought of her. But, no, she thought, she couldn't tell him. Right. And instead Kris looked at the four framed duck prints on the beige wall, then focused on the book-crammed teak bookcase standing on the opposite side. Okay, okay, she told herself. Get a grip. Get to the point. Don't be an idiot. This guy's costing a fortune by the hour. So why are you here?

Instantly, it all came flooding into this tiny room, swirling around her and drowning her in memories. Her smile vanished.

Wearing a tight black skirt and an apricot-color knit top, she shifted in the chair. What is it? Fucking everything, that's what it is! Everything! Kris wanted nothing more than to smile again, but suddenly she was blotting a tear from her left eye. Gazing again out the window and at the mall, she saw a handful of people rush by, evidently late for work. Next came two old women, out for an early stroll. Then two buses dieseled by, one after the other.

"When . . . when . . ."

"Yes?" he pried in his shrinkly way.

"I've been taking hormones for a long time now," said Kris, who still got them quite illegally from her source in California. "My beard is gone, I have breasts now, but . . ." Searching for hope, she turned to him. "But when are things going to get good? When am I going to be happy?"

Dr. Dorsey nodded, jotted a quick note on his clipboard, which rested on his knee, then said, "That's why you're here, Kris. You're residing in an extremely difficult land. Gender dysphoria is—"

"No, don't say that!" she snapped. "Don't use that word *dysphoria*! It makes it sound like I'm sick, like I'm mentally ill. I'm not. I'm just confused and . . . and I'm questioning, but I'm not crazy."

"Of course you're not. I'm sorry. I didn't mean to imply that."

"Yeah, but . . . but . . ." She took a deep breath. "I don't know, there was a big stink about that last year on the Internet. All these trannies objected to that—the use of the word *dysphoria* to describe us—and I mean talk about girlfight girlfight. Maybe it doesn't make sense to you, maybe you don't understand 'cause . . . 'cause, you know, you're straight, but in the T community it's just not PC, not PC at all."

"Kris, please trust me. Of course I understand. And thank you for correcting me."

"Well, I . . . I just want you to know that I'm not crazy and that I think I can be good, and . . . and that I want to be happy."

She was desperate for him to agree, to say, yes, you are good, you are loved, you are worthy of life. And yes, you will be happy. She needed his blessing. His encouragement to keep on. Instead, Dorsey shifted in his chair.

"Kris, sexual expression and gender expression are two totally different things, and their definitions are much broader than society sees them. We've been taught that there is only the male and female, and that the first is masculine and the second is feminine. The first is assigned the blue color, the second pink. And the male is supposed to sexually desire the female, and the female only the male. The spectrum, however, is much broader."

"I know, I know."

"Keep in mind that it wasn't so very long ago when people believed women were supposed to do the cooking and men were supposed to do the yard work, just as they believed that gay men only wanted to wear dresses. But is any of that true?"

"No, of course not."

"Exactly. Everyone, Kris, has the right to their individual place on the continuum. Everyone has the right to contradict what society expects—to be different, to be ambiguous even. And everyone has the right to be honest about who they are." Gently,

Dorsey said, "Kris, you've been quite brave in your life. You've transgressed a boundary society used to say you could not. You were born a boy, but as I look at you now your gender expression is female. That makes you truly a transgendered individual."

"But . . . but do I keep on gender-fucking like this—after all, I do have both breasts and a penis—or do I need to make a decision? I mean, everyone's always asking me if I'm a boy or a girl, if I'm gay or straight."

"You know what? It doesn't matter. Trust me, you don't need a label to be at peace within yourself. I do understand, though, that this is a confusing situation, that it's complicated by another fact. Something terrible happened to you, didn't it?"

Kris laughed and choked back tears. "No shit."

"I think we need to look at that some more."

"What the fuck does that mean, that you want to look at my empty scrotum? That you want to see the boy without balls? The chick with a dick?"

Kris looked at him. The doctor stared back, his face blank and emotionless. Oh, shit, she thought. She was always trying to get some sort of reaction out of him, but clearly she'd overdone it.

"I'm sorry, I guess I'm just a little defensive. I . . . I didn't mean to . . ."

"Kris, all I'm saying is that you have an immense amount of pain surrounding what happened to you—and rightly so. And I think we need to look at that further. Frankly, you haven't dealt completely with your pain, and I think that's causing a lot of the anxiety you're presently experiencing. You need to do that, too, to deal with that pain so you can get to the good stuff in life."

"I know." She closed her eyes and nodded. "I know I have to accept the past before I can go into the future."

"Or enjoy the present."

Recalling the boy side of herself, it all came flooding back with amazing speed and ease. "I was only fifteen when it happened, and I never even got the chance to do it with a guy. Shit, I remember jerking off to pictures of guys but that's as far as things went, as far as—"

"Slow down."

"Sometimes I think I should just give in, that I should just go the whole *M* to *F* route. All they'd have to do is turn my penis inside out and make me a nice little . . . nice . . . well, you know, vagina." She tugged at one of her gold hoops. "On the Internet I read about a hospital out in Colorado they call Trans Central Station, and they've done almost five thousand operations there! For not even ten thousand bucks they make you a vagina that's almost three inches deep, and if you have enough tissue— *corpus spongiosum,* whatever that is—they even make you a functional clitoris."

"Kris, you might in fact decide to have the operation. You might feel better and more complete as a postop transsexual."

"Maybe. I don't know. But I just hate the way our society thinks. Male or female, black or white, straight or gay, innocent or guilty—it's just so . . . so binary!"

"It's very restricting, isn't it? But you know you can decide to stay just the way you are. And that's why you're here. All I want is to help you sort all this out so you can find your own happiness." Dr. Dorsey moved ever so slightly forward, focused all of himself upon Kris, and said, "Let's go back to the beginning again."

"You want all the gory details?" She took a deep breath, because she never talked about it. Never. "It's not pretty, you know. And let me tell you, it hurt like hell, but I'll—"

"No, I want you to start earlier than that. You said last week that you always knew you were gay."

"Right. The truth is that I never wondered if I was 'different' or any of that crap. I always knew I was. I always knew I was gay, right from the start. By that, I don't mean puberty. No, I'm talking age five, maybe six."

"And how did that make you feel?"

"Me? I felt totally normal. It was fucking everybody else that had a problem with it."

"Your—"

Kris held up her hand and just kept barreling along. "I was never masculine, not at all. It just wasn't part of me. I was way at one end of your spectrum, you see. Way at the fem end of things. I feel sorry for gay guys who are more the other way, you know, the butch ones, the masculine types. Sometimes they have a lot to sort out—you know, how to be queer and butch at the same time—whereas with me it was pretty clear-cut. I mean, this stuff," she said, tugging at first her skirt, then her blouse, "comes real natural to me."

He asked it so bluntly that it didn't even hurt: "Do you think you would have dressed in women's clothes if you hadn't been castrated?"

Kris shrugged. "I don't know. Probably. I mean, I'm sure I would have at least done drag. After all, I was awfully interested in my mother's cosmetics and clothes. Even as a kid I was obsessed with the idea of disguise. Of putting something on and becoming someone else. That was what was fun about it."

"Okay, tell me more about your family."

Kris opened her mouth, hesitated, then said, "Unfortunately, they're as good as dead to me."

"Yes, you've said that. You told me how they cut you off after you went to California."

"Right . . ." she said, her voice all but nonexistent. "Most people are born one way and either accept that or struggle with it. I was struggling, of course. A lot. Both with my sexuality and my gender expression. But then there was the accident, which in a weird, awful way opened up everything, all the possibilities, you know?

"So . . . so I went out to California to try living as a woman, and that's when my family disowned me. After the accident the doctors put me on testosterone—I guess technically it was andro-gen—and my parents wanted me to keep taking that and get a pair of fake nuts, but . . . but that just didn't feel right. I've always been very effeminate-looking, so I decided to go that way, toward my natural tendencies and my natural strengths. So I quit the one and started taking estrogen and dressing only in women's clothes. Then, of course, things went from bad to horrible, you know, because of what happened out in L.A. Now my parents tell their friends that I'm dead." She bit her lip, tried not to cry. "They're shits, you know. Real shits. My cousin, the one I'm living with here, is my one and only relative who will talk to me, and we're not getting along so great now either."

"I know. How does—"

"—it make me feel? Awful. Horrible. To be perfectly honest, it killed something deep inside me."

"I'm sorry."

"I mean, how would you feel if your own family told the neighbors that their son died in a car crash? Things were bad enough before . . ." She took a deep breath, tried to stuff away the pain. "Well, let's just say, I'm surprised my own father hasn't already come after me and gunned me down."

"We need to go into all of that at length, of course, but first just tell me about them again, about your parents and brothers and sister. I need some more background. When did they find out you were gay?"

She ran her hand briefly through her blond hair. Her family. Kris sat silent for a few minutes, and then she gave him the stats. Kris was the second oldest of four. Three boys, including herself— or himself. One girl. They lived in Duluth, where Kris's dad worked as a policeman and her mom as a nurse.

"They knew. All of them knew right from the start too. That was the great unspoken truth of my family—little Chris was a fairy. Everyone knew, but no one dared say it."

She continued, explaining how her mother was always tired because she worked the night shift and her father was always, well, strict. Of Irish Catholic background, his job as a cop made him keep odd hours, and so he expected his kids to behave, to be the very model of respectability. Tom and Mike, the two other boys, were the oldest and the youngest, respectively, and both were hockey nuts and champs. And their father's pride. Mary, the third child, was Miss Social and went, of course, from captain of her high-school cheerleading team to homecoming queen.

"How did your brothers and sister treat you?" asked Dr. Dorsey.

"What do you think? For the most part my sister was pretty nice to me, and my brothers, well, they were always hammering on me." Kris smiled. "You know what my big form of rebellion was?"

"What?"

"I never, not once, put on a pair of skates. That's tantamount to being a traitor in Minnesota."

"You did that on purpose?"

"Of course I did. I did it as much to thumb my nose at my dad and my brothers as to protect myself." She lifted up one of her legs. "I mean, look at how skinny these ankles are. I would've been massacred on a hockey rink."

"So you've always been good at taking care of yourself?"

She shrugged. "No, I've always been good at surviving. Somehow I've made it this far, haven't I?"

"Yes, you have."

Quite early on, she explained, Chris had learned which friends were okay and which were not, for there were those who would tolerate him and those who would torment. He learned quickly, too, which school halls were safe for sissies—the ones with teachers around—and which school activities were okay, badminton and football being the two opposite extremes.

"Kids are awfully mean. They're horrible, really. So cruel." Gazing out the window, not really thinking what she was saying but knowing it was some kind of big truth, it just rolled out of Kris's mouth. "I'm amazed at how much I hate straight people."

Dorsey seemed taken aback but struggled not to show it. "Why?"

"Because it's a straight world and I've always had to be on guard. I've always had to do this doublethink crap. I've always had to monitor myself. How would you like to live like that? How would you like worrying all the time what people would do to you, how they would hurt you, if they knew the truth of who you were? I grew up with it. It was always in my head. I was always afraid. And now . . ."

"Now?"

"It's worse. Straight guys think I'm disgusting, but . . ." God, no wonder she was going crazy. "But what's worse is that now gay guys are freaked out by me too. I mean, not even the fucking homos know what to think of me, where to categorize me. And you should see the muscle queens—you know, the ones on steroids—they're the worst, the most intolerant of anyone different from them. I mean, they're as conservative and inflexible in their ways as a Republican housewife. I really scare the shit out of them." She looked down at her broad hands, saw how soft and lovely they'd become. "You know, the truth is that I was always a big fem. Right from the start, from when I was a kid. But . . . but I never wanted to lose my dick and balls. I was just an effeminate gay kid. In fact, I would never have thought about any of this if . . . if . . ."

"So tell me about that night."

For a long time Kris couldn't speak, then she muttered, "It was January, and it was so fucking cold."

As cold as it ever got, pushing past thirty below zero. Then again, that was midwinter Duluth. Co-o-o-ld. It was night and their parents were working, their mom on duty at the hospital until eleven, their dad due back sometime around ten. Mary, Miss Social Butterfly, was off for the night at a friend's house.

"Which left you and Tom and Mike where? Up in your rooms?"

"No, we were downstairs."

"Together?"

Her voice was nearly a whisper. "Yes."

Yes, they were in the living room. The three boys. Together. It was kind of a small room, a sofa, two big old chairs. And a TV in the corner. A TV that had been on for hours. Already they'd watched *Family Ties* and a repeat of *The Cosby Show.*

"Tom was almost seventeen. I'd just turned fifteen. And Mike was eleven. A very loud, very active eleven."

Their mother had made them dinner, a tuna fish hot dish with peas and some crumbled potato chips on top. She'd left it in the oven, just as she always did, and told them when to eat and reminded them of two things.

"Now, you boys, listen up," she had said, lecturing them as she put on a second sweater, then wrapped a scarf around her neck, put on a hat, and finally her heaviest coat. "Don't forget to turn the oven off—I don't want it left on for hours like you did last week. And don't go outside. It's too cold. I mean it, no going out. Am I clear? Do you understand?"

Yes, they'd all replied.

"Gramps and Nanna are just a block away, so you call them if you need anything. Right?"

"Right."

"The number's above the phone."

But it was too much. Three boys locked up inside on the coldest of winter nights. They just got antsy, that was all.

"We ate our dinner, that stupid tuna fish crap," explained Kris with a sneer, "then took our dishes into the kitchen. We got some ice cream and came back to the living room to watch some more TV. It was chocolate ice cream, I'm sure of that, and, you know, we just started horsing around. Mike wanted to sit on the couch; Tom and I told him there wasn't room. Then all of a sudden the two of them were wrestling and a foot came over and kicked my bowl of ice cream. It flipped right over, dumped right in my lap."

Tom and Mike had started laughing, Kris continued, because they knew that Chris was going to get into trouble, big trouble, for making a mess. And so did Chris, which was why he ran into the kitchen, dumped his bowl in the sink, and then charged into the basement. He tore down the narrow wooden steps, over to the old Maytag, and ripped off his jeans and underwear. There was a big pile of laundry, and he hid his clothes beneath it all.

"I . . . I was just standing there in my shirt," continued Kris, forever horrified by the event that had changed her life. "And then I looked over and saw one of my sister's skirts. It was a plaid wool kilt. Blue and white and yellow. It was hanging from a clothesline down there and, I don't know, I just grabbed it. I pulled off the wooden clothespins, then slipped it on. Why not? It was kind of fun."

"Exciting?"

"Yes."

"Sexually exciting?"

"Well . . ." She thought for a moment. "Not really."

"Was this the first time you'd tried on a piece of woman's clothing?"

Kris sat quite still for quite a long time. "No, I'd fooled around with my mom's clothes a few times—you know, her high heels, her bra."

"Then what happened?"

"I put on the skirt and then I started walking around, you know, in the basement. I was just going to wear it for a moment or two, it looked so warm and . . . and my sister always looked so pretty when she wore it, but then . . . Shit, I must have been nuts! What the hell was I thinking? I heard the TV, I thought they were both upstairs! I didn't think they'd come down!"

"But they did."

"Yes," said Kris, her eyes brewing with tears. "I was down there in a T-shirt and my sister's little kilt, and . . . and Tom and Mike were on the stairs." She shook her head, wiped her eyes. "They started screaming, calling me a homo, laughing and saying they were going to tell Mom and Dad and everyone at school! It was like being outed by your own brothers, you know. It was awful! And I was so scared that I didn't know what to do!"

Without thinking Chris had ripped off the skirt, then grabbed a pair of gym shorts from the laundry basket. By then the brothers were laughing and screaming, even pushing Chris around. Chris had no choice. He had to leave. Had to get out of there.

"I thought I could make it down to my grandparents'," explained Kris. "I'd run down there lots of times without a jacket, so I didn't even really think about it. I just went running upstairs and flying out the front door in my T-shirt, those gym shorts, and a pair of socks." Kris blotted her eyes with the back of her hand. "I . . . I wish I could blame it on something. Or someone else. But I guess the only guilty person is . . . me."

"Go on, Kris."

"So I tore down our front walk, down the street. I was running as fast as I could, you know, wanting to get away from it all, wanting to hide for the rest of my life. My parents were going to kill me, I was sure of that. And then . . ." The tears were coming faster. "Then I hit that patch of . . . of ice."

Kris bowed her head into both hands and sobbed. Overwhelmed by the humiliation as well as the horror of it, she couldn't stop, couldn't block the tears. One event on one night had changed the entire rest of her life.

"It's not fair!" she finally managed to say, her face pulsing red and streaked with tears.

"No, of course it's not," replied Dr. Dorsey.

Then came the anger, surging through her with such hate and turpitude that Kris held her hands in front of her, clenching them into the tightest of fists. Using all her strength, thinking of everything she was so pissed about, she squeezed as hard as she could, digging her artificial nails into the palms of her hands.

"You know how fucking mad I am? Do you have any idea at all? Well," she said, unclenching her fists and exposing her punctured and bloodied hands, "let me show you."

At the sight of the blood, Dr. Dorsey sat back, then a moment later glanced at the clock up on his teak bookcase and said, "Well . . . okay, that's enough for today."

Chapter 19

Ignoring this morning's newspaper, Todd sipped his second cup of coffee and stared out at the lake. What if?

What if Todd hadn't seen that guy in the bushes and hadn't called out?

What if the gunman hadn't missed?

What if he tried again to kill Rawlins?

Yes, that had been him last night, the very same guy who'd gunned down Mark Forrest and later telephoned Todd. There was no definitive proof, at least not yet, but Todd was completely sure of it. And now burdened as much by a pile of guilt as a lack of sleep, Todd could barely move. He'd done his damnedest to engage this killer, and in retaliation the killer was evidently doing his damnedest to live up to his threat. And while Todd hadn't understood before, he certainly did now. Yes, go after his lover, that was exactly how to make him suffer.

Dear God, thought Todd, leaning his face into the palms of both hands, if anything happens to Rawlins—particularly now, particularly because of the stupid-ass things I've done—I won't be able to handle it.

It had been a late night. And as much as Todd had just wanted to wrap his arms around Rawlins and whisk him out of there, he'd known that Rawlins was right, that he had to do it all officially. But rather than leaving as Rawlins had wanted—after all, Todd shouldn't have been there in the first place—Todd retreated to his car and waited. And waited.

Rawlins had called in the shooting right away, and it got big attention real quick. The murder of Police Officer Mark Forrest weighed heavy on every cop in town, and within minutes a half dozen police cars had come screaming into the neighborhood. Wasting no time, they searched every yard, cruised every alley, yet discovered nothing but some kids smoking cigarettes in an abandoned garage. Meanwhile, the guys in Car 21—the team from the Bureau of Investigation—arrived and began combing Rawlins's backyard. In hopes of finding the stray bullet that had been meant for Rawlins, they used huge flashlights to search everything—the ground, the side of the neighbor's house, the trees—all to no avail. Even the bullet casing, which they'd hoped would tie into the Forrest case, escaped them.

It was going on 3:00 A.M. before things quieted down, before Todd was able to get Rawlins aside. No, Todd had insisted, Rawlins wasn't spending the night there, least of all by himself. There was some crazy-ass son of a bitch out and about, and Todd wasn't going to leave Rawlins alone. In the end they blew off Lieutenant Holbrook's orders and ended up back at Todd's condo, their fear morphing into sex that was as full of desperation as it was passion.

So what did they get in the end, three, four hours' sleep?

Wondering if the police had dug up anything new on the case, he was just opening the paper when the phone rang. He reached past his coffee and grabbed the cordless. Please, he thought, let it be Rawlins. Letting him walk out of here hadn't been easy, not by any means.

"Hello?" said Todd.

"It's *moi*."

It seemed as if they hadn't spoken last night but days ago, and Todd said, "Hi, Jeff. What's up? Did you find out anything?"

"A bit." He kept his voice low. "Listen, I'm at work, so I can't talk long. But I called one of the bartenders last night, and he said, sure, he remembered Mark Forrest. Apparently a lot of the guys down there knew of him, because last winter Forrest was the cover boy for a feature *Q Monthly* did on gay cops."

"You're kidding. I must have missed that issue," said Todd, making a mental note to dig up that issue.

"I guess besides being a cop he was quite the looker."

"Yeah, he was."

"Well, he was there, at the Gay Times."

Suddenly Todd was very awake, more than he had been yet that morning, and he pressed, "When? In the last few days?"

"That's where the bartender gets a little fuzzy—he's a sweetheart, but he's certainly no rocket scientist, I'll tell you that much. He did one too many chemicals, I do believe. Anyway, he's not positive, but he's pretty sure Mark Forrest was in a day or two before he was killed. Then again, it could've been last week."

"Was he alone?"

"Nope, not this last time, or so says my bartender friend. Forrest usually came in by himself, he said, but the last time he was with some guy. He's sure of that because there was kind of a scene. There was a bachelorette party—about a half dozen women—and they started giggling and laughing because Forrest and this guy were making out in the next booth. Apparently Forrest's friend got all bent out of shape and—"

"This guy, what'd he look like?" demanded Todd.

"I asked, trust me I did, but all I got was that the guy had brown hair."

"Nothing else?"

"Zip."

A pulse of excitement rushed through Todd. It very well might have been him, this guy who'd gunned down Forrest. But even if it weren't, perhaps he knew something about Mark Forrest's last few days.

Todd asked, "Would your friend be willing to talk to me?"

"Maybe, but then again you are a reporter, and I bet he wouldn't want to do anything on TV."

"I just want to talk, that's all."

"Well . . ." Jeff thought a moment. "Well, if you came down when I was there, say, like, tonight or tomorrow night, I could introduce you. But, Toddy, dear, don't get your hopes up. I think I got all there was to get."

"Jeff, thanks. Thanks a million. I'll be in touch."

Todd hung up, then jumped to his feet. He took a quick slug of coffee, next stood at the balcony door overlooking the lake. This wasn't much, but at least it was something, a foothold into Mark Forrest's personal life. So who was this guy that Mark Forrest had been kissing? Had they just picked each other up, or was this someone Forrest had known for a while, perhaps someone he'd even brought home?

Now, there's an idea, thought Todd.

He turned and half trotted across the living room. Reaching the front hall, he grabbed his briefcase, brought it back to the dining room, and, giving it a good shake, dumped it out on the table. Pens and paper clips and scraps of paper spewed out, and there it was, Mark Forrest's address, which Todd had scribbled down just after they'd found his body in the Mississippi. Should he go? Absolutely.

Barely thirty minutes later Todd was pulling down Young Avenue South to a tall, white clapboard house with a front porch, one of thousands like it built in the Twin Cities in the early part of the century. Todd checked the address on the scrap of paper one last time, then climbed out. As he turned from the sidewalk to the front walk, he saw the pot of red geraniums at the base of the porch steps. Had Forrest planted those or had someone else? Someone such as a relative? Todd had learned that Forrest's parents lived south of The Cities, so who was he about to meet, a sister? A brother?

There was only one way to find out, and Todd swung open the screen door, stepped onto the wooden porch, and pressed the doorbell. He hated this kind of cold call, but he had no choice, and he stood there, his hands clasped in front of him as footsteps bustled somewhere inside. A moment later a lace curtain covering the window on the large oak door was pushed aside, and an older woman peered out, her white hair short and curled.

"Yes?" she said through the glass.

The best way was to be terribly up-front about it, and he took a deep breath and said, "I was wondering if I could speak to you for a few minutes about Mark Forrest?"

"I've already talked to the police. I've already told them everything I know." Her brow crinkled in suspicion. "Who are you anyway?"

So Rawlins had been here. Yesterday afternoon either he'd come out here or had sent someone else. Was this then a waste of time?

"My name is Todd Mills. I'm from WLAK TV," he said.

"Oh."

Evidently Todd needed no further introduction. Too midwestern to simply slough him off, she unlocked the door and pulled it open, her eyes running over him. And as she sized him up, Todd studied her as well. No, he realized with a sense of relief, this wasn't a family member. This woman, short with pale skin and plain glasses and wearing blue pants and a white blouse, was sullen, even visibly sad, but her eyes weren't red or watery.

"Sure, I recognize you. You're on Channel Ten," she said, her voice direct and even. "I'm Anna Johnson. I was Mark's landlady."

"He lived here in this house?"

"Sure. He rented my apartment."

Todd glanced over her shoulder, saw the oak staircase, another predominant feature of these homes. "You have an apartment here in the house?"

"Yes, up on the third floor. There's a staircase out back. It's not a big apartment, but it's nice and clean. Mark, bless him, moved in almost a year ago. Nice fellow. Did all my shoveling last winter, and did a real good job too." She paused, then said, "I've been wondering if any of you reporters would come around."

"I'm the first?" Todd casually asked, quite curious to know if the competition had been around.

"Yep." She peered past him toward the street. "Say, I don't want any cameras snooping around my house, okay?"

"Don't worry, I'm here by myself. I'm just trying to understand what happened."

"It's just awful, isn't it?" she said, raising one hand to her chin and shaking her head. "Nice kid like him. A police officer too. I was so happy to have him living here, to have a cop living in my house. And here he gets himself killed!"

"Yeah, it's terrible." Todd hesitated, wondered if she knew Mark was gay. "Could you tell me if any guys used to come around? You know, if Mark had any particularly close male friends?"

"Like a boyfriend? That's what the police asked too. And I told them no, not that I ever saw. Oh, I knew Mark was gay, but I didn't give a bit about that. All that I cared was that he took good care of the apartment, which he certainly did. He was a nice, quiet fellow."

"So you don't remember any guys visiting Mark?"

"No, not any that come to mind. You see, it's small up there, real small. A room with a bed and a kitchenette and bath, that's it. Not much room for entertaining, really. But it's cheap. And Mark took it because he said he was saving up to buy a house. That's what he wanted to do, buy his own place."

"Of course." Already sensing this was going to be a bust, Todd asked, "So you don't remember anyone coming around? You never heard anybody else up there, particularly not in the last few weeks?"

"Nope, not at all. And I would've heard it too. You have to understand, this place is built as tight as a drum. There's a wood floor up there—all maple—and I would've heard if he'd had anyone with him. But he never did. All I ever heard was just one set of footsteps."

"I see," said Todd, quite certain that she had in fact been listening.

He asked her a handful of other questions—was he on time with his rent, was he recently gone more than usual?—none of which shed any light. Then, as discouraged as he was desperate, Todd thanked her and slowly made his way down the front walk and back to his vehicle.

Okay, he pondered, now what?

As he passed around the front of his Cherokee, he looked up and saw a white piece of paper pinned between the windshield and the wiper blade. He immediately scanned the street up and down, but saw not a single car speeding off. He then searched the yards on both sides of the block. No one, not even a dog. Weird, he thought. He'd been standing right up on that porch, right on

Anna Johnson's threshold, and he hadn't heard or noticed a thing out here.

His heart filling with dread, Todd reached for the paper, which was folded in half. But rather than announcing a neighborhood meeting or garage sale, as Todd so hoped, there was one simple typed line that read: Don't forget, asshole, he's still the bait for a trap that you set.

Chapter 20

It was enough to make Todd nauseous, but Rawlins took it in professional stride and told him not to worry.

They met at the curb right outside City Hall, and when Todd passed him the note, which he had handled as little as possible, Rawlins slipped it directly into a plastic bag. With the hope that they could recover a fingerprint, Rawlins said he was going right down to forensics. Speechless, Todd then watched as Rawlins disappeared back into the massive granite building, finding solace only in the fact that Rawlins was, for the time being at least, safely ensconced behind the brutally thick walls of the city's heart.

When Todd finally got to the station shortly before noon, it was clear that the story of Sergeant Forrest's murder was going to sink to the number-two spot on the midday news. Todd, however, couldn't have cared less.

Going directly to his office, he shut his door and sat there, his mind racing for a way to defuse this. Hoping that Forrest's killer would phone, he took virtually every one of his calls, letting none slip into Voice Mail. Then again, undoubtedly the man who had gunned down Mark Forrest and taken a shot at Rawlins suspected that Todd's home and work phones were tapped, as they most definitely had been since eight that morning. Under police advice—namely Rawlins's—any call coming into Todd's office or his cellular phone was immediately traced. Not wanting to lose anything, Todd took it one step further and had a small tape recorder on hand virtually all afternoon. Any time either of his phones rang, the first thing he did was slap the small suction cup with the microphone onto the receiver.

"That's cool, very cool," said Nan, the producer, loving the idea. "Get me a recording of a cop killer's voice, and, no prob, I'll make sure you lead 'em all—the five, six, and ten o'clock."

But no such call came.

As it was, Todd busied himself the rest of the day getting as much information as possible about Mark Forrest. First he called *Q Monthly* and requested the back issue on gay cops, which they said they'd dig out. Following that, he spoke with a public-relations person at the Minneapolis park police, then with Lieutenant Adams, Forrest's superior, and finally with two other police officers who had worked side by side with Forrest and could vouch for his character. Simply, everyone gushed about what a great guy he'd been and how terrible this was, the shooting. By all accounts Park Police Officer Mark Forrest was beloved, a farm boy who worked hard, was without question totally honest, and who got along with everyone. He had no temper, not that anyone knew of. And he'd never been reprimanded, not by any means. That he was gay was almost beside the point. And, no, no one knew if Mark had been dating anyone, least of all some guy with brown hair.

Todd jotted it all down, and it all fit. What everyone said about Mark Forrest matched Todd's initial impressions of the handsome young man Todd had met briefly on the Stone Arch Bridge. Knowing nothing of Forrest's family, Todd had no choice but to be obnoxiously aggressive. He found out where Forrest's mother and father lived, and while all of his instincts told him he should just grab a photographer and head out there, he was reticent to leave the station in case a call came in from the self-identified killer. Instead, he sent Bradley to the farm just outside of Faribault, and he got some footage of the grieving mother and father as they climbed in a car and hurried away.

At the end of the day, unfortunately, Todd had learned nothing new, at least not of any real significance, and he found himself fixated on when Forrest's killer might next emerge. And what he would do. Unbelievable, thought Todd, cursing himself for the hundredth time. He'd been standing right up there on that porch, and that jerk had slithered right on by.

A mere forty minutes before the 5:00 P.M. news, a gas main ruptured in northeast Minneapolis, the explosion ripping open a street. And while no one was killed, a half dozen people, including two kids on bikes, were injured. No doubt about it, it made for very dramatic coverage, and a reporter and photographer rushed to the scene. The 5:00 P.M. news opened with live shots of ambulances screaming down the street, steaming pavement, a ten-foot-deep crater, and, among other things, a bent bike.

"The good news," concluded the evening anchor, Tom Rivers, with his perfectly great broadcaster's voice, "is that at this point none of the injuries appears serious or life-threatening."

At the back of Studio A, Todd was given the cue, and he slipped past the news director, who sat at a bank of computers directing the robotic cameras. Moving toward the news set, Todd stepped over the cables, passed the floor director, then took his position at a desk some fifteen feet to the right of Tom Rivers.

"We'll be having updates throughout this broadcast," continued Rivers. "One of our reporters is now on the way to Hennepin County Medical Center, so we'll keep you posted on the status of those injured."

Todd, tonight wearing a navy-blue sport coat, light-blue shirt, and a solid blue tie, sat down, slipped in his earpiece, and straightened his tie.

A motherlike voice squawked in his ear, "Smooth the front of your hair, Todd."

He did as he was told, then stared straight into the monitor.

"Good," Nan said approvingly.

Todd glanced over at Tom Rivers, saw the anchor look down at a sheaf of papers that was nothing more than a prop, then look up at the TelePrompTer. Okay, thought Todd, here goes.

Staring at the monitor, Rivers read, "Meanwhile, the murder of Minneapolis Park Police Officer Mark Forrest, who was gunned down two days ago on the Stone Arch Bridge in downtown Minneapolis, continues to occupy the full attention of the Minneapolis police force. Here to give us an update is WLAK's investigative reporter, Todd Mills, who in fact witnessed the brutal slaying." Tossing it, he said, "Todd?"

The floor director cued Todd, pointing to him just as a light atop the robotic camera flashed red.

"As of this moment, police continue to search for a suspect in the shooting," began Todd, trying to make things sound interesting but knowing all too well the only real news was that Officer Mark Forrest was still dead.

He then launched into a very brief recap of the story, using part of the Stone Arch Bridge package and explaining how it was not until the following day that Forrest's body was actually found. As a clip of the family farm outside Faribault played, Todd continued, telling how Mark Forrest had left behind two very devoted parents. And then he reported again on the strange phone call he'd received last night from the man who claimed to be the true killer. Certainly, said Todd, that was one of the stranger twists in this story.

In the lobby of the WLAK station, Renee Rogers sat at the main switchboard, thumbing through the latest issue of *McCall's*. In her late fifties, she had pale skin that was very finely etched with wrinkles, professionally dyed auburn hair, and she wore a gray pantsuit with a pink blouse. Having worked at WLAK for nearly seventeen years, she knew this was both the easiest and longest part of the day. By and large the phones quit ringing right before five, yet she had to sit there until six. Things could be worse, she thought, steadying the carefully placed telephone headset as her head tilted back with a big yawn.

The lobby of Channel 10 was an expansive, two-story space, recently redone, the walls painted a slick silver, the floor covered with red carpeting. Renee found it cold and stark, though of course no one asked her and of course she told no one, for she prided herself on knowing her place. If—and granted, she knew that was a big if—someone ever asked, however, among other things she didn't like the four white leather couches surrounding the glass coffee table in the middle of the waiting area. And she really didn't like the shiny black laminate surface of her station. Kind of tacky, not to mention that it showed each and every fingerprint. On the other hand, the video wall, a collection of a dozen screens synchronized to show one image—that of WLAK's continuous broadcast—was rather amazing. The only disadvantage was that she had a tendency to watch what was up there and it made it hard for her to do her work, especially when the soaps were on. Good thing, at least, that the volume was always kept next to nothing.

Glancing up from a recipe claiming to be the world's best nonfat lemon poppy-seed pound cake, she saw the larger-than-life image of Todd Mills filling the screen. She squinted. Handsome. And nice. Always in a rush though. Hard to believe he was gay— certainly didn't look it. Or, as her twenty-year-old niece said, "Oh, for cute, but what a waste, ya know?"

The board in front of her started ringing, and Renee punched a button and said into her headset, "Good afternoon, WLAK Channel 10. How may I direct your call?"

The faint voice on the other end asked, "Would you please write this down?"

Renee's brow wrinkled. "This is WLAK. How may I direct your call?"

"Just write this down, if you'd be so kind."

"I'm sorry, I—"

"Please," said the caller, his voice nervous, even breathless. "I know this is Channel Ten. That's who I'm calling. I just need you to do something for me, all right?"

Renee had had them all. Every type of caller, from the First Lady's personal secretary to a neo-Nazi with a bomb threat. Grace, she thought. That's what you're hired for. You're the first voice of WLAK. And above and beyond everything you have to be polite. Fortunately, that's what she was, yet another native Minnesotan who, no matter what, could always force herself to sound natural and completely unruffled.

"Is there someone you'd like to speak with?" asked Renee, glancing up at the video wall as Todd Mills continued his report.

"I'd just like you to pass on a message. I want you to write it down."

A message. Okay, Renee thought, now we're getting somewhere. A lot of people just wanted to talk or, more precisely, to rant and rave about something WLAK did. Others wanted to leave a message but didn't want to get dumped into Voice Mail, and she couldn't say she blamed them either. Technology just kept getting more impersonal by the day, and she for one hated it.

"Yes, of course," said Renee. "Who is this for?"

"Write this down. Five-five-five, *R-B-G*."

Whoever this nut was, she thought, he certainly couldn't listen very well. Nevertheless, Renee did exactly as she was instructed.

"Read that back to me," demanded the caller.

Good Lord, thought Renee. The nerve. If this person had called even twenty minutes ago, Renee wouldn't have had the time for these kinds of shenanigans. Eager to be done with it, though, Renee did as commanded.

"Five-five-five, *R-B-G*."

"Yes, exactly," said the caller. "Now, you give that to your reporter, to Todd Mills. Tell him that's the car I saw driving away the other night, the night that poor young policeman was killed."

"Oh," gasped Renee, realizing what this was about and just what she had to do. "Just wait, just wait one minute while I—"

"You don't understand, I can't get involved."

There was a click on the other end as the man hung up.

Todd came out of Studio A, gently shutting the door behind him as the news continued live, and she was there, the woman from the front desk. The receptionist—what was her name? And as soon as he saw her standing in the corridor, her eyes moving anxiously about, the headset still perched in her hair with its cord dangling nearly to her knees, his gut clutched.

"Say now, Mr. Mills, a call just—"

"Oh, Jesus, did I miss him?"

"What?" She glanced down at the paper in her hand, then up. "Well . . ."

Desperate, Todd demanded, "Who was it?"

"A man. I don't know his name. He didn't say. He wouldn't. Didn't want to get involved. No, actually, he said he couldn't get involved, whatever that means. Anyway, he just wanted me to give you this."

A piece of paper was thrust at Todd, which he took. "What is this? What—"

"A license-plate number," said the receptionist nervously. "That's . . . that's what he said anyway."

"What do you mean?"

"The caller, the man on the phone. It was a tip caller, and he said he saw a strange car the other night. You know, the night the policeman was killed down by the river. That's the license-plate number."

"Oh, my God."

"I . . . I tried to keep him on the line, but—"

This could be it, the break they needed, and Todd started to dash off. "Thanks!"

"Sure, you bet. Just doin' my job."

As he hurried away, Todd couldn't believe it, this good luck. Who knew what this might prove to be, but what if this was it, the killer's car? And what if, by the grace of God, they were able to catch him before he struck again?

He stopped, called to the woman walking down the hall, saying, "Wait—" But what was her name?

The receptionist stopped, turned around, clutching the cord dangling from her headset. "Renee. That's me. Renee."

"Yes, of course. Did the caller say anything else? Anything else at all?"

"No. No, not really, he just told me to write that number down and give it to you, that's all."

"But you're sure it was a man?"

"Well, I certainly think so. It sure sounded like a man anyway. I'm sorry I couldn't get more information. He just kinda hung up on me."

"This is great. This is wonderful. Thank you very much, Renee."

"You bet."

With that he took off, darting down the narrow hall, around the corner, then into the newsroom, that expansive space filled with a mass of cubicles. Looking at the piece of paper in hand as he headed toward his office, he thought that, yes, this certainly looked like a Minnesota license plate. It had the appropriate sequence of numbers and letters anyway. Now it was just a matter of getting an ID on the plates, which Todd knew would be no problem.

Hurrying into his office, he stopped in the doorway, looked back toward the raised platform of the assignment editor. Just to the side of that, on the monitor that was always going, he saw Michelle Newton, their weather forecaster, coming on. Good, that meant it was a quarter past. He had slightly more than forty-five minutes before he was due back on for the six o'clock.

Todd shut the glass door to his office and dropped himself into his padded desk chair in front of his computer. He hit a couple of keys on the keyboard, the color screen came to life, but, no, there were no messages. He quickly checked both his desk and cell phone, but likewise found nothing. Todd then laid the piece of paper on top of the keyboard and stared at it. Okay, just take this a step at a time, he told himself. This could be nothing. Nothing at all. Just a wild-goose chase.

Forgetting entirely about what might be best for WLAK, Todd dialed a number, got a beeper, and then entered his work number. Less than ten seconds later his desk phone rang, and Todd snatched it up.

"Todd Mills."

"Hey, there. What's up?" Rawlins paused, then added, "Forensics couldn't get a single print but yours off that paper."

"Where are you?"

"Down at CID."

"Good," replied Todd, relieved that Rawlins was still down at the Criminal Investigation Division at City Hall and out of harm's way. "Listen, something's up. That guy didn't call, the supposed killer."

"Yeah, well—"

"But someone else did."

"What?"

"A tip call came in while I was on the air—a man. He said he saw a car the night Forrest was killed."

"No shit? Tell me he got a license-plate number."

"He did, he got one."

"Fabulous. What is it? I'll look it up on CAPRS right now," he said, referring to the Computer-Assisted Police Report System.

"Great." Todd read it off. "Sounds like a Minnesota plate, don't you think?"

"Absolutely." Unable to hide the excitement in his voice, Rawlins said, "Just stay right there, Todd. Don't go anywhere. I'll call you right back. Let's hope this is the break we've been waiting for."

Todd hung up and envisioned Rawlins turning around in his two-person cubicle and using the computer he shared with his partner, Neal Foster. Glancing at his watch, Todd thought that maybe he wouldn't be heading into the studio at six after all. With any luck this might turn into that kind of tip, the superhot kind, that required immediate action.

But if not?

Todd rolled his chair away from his desk and leaned back, closing his eyes, thinking, Christ, for Rawlins's and Rawlins's safety alone they needed to nail this guy ASAP.

If this tip didn't go anywhere, however, Todd would have to go on at six but perhaps not at ten. And then tomorrow? Perhaps he'd go to the park police and try to interview someone there. He'd also make another, more concerted effort to interview Mark Forrest's parents. But should he push to see if the supposedly wonderful Forrest had something else lurking somewhere in his closet? Could he have been involved in any fringe groups involving leather or drugs? Todd didn't relish going down that path, not by any means; the last thing he wanted was to use the underside of the gay world to play off straight stereotypes. But why, he found himself pondering once again, had Todd been drawn into this in

the first place? Why had he been lured that night to the Stone
Arch Bridge? Was it because of all the reporters in the Twin Cities
Todd was the most wonderful and competent? Or was it much
more simple, was it because Todd was gay and the entire metro
area knew it? Todd hated to boil everything down to sexuality,
particularly his, but he couldn't help but suspect the latter. Yes,
and as much as he didn't want to, Mark Forrest's sex life was an
avenue Todd was going to have to explore.

He stared at the phone and thought: Ring. As if on command,
it did just that, cried to be answered. Todd all but leapt forward.

Grabbing the reciever on the first ring, he blurted out,
"Yeah?"

"Bingo," said Rawlins. "The car, a nineteen-sixty-eight Oldsmobile Ninety-Eight, was registered three months ago by a guy
named Christopher Kenney, age twenty-four. Blond hair, blue
eyes."

"What's the name again?"

"Christopher Kenney."

He jotted it down, then asked, "How tall?"

"Five foot seven, weight one hundred and twenty."

"It could be him." The image of the slight figure in the storm
moved through Todd's mind. "It could be our guy."

"Wait, there's more. You know where he lives? South Minneapolis. Can you believe it? He lives at 5241 Turner South."

Todd's mind skipped along, then slammed to a halt. What did
this mean, that they'd known each other?

"My God, Rawlins, that's only something like ten or twelve
blocks from where Forrest lived."

"I know. And get this: It's a reregister—until three months
ago this guy had California plates."

"California?"

"Right. But wait, here's the best part: When I got his plate
number I looked him up on the NCIC," said a smug Rawlins,
referring to the computerized national crime records. "And you
know what?"

"Oh, my God, he's got a record?"

"No shit he's got a record. Like a major-league one. Just over a year ago the Los Angeles Police Department arrested and charged him with the murder of an officer by the name of Dave Ravell."

"A cop?"

"Yep."

"Holy shit."

"Eventually those charges were dropped, but—"

"Hey," said Todd, flipping back into work mode and writing all this down, "we're going to do this just the way we talked about, right?"

"Absolutely. You know that's what I've wanted all along."

Point taken, thought Todd. It was he, Todd, who had screwed up before. He who had been the control freak.

"And Lieutenant Holbrook won't have a problem with it?"

"Ah, he might, but that's my problem. I'll deal with it."

Guessing what the next step would be, Todd asked, "So are you going to get a warrant?"

"No, no. We'd have to formally charge him to get a warrant. But I've already talked to Lieutenant Holbrook, and since this involves a cop-killing he wants me to go over and talk with this guy right away. Unless I absolutely have to, though, he doesn't even want me doing a PC pickup. Not just yet anyway."

Too bad. A probable-cause pickup would definitely give Todd some excellent footage. Nevertheless, his pulse began to quicken. There could still be some great stuff here, and he glanced at his watch, wondered how quickly they could make this happen. Was there a chance in hell he could get something on the six o'clock? He quickly ran through a laundry list of equipment and people he'd need. Yes, it was doable. It was going to be a scramble, no doubt about it, but they could pull it off.

Wanting to make sure he wasn't the one cut out, Todd said, "It's going to take me about five, ten minutes to get out of here. So when are we going to meet? And where?"

"How about twenty minutes at Lyndale and Fifty-second?"

"Great."

"Oh, and Todd," said Rawlins. "The NCIC says this guy frequently wears a disguise."

"What do you mean?"

"I'm not positive, but it sure as hell sounds like he's a drag queen."

Chapter 21

Should she or shouldn't she go?

No, Kris thought as she stood in front of her mirror putting on her lipstick, the answer was absolutely, definitely no. No, no, no, she shouldn't go. Not at all. Girl, of all the dumb-ass things, playing Meals-on-Wheels to some district-court judge and going to that man's apartment was about as dumb as could be.

But of course she was going to go.

Among other things, she had to find out what, if anything, this was all about. Obviously Stuart Hawkins remembered her—how the hell could he not after their little foray—but did he care for her as much as she might for him? That, of course, remained to be learned. Kris, however, was fairly certain of one thing: that the lust, on a scale of one to ten, was way the hell up there. She was no dummy, not after what she'd been through these past few years. Why the hell else would he have requested that she in particular make the Peacock Catering delivery? What other reason could there possibly be? She grinned—a privately catered meal? What a conniving bastard.

She took a Kleenex, laid it between her lips, and pressed down, blotting the deep purplish-red lipstick. She assumed this was a date, but what if it wasn't? What if he just wanted to see her? What if he wanted to show her off? Perhaps he really was having someone else over for dinner, as Travis at Peacock had been told. That was a distinct possibility, one that Kris had to bear in mind. Sure, Kris could arrive with the extravagant meal and there in Mr. Stuart Hawkins's wonderful condominium could be some beautiful woman, a gorgeous rich heiress perhaps. Then again, the story Hawkins had fed Travis could all be a crock, a ruse, a way of getting Kris into the privacy and intimacy of Hawkins's home. And bed.

"Fuck."

She never used to cry, never, but here her eyes were doing it, starting to tear up. What the hell was it, the hormones or the shrink and his probing questions? Whatever, but she couldn't do it, couldn't burst into tears, not now. Her mascara was great, the eyeliner perfect, and she couldn't go screwing it up. No, she had to be heading out. No time for a redo. It was just . . . just . . . well, the other night he'd read her gender expression as female, but what would he do if . . . if . . .

She hadn't been on a date in . . . what was it? Not since that night in L.A. a year and a half ago. And how had things gone then? Dear God, she could still hear the deafening blast of the gun, she could still remember the way his head had exploded. It wasn't supposed to have gone like that, not at all, but things had gotten out of hand. What could she have done otherwise? She'd been hit before. Guys had beaten her. But nothing like that. No, not at all.

Horrified by the memory, Kris stepped out of the bathroom, crossing the small basement room and sitting down on her bed. Her eyes wide open, she stared straight ahead, but she didn't see the pine paneling before her. No, she fell down a bottomless hole, and in her mind's eye she saw him. Dave. She still remembered the first time they saw each other. It was in a coffee shop, and though he'd just gotten off duty, he was still in his police uniform, which hugged those broad shoulders and slim hips. She was undressing him with her eyes when he turned and did the same, clearly visualizing what she might look like without her tight jeans and skimpy top. He was older than her—that much she could tell from a distance—but not over thirty. Sipping her latte, she was sitting at a counter overlooking Melrose, and the next thing she knew he was pulling up a stool next to her. It took all of about fifteen seconds for them to strike up a conversation, and they'd ended up talking for nearly two hours. Everything clicked, everything worked. It was easy, their talk. He was freshly divorced, though why anyone would want to leave that guy she hadn't understood, at least not then. Most importantly, he was funny and she found herself laughing at all his jokes. She also found him enchanting, and when he'd asked her out for the following night, she didn't hesitate, not a blink of a second.

But then, as she'd walked down the street a few minutes later, she found herself wondering how could such a stud like him be attracted to a freak like her? It didn't make sense, not until later.

Over Thai food the next evening, Kris had learned that Dave's wife had dumped him in a bad way, just kicked him right out onto the street—or so he said, trying to laugh it off. Kris had pressed for more details, but he smiled and declined, which was fine, because Kris was content to stare into his dark eyes and dream of what might be. The guy was all beef—thick hairy chest, gorgeous arms. And those wrists, so strong and covered with that dark hair, so very . . . very *guy*. She just wanted him. Wanted his arms wrapped around her, wanted him to hold her and love her and tell her everything would be all right. When he'd dropped her off later that night, they'd parked in front of her apartment and kissed . . . well, hotter and heavier than Kris had ever kissed before. When he started moaning, "God, I've got to have you . . . now," Kris had flushed with panic and barely escaped.

She didn't see him for two weeks after that, not because Dave didn't want to, not for his lack of trying, but because Kris knew it could go nowhere. It wasn't, however, that simple to end. Not by any means. Dave, having been dumped by his wife, wasn't about to be dumped again, not by some young thing like Kris. No. First he called, all sweet talk and everything, saying how much he enjoyed seeing her and asking her to a movie the next night. When Kris declined, he slammed down the phone. The following day he called again, this time begging to get together, and Kris, wanting so much to see him but fearful of where it might go, said she couldn't. He called the day after that as well. And the day after that. Each time he grew more desperate. And more angry.

It broke her heart, doing that to him, pushing him away. After about ten days the calls stopped, and Kris assumed that that was it. The brief affair was over. Dave was history. But then Kris came home one warm California night, climbed up the open staircase to her studio apartment, and there he was, the hunk in police blue. He'd gotten off duty and he stood there, a bottle of red wine in hand.

"Kris, I gotta talk to you," he pleaded, his face all puppy-dog sad. "Can I come in, please?"

At first she thought, No, no way. But then she looked at his eyes, saw that they were all red. Jesus, the hunk had been crying.

"Okay," said Kris, unlocking the door.

So they went into the tiny place. Dave sat down at the kitchen table, took his wallet out of his back pocket, put his holster over on the counter. And told her how messed up he'd made everything. Maybe Kris already guessed, but there was a reason his wife had dumped him.

He volunteered, "She caught me cheating on her."

Kris didn't know why he was telling her this, but she was flattered. Maybe he perceived her as safe, which she was. In any case, Dave said the whole thing was more complicated, and could he please, please tell her? Kris got out two glasses, and then Dave poured them each a towering glass of wine.

"I haven't told anyone about this," he said, and then gulped down most of the glass.

"Dave," said Kris, placing her hand over his. "I don't know what it is, but it's okay."

"No . . . no, it's not."

Kris smiled softly. "Trust me, if you think your life is a mess, you should see mine."

He stared at her, grinning through his teary eyes. "God, how could anyone as beautiful as you have any problems?"

She rolled her eyes, and in a joking voice said, "Maybe I'll tell you about it, big boy."

He leaned over. Puckered his lips. And kissed her ever so gently on her right cheek.

"I've never met anyone as nonjudgmental as you," said Dave. "I mean, I knew that within minutes after we first met. You're just so . . . so sweet."

Shaking her head, Kris pulled away. "No, unfortunately I've

caught a glimpse of the bigger picture—and it's made me humble for the rest of my life."

He took another swig of wine, finishing off the glass, then poured himself some more. He wiped his mouth nervously, looked away. Then turned back to her.

"Kris, the reason my wife kicked me out is that she came home and found me in bed—"

"Dave, I know, you already told me. We all make mistakes."

"—with another guy."

Nothing he could have said would have surprised her more. For a long time she just sat there, overcome with . . . well, shock. Dave? With another guy? How was that possible, and how come Kris had never even guessed?

"Kris," he begged, looking at her desperately, "say something."

"I . . . I . . ."

"Tell me you don't hate me."

She stared at him. "What?"

"My brother's gay, and my father never talked to him again. My wife found out, and she divorced me." He stared at the floor. "I don't think I'm gay, I really don't. Maybe I'm bi, I don't know. I mean, I haven't been able to get you out of my head. I don't know why, but you're all that I can think about. For some reason I'm really attracted to you, Kris. More so than I've been to any other woman, and . . . and I just don't want to . . . don't want to lose you."

Confused, perhaps even terribly anxious—yes, Kris was these. But full of hate? Nothing could have been further from her mind. Hate? Oh, no. Not at all. Compassion and sympathy, yes, but no, never hate, not for that.

Suddenly Kris started laughing: Was this a weird world or what? A half second later she started crying: Was this it, the end of her long road? It came at her like a huge wall of water, a flood of relief that brought so much joy that it terrified her. Dear God in heaven, here was this wonderful, handsome man in front of her, and did they, by some miracle, have one thing in common, namely their sexuality? It was too incredible to be true. She might have done it, done the impossible, found him, a guy who could actually love her for what she was. If he was gay, then he'd be delighted with her, right?

"What's the matter?" demanded Dave, getting all defensive. "Listen, it's not like that's a big part of my life, but I'll leave if you want me to. If you think I'm that horrible, I'll just go."

"No!" cried Kris, lunging out for his hand. "You don't understand—I don't want you to ever go! I don't want to ever lose you!"

That was all it took, just those words. As quick as a flash fire, she was grabbing him, he was clutching her, they were kissing. Their mouths locked, their hands groped, and they caressed and fondled and rubbed as if these were the very last moments of their lives.

But then . . .

"Wait . . ." gasped Kris, pushing back. "There's something I've got to tell you."

"I want you—now!" he said, pulling her back.

"You don't understand—there's something I've got to tell you about me. Something I—"

"Kris, don't you get it? I love you!"

It was as if someone had shot her. No one had ever said anything like that to her, and she collapsed into his arms, crying harder now than she had for a long, long time. He wrapped his large arms around her, kissed her on the cheek, told her how everything would be all right, that he really did love her and that he would never leave her, that he would be hers as long as she would have him. The next instant he was scooping her up and carrying her into the living room, where he put her on the couch. She kicked off her shoes, and then he was stripping, pulling off his blue police uniform, peeling away the world and exposing himself to her.

How, Kris now thought for the millionth time, could everything have gone so quickly from so unbelievably wonderful to so incredibly horrible? Now sitting there on the edge of her small bed in that basement room, she bent forward and started sobbing.

She recalled the passion and lust, then his fury and anger. Yes, she remembered taking his gun, aiming it.

Oh, God, and all that blood. One second he was there, the next, a third of his head was splattered all over her small studio apartment.

Chapter 22

It was seven minutes to six, and Todd hadn't wasted a moment. Having looped around the city on the freeways, he now sped up Lyndale Avenue South.

Hoping that this was it, that this was their guy and they could eliminate the threat against Rawlins so quickly, his energy level was cranked on high, and he said, "This might work out perfectly."

"Yeah, it could be entirely cool," agreed Bradley, the photographer, seated next to him. "I'd just love to get something live, something with a little action."

"We'll see. This might be a bust. This guy might not even be there."

"Ah, come on, man, you've got the best luck of anyone I know."

"Let's hope."

He drove one of WLAK's two unmarked vans, an old blue thing with large tinted windows and scabby-looking rust spots, while close on his tail was one of the shiny white ENG vans with WLAK's logo painted on the side and a large microwave antenna stacked on top. Yes, he'd made sure they were ready for any scenario, whether this be something they fired back live to the station or something Bradley taped with a hidden camera from the rear of his van. If they ended up doing it live, which would be the best, Todd was pretty sure they could get a good signal from here; if not they'd have to double-hop it, bouncing the signal off one of the downtown towers.

Nearing the Boulevard Theatre and yet another Starbucks—

which were sprouting around town as fast as McDonald's once had—Todd turned left on Fifty-second. And there, parked to the side as they had agreed, sat the silver Ford Taurus, in which two men now sat. As soon as Todd pulled up behind it, Rawlins jumped out.

Todd rolled down his window and asked, "Are we still a go?"

"Absolutely." Rawlins came up to the side of the van, squeezed Todd on the arm, then leaned a bit into the window. "Hey, Bradley."

Bradley tipped his head. "You going to get this guy?"

"It would be very great."

No shit it would be very great, thought Todd, more than eager to get this over with, to have the guy who'd taken a potshot at Rawlins behind bars.

Todd nodded toward the Taurus. "Who do you have with you?"

"Officer Tim McNamee."

In case he might need the information later, Todd grabbed a piece of paper, wrote down the name, and asked, "That's all?"

"Nope, a bunch of the guys wanted in on this one. There's a squad car at either end of the block, each car with two cops. There's another one in the alley too. Any problems and we're going to be all over him." Rawlins continued, "My plan is to take it easy. If he's there I simply want to talk to him. Like I said, Holbrook doesn't want me doing a PC pickup just yet, because we don't want him lawyering up on us. But, who knows, things could get a little hot, and we don't want you two hurt and we don't want you getting in the way. So stay clear, okay?"

"Scout's honor," replied Todd.

"What about these other guys?" asked Rawlins, nodding to the white ENG van now pulled up behind Todd.

"They're just insurance in case we go live for the six o'clock," explained Todd. "Don't worry, they're going to stay parked right here until we call them—*if* we call them."

"Perfect." Rawlins looked at the large tinted window in the side of Todd's van. "You're sure no one will be able to see in there?"

"Positive. Bradley will be back there with his camera, but there'll be a curtain pulled around him. You can't see him as long as he's sitting against a dark background."

"Okay."

Todd reached out the van window, grabbed hold of Rawlins's arm. As a homicide investigator, Rawlins usually wasn't at any scenes that were hot. This, however, could very well prove to be—and all because of Todd.

"Be careful," he said, not wanting this, not wanting Rawlins to be the lead man. "If this is the real guy, he's already killed one cop, maybe more, and he's probably the one who took a shot at you. Shouldn't you be wearing a bulletproof vest or something?"

"Don't worry."

"But—"

"Todd, I know what I'm doing."

Todd shrugged, knew he couldn't say a thing, and asked, "So do we go first? Do we drive up and park in front of the house?"

"Sure, but don't stop right in front. Park across the street or something so it doesn't look too obvious. And I don't want you getting out. Agreed?"

"Agreed."

They discussed a few other details, and then Todd started up the van and headed down the street. Two blocks later he turned left on Turner. A solidly middle-class neighborhood on the very edge of the city, the entire area was filled with tiny postwar houses, little boxes lined up one after the other. Number 5241 was almost halfway down the street, built on a small ridge and distinguished from the others only by a large spruce tree in front.

Spotting the car, Todd said, "There's the Ninety-Eight."

As Bradley made sure the black curtain was securely safety-pinned behind him, he asked, "Think you can park where I can get a good shot of both the car and the house?"

"Absolutely."

Todd steered the van into a space across the street and just a bit to the north, which meant that to see the house you had to look over the roof of the parked car. He shut off the engine, grabbed his pad and pen, jotted a couple of notes. The street, he observed, was fairly quiet. Toward the end of the block he saw someone climbing out of a car—a man in a suit, presumably just coming home from work. Through the cracked window, he heard birds chirping, some kids hollering, and caught a whiff of someone grilling. Definitely hamburgers. His stomach growled.

"How's this?" he asked.

"I'm just cleaning my lens," replied Bradley, wiping it with a fine cotton handkerchief. "Ah . . . perfect."

"Get a nice long shot of the house."

"Yes, yes, yes."

Checking his side-view mirror, Todd saw the silver Taurus turn the corner and start down the street. "Here they come."

Something caught his eye and Todd glanced up the street to see some small kids—the noisy ones—being shepherded down the sidewalk by a woman, blond, maybe thirty. They were young kids, not even five, Todd guessed, and he soon realized where they were heading.

"Oh, shit," muttered Todd.

"What?" demanded Bradley, crouched in the back, peering through the lens of his camera.

"Some kids are headed straight for the house."

"Yeah, I see 'em now."

The two children were darting across the yards, racing along, while their mother continued up the sidewalk until she reached 5241 and started up to the house. Todd wondered if Rawlins would simply make a pass for now, if he would continue down the street and come back in a few minutes.

But then things got even more complicated.

"Uh-oh," said Todd, spying someone emerging from the front door. "Here comes someone else."

"Wow!" cooed Bradley. "What a babe."

And that she was, a trim, young blonde in mod black shoes and a tight, tight outfit. A real beauty, no doubt about it, and Todd watched as she stepped out of the house, a small purse and what looked like an overnight bag in hand. The children ran up to her, grabbed onto her legs, and she kissed them on the top of their heads. She said a few quick words to the other woman, the one who'd been out with the kids and who now disappeared into the house. The young woman then continued down to the street and straight toward the Oldsmobile Ninety-Eight.

"Oh, my God," muttered Todd. "That can't be him, can it?"

"What?" snapped Bradley from behind the curtain. "That's no guy. Trust me, I'm the straight one here, and I know a beautiful woman when I see one."

Well, thought Todd, she certainly passed as one, and he watched with fascination as the trim, sexy blonde proceeded around the rear of the car, twisted what looked like a couple of wires, and opened the trunk. She was just rearranging something in the back and tossing in her bag when Rawlins pulled up, parking his car right in front of the Olds so that the two vehicles were radiator to radiator, as if he were going to give the other a jump. Hearing all this, the woman, clearly confused, glanced from around the back of her car. Seeing the two men, a look of concern swept over her. Almost as if she didn't want anyone to see inside the trunk, she slammed it shut, then worked quickly to secure it with the wires. A moment later she darted up to the sidewalk.

Rawlins, as always, was clearly going to be his determined, direct self, and he was already out the door and walking by the time Officer McNamee's car door was even open. Staring at Rawlins, the young woman was about to say something, until she saw McNamee, a tall, bald, muscular man in a police uniform. The clear vision of authority obviously didn't sit well with her, and she bit her lip and took a half-step back.

Even from the van, Todd could hear Rawlins call out, "Good evening, can I speak to you for a moment?"

Like a deer caught in the lights of a marauding vehicle, the woman froze. From the panic etched on her face it was clear that she knew something, but what?

As he moved closer, Rawlins didn't waste a moment of opportunity, glancing through the car windows, looking for something, anything. To really search the car, of course, he needed a warrant, which he didn't have, at least not yet. Instead, he was hoping, Todd knew, simply to spot something of interest in plain view, something incriminating sitting right on the front or back seat.

With McNamee right behind him, Rawlins went directly up to the young woman, pulled out his badge, and identified himself. She stood there, quite paralyzed and biting her bottom lip. Rawlins said something else; the woman hesitantly nodded. Looking confused, he asked another question, and the woman pressed her right hand to her forehead and slowly shook her head. Being quite brazen about the whole thing, Rawlins turned back and peered again into the rear seat. Had something caught his interest?

Watching from the van, Todd couldn't tell what was going on, where this was going, when suddenly the front door of the house opened and the other woman, the one who'd been with the two kids, came quickly out, trotting down the front walk.

"What's the matter? What's going on here?" snapped that woman, her hands on her hips. "Is there a problem?"

Officer McNamee, his voice clear and sharp, said, "We're looking for Christopher Kenney. We just want to—"

"Oh, shit," said the woman, her voice booming as she looked right at the other woman, the young one by the Olds. "What the hell have you done now, Kris?"

In the very same beat, the beautiful young blonde dropped her purse, turned, and fled, dashing desperately away from the Ninety-Eight. Rawlins was so stunned that it took him a moment to realize what was happening, and then he took off after her. McNamee burst into a run as well, albeit a slower one, for he grabbed his walkie-talkie from his belt and started barking into it.

"Come on, that's our guy!" shouted Todd as he grabbed his door handle and shoved open the door.

"Holy shit, I don't fucking believe it!" replied Bradley, clambering over cables and equipment.

There was no way in hell Todd was going to let Rawlins out of his sight, and he jumped out and took off, while Bradley threw open the back of the van and quickly followed, clutching the large, unwieldy Betacam. They charged across the street, up the slope, and around the side of the small house. Then all of a sudden it was everywhere, the wail of not one police siren, but two and possibly three, a terrifying chorus that swept through and inundated the entire neighborhood with a tidal wave of authority. No, thought

Todd as he ran, Christopher Kenney didn't have a chance in hell of getting away.

Racing past a side door, Todd cut into the backyard and to his right saw a flurry of red and white light as a cop car rocketed down the alley.

"Where the hell are they?" gasped Bradley.

Panic started to rise in Todd's throat, until he caught a glimpse of Rawlins leaping a chain-link fence. "There!"

While Bradley briefly paused to get a shot of the speeding squad car, Todd took off. He followed Rawlins's course, running past a single-car garage, through one lawn, straight through a small vegetable garden, and over the low fence. He cut to the right, darted around a garage, ducked down the alley, and there it all was, a vortex of three cop cars, their lights swirling and screaming. And in the center of all that stood a half dozen cops with their guns drawn as Rawlins pinned the young woman to the ground.

"You can't do this to me!" she shrieked, twisting and bucking with panic. "I didn't hurt anyone! Let me go, you asshole!"

"Are you Christopher Kenney?"

"Let me go!"

"Are you—"

"Fuck off!" she screamed as she wrenched one of her manicured hands free and swiped it across Rawlins's neck.

As Todd watched, as Bradley got it all on film, Rawlins tumbled to the side, desperately clutching his neck. Blood. Free-flowing blood. Not that much, but certainly plenty enough to terrify anyone with HIV.

Todd rushed forward.

"No!" shouted Rawlins, holding his hand out like a linebacker. "Stay back! Don't touch me!"

Todd spun to the side, hurried over to Bradley, and demanded, "Give me your handkerchief!"

Grabbing it from Bradley, Todd rushed to Rawlins, who in turn snatched it and pressed it to his neck.

Behind them the young woman burst to her feet and screamed at the cops now encircling her, shouting, "I didn't do it! I didn't hurt anyone!"

She turned to run, but the circle grew tighter and two of the cops lunged after her, seizing her with ease. And then for one long, strange moment all the cops just stood there, staring as her femininity melted away.

"Oh, Jesus!" she sobbed, her voice surprisingly deep.

Rawlins pressed the cloth against his neck and shouted, "One of you guys get a first-aid kit and clean her fingernails—now, on the double!" He then turned to her, demanding, "Are you Christopher Kenney?"

"What if . . . what if I am?"

"I want to ask you some questions. I—"

Kris looked up, mascara streaking down her face, and snapped, "Fuck off! I didn't do anything!"

"Then why the hell," he demanded, exploding, "did someone see your car down by the Mississippi the other night and—"

"That's a lie!"

"And why the hell did you run away?"

"Eat shit! You fucking pigs can't do this to me again! You can't!"

"If you'd just—"

"I'm not going anywhere with you assholes!" she yelled, and then spit into Rawlins's face.

Wiping the slime from his cheek, Rawlins shouted, "That's it! Cuff her, we're taking her in! You're under arrest for—"

"Fuck off!"

"You're under arrest for the murder of Police Officer Mark Forrest!" boomed Rawlins.

"No! No!" Kris screamed.

Two cops descended upon Kris, now easily pinning her arms behind her back and handcuffing her wrists.

"Be careful, for Christ's sake!" shouted Rawlins, who then looked frantically around. "Where the fuck's the first-aid kit? You've got to get her cleaned up right now! Now, damn it all! We need some alcohol! Some disinfectant! What the fuck's taking you so goddamn long? You!" he yelled at the cop who'd gotten a kit from his squad car. "Get the fuck over here—now!"

Todd had never seen this, never seen Rawlins blow, and he

came up behind him, touched him on the elbow, and said, "Rawlins—"

"Don't fucking touch me!" he snapped, ripping his arm away.

Todd jerked back. And there staring at him was not a person, but the Cyclops lens of Todd's own world.

Slapping his open palm over the eye of the camera, he snapped, "Jesus Christ, Bradley, not now!"

Chapter 23

As he paced back and forth in his hotel room, as he clutched at his short brown hair with his right hand, he recalled how desperate he'd been to get Mark Forrest out of his life. But now that the young cop was gone, now that he was dead, dead, dead, he saw it, his error. Oh, sweet Jesus. In his haste to get away that night he'd left something behind that was sure to become a trail as wide as a freeway.

Now what?

Dropping himself on the edge of his bed, the man stared straight ahead, unable to believe this disaster. And unable to eat the other half of the turkey club sandwich he'd ordered from room service. Why the hell had he done it? Why the hell did he have a thing for cops, for handsome guys in uniforms? A couple of years ago he'd been involved with one, but that had also ended in disaster. Just as this one had.

Shit, if only he'd broken things off earlier with Forrest. If only they'd split up after the fight last month.

"Get the fuck away from me!" the man had shouted not five minutes after they'd climbed out of Mark's bed.

"I just wanted your phone number. I just wanted some way of reaching you when—"

"No! You can never call me at home! Never!"

"But—"

And that's when he'd struck him.

He'd always wanted guys, always liked them. The first time he sensed something, though he didn't know what, was when he'd been utterly fascinated by one of his teachers, Mr. Lawson. He couldn't wait to see him every day, made sure that he was in the front row of his science class, was amazed by his strong arms, his warmth. It was a crush, of course, his very first one and totally innocent, though he didn't understand what it was until years later. And later on that thing, that same feeling, stirred within him a lot, particularly in the locker room.

And finally in his junior year of high school he'd consummated that desire with Steve, another kid on the baseball team. After everyone had left they'd done it, right there in the showers, and he'd never experienced something so whole, so complete, a total fusion of his lust and desire, body and mind. After the fact, though, he was horribly confused, for he'd been dating one girl, Teri, and now he felt nothing for her and everything for Steve. A mere six days later, however, it all became perfectly clear just what he should feel, for that was when he and five other guys from the team discovered Steve doing it with some other guy in the shower. The guy—some kid from another school—had fled, but Steve had stood up for himself, which was a mistake, for all of them had descended upon Steve and beat the crap out of him.

They'd all but killed him.

Picturing it all as he now sat in his hotel room, he realized he'd never forget it, would never forget how Steve, naked and bleeding on the floor, had looked up at him, started to say something, and how he, terrified of just what that would be, had kicked Steve so hard that he threw up blood. Steve had spent two weeks in the hospital and was then expelled; all six guys were questioned by school authorities but, as if they were justified, never reprimanded.

The man now closed his eyes, blocked out everything, this pisser of a world around him, and went back to the last time he'd been with Mark Forrest. Yes, handsome. Yes, young. Always half smiling. They'd been in bed, the two of them, right here, right in this very hotel room, right in this fucking bed, making love not thirty minutes before Mark went to meet that stupid reporter. And then he'd ridden with Forrest down to the Stone Arch

Bridge. They'd kissed briefly in Forrest's car; Mark had gotten out. And then . . .

That storm.

There'd been so much rain. And, God, the wind. In his mind's eye he saw him, beautiful Mark Forrest, walking down the Stone Arch Bridge. Alive and so very, very vibrant one moment. So dead the next.

Afterward, after the storm had passed and Mark Forrest was gone, he'd run all the way back to his hotel, making it just in time for her phone call too. So no one could possibly suspect him. He'd gotten away.

Or had he?

Maybe, maybe not, for his singular error, so glaring now, was that he'd left one thing behind. Not a piece of clothing. Not a slip of paper with a telephone number on it. No, what he'd left behind was something far worse: his fingerprints. Shit, he'd forgotten to wipe down the interior of Mark Forrest's car.

Chapter 24

As much as he wanted to call it off, at least for a while, there was no stopping it. As much as Todd wanted to brush away all the television nonsense, then rush to Rawlins and tell him the wound was nothing, no one had been endangered, there was no way Todd could. They were all caught in a rockslide—one that Todd had helped let loose—and both Rawlins and he were swept away, overwhelmed as much by the arrest of Christopher Kenney as by their jobs.

The six o'clock show was well under way, and, in the world of television at least, breaking stories like this were the gifts of the gods.

"We're all set," called Bradley from behind.

Todd was turned the other way, focused on Rawlins, who was filling out some paperwork and conversing with several police officers. As if an artery had been cut instead of his neck being merely scratched, Rawlins continued to keep the handkerchief firmly pressed against his neck.

"Hey, man, come on," pressed Bradley. "We don't want to lose this."

"What?" said Todd, turning around.

"We're ready. Let's do it."

From Bradley's camera a long cable snaked across the green lawn, down between two identical houses, and to the ENG van down on the street. So this was it, thought Todd. They were going to get what they'd come for, a live shot from the scene. Later they'd edit the tape of Christopher Kenney fleeing and resisting the police, perhaps use it on the 10@10 broadcast, but for now they were going to show the police stuffing Kenney into a squad car.

Todd took a deep breath, for this was happening way too fast. He wanted to tell the police to slow down, to wait just a few more seconds, to hold that pose and that suspect right there. But of course that was impossible. Any news that was worth its weight could never wait.

"Here," said Bradley, thrusting out both a stick mike and an earpiece.

Todd took them, grasping the mike and jabbing the small clear plastic device into his ear without even thinking. Just as he was positioning the wire behind his neck and out of sight, a voice started bleating into his ear.

"God, this is so great!"

Todd lifted the mike to his mouth, looked at the camera now trained on him, and said, "Nan?"

"Todd," replied the producer from the station in the distant suburb, "you're the best. I mean, this is so hot. I can't believe it. This guy's a drag queen, isn't he? Isn't that what he is?"

"I . . . I . . ."

"Do you really think he killed that cop? I mean, like, wow! I mean, this is the first gay drag-queen killer I've ever heard of!"

Todd flinched, and all he could say was, "Who said he's gay?"

"Well, he's a drag queen, isn't he?"

"Nan, technically I think a drag queen means someone who's a performer, but the politically correct word for this guy—"

"Oh, come on, Todd."

"—is transgendered."

"Look at him, for Christ's sake! Just look!" she demanded, unable to hide the joy in her voice. "You know, I bet the nationals are going to pick this up."

Nan's words made it all so clear, and suddenly Todd was terrified. Whatever he spit out in the next few minutes would stick. Whatever he said about Chris Kenney, whatever they soon showed on TV, would be how viewers would judge him for weeks, if not forever. And judge him they would, no doubt about it. In particular, if the public now saw Kenney as something different from them, as someone from beyond their world and understanding, they would take his deviance as definitive proof, pronouncing him guilty for the murder of Officer Mark Forrest.

Shit, Todd wanted to pull the plug on Bradley's camera, for he couldn't think, couldn't figure how to come at this.

"Todd!" called Bradley. "We're going to lose him!"

"Don't you dare!" hollered Nan in Todd's earpiece.

Todd turned around, saw them leading the handcuffed Kenney to one of the squad cars.

"Listen," she barked from the control room of the station, "Tom Rivers is going to do a quick lead-in and toss it to you, Todd. We're five seconds away."

It was happening. The producer was doing a countdown, Todd could hear Rivers's voice in his earpiece. And then Todd was live. He opened his mouth, but for a terrifying split second his mind went blank. Nothing. Empty. What the hell was he supposed to say? He stared at the lens.

"Go, Todd! You're on! For Christ's sake, you're live!" screamed Nan via IFB transmission.

They weren't there. The words—they weren't forming. This had never happened before, and all of a sudden his heart took off in a panic. Shit! A second of silence on television was equal to an hour.

"Todd!" Nan shouted.

Todd opened his mouth but . . . but nothing. Then he looked to the side, saw what the camera was also seeing, and then amazingly everything kicked in and his mouth went on autopilot.

"There's been a dramatic breakthrough in the murder of Minneapolis Park Police Officer Mark Forrest," began Todd, his voice somehow smooth, somehow belying his racing heart. "And what you're seeing is a live shot of the arrest of a suspect by the name of Christopher Kenney, who was apprehended not more than five minutes ago by a barrage of Minneapolis police. As you can see, officers are leading Mr. Kenney away as I speak. In a few moments he'll be taken by squad car to the main Minneapolis police department in City Hall, where he will be formally booked for the

murder of Mark Forrest. And while Mr. Kenney is now cooperat-
ing and everything appears to be going smoothly," continued
Todd, as Kenney was placed in a car, "that most definitely was not
the case just a few minutes ago."

As the squad car took off, its lights twirling but its sirens
silent, Bradley brought the camera back over, now completely
focusing on Todd, who went on to explain how an anonymous
caller had telephoned the WLAK station late this afternoon. The
caller, reported Todd, claimed to have seen a strange car by the
Mississippi the night Mark Forrest was gunned down. Todd went
on about how the license-plate number, provided by the tip caller,
had led him and the police here. What started out as simple questioning, however, turned quite dramatic when Kenney fled and
then battled the police. Todd relayed nearly everything in a crisp,
sharp manner, but failed, for some reason even he didn't understand, to mention one important thing. No, he didn't want to
unleash that. Perhaps later. Perhaps on the 10:00 P.M., once he
had more information. But not now.

"I'm sure there'll be more information coming within the next
few hours," concluded Todd, getting ready to toss it back to Tom
Rivers, "but for now—"

"He's in drag!" shrieked Nan into his earpiece. "Jesus Christ,
you gotta tell them that! That's the best part! The juiciest! Todd!
Todd, you couldn't tell from the visual that Kenney was in drag!"

"—that's the latest information. Tune in to the Ten at Ten
report for the very latest. For WLAK, this is Investigative Reporter Todd Mills."

He heard it, her screaming. Via the microwave connection,
Nan Miller's voice was perfectly clear, cursing Todd for what he'd
left out. Todd, however, just stood there, staring at the camera in
silence, waiting for the signal that he was off-air. And eventually
they had no choice, for Todd just stood there motionless and
quiet, forcing them to cut him. As soon as the red light atop
Bradley's camera ceased burning, Todd plucked the earpiece from
his ear and tossed that and the mike at Bradley.

"Hey," said the photographer, catching them both in his left
hand, "you all right?"

Todd shrugged and turned away. Off to the side were two cops, shaking their heads and trying to make sense of all this. One of the other squad cars was now backing up into the alley, turning, and heading slowly away. But where was he? Where was Rawlins? Todd scanned the small backyards, searched for him, yet Rawlins was not to be seen.

Of course. Todd must have missed it, but Rawlins, as the arresting officer, had certainly taken off in the same squad car as Kenney. Shit.

And then Todd just stood there, his mind shifting. Looking around, running it all through his head yet again, from the phone call to the moment of the arrest of Christopher Kenney, he should have been pleased, even thrilled. Any reporter would kill for something so hot. Yes, once again, he'd witnessed virtually every critical step in this bizarre story, from the murder on the Stone Arch Bridge, to the discovery of the body in the Mississippi, and now the arrest of a suspect—a guy in drag, no less—who'd already been once arrested and charged in a cop-killing.

So what felt so wrong?

He couldn't tell, not yet, but every part of Todd's body began to flood with dread. He might be a good investigative reporter, even a great one. But he knew this was way too easy.

Way too insanely easy.

Chapter 25

So what *was* so wrong about all this?

All the way back to the suburban station of WLAK, Todd couldn't shake it, not just the sense that something was off, but that it was flat-out wrong. Nor could he ignore those thoughts even when Nan berated him as soon as he walked into the bunker-like, satellite-dish-enshrined building, where she demanded to know what the hell he'd been doing. Hadn't he heard her? Hadn't he realized how hot this whole thing was? And why, why, why the hell had he ignored her?

"I mean, what were you doing, cutting off early like that?" the producer had screamed. "We're talking about a goddamn drag queen gunning down a cop, for Christ's sake! These are some hot buttons, and that's what you're paid to do: Hit those buttons as hard as you can!"

His voice even and deep and hotly restrained, all Todd could say was, "I'm working on something."

"Yeah, so are the rest of us, and it's called news, big news!" She shook her head. "You realize you blew it, don't you, Todd? You could have scooped this whole thing, been the first to tell the world that this guy is a drag queen, but now you're going to be last. I mean, I'm sure all the other stations are going to feature that on their ten o'clocks. I bet you dollars to doughnuts even that fool Cindy Wilson at Channel Seven is going to beat your ass on this one. And now you know what you're going to have to do? Run like hell just to keep up with her and everyone else, when you could have won this whole thing hands down!"

As he reached his office with her yelling and trailing after him, he stopped at his door and said, "Lay off, Nan. Trust me, something's wrong here, and I want to proceed with just a bit of caution."

"No shit something's wrong! And I know what it—"

Todd put a finger to his lips and said, "Shh."

"Todd—"

Ignoring her, he slipped into his small, glass-walled office just off the main newsroom, closed the door, turned the wand of the white miniblinds so that they shut completely, and stood there rubbing his brow. Stories like this didn't just come your way. No one just gave them away either. And yet . . . yet he couldn't stem the sense that he was being given all this. He witnessed the murder. He found the body. He not only helped find a suspect, but he reported live from the scene of the arrest. As a matter of fact, he'd captured two out of the three major events of this case on film, which was unbelievable.

Exactly: unbelievable.

And, no, it didn't just happen like this.

Todd would have liked to think he was that great, but events over the past few years had left him permanently humble. And wise enough to know that there were two types of truths: the spoken one versus the real. Just last week, Marcia, an old friend from Northwestern University, had shattered yet another one of those supposed truths, this one held not simply by Todd, but by billions around the world. While she'd once been an aspiring actress at Northwestern, she'd eventually abandoned that dream, pursuing something more practical, namely a career as an accountant in suburban Chicago. An instructor of hers from the drama program had finally made it, however, going on to become not a superstar, but certainly a major star in his own right, and this past Tuesday the two of them had reconnected and gone out for a lengthy and gossipy lunch. When the star started talking about one of his more recent films, an action-adventure movie where he'd played the bad guy opposite an actor who was one of the top hunks and biggest superstars in America, Marcia couldn't help but ask.

"I know Tim Chase is married—and, God, his wife's so utterly beautiful—but every now and then you hear those rumors," Marcia began. "I mean, forgive me my 'idol' curiosity, but tell me, is he or isn't he gay?"

The star looked up from his poached-chicken sandwich, shrugged, and said, "I spent something like two months on a set with Tim. And you wouldn't believe what a wonderful person he is—smart, kind, caring. His wife, Gwen Owens, came for a while too—she brought their son for a couple of weeks, and, man, those are the two most devoted parents I've ever seen. They love that little boy and they really love each other, but . . ."

"But?"

"Tim had a same-sex lover, a guy by the name of Rob. A nice guy too. He was on the set for a good chunk of the filming, and Tim and he shared a trailer and were completely open about it on the set. Everyone from the gaffer on up knew."

"But . . . but . . ." Marcia's mouth dropped open. "But what about Gwen Owens?"

"She must know that he likes guys, there's no way she couldn't. There was some kind of big blowup though. She came down, Tim and Rob had a huge fight, and then Rob left. I think it went like that anyway."

"Yeah, but, I mean, just last week there was a big article in the *National Enquirer*—okay, I didn't buy it, I just read it in line at the grocery store—with Tim Chase on the cover. They said he wasn't gay, and then they had a long quote from his wife, who said he was the straightest man she'd ever met."

"That's Hollywood." The star had smiled. "I'm sure his public-relations person wrote the whole thing, her quote and all, and just fed it to them. That's the way these things go."

That afternoon Marcia had called Todd, giggling and saying, "Oh, Todd, I got somethin' real hot here."

When Todd had first heard that story he'd been titillated, as every person—gay and straight, male and female—in the world would be. But now, days later, Todd was pissed. No, his anger had nothing to do with a judgmental belief that since he was out the entire world should be. Rather, now that Todd was out he saw the

crime of the closet all the more, a crime he himself had committed until recently by broadcasting an image of someone he was
not.

No, Tim the megastar was not nice. He was not caring. Nor
was he smart. In fact, he was anything but, for he was perpetuat-
ing a lie. And that lie wasn't simply that you couldn't be gay and
make it in the movies, nor that Middle America didn't want its
movie stars anything less than "perfect," nor even as simple as
being gay meant you couldn't be a good parent. Rather, via the
silver screen it telegraphed to both straight and queer people this
larger-than-life hateful message: *You won't be loved if people find
out you're gay.*

This territory was all too familiar. And horrible. Todd remembered—for God's sake, he'd wanted to die too—the night Michael
was killed and Todd was hauled in for questioning. As if it weren't
bad enough that his lover was dead, in the following days Todd
became instant fodder for a media roast, with the world jumping
to the conclusion that Todd Mills was guilty of murder simply
because he was gay.

So was that what was happening here? Was Todd's reporting
about to unleash upon Christopher Kenney exactly what had been
unleashed upon Todd? And could he morally do that to another
person? More horribly, would the media rush to portray Kenney
as a killer simply because of his gender expression, simply because
he was so very queer? Absolutely, and the fire and brimstone they
were sure to bring down upon a drag queen accused of murdering
a cop would be crushing, of that Todd had no doubt.

So how was Todd supposed to do this? Yes, he had a job to do.
Yes, this was a most shocking case. And, yes, Todd was right at the
epicenter. But as a gay person in the media he had definite, distinct responsibilities. So how could he push this further, how
could he add another dimension to this story without exploiting
the sizzle and gossip of a transgendered person's life, not to mention the fears and stereotypes of straight America as well?

And just what obligation did he have to Christopher Kenney,
if any?

Not thinking if he should or shouldn't, only knowing that

someone had to do something, Todd picked up the telephone and dialed her office number. Fortunately, she picked up right away.

She answered, "Janice Gray."

"It's me," said Todd. "You're working late."

"Oh, hi," she replied with a yawn. "Would you believe I'm just revving up for a late night? I'm going to be here for hours."

"You sure don't sound like it. Say, I don't suppose you were watching TV this evening?"

"Sorry. Were you on? Did I miss something?"

"Kind of." He hesitated—who else could he turn to?—then said, "Janice, I need some advice on transgendered people."

"What's that?" she said, sounding suddenly awake. "You got a question about trannies?"

Chapter 26

Rawlins began to see his error not long after they arrived at City Hall.

Back at the scene he'd been anything but clearheaded, and there'd been, of course, no time to think. And now, given the rigidity of the law—let alone the intensity of the situation—there was no going back. While Officer McNamee escorted Kenney into City Hall via the sally port—the police entrance on the east side of the building—and up to the CID on the second floor, Rawlins slipped away, unable to shake a sense of dread of where this thing would go over the next thirty-six hours.

No longer pressing the bloodied handkerchief to his neck, Rawlins went into the men's room and headed straight for the mirror over the sink, where he examined the scratches, three of them, on the left side of his neck. The bleeding had stopped long ago, thank God. And really there hadn't been that much blood, for the scratches weren't that deep. It wasn't as if Kenney had gouged him or anything. There'd been no spurting artery, no spray of blood. Now thinking about it, he really doubted whether Kenney himself had been exposed to Rawlins's blood. For starters, Kenney would have had to have open wounds on his own fingertips, which was doubtful, though somehow Rawlins would have to check on that.

Nevertheless, the struggle had still scared the shit out of Rawlins. He'd seen the blood and all he could think about was how to control it, which was why he'd overreacted. And why he'd taken the wrong steps. No two ways about it, he shouldn't have arrested him. Not yet anyway, for as of right now they didn't have it, enough evidence. Even he could see that.

Rawlins took a deep breath, exhaled, then washed his hands. He grabbed a paper towel, dampened that, then blotted the wound, which looked completely clean. The tiniest bit of blood stained the towel, but nothing to panic about. It would scab over immediately. So don't worry, he told himself. No damage done. Just get on with it and make the most of the present situation. It was just that . . . that . . .

"Oh, Christ," muttered Rawlins, shaking his head.

He wondered how long he could take this. Supposing that he was going to be HIV-positive if not for the rest of his life, then for years to come, he wondered how long he could take the pressure, the worry, the secrecy. A few years back it had been such a relief to come out as a gay man, but now he was right back there. No, actually he wasn't back in the closet. Rather, thanks to HIV he'd been tossed in some hideous dungeon from which he might never escape. Shit, he just wanted to tell someone on the force about his health. But who? And when? Or perhaps he should just ask for a desk job. Then again, knowing him he'd get the mother of all paper cuts and infect half the people in his office.

He tossed the used paper towels in the garbage, then, just in case he started to bleed again, stepped into a toilet stall and grabbed some tissue and stuffed it in his pocket. Okay, he thought. You know what you have to do.

A few minutes later Rawlins sat next to Officer McNamee in a small, windowless office, one of only several in the homicide division. In front of them, on the screen of a color television housed in a golden-oak home-entertainment center, was the image of a person, head bowed, blond hair disheveled, body completely still. The person sniffled once, and the sound was picked up clearly and precisely.

"So," said Rawlins, nodding at Kenney, "what's he been doing?"

"Nothing," replied McNamee. "Hasn't moved a muscle."

The interview room was right next door, a small chamber only some six feet by eight with a round table right in the middle. On the table sat two glasses and a sweating pitcher of ice water, and around the table were four simple, armless office chairs, the fabric on the seats a dark maroon. The walls were plain, a nondescript beige vinyl wallpaper covering them, and a single heating and air-conditioning vent was mounted halfway up one wall. Hidden in the vent was the video camera.

Rawlins glanced at his watch. Kenney had been sitting in there for seventeen minutes. Usually he liked to let them sit longer, sometimes over thirty minutes, to give them a taste of incarceration. After they'd sweated it out some, they were usually more inclined to talk. But not this one. Rawlins could see him shutting down by the second.

"Okay, here goes," said Rawlins, grabbing a microcassette recorder.

"Don't forget to smile for the camera," cracked McNamee.

Rawlins ducked out of the office, stepped to the next door, which was only inches away, tapped twice, and entered. Kenney didn't flinch. Rather, he sat there in a state of shock, one leg crossed over the other, his arms wrapped around his waist, his head hung. A single, narrow streak of mascara curled down his young cheek.

Rawlins placed the small recorder in the middle of the table, pushed the RECORD button, and said, "Good evening, my name is Sergeant Steve Rawlins. I'm a homicide investigator with the Minneapolis police, and we're here at the Minneapolis City Hall on the second floor. Our conversation is being recorded. Can you tell me your name, please?"

"Kris Kenney," she said quite faintly, without lifting her head.

Rawlins glanced down at a piece of paper. "Christopher Louis Kenney?"

She shrugged.

"Please speak out loud so the recorder will pick up your voice," said Rawlins.

"Well, it used to be Christopher Kenney. I'm in the, um, process of changing it. I go by *Kris* now. *Kris* with a *K.*"

"And you can read and write English?"

Kris nodded.

"Please say your response out loud. Can you read and write English?"

"Yes. Yes, I can."

"And you're comfortable and have water?"

"Yes."

"Can you tell me where you live?"

"In south Minneapolis. I live with my cousin at 5241 Turner Avenue South."

"I see," said Rawlins, hoping to keep this warmup going as long as possible. "Have you lived there for long?"

"No."

"Can you tell me how old you are and where you were born?"

Kris shifted in her seat, glanced up once with narrowed, angry eyes, and said, "I'm twenty-four. I was born in Duluth."

"And you went to school there?"

"Yes, I went to school there."

"Do your parents still live in Duluth?"

"I suppose so."

"Do you have any brothers and sisters?"

"Two brothers, one sister."

In the hope of gaining his trust, Rawlins continued with this series of banal questions, asking, "Did you go to college?"

"No."

"Do you have a job?"

"Not really."

But when, he wondered, should he play the gay card? Eventually he had to, of course, because it was far too valuable a tool to ignore. He considered waiting, then dropping some I'm-a-member-of-the-tribe-too line when he needed to bring Kenney back, to make him feel as if he had a friend in Rawlins. But, no, he should work it in now, because one of the earliest things Rawlins had learned as an investigator was how critical it was to build rapport. The sooner the better. If Rawlins could do that, make Kenney believe he had a comrade in Rawlins, perhaps then he'd forgo a lawyer, which of course would be ideal.

Referring to the mega-gay complex in downtown Minneapolis,

Rawlins said, "I go to the Gay Times in downtown Minneapolis. Haven't I seen you down there?"

For the first time Kris looked up. Cocking her painted right eyebrow, she stared at Rawlins for a long, ponderous moment. Then Kris poured herself a glass of water, took a sip, and leaned toward the small recorder.

"That's right, I think we have met," said Kris, quite clearly. "But I don't think it was down at the Times. No, I think it was in Loring Park on one dark night. After all, isn't that where all the homosexuals go to have sex? And aren't you the old troll who crept out and paid me twenty dollars for that blow job?" Kris forced a smile. "How did I do? Was it worth it, sweetheart?"

Oh, fuck. Rawlins sensed a rush of redness climb from his chest and up his neck, then push across his face. Fully aware that this was also being videotaped, he bent over and shielded his face as if he were looking at his notes.

Rawlins cleared his throat and said, "No, you're mistaken."

"Really? I could have sworn you were the one with that miniature dick. Then again, maybe it was a different cop. After all, it gets awfully dark under that bridge, don't you think?"

Struggling to maintain control, which he clearly wasn't, Rawlins cleared his throat and asked, "So, Kris, how long ago did you move from Duluth to Minneapolis?"

"I didn't move here from—" Kris shook her head, looked away, then stared back. "Would you quit fucking around with me and just get to the point?"

Okay, thought Rawlins, so he knows how these things go. He's been through this at least once, of course, if not more.

"Certainly."

What they'd talked about so far was nothing, a failed attempt on Rawlins's part to build trust. He had to be careful though. He didn't want to read Kenney the Miranda warning, not just yet, because then he'd probably lawyer up on him. At the same time, whatever Rawlins asked him now would not be admissible in court, not until Kenney had been Mirandized. However, it was a different matter if he didn't ask Kenney any questions but Kenney simply volunteered information.

"There was a murder down on the Stone Arch Bridge the other night," said Rawlins, choosing his words. "A police officer was killed."

Kris glared at him. "So?"

"I wanted to hear what you had to say about it. Things apparently got out of hand. There was a big storm, and—"

"You know what," said Kris, choosing her words equally carefully. "You can eat shit. I'm not saying anything."

No, thought Rawlins, taking a deep breath, he didn't have any choice. Time to go to the next step.

"I wish to inform you that you have been arrested for the murder of Park Police Officer Sergeant Mark Forrest," began Rawlins, who then read him the Miranda warning. "Can you tell me what you know about this murder?"

Kris leaned forward, put both her elbows on the table, and buried her face in her hands. Then she bowed her head farther down so that her hands slid into her tousled blond hair.

Into the table, Kris said, "This is bullshit."

"What's bullshit?"

"I didn't do anything. I didn't hurt anyone."

"Did you see anything?"

"No!" shouted Kris, jerking her head up.

He was going to lose him any second now, that much was obvious, and Rawlins stepped up the pace, asking, "Where were you two days ago, on the night of July tenth?"

"I saw my shrink, and then . . . then . . ." Kris looked away and shook her head in disgust. "Oh, shit."

"What kind of car do you own?"

Kris looked away and was totally silent.

"Do you own an Oldsmobile Ninety-Eight? Minnesota license-plate number five-five-five RBG?"

Kris sat there, staring at the wall and biting her lip.

"What do you have in the trunk of your car?"

She quickly looked back, her forehead wrinkled downward in confusion and surprise. "What the fuck are you talking about?"

"What is in the trunk of your Oldsmobile Ninety-Eight?"

"I don't know. Nothing. Just junk."

Rawlins went on the offensive, stating, "Kris, when I first approached you in front of your home you were putting something in the back of your Oldsmobile Ninety-Eight. Then you quickly shut it and moved up onto the sidewalk. Tell me, what's in there? A weapon of some sort? A gun?"

Wordless, confused, and now afraid, her head shook back and forth, yet she said nothing.

"Kris, we're in the process of getting a search warrant for your home and your car. Once we have that warrant, our investigators will go over everything. They'll look for hairs, for bits of fabric, and they'll spray anything suspicious with luminol. Do you know what that is? Luminol? It's a chemical that changes color if it touches blood or touches where blood has been, even if that blood has been scrubbed away. Perhaps we won't need it though. Perhaps we'll get lucky and find a few pure blood samples. Just a few drops, that's all we need. And if we find any we'll have it tested. And you know what? If the DNA matches Officer Forrest's, then you have a big problem."

"Oh, shit . . . You guys are out to get me, aren't you? You're trying to trap me, right?" she gasped, her eyes wide. "I . . . I need to make a phone call. I get to make a phone call. I want to do that now."

"You have to be booked first." Rawlins tried to keep it going just a bit more. "Is there anything else you can tell me?"

"No. No, I'm not saying anything until I have a lawyer."

"Certainly."

"Wait . . ." Kris thought for a moment. "I want this recorded. I want to make this official."

Rawlins leaned forward, hoping this was gold. "Yes?"

Kris leaned toward the small recorder and said, "I have to have a private cell. I don't want to be with anyone else. My name is Kris Kenney, and I'm a transgender person. If you put me in a cell with a bunch of guys they're gong to rape the shit out of me. Am I clear?"

"Absolutely," said Rawlins, unable to hide his disappointment. "Don't worry, I can guarantee that for the next thirty-six hours you'll have a cell all to yourself."

"I mean it. If any guys in the prison here hurt me, I'm going to sue the Minneapolis police department for every fucking dime it's got."

Rawlins saw the hate in Kenney's eyes, then clicked off the recorder and pushed back his chair. "Come on, Officer McNamee will take you down."

It wasn't a quick process, but it wasn't hard. All she had to do was let herself be shepherded along. Arms up. Arms down. Fingers here. That one there. Look this way. Turn the other. Ink and photograph.

Her hands cuffed behind her back, Kris was led out of CID by some oaf of a cop and down the grand marble staircase of City Hall. About three steps from the bottom, she unknowingly walked through an infrared beam, which triggered a buzzer at the guard desk below. The guard looked their way, checking to make sure all was well this evening, then turned back to his magazine.

She said nothing as she was led through a series of small halls, then around a corner where a line of cops and cuffed suspects waited in front of a heavy metal door labeled JAIL INTAKE.

"Ah, crap," muttered McNamee. "This might take a while."

And it did, nearly forty minutes. Eventually, though, Kris was led up to the door and buzzed into a small room, where she was officially turned over to the Hennepin County Sheriff. Once she was thoroughly and completely searched, the deputy buzzed her into the next hall, and the process of booking began. In sequence, her personal information was taken, she was next carefully finger-printed—her fingers rolled in ink one by one—and lastly photographed. Only then was Kris shunted onto a heavy, secure prisoner elevator and taken to the jail on the fifth floor.

What seemed like hours later she was finally allowed her phone call. Calling from an outgoing-only wall phone, Kris dialed the number without hesitation. No, she'd never forgot this number. It would be part of her for the rest of her life.

Her lawyer in Los Angeles picked up halfway through the second ring, with a frustrated, "Hello?"

The operator chimed in, "I have a collect call from Kris Kenney. Will you accept the charges?"

"What? Oh, sure. Yes, I'll pay."

The operator clicked off, and Kris, feeling relieved for the first time since her arrest, said, "Joan, it's me."

"Kris? Oh, my God. How are you, hon? Where are you?" A honk of a horn drowned out everything, and then Joan Ryan said, "Shit, you have to speak loud—I can barely hear you. You wouldn't believe the traffic I'm in. I've been driving five miles an hour for the last forty minutes. It's awful. Anyway, I haven't heard from you in—"

"Joan, it's happening again."

"What do you mean, hon? What's happening? Are you in trouble or something?"

"Yeah. It's . . . it's started all over again."

"What? Where are you? Here in L.A.? Listen, I'm going to meet someone for dinner, but I'm free later on. Want to have a drink? I know a great place for martinis. Wait, no, you're a margarita girl, aren't you?"

"Joan, I'm in Minneapolis."

"Minneapolis? But—"

"A cop was killed, and . . . and the police picked me up."

"What!"

"It happened just a little while ago, and . . . and . . ." Kris clutched the phone and suddenly started crying. "Joan, I'm scared. I'm really scared. They're going to get me this time, I know they are."

Halfway across the country and above the din of freeway mayhem, Joan bellowed, "Okay, the traffic's not moving an inch. I'm just sitting here now, so tell me everything. And I mean everything. None of your fancy stuff either. Am I clear, hon?"

"Yes, but . . . but I really don't know much."

It took only a quick couple of minutes for Kris to go through it all. A cop was killed—a young guy—and, no, she didn't have an alibi, at least not yet, though she'd get to work on that. Then late this afternoon she was leaving her house and . . . and the fucking cops swooped down. She had no idea what they knew or didn't know, but they were mean fuckers and didn't waste a second. She ran—okay, so she'd panicked—and then they handcuffed her and everything and hauled her ass down to City Hall. She'd been interrogated, booked, and now they were tossing her ass in jail.

"Wait a minute," demanded Joan. "You mean they arrested you? They formally charged you with this guy's murder?"

"Yes."

"Oh, brother. Obviously they've got something then."

"But what? I thought we'd taken care of everything," she said, trying not to cry. "I bet they know all about California. I bet they know, and—"

"Listen, don't panic."

"—and this time they're going to get me!"

"I can't believe this," said Joan. "Yeah, they probably do know about California. They probably know every little detail. And they're probably pissed that I got you off. So I'm sure—"

"Joan, you gotta come out here! You gotta help me!"

"I'll do what I can, babe, but—"

"Joan!"

"Listen, Kris, I'm in Los Angeles. And I'm a California attorney. I'm not licensed to practice anywhere else, hon."

Kris turned around to make sure none of the deputies was listening, then in a muffled voice said, "Listen, sister, you better find me someone. If it weren't for you I wouldn't be in any of this shit. This is all your fault, and I can ruin you, you know. All I gotta do is tell someone where I've been gettin' all my hormones and—"

"That's enough!" she snapped. "You'd never do that, and you know it."

Sheepishly, she replied, "Of course I wouldn't."

"Just be cool. Just calm down. I don't know anyone out there, but let me see what I can do."

Chapter 27

Once he'd spoken to Janice, Todd sat down at his desk and stared at the wall. He thought of himself and his closeted days, he thought of Tim the film star and the false image he projected, and he thought of Christopher/Kris. What did it all imply, that every gay person was a pathological liar?

Certainly not, thought Todd. Nor were gays innate liars either. He wasn't enough of a fool, however, to not recognize how easily and naturally all gays could lie—just as he had done for almost all his adult life—simply because their safety had depended on it for so very, very long. As a survival technique over the centuries gay people had learned what truth to give to which person. And when. If at all. Which meant getting to the truth of Kenney wasn't going to be an easy process. Nor was it going to be easy regarding Mark Forrest—what were the secrets of his sex life? Todd now saw it more clearly than ever, understood that his hunt for the truth would probably entail peeling away many layers of many lies.

Reaching for a legal pad on the side of his desk, Todd read down his notes until he came to the name of the cop killed in California. Next turning to his computer, he punched a couple of keys and his screen throbbed to colorful life. Disregarding the first image that surfaced—that of a half-finished game of solitaire he'd been playing a couple of days ago—Todd plunged on. Like all things in this age, his hunt would start here.

The Minneapolis/St. Paul area was in the top fifteen large-market television category, particularly now that it was feeding its programming via satellite to a Canadian cable company. In terms of quality, however, it was considered to be in the top three, vying not against New York or Chicago or Los Angeles, but Atlanta and Denver, and, according to Minnesota chauvinists and maybe just a few unbiased others, actually winning. What that primarily meant to Todd was that not only were the production standards high at WLAK, but that he had access to a vast array of the best equipment and services, such as almost every data base available in the country. Thinking he could later get from Rawlins a printout from the National Crime Information Center—which would include relatively dry, straightforward information, from police wants to fingerprint details like central-pocket loop whorls—Todd decided to start elsewhere. He typed in his user name and password, the computer dialed in, and the vast world of Lexis-Nexis opened onto Todd's desk.

It didn't take long to get things going and find what he wanted. He had two initial options of how to enter the system— *News* or *People*—and he chose the first; if nothing turned up he'd later search the *People* section for mention of Kenney. His next choice was whether to peruse magazines, major papers, wires, or newsletters, and his automatic choice was to go in on *Newspapers.* When a mostly blank screen appeared before him, Todd entered a series of keywords, typing: *Kenney and Ravell and police and murder.* He paused a moment, considered adding a couple of additional keywords, but then decided against it. For now he wanted as broad a search as possible; he'd be more specific later when and if he wanted to narrow his hunt. He hit the ENTER key, then waited as the computer system flashed the words: *Nexis is working on the displayed request.* In the next few seconds Todd feared that Lexis-Nexis would flash back that it had no stories, but instead Todd got a total of nine hits.

Immediately Todd punched the CITE function key at the top of his keyboard, and nine blips appeared in chronological order, listing the journal, the date of the story, the headline, and a synopsis of the text. Quickly scrolling through them all, Todd noted that seven were from the *Los Angeles Times* and two from the *Duluth Tribune.* Apparently, thought Todd, settling into this, there was no lack of information on whatever had taken place in California. The question was how it would or wouldn't tie in to the murder of Sergeant Mark Forrest here in Minneapolis, and most importantly whether or not it would indicate if Kenney was a fledgling serial killer. If so, if Kenney was making a morose career of this kind of murder, were there just these two killings, or had he perhaps left a trail of dead police officers across the country? That, Todd realized, was something he'd have to check into—a listing, including dates and locations, of cops killed over the last couple of years.

Completely unaware of what he would find yet intuitively certain that this hunt was going to take him somewhere, a rush of excitement swelled through Todd. He glanced at his watch, saw that it wasn't even eight-thirty, which meant he had plenty of time before the 10@10 broadcast. He switched from the synopses to the full texts, and the keywords he had entered stared out at him in bold typeface each and every time they appeared in the text of the stories. Starting with the first article, which appeared the morning after the murder of Los Angeles cop Dave Ravell a year and a half ago, Todd read them in order, one after the other.

In the beginning, Todd understood, the case seemed pretty open and shut—or so it was portrayed by the media. On a pleasant Saturday night in Los Angeles, a series of screams from an efficiency apartment rented to Christopher Louis Kenney broke the stillness. Moments later a single gunshot exploded. There was a moment of quiet, then one large shriek. The neighbor across the open-air landing, a guy by the name of Tom Babcock, heard the shot, the screams, and rushed over. He banged on the door, hollered to see if everything was all right, then opened the door, which was unlocked. Sobbing on the floor in a skimpy blood-spattered dress was Kenney, whom everyone in the apartment building actually believed to be a beautiful twentysomething girl by the name of Kris. Across from Kenney, slumped on the couch, was the body of a young man, Sergeant David Ravell, his blue police shirt and several pairs of shoes—both his and hers—on the floor. A third of David's head was blown away from a gunshot wound, and blood was pumping from the body onto the couch and floor. On the carpet in front of Dave lay a pistol. This was what the neighbor saw and also exactly what the police found less than four minutes later when a nearby squad car responded to the neighbor's 911 call. As far as the two cops could tell, Kenney had not moved an inch, for none of the blood around her was smeared. Rather she just sat there, eyes and mouth opened in horrified shock. In fact, she wouldn't move, even when called to, and they had to lift her away.

So far, thought Todd, scrolling from one article to the next, it seemed about as straightforward as could be. One body. One gun. One obvious suspect. It was no wonder that Christopher Louis Kenney, a.k.a. Kris, was booked and charged that very night with the murder of Police Officer Dave Ravell. And, given that this was all about a cop-killing, it was completely understandable why he was held without bail. But the truth, Todd knew from both his personal as well as his professional lives, was rarely a superficial thing, not something that lay like an oil slick on the surface of deep waters. Particularly in something so complicated as death.

Yet . . .

With each sentence Todd read, it looked more and more certain that Kenney had in fact killed Sergeant Ravell. The medical examiner's report, which came back the next day, was equally damning. According to the *Los Angeles Times* in a subsequent article, the M.E.'s office confirmed beyond a doubt not only that the weapon used to kill Dave Ravell was police issue, but that in fact Kenney's fingerprints were on the handle of the gun. Mention was then made of Kenney's sexuality. Yes, he'd been dressed as a woman when the murder was committed. And, yes, he was gay, the very mention of which made Todd flinch, for it was something about the way it was phrased. Or was it the placement of the sexual revelation in the story? For whatever reason, though, the reporter's wording made it sound as if Kenney was guilty simply because he was homosexual, which in turn reminded Todd of older movies and books where queer people were portrayed as one of two aberrations: either the repulsive villain who couldn't control himself or the pathetic, limp-wristed victim who more or less deserved to be killed.

So how, wondered Todd, flipping to the next article, did they know Kenney was gay? Had Kenney simply told them? Or had the media jumped to conclusions, assuming that since he was dressed as a woman he was homosexual? Todd would have to follow up on that, for a man in a skirt didn't equal a homo. Absolutely not. The spectrum of cross-dressing was much broader than that, with heterosexual transvestites—straights who cross-dressed as a way to arouse themselves sexually—on one end, and transsexuals—those who'd had sexual reassignment—on the other.

Todd sat back for a moment and rubbed his eyes. Wait a minute, he thought, what the hell had Sergeant Ravell been doing there in Kenney's apartment in the first place? Most murders, of course, took place in the heat of passion. So if the two of them, Christopher Kenney and Dave Ravell, had been sexually intimate, just what was the nature of their relationship?

There was no telling yet how far this story would actually go. He'd do the story at ten, then follow-up once or twice tomorrow, but experience had told him the public's attention would soon start to lag. And before that happened, to be sure, WLAK management would sure as hell pull Todd from the story. That meant that at best Todd would have only until Mark Forrest's funeral— which would be attended by family and friends and thousands of cops and would be covered at length by all the media, print and broadcast—to come up with something that would keep this thing alive. Broadcast journalism—in particular, television—was getting more and more shit these days for its lack of depth in reporting, but that, Todd felt, said as much about the American public's attention span as anything else.

Returning to the screen, Todd read on about the murder in Los Angeles. Sergeant Dave Ravell had been recently divorced— and what, Todd mused, was the story there?—and was survived only by his mother, Roseanne, who was struck so hard by the news that she was immediately put on medication, and by his younger brother, Ron, who was described as "shattered." Hoping they wouldn't be too hard to reach and that they would agree to talk to him, Todd jotted down their names, then continued. By the afternoon of the following day, Kenney had hired an attorney, Joan

Ryan, who came forward, insisting absolutely and completely that Christopher Louis Kenney was innocent.

"There was a struggle involving the weapon, but Christopher most definitely did not pull the trigger. Clearly this is not a case of murder but suicide," she was quoted in the *Los Angeles Times*. "I've met at length with my client, and I intend to prove his innocence in a court of law."

Todd next came to an article in the *Duluth Tribune* reporting that one of northern Minnesota's native sons had been arrested in California for killing a cop. Again there was mention both of young Christopher's sexuality and that he was presumed by all in Los Angeles to be a woman, leaving readers to cast their own stones. The damage to the Kenney family reputation, though, surely had to have been significant, for his parents, Marie and Joseph, were identified, specifically that Joseph had served with the Duluth police for over twenty-five years. It was a fact that jumped out at Todd, definitely suggesting another avenue to explore. On his pad of paper Todd jotted: What is Kenney's relationship with father? Was there any physical abuse? What does father think of gays?

As surely and easily as the case had been built against Christopher Louis Kenney, however, it unraveled just as quickly. A mere four days after the murder and just three days after the medical examiner's report, the medical examiner himself was stopped for driving under the influence. It was a scandal that swept across the front pages of the papers, and it was more than enough ammo for attorney Joan Ryan—"For God's sake," she was quoted, "what kind of butchering has he been doing? How many autopsies has this man done while drunk?"—to call for a prosecuting attorney and medical examiner from another city to reevaluate the case. Which was exactly what took place. Not even twenty-four hours after Sergeant Dave Ravell was laid to rest with great mourning from thousands of the L.A.P.D., his body was exhumed from the dark and placed again in the scrutiny of light.

And the findings of the second report couldn't have been more shocking.

Much to the chagrin of the police and the horror of the Ravell family, the second medical examiner supported Christopher Louis Kenney's claims. Both men were right-handed—indeed, only the prints of Christopher's right hand were found on the gun—yet the bullet wound was not on the left side of Ravell's head, but on the right. Furthermore, the powder burns, the angle of the bullet, and the immense damage to the skull, which was horribly shattered, confirmed that the weapon had been fired point-blank. This raised considerable doubt on Kenney's ability to move around to Ravell's right side and fire the gun, then sit down opposite him. And while Kenney was splattered with blood, he'd definitely not been smeared nor had he left any bloody tracks, as would have been the case had he physically traversed the scene. Furthermore, Sergeant Dave Ravell's personal medical files confirmed that he was distraught over his divorce and that he was not only taking Prozac for depression but had been identified as suicidal. And finally, someone looked up and spoke with Ravell's former wife, who admitted that she and her husband had divorced over issues of his sexuality, specifically his homosexuality. In no uncertain terms she told the investigators that she dumped her husband when she found him in bed with a FedEx man.

"What we have here," pronounced Joan Ryan in an interview to all the press, "is clearly a case of a confused cop who could not come to terms with his being gay. He and my client, who cared deeply for him, were beginning a relationship, but unfortunately Mr. Ravell felt it easier to take his own life than to face the truth. Sadly, this is all about homophobia and self-hate."

That afternoon the judge tossed out the case, feeling that guilt beyond a reasonable doubt could not be established, and Christopher Louis Kenney was released.

The second-to-the-last article was again from the *Duluth Tribune,* a short piece that reported that the charges against Kenney had been dropped. When asked how he felt about all this, Kenney's father, Officer Joseph Kenney, simply said, "As far as I'm concerned, my son is dead."

Moving on, Todd came to the final article in the data base, which was dated the very next day:

9TH STORY of Level 1 printed in FULL format
Copyright Times Mirror Company
Los Angeles Times
Home Edition
SECTION: Metro; Part B, Page 24
LENGTH: 265 words
HEADLINE: More Difficulties for Policeman's Family
BODY:

Roseanne Ravell, age 63, mother of Sergeant Dave Ravell, who died last week of an apparently self-inflicted gunshot wound, suffered a debilitating stroke Friday afternoon at her home in Los Angeles. Her only surviving relative, her son, Ron, was at her side when she collapsed in her living room. Thanks in large part to her son's efforts and those of an emergency medical team who were summoned, Mrs. Ravell was quickly stabilized and rushed to a nearby hospital.

Since the death of her son Sergeant Ravell, in what at first was widely believed to be a homicide, Mrs. Ravell had been on medication and under the supervision of her doctor. Friday afternoon, however, reporters descended upon her house, telling her that the charges against Christopher Louis Kenney, the young man dressed as a woman who had been arrested for Sergeant Ravell's murder, were dismissed and he was being released. When asked if she thought her son was gay and that he had killed himself, Mrs. Ravell burst into tears and retreated into her house. Approximately one hour later Mrs. Ravell suffered her stroke.

The story went on to recapitulate the strange events of the prior week, noting that Christopher Kenney's release was prompted when the initial report from the medical examiner was found to be faulty. The reporter went into detail about the drunk medical examiner, who had been relieved of his duties without pay pending an investigation, and added a quote from Kenney's attor-

ney, Joan Ryan, who regretted the entire tragedy. The story concluded with a few words about and from Ron Ravell.

> This leaves Ron Ravell, age 28, just sixteen months
> younger than his brother Dave, to deal with the family
> tragedy. Nine years earlier his father, Thomas Ravell, was
> killed in an automobile accident.
> "As far as I'm concerned," said Ron Ravell, "Chris
> Kenney killed not only my brother, but also robbed my
> mother of her life. Her stroke was massive and she will
> only partially recover. The doctors say she will need full-
> time care from now on, the cost of which, hopefully, will
> be covered by the settlement from Dave's life insurance.
> As far as my brother, I know he didn't kill himself over
> questions of sexuality. I'm gay, and Dave had virtually no
> issues with that. Besides, this is California, these are the
> nineties. Being gay is just not enough of a reason to blow
> your brains out. And now my mother's life is ruined all
> because of this. It's horrible, senseless."

And that, thought Todd, reading and rereading the last few
sentences, was an extremely valid point. Not only was Sergeant
Dave Ravell apparently close to his brother, who was openly gay,
but surely he knew numerous gay people. Undoubtedly he came
across them on a daily basis. After all, he lived in L.A. There were
millions of queers out there. Hollywood was swarming with them.
All you had to do was drive down Santa Monica Boulevard at night
to see scores of gay men strolling along holding hands. So what
could possibly have been the big deal? What could he have been
so upset about?

The sad truth was that perhaps now there would never be any
knowing.

While right then and there it seemed impossible to Todd that
a California man could commit suicide over sexuality issues, Todd
could in fact empathize. Not so very long ago there had been a
time in his own life when it seemed as if the world hinged on
Todd's sexuality. His own homophobia had led him down some

path into a dark cave where his fears had grown to nightmarish proportions. He'd been terrified what his friends and family would think if they knew the truth about him, how they would react, how they would reject him, how hurt and supposedly disappointed his father would have been. Later he'd been fearful not only of losing his job but ending his career in broadcast. And he'd been upset that if he didn't marry and have kids the family would die out. It had all seemed so monumental, so insurmountable.

Yet now all that was gone, disappeared as if it had been that and only that, a hideous nightmare, vanquished by some kind of light.

So, Dave Ravell, who were you? And what were you doing there with Christopher Louis Kenney?

Staring at this, the last article, Todd knew there was only one place to dig and that he had in fact found it: the younger brother who not only knew Sergeant Dave Ravell better than anyone else, but who was also quite sure of Kenney's guilt.

And maybe, just maybe, Ron Ravell would finally prove to be right.

Chapter 28

Just as he did nearly every morning on his way to work, Douglas Simms stopped for breakfast at a small skyway deli overlooking Third Avenue. It was just past eight.

"A glazed doughnut," he requested as he pushed his glasses up.

"Yes, yes, of course," said the short, gray-haired woman behind the counter. "And a Coke."

"A jumbo."

"Sure, just like always. That'll be—"

"I know," interrupted Simms, slapping down the exact amount.

He carried his doughnut and towering drink to a white Formica booth by the window, glanced down at the street, and sat down. Forgoing a straw as he always did, he took a long gulp of the soda, letting the cool beverage twirl down to his gut. Work was going to be a madhouse this morning, and Judge Hawkins was sure to be on a tirade, probably the worst one yet. But then again, the good judge should be scared as hell, shouldn't he?

Simms took a bite of the doughnut, which was fresh and sweet and sticky, and shook his head. He knew what to expect. He knew how the litany would go. Do this. Get that. Look that up. Call so-and-so. Make sure I have this. Write that up by noon. And change the fucking world, goddamn it all! Hawkins was always the worst in the morning, the crabbiest and bossiest. On top of that, for the past few days everyone had been so uptight over the cop-killing.

But—a small grin on Simms's lips—they'd already caught

some guy, hadn't they? Well? Yes, he'd seen it last night on the late news, and then it was the cover story in this morning's paper. Thank God. Life was going to be ever so much easier now.

He took another long slug of Coke, closing his eyes as he sucked on the rim of the paper cup. Putting the beverage down, he quickly gobbled up the rest of the doughnut, then licked the sugary glaze off his fingertips. At the next table two corporate types drinking coffee got up, leaving behind the paper, which Simms quickly snatched. He'd read the paper at home, stared and stared at it with immense amusement, but still he couldn't get enough.

Now spreading the wrinkled pages on the Formica before him, Simms burst into a grin. There, staring up at him from the front page, was a police photo of the accused, the guy who'd been picked up for the murder of Officer Mark Forrest. It was a thin, young face, the hair blond and disheveled. A face Simms most surely knew. And then there was the clincher, the caption that read: *Disguised as woman, suspect arrested in cop-killing.*

Oh, Christ, laughed Simms out loud. This really was too perfect. Too fucking perfect. Could things possibly be working out any better?

Chapter 29

Todd was at the station by eight-thirty that morning. Grabbing a cup of coffee, he disappeared into his office and closed the mini-blinds on the glass wall, then sat in his chair and yawned. He'd slept alone and slept horribly, for Rawlins had reverted to Lieutenant Holbrook's orders and had stayed at his duplex last night.

But now, presuming that the threat against Rawlins was allayed by the arrest of Kenney, Todd had to focus on his story and just where it was going. No doubt about it, he needed more for tonight. More precisely, he needed something different and fresh. And so naturally he turned to what he had been working on yesterday evening.

It never happened this easily though.

When you were backgrounding someone you weren't supposed to just call up directory information and get his phone number in a flash. Usually you had to refer to the Department of Motor Vehicles or, if the person lived in another city, one of the on-line data bases like Autotrak that listed all the public information on a person, from phone number to street address, social-security number to neighbors. And it was supposed to take one of WLAK's researchers days to accomplish.

Instead, Todd simply dialed Los Angeles information, asked for and got the telephone number for the only Ronald Ravell listed. Wasting not a moment, Todd dialed that number; Ron Ravell's phone rang four times before his Voice Mail picked up. It was only then that Todd realized how early it was in Los Angeles, just after six-thirty.

"Hi, my name is Todd Mills," he said, deciding that brevity—
i.e., leaving out that he was a reporter—was perhaps the best way
to catch this guy's interest. "I'm sorry for calling so early, but I'm
trying to reach Ron Ravell, whose brother was Dave Ravell. I'm
assuming that's you, and I'm hoping that we can talk regarding
Christopher Kenney. Would you please call me collect?"

Todd left his cell-phone number, then hung up. Perhaps the
guy was in the shower. Perhaps he'd already gone to work. Or
perhaps the poor bastard was still asleep. So should Todd wait
around, say a half hour or so, to see if he called back? No, he
couldn't afford to waste the time.

He slammed down the last of his coffee, then took off. As
always, no one inquired where he was going, what he was doing.
For all management knew, Todd was going to the gym.

As it was, he drove back into town, heading directly to south
Minneapolis. Pulling up to the house where Mark Forrest had
lived on Young Avenue, Todd hoped he'd find Forrest's landlady,
Anna Johnson, at home. It was only last night that Todd realized
how slanted he'd been thus far in his thinking, namely, how focused he'd been on one thing and one thing alone when he'd
come here before.

His realization started last night not with the arrest of Christopher Kenney, but with his phone conversation with Janice. Like
other times before, he'd been looking for more than an answer to
a specific question. No doubt about it, he often called her wanting
one thing and one thing only: her nurturing.

Not just gay men but all men were shit at it. At soothing. At
stroking. At giving.

If Todd had a specific problem, a complex question of any
sort, he turned to Rawlins for his opinions. But when his confidence was waning he turned to Janice, not simply for her school-
ing, but for her mothering. Increasingly, Todd was realizing that
guys, including himself, just didn't get it, didn't know how to do it.
Giving selflessly wasn't a natural, an automatic.

And that was what he'd come here this morning to ask Anna
Johnson. Todd had been so focused on Mark Forrest's sex life, so
preoccupied with the guy he might have been sleeping with, that

he'd overlooked the other possibility altogether. Namely, if Anna Johnson didn't know if Mark Forrest had a boyfriend, what about a close, close female friend? A close female friend to whom he might spill all?

In other words, did he have a fag hag?

He climbed out of his truck and headed up to the tall clapboard house, the warmth of the day quickly embracing him. Squinting, he peered up at the Palladian window right below the peak of the house and tried to imagine Forrest's life up there. No, regardless of how out he was, Todd didn't think he'd bring anyone home either, not with a landlady sleeping right beneath you.

Opening the screen door, he crossed the porch and rang the doorbell. A few moments later she again came to the door, pulled aside the lace curtain covering the glass. This time, recognizing Todd, she opened the door right away.

"Hi, Mrs. Johnson," began Todd. "I'm sorry for bothering you, but—"

"I saw you on TV last night. Saw the whole thing live," she said, interrupting. "So they got the guy who did it, did they? Arrested him, huh? My, my, my. Poor Mark, what a shame."

"Well, the police do have a suspect, but they're still trying to decide if—"

"And dressed up all like a girl—heavens!"

Todd said, "Did you ever see her here?"

"Heavens no! Never saw anyone like that thing, that's for sure. I mean, I'd remember her, no doubt in my mind about that."

"Certainly." Todd glanced to his left at the assemblage of old porch furniture, then looked back at her. "Last time I was here I asked if you remembered any guys coming around to see Mark."

"That's right, and I still can't recall a one."

"I'm sure of that. But what about any women? And I'm not talking about her, the one you saw on TV last night."

"Well, like I said, she wasn't here, that's for sure. But, no, I can't really recall any other girls coming over." She put her hand to her chin, thought a moment, then shook her head. "Nope. Like I was telling you, nobody really came over. I mean, it's a nice little apartment, but it's just one room. One room, that's all. Not much for entertaining."

Oh, crap, thought Todd. Why hadn't he just called? Why had he come all the way over here?

Out of desperation he asked one last time, "So you don't remember seeing him with anyone? You don't even know who his friends were?"

"No, Mark wasn't here much except to sleep. He worked a lot, you know. And he was always going to the gym. And he did stay out late. I mean, when he wasn't working he usually didn't come home until the bars closed, you know, after one."

"I see."

So, thought Todd, she knew of what she spoke. More of a snoop than she actually let on to, she really did keep tabs on Forrest's comings and goings. What else did she know, and how could Todd get it out of her?

"Didn't anyone help him move in?"

"Say now," she said, her eyes widening, "there was this young girl. Cute thing. Dark hair, big smile. He came to look at the apartment twice, and she was with him the second time."

Bingo, thought Todd. He'd brought her along for her approval.

He asked, "Do you remember her name?"

"Well, no. I mean, that was so long ago, last fall, and . . ." Stumbling into thought, she stopped, put her hand to her mouth. "Wait a minute. I think he put her down on his application. Come on."

For the first time she swung the front door wide, then turned and bustled through the house. Todd followed, passing from the small entry, past the oak staircase, through the living room with its dark-oak built-ins and fireplace, around and through the dining room, and finally into the kitchen. It wasn't that large a space, with an electric range, a large porcelain sink, and cabinets painted a pale yellow. Looking at the linoleum and the countertops, both of which had been cleaned so many times that their patterns had been scrubbed away, Todd guessed that the kitchen hadn't been remodeled since the early sixties.

"I've got it all over here," she said as much to Todd as to herself.

Anna Johnson went directly to a brown accordion-type file that sat on a shelf beneath an old wall phone, a rotary one. Licking her right index finger, she thumbed through the file, came to one pocket, reached in, and pulled out a piece of paper. Through her plain glasses, she squinted at the writing, flipped it over, then smiled.

"Yes, Mark did put her down as a reference. He wrote her name right here—Maureen Shea. Of course that's it, I remember now. See? This is his handwriting, and here's her name, Maureen Shea. He wrote that she's a friend. And look, here's her telephone number."

Shea? Why the hell was that name familiar? He couldn't place it, not right offhand, but he was sure he'd heard of her before. In any case, he was thrilled. He didn't know where it would lead, but, grinning, he was sure that Rawlins and his crew hadn't come up with this.

"I wish I were as organized as you," said Todd.

"All you have to do is file things, that's all."

"Can I see it?"

Anna Johnson proudly handed it to him. "Sure."

He took the rental application, ran his eyes over it, and found an odd sensation running up his spine. This was Mark Forrest's handwriting, small and neat and tight. Recalling the handsome young man he'd so briefly met on the Stone Arch Bridge, Todd realized that while Mark projected a bold, broad image, this writing indicated someone who was inwardly careful, perhaps even meticulous, which meshed of course with Anna Johnson's description of him and the apartment he kept here.

Todd took a pen and paper from his shirt pocket, jotting down not only Maureen Shea's phone number, but also the address of the apartment where Forrest had lived for, he claimed, two years. Scanning the application, he saw nothing else of interest.

"This is very, very helpful," said Todd, handing it back to her. "Thank you."

"Oh, you bet."

As she escorted him out, Todd ran through it all in his head. He'd start with Maureen Shea and see what he could learn from her. If his crude theory was even partly correct, she'd definitely have some insights into Forrest's personal life. And then after he spoke with her, he'd swing by the apartment where Forrest used to live. So why had he left there—perhaps to save money by moving into a smaller place? Or could he possibly have been living with some guy and walked out on him? A guy who might be consumed with anger?

"Say now, Mr. Mills," said Anna Johnson, just as Todd was heading out the front door. "There is just one more thing. Actually, I was talking with my neighbor friend and she mentioned it."

"What's that?" asked Todd, turning around on the threshold.

"Well, I think there's another fellow down the street. On the corner, you know."

"Another fellow?"

"You know, another gay fellow. He lives down in the little white bungalow on the corner. I didn't mention him before because he never came over, not here anyway."

Another gay man down the block? Todd didn't know whether to be interested or offended that someone's sexuality was neighborhood gossip.

He asked, "Do you know if Mark ever went down to see him?"

"No, I don't, but my friend thinks she saw them talking once." She thought for a second. "You don't suppose they knew each other, Mark and this fellow?"

"I don't know, but I'll keep that in mind." Todd held up the piece of paper. "Thanks for Maureen's name and number."

She leaned toward Todd and half whispered, "Just don't tell her you got it from me, okay?"

"Right."

Walking down the concrete walk, Todd glanced at the billowing clouds in the sky, saw one huge puff atop another. He headed straight for his car, got in, and immediately reached for his cellular phone. Glancing at the number, he dialed it immediately.

After four rings her answering machine picked up, and her

voice, bright and energetic, said, "*Hi, this is Maureen Shea. I'm away from the phone, but leave a message and I'll get back to you, hopefully within the hour. Thanks, and have a great day!*"

Todd cleared his throat and after the beep said, "Hi, this is Todd Mills from WLAK TV. I was wondering if I could speak to you about Mark Forrest. Would you please call me at your earliest convenience?"

Todd left his cell number, folded up the compact phone, then started up his Jeep. At this point there wasn't much else he could do but return to the station. And then? With any luck he'd get calls from both Maureen Shea and Ron Ravell.

As he started down the block he glanced at the small yards in front of the houses, saw the vibrant green grass and the shrubs, mostly lilacs and evergreens. Midwesterners still weren't among the most creative gardeners, their roots stemming from corn and wheat, but then again whatever grew here had to withstand more than a 125-degree temperature swing.

The house on the corner stuck out not only because, unlike the other tall farmhouselike clapboard houses, it was short and stuccoed, but because there were roses, lots of them in a variety of colors, in the front yard. Thriving roses, which in this climate was no small feat, since not only did they have to be tended to all summer, but buried beneath straw every winter. Okay, thought Todd as he pulled to a stop, so maybe a queer person does live here. In any case, it was someone making an effort.

But wait a minute. Just because this person might be gay— yes, the flowers are fabulous, the house perfectly maintained— doesn't mean he knew Mark Forrest. Not by any means. And it doesn't mean he knew anything about either Forrest's life or end. Yet . . .

In spite of himself, Todd turned off the Cherokee and got out. Whoever gardened like this was dumping all their love into these flowers, and it showed. Along the walk to the front door, an extravaganza of red and yellow and peach-color roses blossomed, and Todd admired them all as he went up to the house. It was the only structure on the block without a front porch, and to the side of the arched door was a mail slot with a few outgoing letters and a doorbell, which he rang. This could be entirely stupid, but on the other hand it couldn't hurt.

Nothing happened and no one came to the door, however. Todd stood there for a minute or so, rang again. And waited. Evidently whoever lived here was already at work, which made complete sense. Todd peered through a small window in the door, next leaned to the side and looked in the living room. No one, not a sign of life. He glanced at the house next door, then turned around and checked to see if anyone was out and about. Confident that he was unobserved, he plucked from the mail slot the stack of three or four letters left there for pick-up. Quickly sorting through them, he saw that one was a gas bill, another an electric, the others just plain white envelopes. Written in the top left corner of all of them, the handwriting even and perfect, was the return address for this house on Young Avenue and the name of the sender, Douglas Simms.

Todd stuck the stack of envelopes back in the slot, then headed to his car. He'd make a note of this guy and his address. After all, who knew. Perhaps it wasn't such a far stretch that two gay guys on the same block knew each other.

Chapter 30

Shortly before noon Rawlins headed through the broad, dark tunnel that swooped beneath Fifth Street from City Hall to Government Center. Clutching a file that was sure to grow thicker by the day, he focused ahead on the dramatic wall of water that tumbled from an overhead plaza into the middle of this subterranean passage.

Okay, he was exhausted. And out of sync. Either it was because he didn't get enough rest—it was well after one in the morning by the time he got home—or because he was nervous about where this entire cop-killing thing was going.

Now, he pondered as his feet slapped the red-brick pavers, all he could do was hope that this meeting went well. Fortunately they'd had a major break. Once they'd obtained a search warrant, they'd gone through Kenney's car and late last night found—thank God—something incredible: a yellow rain slicker. And not just any old yellow rain slicker, but one that showed evidence of blood. That would do it, wouldn't it?

Hoping it was enough to cover his ass, he rode the escalators up a couple of floors to the courtyard, an enormous glass atrium that was flanked on two long sides by matching twenty-four-story red granite towers. Stepping off the mechanical stairs, he immediately came upon a round information desk, on which sat a small Plexiglas picture stand holding this week's schedule. And there it was, written in blue marker: Civil and Criminal Signing Judge: Brown 1850.

"Oh, shit," muttered Rawlins, rubbing his brow.

Judge Brown was known as a stickler for detail, a judge who was reticent to tie up the courts with a case that was not sure to be successfully prosecuted. Just a couple of months ago Rawlins had heard that she'd been dissatisfied with the evidence presented her and had refused to sign a formal complaint, thereby halting a case in its tracks by not allowing it to be arraigned. So were they going to be able to pull this one off; would the prosecuting attorney be able to draft a formal complaint that would fly past Judge Brown's scrutiny?

Time would soon tell, he thought, skirting a long, placid fountain. Making his way toward the Court Tower, he boarded an elevator and rode it up to the seventeenth floor.

Thankful that the sinus infection that had plagued him for so long—and which had in fact led to his discovery of his HIV status—was now long gone, he got out without a trace of dizziness. Heading along the hallway, he peered through the glass wall, which had been added because there had been so many jumpers. Shuddering, he recalled how he, too, had once considered taking such a fatal leap, one from Todd's balcony. And how he probably would have had Todd not tackled him with a kind of desperate love.

Turning away from the memories of that horrible night, he headed toward a receptionist, yet another Minnesota blonde—her hair thick and long, her face broad and cute—who sat behind a shield of bulletproof glass.

"Hi, I have an appointment with Denise Daylen."

"Please sign in," said the young woman, pushing a register through a slot at the bottom of the window.

While Rawlins signed in, the receptionist telephoned to the back, and it was only moments before a side door opened and a black woman in a gray suit stepped out.

"Steve?"

"Hi, Denise."

With a broad, warm smile, she extended her hand and said, "Long time no see."

"Yeah, well, I've been catching 'em."

"I know you have—trust me, I keep up with your career." She opened the door wide. "Come on back."

A slender, rather plain woman with straight hair pulled back into a tight bun, Denise Daylen was one of Hennepin County's senior prosecuting attorneys. Rawlins had worked with her—what was it—something like two or three years ago when some nut she had successfully prosecuted for theft began stalking and threatening her and her husband. He'd admired her strength back then— she wouldn't be intimidated, even when the creep had killed her dog—and was glad to learn earlier today that the assigning attorney had passed this case directly on to her.

Rawlins followed her down one narrow corridor and around a corner. Reaching her office, they entered a small space filled with a desk, three or four bookcases packed with books and papers, and a window that looked east toward the inflated hump of the Metrodome, the University of Minnesota, and eventually St. Paul. As Daylen sat behind her desk and slipped on a pair of large glasses, Rawlins pulled up a wooden chair.

"Here's my report," he said, opening the file and taking out a sheaf of papers and forms. "And the NCIC printout on him."

This was the part he hated, the part that reeked of his grade-school days—sitting and waiting to see if he'd passed.

"Anything new since we spoke?" she asked, referring to their lengthy phone call some forty-five minutes ago.

"Ah, no. Not since the yellow raincoat," he said, trying to keep that front and foremost. "Like I said, Kenney let it slip that he was seeing a shrink, but I don't have a name yet."

"That's definitely one to follow up on."

"Right. There's a gender program at the U—I'm going to check there first."

"Good idea."

"Oh, the B of I guys are almost finished going over Forrest's car."

"And?"

"Well, they've gotten a lot of prints besides Forrest's, including some that look pretty fresh. We'll run 'em, but God only knows if we'll get a match." It was a long shot, of course—if by chance one of the sets of fingerprints belonged to the killer, the killer had to have a previous record for his prints to be on computerized file. "Otherwise, I think we went over everything. Everything in my report just backs up what I said. We'll be able to formally charge him, won't we?"

"I'm getting a lot of pressure from above to do exactly that," she said, pointing upward as if to God but instead just to the floor overhead. "Not only the judges either, but your folks across the street too."

He had no doubt about that. Every cop on the force wanted this over with as quickly as possible, for nothing shook the force to the core more than a murder of one of their brothers. Rawlins had heard that over four thousand officers from as far away as the Dakotas and Canada would attend Mark Forrest's funeral.

She opened his report and began thumbing through the papers. "But—"

"No, no, no. Don't say that. Don't say *But.*" Rawlins leaned forward, grabbing the edge of her desk. "Denise, trust me. This is our guy. I'm positive."

"I hope you're right, I hope he's the right one, I really do." She shrugged. "Listen, Rawlins, I want to make this stick too—that's my job, to make sure the guilty ones get put behind bars—but right now we don't have it. Not the way I see it. Not yet anyway."

"Someone saw his car parked down by the river the night of the murder. That's how I got his license plate."

"Okay, who?" she pressed, looking at him over the tops of her glasses.

"It was an anonymous tip to a television reporter."

"Right, and that's problem one—we need a witness who's willing to come forward. A witness who actually saw the car."

"The reporter who got the call will testify," said Rawlins, sure as hell that Todd would.

"Did he actually speak to this person?"

Rawlins hesitated, then admitted, "No. I think it was the receptionist at Channel Ten."

"Well, find out for sure. And get a statement from that person." Daylen looked down at the papers. "Still, that's not very good. We really need more than that. I mean, we want someone who can swear on a stack of Bibles a mile high they saw Kenney's car down by the river. Even with that, it's rather circumstantial— just because he might have been down by the river doesn't mean he pulled the trigger. If we can't find someone who saw him fire the gun, then we at least need someone who can place Kenney on the Stone Arch Bridge at approximately the time Sergeant Forrest was killed." Daylen hesitated, then asked, "This reporter—it's Todd Mills, right?"

Rawlins nodded.

"And rumor has it that he's your . . ."

Rawlins nodded again. "Boyfriend."

"Okay." She took a deep breath and pursed her lips, obviously mulling how to put this.

Rawlins guessed her thoughts and said, "Don't worry. At first we were trading information, which was helpful, but now—"

"Now you can't tell him a thing—*nada,* zip."

"I know, I know. Trust me, Lieutenant Holbrook has been all over me about it."

"You know how these things work, Rawlins. You say something to someone in the media, no matter how innocuous, and it gets passed along and twisted around. You have to be very careful. In fact—and I couldn't be more serious—from now on I don't want you talking about this case with Todd Mills in anything but a formal interview, one that's recorded. Am I clear? I don't want anything we're working on leaked to the press, no matter how inadvertently."

"Absolutely, but—"

"I mean it, if you leak anything to Mills I'll see to it that you're off this case in two seconds flat."

"Sure, but you know he's the one who was there when Forrest was killed. He saw the whole thing."

"Right, I saw his report on TV. Pretty dramatic stuff, I know, but he can't ID this guy, can he? That right?"

"Doubtful. Very doubtful," admitted Rawlins. "The perp was wearing a jacket with a hood, his face was covered, and it was storming like all hell. Todd can testify about the guy's height and weight, which by the way match Kenney's, but—"

"What about the face? We need something definitive."

"Listen, Todd's coming in this afternoon to take a look at Kenney. Maybe he'll remember something. Maybe he did see the guy's face or . . . or a spot or a scar on the guy's hand."

"Let's hope so." She looked at Rawlins's report, turned a page, and jotted something in the margin. "And while he's down there take him into one of the interview rooms and get a formal statement from him as well, okay?"

"Sure." Pushing what he hoped would be the clincher, he asked, "Now, what about the yellow raincoat?"

"Yeah, what about it? You sure you didn't touch it before you got a search warrant?"

"Positive."

Rawlins sat back, rubbed his eyes, shook his head. Lawyers— they were such a pain. He knew that Daylen was being careful, that she had to be, but, Jesus Christ, they were always panicky, always bringing up the absurd. What kind of fools did they take cops for?

Rawlins, his calculated speech belying his frustration, said, "It went like this: Kenney was standing by the back of his car when I went up to him. The trunk was closed. Kenney then took off and we apprehended and arrested him. While I took Kenney down-town, another police officer got a search warrant. In the mean-time, I had two cop cars sitting on the house and the Olds. After I interviewed Kenney, we went back with the warrant and—"

"Okay, okay. I get the picture," said Daylen, raising her hand for Rawlins to stop. "I just don't want this slicker tossed out on a technicality. After all, it's probably going to be our best piece of evidence."

"Trust me, there won't be a problem." Rawlins thought for a second, recalling the scene and just who had been there. "Mills and his crew were filming when I first went up to the car. If need be, we can subpoena his tape."

"Excellent." She read something once, twice. "There's just something I don't like about this."

"What?"

"You say that the trunk didn't have a lock on it, that it was held shut by a wire."

He knew this would be a problem, and he reluctantly admitted, "A twisted coat hanger, actually."

"Which means anyone had access to it."

"I suppose, but—"

"My job is to prove him guilty beyond a doubt. And trust me, the defense will be all over this one. They'll lunge at any angle that looks weak and—"

"Denise, we sprayed luminol on the raincoat, and—"

"I know, blood came up."

"Not a tiny bit either, but a lot. A big splotch of it fluoresced as a matter of fact."

"So maybe he cut himself last week on his umbrella?"

"The lab says that because it came up so strongly, it looks like the blood had recently been washed from the front of the coat."

"But that's just a guess, albeit an educated one."

"Jesus Christ," said Rawlins, leaning onto the desk, "we got a sample of blood from just inside the right sleeve!"

"Rawlins, trust me," said Daylen, looking up at him again. "We're on the same side, but it's going to be a hell of a battle. An uphill battle. I just want to make sure that raincoat looks as damning as hell in court."

Rawlins sat back in his chair, stared past Denise and out the window. But rather than seeing a few white clouds set against a rich blue sky, he saw, to his dismay, precisely where this thing was going. Oh, fuck. If she didn't care for what they'd already discussed, then she really wasn't going to like this.

Trying not to sound defeated, at least not yet, he admitted, "The coat's down in the serology lab, and they've got this all on a rush. If the blood matches Forrest's, we've got it, don't we?"

"If we get a DNA match, sure. That would certainly be enough to formally charge Kenney. Everyone's so worked up about this that that would certainly be enough to put him on trial—and probably convict him too."

"There's only one problem," muttered Rawlins, clenching his

fists, for this was the part she wasn't going to like. "I just spoke with serology before coming over here, and the blood sample's not big enough."

"What?" she snapped. "I thought we were one of the few places that had one of these labs for DNA testing and everything. What have they been bragging about anyway? I mean, that joint cost millions."

"I know, but their equipment isn't powerful enough for the size of the sample we got." He added, "They're going to have to send it out."

"And how long's that going to take?"

"Ten days."

"Oh, shit," moaned Daylen, sitting back.

The problem, Rawlins knew, was that they had but thirty-six hours to formally charge Kenney, and the clock had started ticking today at 12:01 A.M. Even a twenty-four extension, which they would certainly be able to get, would do next to nothing.

"We're going to have to let him go, aren't we?" said Rawlins, staring down at the floor and shaking his head.

"Right now it doesn't look good."

"God, I'm going to have to really hustle."

"Yep." Daylen thought for a moment, took off her glasses, and said, "Listen, you guys have to get statements from Mills, from the receptionist at Channel Ten, and also from Kenney's cousin, the one he lives with."

"Yeah, I've got her coming down this afternoon too. I thought a formal interview with her might rattle something loose."

"It's just an idea, but make sure this cousin has an alibi for that night. You never know . . ."

He hadn't thought about that, considered the possibility that it might have been Kenney's cousin down there on the Stone Arch Bridge. While Todd had presumed it had been a guy, couldn't it have been a woman cloaked by that yellow slicker? A possibility, albeit a stretch.

"And keep at this shrink thing. Maybe Kenney confessed something to his therapist."

"Perhaps." Rawlins continued, saying, "I've been poring over everything I can get on what happened in California."

"You mean the cop-killing out there, the one Kenney was initially charged with?"

"Right. You'll see in my report and everything. I mean, it's clear why they let him go back then—they didn't have anything concrete."

"Which is exactly like now."

Rawlins nodded. "A little too familiar, wouldn't you say?"

"Actually . . . yes." Daylen slipped her glasses back on and looked through the papers. "Did you turn up anything else after you got the search warrant?"

Rawlins shook his head. "Nope."

They had searched not only the car but the house, yet they'd discovered no weapon, no additional article of clothing with blood on it, nor any evidence whatsoever linking Kenney to Officer Mark Forrest, not so much as even a phone number. Hoping he'd hit pay dirt, Rawlins had seized the answering machine attached to Kenney's private phone line in his basement room, but that, too, had yielded nothing.

"Aside from Kenney's, we got a couple of partial prints from the Olds," added Rawlins. "Maybe we'll get lucky."

"If they match Mark Forrest's prints, then we're in business. Big business." She looked at him, her brow raised in doubt. "You gotta get me something that'll link Christopher Kenney to Mark Forrest, something that'll prove Kenney knew him or contacted him or—"

"I'm trying."

"Between you and me, let me say this, Rawlins: I'm willing to stick my neck out on this one. Because this is about a cop-killing and this Kenney guy has already been arrested once for something like this, I'm willing to write up a charge even if we're only, say, seventy-five percent there. But frankly, we're only sixty percent there right now. You gotta get me something more, or," she said, glancing at her watch, "we're going to have to let Kenney go at noon tomorrow."

Pushing himself to his feet, Rawlins knew they needed a break or a lead, something to spin them off in a new direction. And they needed it soon.

"I don't know what," began Rawlins, "but I'm going to come up with it. You can trust me on that one. In fact, you can plan on writing this all up tomorrow morning. That way I'll still have time to get it to the signing judge."

As the Hennepin County prosecuting attorney handling this case, Denise Daylen had to first write up the complaint against Christopher Louis Kenney. Then Rawlins had to take the documents to the signing judge on duty, Judge Brown, who would review the documents, ask a few questions, and if she thought the evidence sufficient, sign the complaint and formalize the charges. Only then would Kenney be officially arraigned, whereupon the judge would surely find probable cause and set bail.

Given that a cop was killed, though, Rawlins doubted any judge would set bail. Or if she or he did, it would certainly be astronomically high.

"Good." Closing the report on her desk, Daylen looked up at Rawlins and said, "I spoke with the signing judge just before you came in, and he's very, very interested in this case."

Rawlins stopped and stared at her. "*He?* I thought Judge Brown—Judge *Sharon* Brown—was on duty this week."

"Well, she was until this morning. I don't know what's going on up there, but as of about ten this morning the rotation schedule changed and Judge Stuart Hawkins took over."

"No shit?"

"Yeah, and right now they don't get any bigger than him. Trust me, he's quite hot to trot on this thing, which, by the by, is why I'm willing to press charges even if we're a bit short of evidence."

"Good. Very good. In fact, aside from the raincoat, that's the best news I've heard all morning," said Rawlins, heading for the door.

Chapter 31

Clenching her eyes shut, Kris knew she shouldn't have come back to Minnesota. Everything she hated about herself was here.

No, after what had happened in California, she should have kept going. Escaped to a place where no one would ever have found her. Hawaii. Thailand. Katmandu. New Delhi. Someplace far, far away. Instead, she'd returned if not to Duluth, then to her home state, and now she'd been caught. How could she have been so absolutely stupid? This was it. All her life she hadn't felt simply shunned and rejected, but pursued. And hunted. In California she'd escaped, but now they had her once again, and perhaps this time they'd really do it, succeed in destroying her.

She opened her eyes, horrified that she was here in this small cell on the fifth floor of City Hall, a tiny hole not much more than six by eight, the walls and even the ceiling covered with steel. On one side hung a steel platform covered with the skimpy mattress on which she now sat. On the other stood a stainless-steel sink and toilet, the two of them combined into a stumpy little tower, the sink on top, the lidless toilet protruding from the bottom. The only window, a small glass one in the door, was covered from the outside with a piece of paper, on which was written: *The Truth Will Set You Free!*

In the upper corner of the cell was a video camera mounted behind a shield of glass and steel, and she looked up at it and screamed at the top of her lungs, "Fuck you! Fuck you! Fuck you!"

This was a cruel place, this Minnesota.

Never had Kris been anywhere so ruled by climate, never had she heard of a city or a state where a person's mood was defined by temperature, humidity, dew point, windchill. And by light—sunlight—from the wonderfully long summer days when the glory seemed to never fade, to the short, cruel days of winter when getting out of bed was like crawling out of a black cave into a black cave. In equally severe but southern climes like Florida, Georgia, Texas, Arizona, they'd conquered their cruelty with air-conditioning, so much so that people complained not about the severity, but the monotony. But not here. Not in Minnesota. In these northern plains the winds came up, the storms blew in, things heated up, they chilled down. They blew away, they froze. And thus people's lives were defined, just as hers had been.

Bringing her knees up to her chest as she sat on the bunk, she clutched her arms around her legs, bowed her head forward, and closed her eyes. Recalling happier times, Kris was taken back to the summers of her youth, when the blue sea of Lake Superior would stretch and stretch forever until it somehow melded with the heavens and did a Möbius flip of sorts, looping back over Duluth in endless delight. Those summers seemed to never want to end, but of course they always did, and all too soon as well, the sun dropping from a beacon of strength to a weak orb that skimmed just above the horizon.

Kris reached around and down to her crotch, feeling her empty sack. If she'd had the voice of a bird and if these were Venetian times, she might have enjoyed life as a castrato. As it was, the world today saw her not as a gift but a monster.

It had been so cold.

Tumbling back through time, she started crying. *This kilt's kind of cool,* Chris had thought, picking it up in the laundry room. *I wonder what it would feel like?*

What a fool. What a complete idiot. If she could only do it over, that one moment, that one act. It had changed so much. Everything really. Her brothers had come down, spied their brother Christopher in a skirt, and started screaming and shouting the worst of all possible curses: *"Homo!"* And little Chris had torn away the skirt, pulled on the gym shorts, and run out, dashing through the frigid night to his grandparents'.

Then, of course, he'd fallen. What a sissy. Couldn't even make a dash through the winter night without tumbling.

As if she were watching a video that she could play over and over again, Kris had conjured it up countless times, how Chris had torn through the subzero night, his stocking feet running over that dry, packed snow, the cold biting at his lungs and turning his tears into icicles. *God, they know. Now what?* He'd been running so quickly that he hadn't seen it, the patch of ice lingering beneath the snow, a film of ice so thin as to be invisible. His feet had hit it, shot right out, and swung way above his head. There was no way Chris had been able to catch himself, and he'd fallen back and smacked his head so hard that everything had gone black. *I've got to get up,* Kris remembered thinking. *It's thirty below.* But of course Chris hadn't been able to move and had slipped away. If a neighbor hadn't spotted him lying on the sidewalk nearly thirty minutes later, he would have died. How many times had he wished that he had?

Oh, fuck, thought Kris, sitting in her cell. Only in Minnesota could you freeze your balls off, quite literally so.

That night they'd rushed Chris to the very hospital where his mother was working, treated him for hypothermia, and amputated not only the frostbitten tips of three fingers and two toes, but his testicles, which had flopped exposed from his gym shorts. And thus his fate was cast. Which was why a few years ago he'd moved to California, where he met Joan Ryan, first his transgender mentor and later his lawyer, started on hormones, and tried his best to become Kris.

It might have worked too. No, it had been working. She was on her way to being happy. Yes, Kris was going to be whole. Loving and loved. Not the tragic outcast. And for a few fleeting minutes, when Dave had taken her into his embrace and pledged himself to her, Kris had seen it too—happiness, pure and unbridled. For the briefest of moments she sensed that the hard times were over and that Dave was hers and she was his. An honest man and a string of pearls, that was all she wanted out of life. But it had been so fleeting, so brief, the love she felt for him and he for her and the future she clearly saw for them both, because then Dave's groping hand had discovered her truth—her erect penis—and in a single second he'd gone crazy.

His eyes crazed with horror, he had stared at Kris.

"You fucking freak!" he had screamed, leaping away from her.

He'd then brought back one of those massively guy arms and punched her in the jaw. Kris had gone tumbling from the couch, screaming and falling to the floor in the tiny living room. She'd looked up, seen the vile hate in his eyes.

"No!" she had begged. "Please! I love you!"

When he started toward her, when Kris was sure that he meant her only the worst harm, she scrambled backward toward the kitchen, grabbing one of the chairs, pulling herself up. And as he charged toward her, she had no choice but to lunge for his gun, which lay so innocently in Dave's gun belt on the kitchen counter.

"Stop!" Kris had screamed through her tears. "Stop or I'm going to blow your fucking head off!"

What a disaster. What an explosion. She could still see it—she'd always see it—how his head had exploded, bursting with shattered bone and juicy cartilage. The fountain of blood. Could it have been more horrific?

Slumped in her cell, she was lost all over again in the terror of that night and how everything had gone so wrong, when she heard the deep buzz of electromagnets. The next second her door swung in, and a detention deputy, an older man with no hair and a large waist, stood there.

"Someone here to see you," he pronounced.

She wiped her eyes, then uncurled her legs and swung them to the floor. She fussed a bit with her hair, blotted her lips, but there wasn't much to be done. She hadn't slept more than an hour or two last night—some nut down the hall had screamed half the night—and, besides, there was no mirror. Plus she was wearing the same clothes she'd been arrested in last night. Oh, Christ, girl. You're not making a good fashion statement, no, not at all.

"This way," grumbled the guard.

As soon as Kris neared the door, the deputy took her by the

left arm, his thick old fingers sinking into her soft skin. He let the cell swing shut, then steered her down the corridor past cell door after cell door. Glancing once to her right, Kris saw a face filling the small window of one of the cell doors, the nose and mouth smashed against the glass, the eyes stretched wide in jealous curse.

Moving on through a maze of hallways and gates, all that Kris was aware of was the buzzing of locks, the clanging of doors.

"Right here," he said, pushing Kris into a room.

Stumbling into a small, windowless chamber with a low ceiling, Kris focused on a woman standing there. Tall and thin, a narrow face with short brown hair. Yes, attractive too. And it ran through Kris's mind: *T?* No. She sensed it as quickly as she thought it. The shoulders are too narrow, the hips too big, the feet too small. This one's a dyke. But who?

The door behind them shut, and only then did Kris notice the small table with two chairs, one on each side.

"Good morning, Kris. My name's Janice Gray, and I'm—"

"Let me guess," interrupted Kris. "You're my new attorney."

Bristling, the woman looked her up and down, then after a long moment finally said, "That depends."

"You know my attorney, Joan Ryan, don't you? She sent you, didn't she?"

"No."

Her brow knit, Kris asked, "Then why the hell are you here?"

"Let's just say I'm a transgender ally."

"Oh, for quaint. SuperDyke to the rescue—I'm saved," quipped Kris. "Heavens, you are a dyke, aren't you?"

"Fuck off."

"Yep, you are," she said with a nervous laugh. "So tell me, how're you gonna get me out of here?"

"No," said Janice, shaking her head and crossing her arms. "That's not how I work. First of all, you're the one in a shitload of trouble. Second, I haven't decided whether or not to take you on."

"Well, in that case, doll, I'm not sure if I want you either." Kris studied her, wondered if Janice could get her off as Joan had. "In fact, before I even let you think of representing me, I want you to take a good look at me. God knows I look like shit, but check me out from head to toe. Just do it . . . that's right, that's good. Now look straight into these eyes of mine and tell me one thing: Do you see a sicko psycho killer?"

Chapter 32

The big news that all the media—radio, television, newspaper—
were covering was the discovery of the raincoat in the trunk of
Christopher Kenney's Oldsmobile. And not just any old yellow
raincoat, but a yellow raincoat with blood on it. Like a lynch mob,
the media was working itself into a frenzy, with some of the local
radio talk-show hosts speculating that this was it, the cops had
their killer and Kenney would be locked away for the rest of his or
her or its life. The only question remaining was where to incarcer-
ate him, the men's or the women's prison? Or how about the
pound? One disc jockey even told the first Christopher Kenney
joke: "How many drag queens does it take to kill a . . ."

Todd wanted more, of course, for his story tonight. More precisely, he wanted something different. Determined to get just
that, after lunch he sat down in his office and tried Maureen
Shea's number another time.

And once again he got the energetic message: *"Hi, this is
Maureen Shea. I'm away from the phone, but leave a message and
I'll get back to you, hopefully within the hour. Thanks, and have a
great day!"*

Still trying to figure out why he knew her name, he hung up
without leaving a message. He most definitely wanted to talk with
her, but what was this bit about calling back within the hour, and
why hadn't she? Either it was a ploy of some sort or she was
avoiding him, which was a distinct possibility. He guessed that in
the message he'd already left he shouldn't have told her that he
was from WLAK; letting someone know he was from the media

usually worked for him. In this case, though, Todd suspected it wasn't.

He was just rolling his chair across the small room when his cellular phone, lying by his computer, started to ring. He looked at it, hoped this was one of the calls he was waiting for, and grabbed it.

"Hi, this is Todd Mills."

"Hello, this is the operator. Will you accept a collect call from Ron Ravell?"

"Absolutely."

Thrilled, Todd reached for a pen and pad. Now the trick wouldn't simply be keeping him on the line, but also getting him to cooperate. He'd kill to get this guy on film.

The connection went through, and Todd jumped right in, saying, "Hi, Mr. Ravell. Thank you very much for calling back."

"Sure . . ." replied the hesitant voice. "But who are you?" A bit of silence. "And what do you want?"

"My name is Todd Mills, and I'm an investigative reporter for WLAK TV in Minneapolis. I called this morning trying to reach Ron Ravell, the younger brother of Police Officer Dave Ravell. Am I speaking to the right person?"

"Yes, but—"

Wanting to hook him and hook him fast, Todd interrupted, saying, "I'm wondering if you'd be willing to answer a few questions for me about Christopher Louis Kenney, the man who was accused of murdering your brother?"

There was a long, cautious pause, a deep breath. "Like what?"

"Last night Christopher Kenney was arrested here in Minneapolis in conjunction with—"

"Oh, my God," Ron Ravell gasped, his voice cracking. "He did it again, didn't he? He killed another cop, right?"

"It hasn't been proven yet, of course, but a police officer was murdered several days ago, and it appears that Kenney will be charged with that crime."

They talked for nearly fifteen minutes, Todd running through the whole situation, then scribbling down nearly every detail he could get from Ravell.

"Ron," said Todd as they wrapped up their conversation, "I'd very much like to get you on camera. Would you be willing to do that?"

"Sure, but how? I mean, I'm out in California. What are you going to do, come out here?"

"Actually, our operations department could set up some satellite time with WLAK's affiliate out there in L.A., and then we'd be able to shoot you directly from there. Would you be willing? It wouldn't take very long. I'd be here at WLAK, and all you'd have to do is go into the studio out there."

After some hesitation Ron Ravell agreed, and while Todd was hoping they could still do it that afternoon, on such short notice it couldn't be set up until that evening at nine Central Standard Time. In the ensuing time Todd dashed downtown for the formal tape-recorded interview that Rawlins had requested, then hurried back and pulled together an update for the six o'clock news.

And now he sat in one of the large edit bays, a dimly lit glassed-in booth filled with monitors and control boards and taping equipment. If all went as it was supposed to, the satellite connection with WLAK's affiliate would take place in just thirty seconds.

On the other side of the edit bay, Bradley focused a Betacam—a new 300-A that needed hardly any light because of a new microchip—and said, "Okay, we're all set."

"Great," replied Todd, who now wore a blue oxford shirt and a navy and yellow striped tie. "Can you leave it running, or do you need to stay?"

"Oh, I'll stay," he said, squinting as he made the last adjustments. "I just want to make sure you keep in focus."

Todd had no idea, of course, what type of interview Ron Ravell would be—he had sounded reticent on the phone, so he might not be too forthcoming—which was why Todd had decided on a reversal. Having himself taped as well, Todd had learned the hard way, would give him a few extra guarantees. If in response to a question like "Do you think Kenney should be put away for life?" Ravell merely replied with a nonanswer like "Well . . ." or "Yes, but . . ." or simply "Absolutely," then at least they'd be able to edit in Todd and his words, which would give context to the reply. After all, Todd never did any self-editing during an actual interview like this. It wasn't until later, once they had it all on tape, that Bradley and he would go over this whole thing frame by frame, picking and choosing, cutting and butting one thing up against another, to get just the right play.

Turning his attention to the router switches, Todd flicked one of the black buttons and saw the monitor in front of him fill with snow. Suddenly the screen went from a blizzard to a rainbow of colored bars, indicating that the uplink to the satellite was taking place. Immediately thereafter the L.A. station's call letters appeared and the ten-second countdown began. Todd quickly shoved a Beta tape into a recorder and picked up not an earpiece but a telephone receiver. He had all of ten minutes for the interview, which was about as long a satellite interview as he ever conducted, and all he hoped to snag in that time was a sound byte of some sort from Ron Ravell. If he didn't get a pithy, dramatic statement in that time—his personal rule was never one longer than nineteen seconds—he wouldn't get one no matter how long the interview.

Suddenly the colored bars vanished and the image of a young man appeared on the monitor before Todd. He was a nice-enough looking guy, chestnut hair, striking eyebrows, and a broad, clear face. Seated in what looked like the L.A. station's newsroom, he wore a blue sport jacket and a tie and white shirt.

"Hi, Ron, it's me, Todd Mills."

Spooked by the clarity of the sound, Ron jumped and looked around as if a ghost had just whispered in his ear. With his right hand he then nervously pressed the earpiece deeper into his ear, while with his left he touched the lav mike pinned to the lapel of his sport coat.

"You look great," said Todd into the phone as he stared at the monitor. "I can see you perfectly."

"Oh, good," replied Ron, glancing around, not sure what to do. "Hi."

"I'm sorry you can't see me, too, but all you have to do is look right into the camera," instructed Todd.

Ron's hands settled back into his lap and he turned his eyes straight ahead. "Sure."

"That's perfect. I just want to say thank you for coming today. I really appreciate it."

"Of course."

This wasn't good, thought Todd. He had to get him talking. Get him to reply in more complete statements. And so Todd continued the banter.

"Did you have any trouble finding the station?"

"No. No, I knew right where it was."

"Good. And what's the weather like out there?"

"Warm."

"Smoggy?"

"No, not too bad."

"Well, it's hotter than hell out here," said Todd, avoiding Minnesota's most famous, or rather infamous, quality: winter. "Humid, too, which I can't stand."

Ron smiled. "That's what I hear, that it can get pretty bad out there in the summer."

And then, boom: "Ron, I can't imagine what it's like to lose a brother to violence."

It was Todd's method, his trick. Relax them, get them to loosen their guard, then hit them with a horribly honest yet horribly sympathetic statement. And it worked. Just like a surgeon sticking in a knife at the opportune moment, Todd's words cut through any defenses Ron Ravell might have had, slicing through to Ron's true thoughts and feelings.

Right off the bat Ravell blurted a sound byte Todd had only dreamed of getting: "It's been awful. Christopher Kenney is a monster, a cold-blooded murderer, and I'll never forgive him for killing my brother."

It shocked even Todd that he got something so easily and so quickly, and for a moment he didn't know what to do. That was it. All he needed. The next instant, though, a rush of excitement whizzed through him. This was a hot one. And instinctively he knew there was more where that came from.

He countered, "Los Angeles officials, however, ruled that

your brother died from a self-inflicted gunshot wound to the head. Why do you believe otherwise?"

"There was no way Dave would have killed himself. Dave was just sixteen months older than me and we were very close. He was upset over his recent divorce, but that was it."

Okay, thought Todd. He wanted to get him to say it again, what Todd had earlier read about. It was tacky and insensitive of Todd to ask, but he pushed aside any hesitation. He had a job to do. If Ron got pissed off and ended the interview, then so be it. Todd already had what he needed.

"Ron, was your brother gay?"

Ravell's brow wrinkled downward, and then he said it just the way he had a couple of years ago for the papers: "Maybe, maybe not. But I can tell you one thing for sure: Dave didn't kill himself over questions of his sexuality."

"Why do you say that?"

"Because I'm gay, and Dave had virtually no problems with it. Who knows, maybe he was struggling with some sexuality issues. He never mentioned anything, but there are plenty of families where all the kids are gay."

"So you're quite certain—"

"I'm quite certain," interrupted Ravell, springing to verbosity as if he'd been waiting desperately for this opportunity, "that Dave was murdered by that drag queen."

"Christopher Louis Kenney?"

"Yes. Dave was killed in that pervert's apartment, and I'm quite certain that Kenney was the one who fired the gun at my brother."

Suddenly Todd found himself in the position of trying to keep up with Ravell, and staring at the monitor, he said, "As I told you earlier, Christopher Kenney was arrested just last night in Minneapolis in conjunction with the murder of Minneapolis Park Police Officer Mark Forrest."

"I'm not surprised."

"But why do you think your brother was murdered, Ron, when the Los Angeles authorities believe otherwise?"

"Because the evidence is overwhelming."

"What do you mean? Can you be specific?"

"Dave was at Kenney's apartment, there was no one else there. Kenney's fingerprints were on the handle of the gun that killed Dave. And when someone—a neighbor—came in after the shot, he found Kenney just sitting there, staring at my brother, the gun on the floor between them."

"Yes, but what happened? Why did the Los Angeles authorities rule this a suicide, and why did the prosecuting attorney drop the charges against Christopher Kenney?"

"They ruled it a suicide because the Los Angeles police and the medical examiner screwed up right from the beginning. First the police failed to do some kind of test, and—"

"Wait a minute," interrupted Todd, leaning forward, his eyes fixed on Ron's image. "I haven't heard about this. They failed to do what?"

"There's some kind of test that shows if a suspect has fired a gun. They should've done it, but they didn't."

"You mean they didn't do a paraffin test?"

"Exactly."

Incredulous, Todd sat there shaking his head. A paraffin test, which would have shown if there was gunpowder residue on Kenney's hands, should have been done right away, the moment he was brought in. Was Ron Ravell now saying it hadn't been done at all? If so, that would be ridiculous. And why the hell hadn't Todd seen mention of this screwup in any of the newspaper articles he'd read on Lexis-Nexis?

Todd said, "But that should have been routine."

"I know, that's what I was told too. Somehow they messed up though. There were too many cops involved. One guy thought the other had the test done, the other guy thought a third guy was taking care of it. You know, it was just a total screwup, and no one realized the test hadn't been done until three or four days later."

"And that's way too late," said Todd, knowing that you had a few hours, not a few days, before the residue was washed away by something as simple as hand soap. "That wasn't in the papers at all, was it?"

"Of course not. You think the cops would let out something like that?"

"Frankly, I'm really shocked."

"It's terrible. And then to top it off, the medical examiner who filed the initial report was arrested a day or two later for drunk driving. Everything he'd been working on was discredited, including the case he'd built against Kenney."

"I did read about that." Todd took a deep breath, gathered his thoughts, and, staring at the video image of Ravell on the monitor, said, "So the charges against Kenney were dropped because the prosecutor didn't believe he could prove his guilt beyond a reasonable doubt?"

"Exactly. And the reason he couldn't prove Kenney's guilt was because between the cops and the medical examiner all the evidence was either lost or ruined."

"I see, but—"

"And an hour after that," interrupted Kenney, "my mother . . . my mother . . ." He bowed his head slightly and pinched the bridge of his nose with his right hand as if to forestall any tears. "She was crushed by Dave's death. She'd been on medication ever since he was killed. But then an . . . an hour after she heard the news that Kenney was going free she had this horrible stroke."

This was good. Excellent. All of it he could use.

Todd said, "I'm sorry."

"It was horrible." His eyes red with grief, Ravell stared back up at the camera. "I've been waiting for this to happen. I hate to say it, but I've been waiting for Kenney to kill again. I knew he would."

Sometimes you got nothing, thought Todd. Sometimes you got an avalanche, almost more than you could use. And this was clearly the second.

Wondering what a more moderate statement might elicit, Todd said, "Well, the authorities here in Hennepin County certainly have a challenging case. Kenney's being held at City Hall jail, but he hasn't yet been formally charged with first-degree murder, which he would be since a police officer was killed. That, I'm sure, will only happen when and if the prosecutor's office determines they have sufficient evidence against Kenney."

As if spent, Ravell quietly shook his head on-screen, his face drawn and achingly sad, and said, "Dear God, it would be a crime if they let him go again."

Todd asked him several other questions, none of which elicited anything insightful, and then closed him out, saying, "Ron, we have only a few more moments of satellite time, but I want to thank you very much for joining me and sharing your opinions. And my condolences to you for the tragedies you have suffered."

"Thank you."

Okay, thought Todd, but was the door still open? "Can I give you a call if anything else comes up?"

"Of course. You might have to leave a message. I travel a lot—I'm a flight attendant out here—but I check my messages all the time."

"Listen, you take care," concluded Todd. "We'll all be curious to see how this thing ends."

A sad expression on his face, Ron Ravell shrugged and said, "I just hope the legal system doesn't let us down again."

The next instant the satellite connection was severed and the monitor in front of Todd snapped into a blizzard of snow. Todd then hung up the phone, flicked off the router switch, and popped out the Beta tape.

"That was kind of incredible," said Bradley, turning off the camera focused on Todd.

"No kidding. I still can't believe they didn't do a paraffin test. That's just outrageous. The cops have done that on every murder I've ever covered." He thought for a moment. "But I don't think I want to touch that yet. I have to check it out, get confirmation from the L.A. police, so maybe that's something for tomorrow night's story."

Right. Keeping a story like this going was harder than hell, but a major mistake like that by the Los Angeles police—particularly if it had never been reported—was ample material for another story or two. Before touching that one, though, he really did need to do some research and conduct a few more interviews.

He could see it now, how he'd do his next piece on the murder of Mark Forrest. They'd start out with the image of Ron, his harsh words. Then they'd cut to a variety of other images, footage that a producer had already requested from their L.A. affiliate and was due to come to WLAK on tomorrow morning's feed. Todd already knew they were going to get shots of Dave Ravell's body being carted from Kenney's apartment and then of course shots of Dave Ravell's funeral. There'd be tons of that footage. Todd would also ask the producer to get images of Ravell in his police uniform and of his mother as well. Perhaps all three—Dave, Ron, and Mom. Maybe he'd get a sound byte from the L.A. investigator. And music. Yes, absolutely. There had to be music in tonight's package. From watching Spielberg movies Todd had learned the importance of music to stir the emotions. But what could he use? In these midwestern parts any cop funeral was accompanied by a bagpiper, and he presumed that was the case in California as well.

Right, to wrap the whole thing up he'd show Ravell's body being lowered into the ground as a lone, mournful bagpiper toiled away. And the final sound wouldn't be Ron Ravell's condemning words of Kenney, but Todd wondering how this mystery was yet to unfold.

Chapter 33

It took him a long time to go to sleep that night, not because he was nervous or upset, but because he finally knew what he was going to do next. What he had to do. After days of sitting in this room, he'd finally come to the realization that he had no other choice, that there was no other way to end this.

He'd been out of his room at the Redmont only a scant few times since the night Forrest had died. He'd ordered room service three times. He hadn't let the maids in to clean. No, mostly what he'd done was watch the news—the sunrise, early, midday, five o'clock, six, and late-night broadcasts to see what that fool Mills had to say. And he hadn't spoken to anyone but her, of course, and only then because she kept phoning, so worried was she about how things were going. Well, fuck her, the stupid bitch. Couldn't she tell? Couldn't she see that things were all fucked up?

He rolled onto his left shoulder. Just get some sleep. Tomorrow's going to be another big, big day. And you need your sleep, you most certainly do. Just gotta be sharp as a tack. Just gotta keep the ball rolling down that big, bad hill. Yes, it was time to act, no doubt about it. Hoping it would lull him to sleep, he chanted: "GMF, GMF, GMF . . ."

He tossed the other way, squirming and now rolling onto his right shoulder. Was this a dream or was it a nightmare? At this point he had no idea. But, oh, shit. Why had he done it? And why the hell hadn't he met Mark Forrest before her, before she'd wormed her way into his life?

He still couldn't believe it. Believe that he'd gotten away. After all, everyone thought they knew what was going on, but no one knew what he did, now, did they?

Chapter 34

By the next morning Rawlins had everything he was going to get, at least in the time he had. They hadn't been able to get a match on the fingerprints they'd recovered from Mark Forrest's car, there were no more interviews left, and there were no more trails that could be followed before noon today when Kenney's thirty-six hours expired. Either they had him now or they didn't.

Tucked into his manila folder were formal statements from Todd, from Christopher Kenney's cousin, and from an L.A.P.D. homicide investigator who'd worked on the Dave Ravell case. Additionally there was the preliminary blood work that showed that the blood found on the yellow rain slicker was the same type, B-positive, as Mark Forrest's. For now it was the best Rawlins could do. The hoped-for ace in the hole—a direct DNA match to Forrest's blood—was going to take another fifteen days.

"This is good, but it sure isn't perfect," said Denise Daylen as she rose from behind her desk and handed him the formal complaint against Christopher Louis Kenney. "What about Kenney's therapist? Anything there yet?"

"No, nothing. Not even a name. And at the U they won't even tell me if Kenney's part of their gender program." Rawlins rubbed his face and said, "I was up a good part of the night working on all this."

"I don't doubt it."

He tugged at his dark gray sport coat, then fidgeted with his tie. "So you think he'll sign it?"

"Well, Judge Hawkins certainly isn't going to ignore the fact that Kenney has already been arrested in conjunction with a cop-killing." Escorting him to her door, she kept her voice low as she whispered, "Frankly, I wouldn't have written this one up if it was anyone else but Hawkins. Stopping this one certainly wouldn't make him look good, that's for sure, what with all the get-tough-on-crime talk and everything."

"Well, wish me luck."

"Break a leg."

Carrying the NCIC printout, various forms, his report, and now the formal complaint, Rawlins headed for the elevators. Riding the lift up a single floor, he got out and went around to the receptionist, who was squirreled away behind bulletproof glass. Eventually Hawkins's administrative clerk, Marge, an older woman with short, curled hair, came out to get him.

"Good morning," said Marge. "This way, please. The judge is expecting you."

Rawlins took a deep breath and followed her, hoping like hell that, at last, this was it, the end of the beginning.

Chapter 35

Todd was slow getting to the station that morning mostly because he'd slept like crap the night before. Jazzed by the satellite interview with Ron Ravell, worried about Rawlins, he hadn't been the least bit tired and had ended up reading until the early hours.

He pretty much knew how he was going to do the story, how he was going to edit down the interview for the five o'clock. He'd already spoken with both a producer and an assignment editor, telling them how great Ravell was, and Todd was pretty sure the piece would be one of the top leads tonight. That, however, wouldn't be fully decided until the editorial meeting later this morning.

Now driving out of the garage, he steered down the ramp, one hand on the wheel, the other holding his third cup of coffee. Coming around the building and reaching the road, he turned left on Dean Parkway, a tree-studded stretch of roadway with meandering bike and pedestrian paths. Two blocks later he turned left, heading up a small hill toward Cedar Lake.

And that's when he saw it, the Lakes Real Estate Agency sign hanging in front of a one-story house. Staring at the listing agent's name on the for-sale sign, he realized why, of course, her name had seemed familiar. He'd never met her, they probably didn't even have any friends in common, but he'd seen her name on a handful of signs just like this one. Of course, Maureen Shea was a real-estate agent.

He veered immediately to the right and slammed on the brakes. Reaching into his briefcase, which sat on the passenger seat, he pawed through his papers until he found it, her number. He glanced at it, then at the small number at the bottom of the sign. They were one and the same. Yes, a real-estate agent. No wonder she promised her very, very best to call back within the hour—that is, if you were a buyer and not a reporter.

Well, screw that. Todd flipped open his phone and dialed the main number at the top of the sign.

A woman answered. "Good morning, Lakes Real Estate. How may I help you?"

"Can you tell me where you're located?"

"Certainly, sir. We're in the Lakes Village Shopping Mall on Lake Street."

Exactly, thought Todd. The strip mall not three blocks from his condo.

"And is Maureen Shea in this morning?" he asked.

"Yes, she is. Would you like me to connect you?"

"No, that's okay," he said, quickly hanging up.

He spun around and, driving considerably faster, headed back down to Dean Parkway and out to Lake Street. He turned right past his building, continued on, and steered into the strip mall not more than three minutes later. Lakes Real Estate was right next door to a bakery Todd had shopped at a handful of times.

Todd parked and went in, swinging open the glass door and entering a reception area filled with a couch and a handful of large plants. An attractive woman with blondish hair and brown glasses looked up from a reception desk.

"Good morning," she said with a pleasant smile.

Since he'd just spoken to her, Todd lowered his voice slightly and said, "I just drove by a house that you all are selling. I believe Maureen Shea's the listing agent. Would it be possible to speak with her?"

"Of course."

Without further question the woman picked up her phone and called back to Maureen's office. And within less than a minute—after all, it wasn't every day that a potential buyer simply walked in off the street—a trim, attractive woman appeared. With thick, black hair and wearing black pants and a grayish top, she bore a smile that seemed strained.

"Hi, I'm Maureen," she said, extending her hand. "Thanks so much for coming in. Are you looking for a house?"

"Hi, Maureen." He hesitated, then said, "I'm Todd Mills."

Her smiled vanished, and her hand fell to her side. "Oh."

"I'm sorry about Mark."

Not at all pleased, she looked away, mumbled, "I . . . I . . ."

"And I'm sorry for just stopping in like this, but I'd very much like to speak to you. Do you have a couple of minutes?"

"I'm . . . I'm sorry, but I'm very busy. Mark's death has been very difficult for me, and this is my first time in the office in a couple of days, and—"

"Please. It's important, obviously."

She looked up at him. "But I thought they already caught the guy who did it."

"They have a suspect, that's all."

She thought for a moment, then without a trace of enthusiasm said, "Okay, but I really don't have much time."

Todd followed her down a short hall to the first door, which led into a small conference room filled with a table and chairs and prints of antique cars on each of the four walls. Maureen sat down and pointed to one of the seats opposite her.

"Lookit, Mr. Mills," she began, "I'll be real frank about this. I didn't call you back because I don't want Mark's death sensationalized."

"Of course not. Neither do I." Assessing that he needed to be just as frank, he said, "Please don't forget that I was right there, that I witnessed the shooting. I've done a number of stories on it already, but, trust me, it hasn't been easy."

She stared at him, seemed about to ask a question—and Todd knew exactly which one—then caught herself.

Trying to keep this going, Todd said, "If I understand correctly, you two were very good friends."

"Who told you that?"

"A friend of his."

"Oh." Satisfied, Maureen paused, looked away. "Well, we were close. Very close. We saw each other only about once a week, but we talked every day, sometimes twice a day. He was my pal, my bud."

"I see."

"Do you know how great it is for a straight woman to have a gay man as a best friend? I mean, there was no sexual tension between us. Just friendship . . . and love."

"Of course. I hardly met him, but he seemed like a great guy."

"The best." Starting to cry even as she smiled, she wiped a tear away, then said, "I was helping him look for a house. That's what he really wanted, his own place."

"Maureen, was Mark dating anyone?"

"Oh, brother, that's a complicated question."

"What do you mean?"

"A guy as gorgeous as him could've had anyone. I mean, really. Gay men and straight women were always hitting on him. Instead, he goes and falls for that jerk."

Todd tried to rein it in, his excitement, softly asking, "Who?"

"Oh, this stupid closet case. Some guy who travels here on business."

"Did you ever meet him?"

"No, never. I wanted to, but Mark said the guy was too scared, that it was too big a step." She shook her head. "It was all wrong. A guy as great as Mark deserved the best, someone who was around all the time, not some uptight jerk who was only around once a month."

"What about his name? Did Mark ever tell—"

"Russ."

"Russ?"

"Yeah, that's all Mark ever told me, that he was going down to the Redmont because Russ was in town. I have no idea of his last name."

Excellent, thought Todd. That should be enough to find him, definitely so, particularly with Rawlins's aid.

"That might be very helpful to the police," Todd said. "Do you mind if I pass that along?"

"Not at all, not if you think it might help."

"Anything else?"

"No, not really. Listen, I don't know what you're looking for—"

"Neither do I."

"—but I sure as hell hope that once you find it you treat it with care."

"I promise I will."

He thanked her again, then started to get up. And then, reticent but needing to know, she asked it, the question she'd earlier stuffed and the one they always asked.

"Mark wasn't in a lot of pain, was he? He didn't suffer, did he?"

"No, not at all. It happened very quickly. I'm not even sure he knew."

"Thanks."

Leaving her sitting in the small conference room, Todd had no idea where this information would take him, but he had a gut feeling it would be someplace interesting. This might be just a piece, a singular part of a puzzle, but the more anyone understood about Mark Forrest, the more quickly this might be wrapped up. Or so he hoped.

Emerging from the cool air-conditioning, he stepped into the day that was rapidly growing more hot and humid. On the early-morning news he'd heard that a huge storm was blowing in from the Dakotas, and Todd didn't doubt it, not one bit. Something was going to break.

He was just reaching into his pocket for his keys when he heard steps behind him.

"Todd?"

He turned, saw Maureen Shea pulling her dark hair from her face, then shielding her eyes from the bright sun.

"Yes?" he said.

"Well, there's just one other thing." She looked across the parking lot, grinned, then looked back at him. "I don't know if they really did or not, but Mark said he and Russ always tried to stay in one particular room at the Redmont."

"Which one, the Princess Suite?"

"No," she replied with a small laugh. "Room 469."

Todd couldn't hide his own amusement, but in the moment that he groped for some witty reply a distant phone started ringing. Both Maureen and he glanced back toward her office, then turned and looked at his Grand Cherokee.

"That's mine," he said, fumbling to open the door. "Thanks again, Maureen!"

"You bet."

Pulling open the door as quickly as he could, Todd leaned across and grabbed his phone from the passenger seat.

He said, "Todd Mills."

"Listen up," said a deep voice. "It's me. Don't tell anyone I called, just get your ass down to City Hall, the main entrance. Now—on the fucking double. Got it?"

"But—"

"And bring one of your camera guys."

"Okay, but I really need to talk to you."

"Later. Just get down to City Hall. You're not going to believe it—they're letting Kenney go."

Chapter 36

Thirty minutes later, thanks to the tip, Todd and Bradley were the only ones from the media standing there in the sultry summer air. No one else knew. Not yet anyway. And they were right outside the main doors of the granite fortress of bureaucracy when Christopher Louis Kenney came tramping out of City Hall, escorted by none other than his attorney and Todd's closest friend, Janice Gray.

Oh, God, thought Todd, spying Janice. I don't want to be doing this. I really don't. But did he have a choice? Of course not. He had all of a few seconds to get what he needed—a sound byte from the accused, who was also now the liberated. To do that, to get Kenney to say something outrageous, something that would pop on television, Todd was going to have to be obnoxious, repulsively so.

Todd took a deep breath and said, "Here they come, Bradley."

"Oh, yes. Oh, yes, indeed," said the photographer, his camera on his shoulder, his eye on the lens, and his finger on the trigger.

"Chris! Janice!" called Todd, wiping the perspiration from his brow, then stepping quickly toward them, a stick mike in hand. "Over here!"

The two of them turned their heads as much in surprise as in shock. As soon as Chris saw the camera focused on him, he bowed his head. Janice, playing the good attorney, stepped in direct line of the lens.

"Oh, shit," moaned Janice, stepping into the hot sunlight.

"What the hell are you doing here, Todd? How did you find out already? Or is that an exceedingly dumb question?"

"I'm sorry, Janice. I really don't want to be doing this."

"Then don't."

"The choice isn't mine." He took a deep breath, forced himself to ask, "Will you comment on your client's release?"

"Knock it off, Todd! Just turn the camera off and leave us alone, okay?"

As his stomach twisted into a knot, he said, "Sorry, I can't."

"Don't be an asshole!" she shouted, moving along and shaking her head in disgust. "You know what I've never told you, Todd? I hate the media. Particularly television. You people are such bottom feeders."

It stung, no doubt about it, but Todd pushed past it, saying, "Janice, I didn't ask you to represent him, for God's sake. I only asked you a few questions. It was your idea to go down and check on him to make sure he—"

"*She.* You can refer to Kris as *she,* got it?"

"So how did you get Kenney out?" demanded Todd, keeping up with her. "What did you have to do?"

"Kris Kenney was released because the evidence against her was purely circumstantial. End of statement."

"Congratulations, Janice."

"Eat shit, Todd. We both know I'm involved in this only because of you. And between you and me and strictly off the record—" She stopped, glanced at Bradley's camera, then stared right at Todd and raised her finger. "And I mean off the record— if you use any of this I'll never speak to you again, so help me God. Got it?"

He had no doubt she meant it, too, and he turned to Bradley and said, "Turn the camera off."

"Well," began Janice, "I didn't even have to make any protests. The judge tossed this one out on his own."

"I see."

"No, Todd, I don't think you do. I don't think you truly understand what's going on here."

Janice then turned and shepherded Kris onward. Todd in turn

shouted at Bradley to start filming again, then rushed after them. A mother and her daughter on the sidewalk scurried away. Someone else stopped and stared. A cop looked on from his squad car.

Darting in front of them, Todd blurted, "Kris, I hear they let you go because of a lack of evidence. Does that mean you actually didn't kill Officer Mark Forrest?"

As she walked Janice shouted, "Shut up, Todd!"

"But what about your raincoat, Kris?" pressed Todd. "What about Forrest's blood on your raincoat?"

"Stop it!"

Kris said, "I—"

"Don't say a thing!" Janice advised, hurrying faster.

Desperate not to lose her, the worst of his journalistic instincts kicked in, and he shouted, "Did you dress up for them both, Kris? Were both Dave Ravell and Mark Forrest into drag queens? Is that what it was? Were you lovers with them?"

Kris flinched as if someone had just hurled a stone at her. The next instant she twisted out of Janice's tight grasp, turning on Todd with a vicious face.

"I knew Dave Ravell and I loved him. But I didn't hurt him. And I didn't hurt this faggot named Forrest either. Hell, I didn't even know him!" she shouted. "As for me, I'm not straight and I'm not gay, do you understand? My name is Kris with a *K* and I'm *queer*, very fucking *queer!*"

Stunned, Todd didn't move. Unfortunately that was it, exactly what he needed for the six o'clock.

"Are you happy now, Todd?" asked Janice, shaking her head. "You're going to make all us 'deviants' look really good on the news tonight, aren't you?"

Standing there, he watched them hurry away, Janice leading the way through the heat and across the street. He took a deep breath, mopped his brow, then turned to his photographer.

"Bradley, I think I need to have that tape. Do you mind?"

"Hell, no," he replied, popping it out of his Betacam and handing it over.

"Thanks," said Todd, most definitely wanting to be in control of it. "I've got to talk to Rawlins, so I'll meet you back at the station."

God, he thought as he headed into City Hall, sometimes he really hated this job. And himself.

Chapter 37

Preoccupied with what had just transpired in Government Center and at City Hall—Jesus, was she going to give it to Todd when she next saw him!—Janice sped out of downtown Minneapolis. Driving her new maroon Honda Accord south on 35W, the air-conditioning began to cool her brow but not her temper. Why the hell had the judge refused to sign the complaint? Why the hell had Todd been lurking on the street? And why the hell had she ever gotten involved in this?

"That jail sucked," said Kris, in the passenger seat next to her. "I was really afraid, you know."

"Well, you should have been."

"I suppose I should say thank you."

Janice shook her head as she reached to the dashboard for her sunglasses, which she slipped on. "I didn't do anything."

"You got me out."

"No, I didn't."

"But—"

"Listen," instructed Janice, as she switched lanes and shifted into fifth gear, "it doesn't happen very often, but for some reason the judge refused to sign the complaint against you. That means the only reason you were released was because your thirty-six hours were up and they couldn't legally hold you any longer." Janice shook her head. "But that doesn't mean this is over, not by any means. The cops are going to continue working big time on this, of course. And you're still the primary suspect, you realize.

That means they could still come get you, particularly if they get something incriminating from those DNA tests."

Kris shrugged. "They won't."

Janice glanced over at her. "How do you know that?"

"Because I didn't do it," she said rather casually. "I didn't kill this Forrest guy. Like I told you, I never even met him."

"Can I be sure of that?"

"Absolutely."

"Well, just realize they might come get you for more questioning. Or they might show up with an arrest warrant."

"Then what do we do?"

"Beats me."

Janice hated to think it. Hated to assign this sense of uneasiness she'd had all along to something like a woman's intuition. But ever since she'd met Kris she'd felt something was screwy here. Maybe Janice simply didn't know enough about the case, which she certainly didn't. Or maybe Janice just didn't know Kris well enough, which was also true.

"Kris, I don't want to say you've been lying to me, but there's a hell of a lot I don't know about either you or this case, not to mention the trouble you were in in California. And I'm not so sure if—"

"You don't like me, do you?"

Shit, and Janice thought she was up-front?

"Kris, I don't even know you."

"That's what everyone says, that they don't know me. But that's bullshit, total bullshit. You say you're a tranny ally, but the reason you don't think you know me is that you don't know how to. You're just like everyone else. I mean, you can't put a label on me. That's why no one believes me—because no one can believe their eyes when they look at me. People look at me and see a young woman, but then they think, wait a minute, that's a guy, that's a trick, this is deceitful, that person's a lie."

"Kris, please—"

"I'm the only one telling the truth around here. I'm the only one expressing how I truly feel."

"Watch it," warned Janice, "you're talking to a woman who's living life just the way she wants to."

"But I confuse you, don't I? And I probably scare you, right? I mean, I bet you don't know whether to ignore me because I've got a penis, be attracted to me because of my feminine body, or—"

"Okay, okay."

Kris took a deep breath, then said, "Judge Hawkins was the guy who refused to sign that piece of paper, right?"

"The complaint? Yeah, that was him." As Janice steered toward the Forty-sixth Street exit, she eyed her passenger. "So?"

Kris sat there grinning as she said, "So nothing."

"What's that mean?"

"It means . . . nothing."

Janice took the exit, steering up the ramp, then turning right and heading west. "What the hell are you saying?"

"Too much, I suppose," Kris said with a shrug. "I mean, people always talk about me behind my back, but I don't talk about them. I never—"

"Kris—"

"Forget it. I already said too much. I just want you to know there are other people around who aren't being honest."

"I don't like this."

She certainly didn't. There was more here, that much was obvious. Perhaps an entire dimension that Janice hadn't even been aware of. Perhaps a dynamic she hadn't even imagined or considered possible.

"Oh, my God, don't tell me you know Judge Hawkins?" demanded Janice.

"Nothing. Just forget it."

"Absolutely not."

"That was stupid of me. I shouldn't have brought it up."

"Oh, yes, you should have. If you're talking about something that involves a judge who's active in your case, then this is absolutely something I need to know."

"I don't want to rat on anyone. It's not cool."

Janice stopped at a red light, looked over at her young client, and in a loud voice said, "Jesus Christ, Kris, do you realize what you're saying? If Hawkins is gay or something like that and if he refused to sign the complaint because of some connection between you two, then this whole thing could explode so big you won't even know what hit you. I want to know—I need to know—every little detail about what—"

"Okay, okay. Just back off, would you? Maybe it is something I'm going to have to tell. I don't know. But I don't really want to talk about it now. I'm exhausted, okay? Really wiped out, you know. And besides, I'm not sure how relevant it is." She put a hand to her forehead. "Just take me home, would you?"

The light popped green, and Janice stomped on the gas. "With pleasure."

Driving her small red car much too quickly, Janice sped down Forty-sixth, continuing all the way up to Lyndale, where she turned left. There was a lot Janice wanted to say, an entire diatribe. Instead, she took a deep breath and forced herself to calm down.

Finally she said, "Look, maybe we need to back up a bit. Maybe I need to get to know you better—and you me." She glanced at Kris through her dark glasses. "And maybe you need to tell me everything you know about Judge Hawkins."

"Perhaps."

Janice passed a public library on her right, the Boulevard Theatre on her left, then turned right into a small parking lot attached to a café.

Pulling into a space, she said, "Come on, let's get a cup of coffee and start over."

Not budging, Kris stared at her and replied, "Well, you're not making a very good start. If you would've asked I would've told you: I don't drink coffee."

"Then . . . then you can get some tea. Or juice. Or a pop. Shit, I don't care. They have sandwiches—you can get whatever you want. Come on, I'm buying."

"Uh-uh."

Janice closed her eyes, took a deep breath, and leaned forward in the driver's seat. "Kris, please. I'm trying."

"No, I'm not going anywhere public. In case you haven't noticed, I look like shit. I've been in jail for two nights, I haven't had a shower, and I look like a drag queen just off a pig farm. Sorry, girlfriend, I'm not going in there. This isn't about you. It's about vanity."

"Oh, shit."

Janice didn't say anything more. She nearly left the key in the ignition, thought better of it, and plucked it out. She then got out of the car, slammed the door, and walked up the side of the building, a long brick structure morphed from a hair salon into a coffee shop.

From behind, Kris hollered, "Hey, I'll take a mineral water, lemon if they got it."

Nodding as she walked, Janice felt as if her head was going to split. How the hell was she supposed to handle this? As if Kris's case weren't strange enough, this stuff about Hawkins—whatever it was—was more than a tad disturbing.

As she pulled open the door, she glanced at her watch. She had an enormous pile of work back at the office. Sure, this was a big case, but why, why, why hadn't she given Kris ten bucks and sent her packing in a cab? Given Janice's hourly fee, this was surely going to be the most expensive ride Kris would ever take. Then again, they hadn't discussed Janice's fees and just what Kris might be able to afford, if anything.

About half of the ten or fifteen tables were filled with people sipping coffee and reading newspapers or gabbing. Who were these people that could hang out like this in the middle of the day, she wondered, and why wasn't she one of them? Perplexed yet again, Janice turned to the right and went up to the glass case holding muffins and random pastries.

"What can I get you?" said the guy, a small man in his twenties with birdlike arms and legs.

Janice looked up at the menu board and said, "I'll have . . . I'll have a cappuccino."

"Short or tall?"

"Short."

"For here or to go?"

"To go."

He glanced over the countertop toward her right hand. "Do you have your own travel mug?"

"No," she said, lifting up her keys.

"Oh, okay."

Bemoaning the days of a simple cup of black coffee, she was almost loath to ask, "Can you make it with skim?"

"Ah . . . sure."

"Oh, and a lemon mineral water too."

So did she really trust Kris?

Janice usually had excellent instincts, but for some reason she was lost here. Kris Kenney could be speaking the gospel. Then again, she could be full of shit, a compulsive liar from the start. She did believe her, though, when she said she didn't kill Mark Forrest. But if Kris hadn't killed him or that cop out in California, then what the hell was going on? Why had someone reported her Olds down near the Stone Arch Bridge, and why had a yellow raincoat been found in the trunk—with blood on it, no less? Coincidences, though, always made Janice uneasy. Particularly—especially—double-coincidences.

Janice paid up and took the drinks. This was going to take time to sort out, no doubt about that. It was going to take hours of conversation with Kris and with others as well. Kris had been released from jail today, but the cops would be back, of that Janice was sure. In most eyes, to be a suspect in not one but two cop-killings was tantamount to being guilty, but if Kris really wasn't, then Janice would have to do more than merely provide reasonable doubt. No, to secure Kris's release yet another time Janice would have to do her best to locate the real killer.

Pushing open the door, Janice stepped out into the hot sun, coffee in one hand, her car keys and the bottle of mineral water in the other. She gazed up at the sky, saw less blue than before and more clouds, these ones huge, billowing things that looked like exploded marshmallows. You could always sense a storm in Minnesota, and she was sure one was going to hit, just as predicted. Oh, well, her tomatoes needed the rain, didn't they?

Looking ahead, she saw a dark blue van parked so that it blocked her car from view. As she walked on, Janice pondered whether the two of them should just sit here in the parking lot and have it out, or whether Kris and she should go back downtown to Janice's office and hash things out in a more formal environment. No, the second wouldn't work, realized Janice, because Kris wouldn't go anywhere, not until she had her shower. What a princess.

As Janice made her way around the rear of the blue van, some of her cappuccino sloshed out. She paused, licked the back of her hand. As she did so, she glanced at the rear of her Honda. No Kris, at least not that Janice could see. Must be asleep, thought Janice. Kris was probably exhausted from the stress—God only knew she should be—and had put down the back of her seat. Probably out like a light too.

A grumbling in the sky caused Janice to look up. Was the storm here already? No, most of the sky was still clear, and she took another quick sip of her drink, then moved around the rear of the Accord. Without realizing it until just about then, it struck her that she was going to have to see this one through, that she couldn't bail on Kris, not now.

"Here's your water," called Janice, coming up on the passenger side of the car. "And, yes, they had lemon."

Reaching the passenger door, however, Janice looked in. The window was up. And the seat was empty. Oh, crap. Had Kris decided to walk the rest of the way home?

Hearing the fleeting sound of shoes sliding over gravel, Janice began to turn around, saying, "Kris?"

But Janice, not suspecting, was much too slow. She caught a glimmer of a figure, someone racing up behind her. And the next instant she felt it—the brutal strike against the back of her head.

As the day fell dark and she collapsed to the ground, all she could think was, Don't spill the coffee.

But of course she did.

Chapter 38

As Rawlins and he stood just outside Dayton's department store, Todd dialed the hotel on his cellular phone.

A man's voice answered, saying, "Hotel Redmont, how may I direct your call?"

"Yes, I'd like to speak to Mr. Russ . . . Mr. Russ . . ." began Todd. "Oh, good grief. I can't believe I've forgotten his last name. He's in Room 469."

"Let me see," said the operator, as his fingers apparently flew across a keyboard. "Yes, that would be Mr. Russ Fugle."

"Exactly."

"One moment please."

Todd, however, hung up immediately, slipped his phone back into his shirt pocket, and to Rawlins said, "Russ Fugle—that's our guy."

"Let's go."

Darting around a couple of taxis, they half jogged across Seventh Street. As they neared the main entrance of the Hotel Redmont, a towering hotel not yet five years old, a doorman greeted them and pulled open the glass door.

"Thank you," said Todd.

As if they were guests, Rawlins and he immediately veered to the left, passing through the beige marble lobby and going straight to the bank of three elevators. Stepping into the brass-trimmed lift, they rose to the fourth floor. As they did so, Rawlins reached beneath his sport coat, pulled out his gun, checked it, then slipped the weapon back into his holster.

"Remember, let me do the talking," said Rawlins.

"Sure, whatever you say, butch."

Stopping at the fourth floor, the lift opened onto a long hallway void of guests and service people. Brass light fixtures lined either side of the corridor, and Todd and Rawlins wasted no time going down it and turning to the right. Room 469 was third from the end, and they approached it in complete silence.

Zeroing in, Todd watched as Rawlins went right up to the door and placed his ear against it. He stood for a long while, then, apparently unable to hear anything, pulled back and knocked. But there was no response. If he was in there, Russ Fugle didn't call back, didn't even flinch.

Noticing a band of light at the bottom of the door, Todd dropped to his knees and bent down. Spying into the room, he could tell that the curtains were open and that sunlight was flooding into the room. He saw teal carpeting, what looked like a wastebasket, perhaps a dresser, the corner of a bed. But no one quietly moving about in the room.

Rawlins knocked again and said, "Room service." He pounded harder. "Room service for Mr. Russ Fugle."

With one side of his face pressed against the carpet, Todd continued to stare beneath the door. He half expected to see the guy standing there as still as a statue. Instead, he saw nothing. Nor were there any sounds of any kind, no running shower, no blaring TV.

"Come on," said Rawlins, reaching down and nudging Todd on the shoulder. "He's not here."

Rising to his feet, Todd said, "We need to find out when he checked in and how long he plans on staying."

"Yeah, it's time to have a little talk with the hotel manager."

Chapter 39

It was a pothole that woke Janice.

Minnesota was famous for them. Winter and road repairs, those were the two seasons, or so they said, so went the perpetual joke. And so many road cavities had bloomed this past spring that the crews would be working until the first frost trying to patch them with rich, hot asphalt.

As it was, the vehicle hit a craterlike hollow, Janice was thrown slightly into the air. And her eyes opened. Opened but saw nothing, only black.

Oh, my God!

She went to scream, but something was there, tied across her mouth. She cried out anyway, her muffled pleas going nowhere, echoing only in her terrified head. Lying on her stomach, she struggled to move her hands, her arms, but realized she couldn't, for they were strapped behind her back. Nor could she move her legs, for they were bound at the ankles. Lying there on some kind of short carpeting, a tidal wave of panic swept through her, and she tried to roll over, to flop about, to twist, turn. *Jesus Christ, help! Someone!* Her heart flooded with adrenaline, and she kicked and bucked, screamed and cried out. All to no avail. Her stomach started to whirl and heave, but no. *No!* The very thought of it made her crazy, for if she vomited, that would be it, she would drown in a pool of her own fear.

Just relax, she told herself, trying to calm her gut and trying to slow her heart, which was in fact shooting along, desperately hunting for some hoped-for peaceful destination. You're alive. Yes, you are. You've been taken. Someone has kidnapped you—dear God in heaven, Kris?—and you're in some kind of car.

No, not a car.

It was a vehicle of some sort. They were moving. She could hear the road, the rolling of wheels. The rumble of a paved road gone sour. But this was much too large a space. Right. She rolled onto one side, then back on the other. She wasn't in a car. Or was she? Oh, shit. A trunk. Had she been knocked over the head, tied up, and tossed in the trunk of her Accord? Now her heart churned like a water balloon, welling and nearing explosion. Locked in a trunk and no way to holler out? No way to crawl out? She'd rather drown, her arms scrambling, legs kicking. She'd rather go down in a plane crash, smashed in the mayhem. Just not closed in. Just not boxed in. Anything but her nightmare of nightmares: buried alive.

She began to cry. The tears, though, had nowhere to roll, no way to wick themselves away. Her eyes were covered with plastic. No, tape. Sealed. And she felt the salty water puddling against her, damned in and building. That was when she turned her head. That was when she saw it. The light. Nothing direct. Just brightness. And not a little pinprick of it either. But a full swath of powerful, beautiful sunlight burning through the translucent tape.

Okay. Relax. You're not locked in a trunk. You're not boxed in some little, cramped space. This is no coffin on wheels. You're not even in your Honda. This can't be it. Your car's not nearly this big.

It was some other kind of vehicle. Again she felt the short nubs of a carpet against her cheek. So this wasn't a truck. No, the sounds from outside were muffled, which meant she was in some kind of enclosed space. The back of some sort of car? Yes. A station wagon of sorts. Moving her bound legs as one, she swung them from side to side. Then hit something metal. Probing it dumbly and blindly with her feet, she realized it was the base of a seat. That meant she wasn't in a station wagon. That could mean only one thing: This was a van. She was in the back, thrown on the floor.

While it didn't make any sense, just getting some semblance of the present reality soothed her, stilled her tears, slowed her heart, calmed her stomach. And in her typical, orderly way, she made a mental list of what she knew. She was in the back of a van. On the floor of said vehicle.

Wait a minute. Hadn't there been a dark-blue van next to her car when she'd come out of the coffee shop? Yes. But what about Kris? Where the hell was she? Behind the wheel and now driving or . . .

Okay, one stolen van. And her eyes were covered with some kind of plastic tape. Plastic packaging tape that allowed some light in. A rag or T-shirt was tied across her mouth. Her hands were strapped behind her back, most likely with tape too. And her feet as well. And the vehicle was moving, for Janice could hear the roar of the engine, sense the pocked complexion of the Minnesota road. Exactly. And even as she thought that, she felt the van slow, sway to one side. Then churn and groan as it accelerated. The speed seemed to increase. And increase. The vehicle seemed to be rising. The pavement smoothing into a steady hum.

A highway, realized Janice. They'd just sped up a ramp and had entered one of the freeways. But which? Had they merely gone south on Lyndale and proceeded onto 35W South, or had they turned another way and were headed west on 62? Or was it 94? Could they be on their way to St. Paul? Or had Janice been unconscious for hours and were they somewhere in Wisconsin or Iowa?

With no other cues—no roar of a jet from the airport, no toll of a bell from the Basilica, no sounds of bikers in the park—there was no way of telling. And, no, she thought as she twisted her wrists ever so slightly, there would be no breaking loose anyway.

If she was going to free herself, it wasn't going to be by force. No, the only way she was going to get out of this was the way she got out of everything: talk. Big talk. Big stupid, lawyerly talk. But to do that she was not only going to have to get the gag out of her mouth, she was going to have to understand what was happening. Which meant she was right back at square one: What the hell was going on? Just please, she prayed, don't let it be Kris who has done this. It can't be. Kris isn't that stupid, that desperate.

Suddenly—yes, from up front, from the dashboard—there

was a click of a radio. The next moment music began to play. Rock. Yes, Alanis Morissette.

And then a hoarse, wispy voice said, "You comfortable back there?"

Stunned, Janice didn't move. Didn't even try to curse or scream out.

"Well, don't worry. We'll be there pretty soon."

Janice couldn't tell if the voice, so nondescript, so noncommittal, was that of a man or a woman. Christopher or Kris. Or neither?

She lay completely still. She had to think. Had to figure this out before they arrived wherever they were going, because God only knew how long she'd have then.

They rounded a long, arching corner, and Janice heard a nearby thud as something shifted. What was it, a suitcase? A box? Desperate to find out, she started to roll, twisting across the back of the van. It took all of two turns before she collided not with a thing but with the soft folds of another body. Dear God, someone else was back here, and Janice flinched, blurted something through the gag. There was, however, no response. Janice nudged the person with her knees, then with her shoulders, yet she got nothing back, not a muffled plea, nor even a terrified sob. She rolled herself closer, poked at her secret sharer one more time. And again nothing, only a lifeless corpse. Finally, she moved as close as she could and blindly nudged at the other with her nose, sensing first a thin arm, next a smallish breast, then lastly a mass of short hair.

Oh, my God, silently screamed Janice, her heart beating maniacally, wasn't this in fact Kris . . . and wasn't she dead?

Chapter 40

The release of Christopher Louis Kenney shocked everyone, and the news spread not only up and down the nineteenth floor but through Government Center as fast as e-mail could carry it. No one really understood why Judge Stuart Hawkins had refused to sign the complaint against Kenney.

No one except Douglas Simms.

Disgusted, he'd left his office as soon as he'd heard, and now Simms sat in the basement level cafeteria of Government Center sipping his second large Coke. So what was he supposed to do? How in the hell was he supposed to handle this? He knew perfectly well what had taken place, both back at that fund-raiser weeks ago and again today.

Well, fuck Hawkins, thought Simms, slamming down the last bit of Coke. He sucked on the ice cubes, spit them back into the tall paper cup. Then pushing back his chair, he rose to his feet, a rush swirling through his body and a grin crossing his face. There was no way in hell he was going back to work today. Nope. And there was no way he was going back tomorrow or the day after. Letting Christopher Kenney go free today was a mistake that couldn't be made.

Wearing a cheap blue suit, he rode the escalator up one floor, then left the building. The summer air was thick, turgid even, and the temperature was climbing high, the humidity pumping up, covering Minnesota as if with a tropical blanket. Simms glanced into the sky, saw enormous clouds billowing up into the heavens.

There was a wind, sultry yet strong, and Simms knew the heat would soon break. It always did.

His heart pounding—had it really come to this?—Simms jogged across Fifth Avenue and ducked into the parking ramp. He climbed the stairs three levels and, huffing and sweating, made his way up the sloping concrete floor toward his car, a small white sedan. Taking out his keys, he unlocked the door, took off his suit coat, and tossed it in the backseat, then climbed in. A dense, suffocating cloud of heat embraced him. He gasped.

Was he really going to do this, really going to quit? Damn right. He'd wanted nothing more than to be Hawkins's campaign manager, and he'd have been perfect. But there was no way in hell he wanted anything more to do with Judge Stuart Hawkins. Not now. Not after today.

Douglas Simms revved up his car. He'd been ready to blackmail Hawkins, per se—make me your campaign manager or I might be inclined to blab about your young girlfriend—but not anymore. Allowing a murder suspect to simply walk out of here was too gross an injunction.

Nope, there was no way in hell he was going down any kind of political path with Stuart Hawkins.

Chapter 41

As they waited for the hotel elevator on the fourth floor, Todd said, "I'm not sure Janice is going to speak to me ever again. Or you, for that matter."

"She was that pissed?" asked Rawlins.

"Furious. Bradley and I were standing right outside City Hall when they came out."

A chime announced the arrival of the lift, and just as the doors eased open a man with short brown hair stepped out. Clutching a can of soda, the guy kept his head bowed as he moved quickly past them and started down the hall.

Todd followed Rawlins into the lift, but instead of hitting the button for the ground floor, he pressed the one to hold the doors open. It was only a sense, but he peered after the guy. He wasn't too tall. Not too old. Broad-shouldered. And attractive. When the stranger glanced nervously over his shoulder and their eyes met and held for a flash of a knowing second, Todd knew.

"Russ?" called Todd.

The guy took off, bolting down the corridor. Without a moment's hesitation Todd and Rawlins broke into a run as well, bursting from the elevator and running after him as fast as they could. This was him, Russ Fugle, the one they wanted, and he had, Todd knew now more than ever, some kind of truth, not just to Mark Forrest's life but also his death. And there was no way in hell Todd was going to let that truth now escape.

"Police! Stop!" bellowed Rawlins, reaching into his jacket for his gun.

Going all the faster, Russ threw aside his open can of soda and tore down the corridor to the right. By the time Todd and Rawlins rounded the corner, Russ was almost to his room, fumbling for his plastic key, trying to get it out, then desperately attempting to cram it into the lock. Terrified, he looked back as they closed in, then finally got the door unlocked, heaved it open, and darted inside.

Shit, thought Todd, he's got a gun in there.

Just as the door was slamming shut, Rawlins and Todd threw themselves against it. Under their force and weight the door exploded inward, and Russ Fugle went flying back, tumbling to the floor. Seizing the moment, Rawlins barreled in and was all over Fugle within seconds, shouting, then shoving, next dragging.

"Police!" he shouted. "Don't move!"

And before Todd knew it, Rawlins was sitting on Russ Fugle's back and pinning him facedown to the floor of his hotel room.

"Please!" begged Fugle, his face pressed into the carpet at the foot of the bed. "I didn't do it! I didn't kill Mark!"

"Then who did?" demanded Rawlins.

Coming up on the side, Todd looked at Fugle's profile, saw the thick sideburns, the dark brown hair. His eyes ran over the broad hands splayed on the floor, hands that were not only thick but had a trail of dark hair running over the back of them. And in a flash Todd knew this guy hadn't been the one.

"That's not him," said Todd. "That's not the guy I saw on the bridge."

Rawlins sat back and cursed. "Crap."

"He's right, it wasn't me!"

"Get off him, Rawlins."

"Do you have a gun?" asked Rawlins. "Or a weapon of any sort?"

"No, of course not! Nothing, I've got nothing!"

"Okay, then, just don't do anything fast," Rawlins said as he rose to his feet, gun in hand.

Russ Fugle lay there, then slowly rolled over. Shaking, he looked at Rawlins, then Todd, and next pushed himself up.

"You just sit there, right there on the end of the bed," ordered Rawlins, "and tell us what's going on."

Todd watched as Fugle did as he was told. No, this wasn't the guy in the yellow raincoat, the one who'd gunned down Forrest and taken a shot at Todd. Of that Todd was completely sure. But why was he so afraid? What did he know? Could he possibly be the guy who'd been lurking behind Rawlins's house and had fired on him?

"You were Mark Forrest's lover, weren't you?" asked Todd.

He bowed his head. "Yeah."

"And you were with him that night, weren't you?"

"Yeah."

"At the river?" asked Rawlins.

Fugle nodded, then, starting to weep, he bowed his head and covered his eyes with his left hand. "Oh, God. I've just been so afraid. You don't know what it's been like. She's been calling and calling, and—"

"Who?" demanded Rawlins. "Kris Kenney?"

"What?" said Fugle, looking up, his face washed with confusion.

It was right then that Todd understood. He'd been afraid like that, terrified to come forward because of all the truths it would force to the surface. Yes, he'd done as Russ Fugle had done. He'd been in exactly the same position as this closeted man right before him, tangled in a web of lies from which there seemed to be no escape.

Todd said, "You're married, aren't you?"

Biting his bottom lip, Fugle nodded. "Yeah . . ." He took a deep breath and motioned toward the phone. "She keeps calling. My wife—she doesn't know, doesn't have any idea."

"About Mark?" asked Todd.

"Exactly. She thinks I keep coming here on business, which is only partly true."

Not only was this guy stressed to the max, but Todd could see he was exhausted, worn out from all the lies that he'd apparently told and told well. And it was the weight of Mark Forrest's death that was proving unbearable and demanding that all the truths finally come to light.

"You know something," began Todd, "but you haven't come forward because—"

"I've got two boys! Two little boys, seven and ten!"

"Because that would mean outing yourself."

Fugle slowly nodded, then said, "I thought about leaving my wife for Mark—that's what he wanted, that's kind of what we were working toward—but now he's dead and . . . and . . ."

Rawlins gently said, "Tell us what you know."

"I went down there with Mark. To the river. I drove down there with him. He told me to wait in the car while he went to meet with you," he said, wiping his eyes and then looking up at Todd. "Then there was that storm, all the lightning and thunder and that wind. I stayed in the car through it all. But then Mark didn't come back. The rain stopped and I started to get worried about him, you know, like he might've gotten hurt in the storm. I saw someone come running off the bridge and take off, and then I got out and went down the bridge. I looked out, and there was Mark's body floating . . . floating facedown in the river . . . and . . . and you," he said, again looking at Todd, "were on the ground. I thought you were dead too. I was so scared I ran all the way back to the hotel."

"The person you saw come running off the bridge—it was him, wasn't it, the guy in the yellow raincoat?" asked Todd, sensing the truth was finally within reach.

"Yes."

Rawlins said, "What did he look like?"

"I . . . I don't know. I couldn't really see his face."

"What about his car?"

"He'd put mud on the license plates, but the rain washed part of it off. It was a rental car from Enterprise—I saw their sticker, you know, the *e* they put on the bumper. It was a white Toyota. I couldn't make out the numbers, but I did see the last three letters on the rear plates." Fugle motioned toward the desk. "I've been so afraid I'd forget it that I've been writing it over and over: *GMF*."

Yes, thought Todd. License plates up here consisted of three numbers followed by three letters. So they had half of the license plate for a white Toyota from Enterprise rental cars.

His phone began to ring. Pulling it from his pocket, he glanced at Rawlins, who was glaring at him. This might be one of the producers at the station. Or it might be something like Minnesota Public Radio asking for a donation. Then again, it very well might be Janice calling to yell at him.

Answering, he said, "Todd Mills."

"Todd! Todd, it's me, Janice! I'm in trouble and—"

Chapter 42

"I'm in trouble and—"

His deep, rich voice called, "Janice?"

"Todd!" she screamed.

Janice's captor grabbed her by the hair and yanked her back. Losing her balance, she cried out as she was pulled from the phone booth.

"Todd!"

"Janice!" he shouted as the receiver flew out of her hand.

While the tape around her ankles had been cut away and the cloth gagging her mouth ripped off, her eyes were still covered. Her hands were strapped tightly behind her back as well, and, with no way of catching herself, she fell backward, landing first on her rear, then falling on her back.

In front of her, the captor grabbed the phone, and speaking in a soft, wispy voice, said, "Listen, asshole, there's an old gas station at the Crow Island exit off Thirty-five W South. If you ever want to see your friend Janice alive again, go to the phone booth behind it. And come alone, asshole. I mean it—do as I say, or this is one dead fucking bitch." There was a moment of silence, and he laughed, saying, "Yeah, it's me, Kris."

Lying on the old pavement—yes, old, broken pavement, she thought, one tiny, sane corner of her mind making note of everything, including the bits of gravel and broken glass—Janice heard him slam down the receiver. Next came the sound of feet dashing over gravel. Finally, Janice blindly sensed her unseen abductor descending upon her.

"Everything's going perfectly," he said, his voice hoarse. "He'll be here right on schedule."

She shouted, "Why the hell did you tell him that?"

"Tell him what?"

"That you're Kris. You're not her—she's back in the van!"

"How very perceptive of you."

"Is she dead? Did you kill her?"

He laughed. "Perhaps."

"Whoever you are, please don't do this!"

"You talk too fucking much!"

"Please!" she begged, struggling to get up and perhaps, somehow, get away. "I can help you, I really can!"

"Shut up!" he yelled, slapping her on the cheek.

Janice screamed, fell back to the ground. Just as quickly, she felt his fingers digging into her arm.

"Get the fuck up!" he demanded.

"Ow!"

"Come on!"

Janice didn't so much get up as was lifted to her feet. And once yanked upright, she was shoved on. Jesus Christ, she thought, stumbling along and fearing the worst, fearing every horror story she'd ever read in the paper, seen on television, or heard in court. All the ax murders, the tortures, the vivisections whizzed through her mind. What the hell was this all about? And why in God's name wasn't anyone stopping? Why couldn't any stupid passing motorist see what was happening?

"Get in!" he demanded, pushing her forward.

Thrown ahead, she sightlessly trudged on until her shin hit the running board of the van and she fell forward, tumbling face-first through an open door. Twisting to the side at the last moment, she toppled onto the floor of the van, breaking the fall with her shoulder.

Janice pleaded, "Who are you? Please, I can make things right. I can—"

"Shut up!" he ordered.

The next instant Janice heard him charge up behind her, then felt his powerful hand as he grabbed her by the arm and flipped her over. Janice shrieked, sure that he was about to strike her. Instead, he dropped himself upon her. She bucked once, twice, then felt something jabbed into her mouth. Cloth. Some kind of rag. She screamed as loud as she could, but of course the gag did its job, corking her fear back in her body. She twisted to the side, kicked with her feet, her right foot connecting squarely with his ribs.

"You bitch!"

He punched her, his fist landing square in her gut. In a millisecond all the air seemed to explode out of every little corner of her gut, and when she breathed back in, she couldn't get her breath. Or not enough. It was as if she'd sucked the cotton gag all the way down her throat. She went to scream, but nothing came out. Panicking, her body flushing with heat, she sucked in through her nose, pulled and pulled and pulled with every muscle in her body until her nostrils shriveled up and collapsed. Desperate, she tried again, then again, her lungs tasting oxygen, killing for more. But her head felt light, her mind breezy, and it was not until a minute or two later, lying completely still on the floor of the van, that she felt as if she wouldn't pass out.

And only then did she realize that her feet were once again bound, the door to the van was shut, and the vehicle was once again driving off, bouncing and swaying down some road.

"How you doin' back there, huh?" called her mad driver.

Rocking back and forth on the floor, Janice struggled not to cry, not to burst into hysterical sobs. You can't, you can't, you can't, she chanted. Just gotta breathe. Just gotta stay alive. One minute, one moment, at a time. She turned her attention to the other body back here, that of Kris, and struggled to hear anything, even the faintest sign of life. There was, however, nothing, not a moan, not even a single breath.

"You say you're fine? Well, that's good," he laughed, "because things are gonna get real interesting now. Just you wait. It's going so perfectly, really so great. Your friend, that reporter, that Todd Mills—he's on his way. You did a good job back there, Janice. He's gonna come runnin', I'm sure of it, aren't you?"

Oh, God, thought Janice, lying there, all of her wrapped and twisted and bound in fear. Not him too. Please, not Todd.

"And, trust me, you're going to give him a really great story. I mean, a perfect one for TV. He's gonna come running, running real fast—and you know what? You know what he's gonna find?" He cackled. "Oh, this time it's going so very right. He's gonna find one very dead lawyer!"

Her eyes sealed behind the blindfold, Janice clasped her eyelids shut. In the dark of the dark, she saw it all now. Saw the movie of what was to happen, how this was to play out. Some country place. A single shot. Maybe two. All set up for Todd to discover.

Chapter 43

Like half-cooked oatmeal smeared across a tabletop, the sprawl of the Twin Cities went on and on, ruining the rolling landscape of what was once known as Black Dog but rechristened in these days of mediocrity as Burnsville. It seemed to Todd that it was taking forever to get beyond the strip malls and acres and acres of identical houses slapped up all ticky-tacky. Never before had Todd hated them so much.

Russ Fugle had been completely cooperative; they'd left him at the downtown police station so another officer could take his formal statement. From there Rawlins had wanted to take his car, his silver Taurus with the police siren that he could slap on the roof. Todd, however, had been adamant: They had to take his Cherokee. The caller had insisted Todd come alone—which Rawlins absolutely forbade—so at least Todd had to be driving his car.

"It shouldn't take them too long to get a trace on that car," said Rawlins, seated in the passenger seat.

"Yeah, but how long's that going to be?" And what good, wondered Todd as he sped southward at over eighty, would that do? "Shit, I can't believe this. It's my fault, all my fault. Janice is involved in this only because of me."

"Why? You just asked her a few things."

"Yeah, but . . ."

He just wished to hell he hadn't called her in the first place. True, after that it was her idea that someone from the queer community at large should check on Kris. And it was her idea, too, that she herself should do just that, see how Kris was doing and make sure the county wasn't going to assign her a transphobic defense attorney. In her typical caring fashion, though, Janice had done all that and more, becoming Kris Kenney's de facto lawyer. Still, Todd couldn't help but feel horribly responsible, and Janice herself had said as much.

"Okay, go through it again," said Rawlins. "Go over it word by word."

With the air-conditioning cranked on high, Todd gripped the wheel in both hands and said, "I answered the phone, and it was her."

"Right."

"She said she was in trouble, she needed me."

"And then?"

"Then . . . then I think I said her name or something." It had all happened so quickly; just what had been said? "And then she screamed my name back."

"That was it, that was all?"

Todd replayed it in his memory, then nodded and replied, "All that Janice said, anyway."

"Then Kris got on?"

"Yes. She said go to the gas station at the Crow Island exit. An old gas station. She said go there and then to the phone booth behind it. She said if I ever wanted to see Janice alive again, I should go there. And alone. She stressed that part—alone." Todd touched his brow. "Oh, God, I hope we're not making some kind of mistake by bringing you along."

"Let me handle that."

"Then I asked if it was her, Kris. I couldn't tell because the voice was kind of deep."

"Yeah, well, maybe none of us has ever heard her real voice before. I caught a glimmer of it when I was interviewing her—it was deep, kind of hoarse-sounding."

Glancing out the right side of the vehicle, Todd shook his head and said, "What the hell's going on?"

Oh, God, dear God, prayed Todd. In his mind's eyes he saw Mark Forrest. Saw his body taking the bullet. The burst of blood. Please. Please, not Janice. Not her too.

"You don't think she's already hurt Janice, do you?" demanded Todd, his foot weighing heavier than ever on the accelerator.

"Probably not, but who knows."

"This just doesn't make any sense," said Todd, pounding the steering wheel with one fist. "Why would Kris want to hurt her? Janice is her lawyer. Janice got her out of jail. It doesn't fit the other killings. The others were cops."

"Maybe Janice figured something out."

"Maybe . . ."

"One thing for sure, it's not a plea for help."

"No." And then of course the answer stared right back at Todd with grotesque clarity. "Oh, shit. I'm her witness. Kris has been setting this up—setting me up—all along. You know, feeding me the entire story. That's why I've been at all the right places at precisely all the right times." And as soon as he said it, he realized what it meant. "This is not good, not good at all. Kris called because she wants me to witness whatever she's going to do to Janice."

Like murder her, he thought.

Todd couldn't go any faster. The freeway narrowed from three to two lanes, transformed into Interstate 35, and became bloated with cars and trucks and semis. Todd swerved around a van, a tan thing packed with parents and kids and camping gear, undoubtedly a family unit returning from some northern lake. He charged past a long UPS semi. Then swerved around a red pickup. Someone leaned on the horn. Todd, after all, was going over eighty-five.

"Look at that," said Rawlins, tapping the side window.

On the right, off to the west, the blue sky and billowing clouds gave way to a black band of clouds: the cold front. Solid and ominous, it was marching their way like some gigantic starship.

Todd glanced over. "Looks like the forecasters are going to be right for once."

Yes, heavy rains. High winds. Thunderstorms and hail. A heavy mass of cold air was descending from the Canadian plains, sweeping across the Dakotas and descending upon Minnesota. Something big was going to hit, there was no doubt about that.

Something that was going to do its damnedest to bulldoze out the thick, tropical air now settled here. No doubt about it, this was primo tornado stuff.

Todd just hoped to hell they found Janice before it hit.

The urban sprawl finally gave way to corn, endless fields of green stalks as tall as a person and stretching as far as the eye could see. You could drive for days and days in almost any direction, Todd knew, and ninety percent of what you'd see in these midwestern plains would be corn, corn, corn. And the sea of green fronds didn't now simply sway this way and that in casual summer bliss. No. All of it was bent to the east in a forced bow to Mother Nature's prowess and the storm she was brewing for the area.

It was almost another fifteen miles to the Crow Island exit, and when they finally reached it Rawlins pulled out his gun and hunkered down beneath the dashboard. Using a sheet they'd brought along for this purpose, he covered himself.

Shooting down the exit ramp, Todd barreled down on a stop sign and slammed on the brakes. In a part of the country where entire regions from the Great Lakes on westward had been mapped out in a grid of vast and distinct parcels, Crow Island Road ran exactly east and west and exactly perpendicular to I-35. It wasn't much of a road of course. Two lanes. Something that now stretched in either direction from farm to farm to farm and, presumably, eventually to someplace with an island once inhabited by a tribe of that name, a tribe that had long been obliterated.

But there wasn't any gas station. Ahead and on the right was only one thing: more corn.

"Shit!" cursed Todd. "There's nothing here!"

"What?" demanded Rawlins, staying low.

He looked the other way, then said, "Hang on."

Todd stomped on the gas and, tires squealing, sped to the left, passing beneath a bridge and the interstate's ribbons of concrete. Finally, there it stood, a white hulking skeleton of a gas station, now boarded up and rusting.

"There it is!" said Todd.

"Any cars? Anyone around?"

As he drove madly toward the building, his eyes swept the area. "No, not that I can see."

A faded sign featuring a red flying horse still stood out front, but the business had long since died, the pumps long ago yanked, the windows long ago boarded over. Yet a much smaller, much newer sign posted out front pointed to the rear of the place: PHONE. Undoubtedly left active as a concession to the desolate area and this Jekyll and Hyde climate that flipped biannually from blizzard to tornado, it was a means to call for help. Just as Janice had so recently done.

Todd swooped down on the place, the rear of the Cherokee skidding as he drove off the road and around the building.

"There's the phone."

"Take it easy, take it slow," coached Rawlins, still crouched in hiding. "Any sign of anyone or anything?"

"No, nothing."

He steered a definite arc toward the booth, then slammed on the brakes. Glancing quickly around, he then threw open the door and leapt out into the hot air.

"Hello?" called Todd into the thick, heaving wind. "Janice? Anyone!"

His eyes ran over the glass booth—or what remained of it—then scanned the building. Hurrying forward, Todd saw a couple of huge, rusty barrels, a door with a padlock on it. A small boarded window. Some paper flapping, tumbling along. And behind him and just off the concrete apron of the old filling station, corn as thick as an Amazon jungle.

What the hell was supposed to happen now? Could someone be hiding in the building? Crouched in the corn?

"Janice!" he shouted as loud as he could.

He turned back to the phone booth. Was he supposed to wait for a call and further instructions? Stepping closer, he saw it flapping there. A small piece of paper. Todd tore forward.

"Don't!" shouted a huge voice behind him.

Todd froze.

Emerging from the Jeep, Rawlins said, "Don't touch anything!"

"But . . ."

Todd looked back, saw Rawlins, his gun pulled, scanning from side to side as he rushed over. Yes, of course. Fingerprints. Perhaps a shred of clothing. Footprints. Something to later prove what had already happened here today. But who cared what might be important later. Right now there was only one preeminent thing: finding Janice.

Todd took a deep breath, tried to gather his patience, and said, "Kris left something." He saw it trapped between the receiver and the hook. "A note."

Rawlins, flipping into training so thorough it was instinctual, moved quickly over, scanning the ground, the building, the phone booth. With knowing, professional eyes, he checked the small structure with the broken-glass walls. Lastly, he spun around, his eyes beating the stalks of corn. Satisfied, he slipped his gun back into his shoulder holster, then pulled a tissue from the pocket of his shirt.

Todd moved after him, but Rawlins held out his hand, saying, "Let me do this."

Todd watched as Rawlins slipped into the booth, careful not to touch what was left of the sliding door or the walls. Grasping the receiver with the tissue, he then slipped out the note, holding it gingerly between two fingers.

"What's it say?" demanded Todd.

Rawlins slipped back out, then flipped the paper open. Todd rushed to his side, seeing a mere few words and then a pattern of lines.

The note read: Come here if you want to see Janice again.

Todd's eyes fell downward, realized what the pattern was. "That's a map. That's Crow Island," he said, pointing to the most major of lines. "And there, you go up Crow Island about a mile to that road, take a left. Then a right." His heart was pounding so hard it seemed that he could hear it. "Come on!"

"Oh, God . . ." moaned Rawlins, not moving. "Oh, dear God."

"What?"

"This isn't good. Not good at all." Rawlins closed his eyes, then opened them and looked straight at Todd. "It doesn't say to go there if we want to see Janice *alive* again."

Todd realized the terrible difference, just as he realized the deep, hard pounding he was hearing wasn't his heart.

No, it was the approaching storm.

Chapter 44

The smell of rain.

Janice got a whiff of it as soon as the man slid open the door of the van, the air rich and earthy and seductive. Ozone, some said. The scent of positive ions, claimed others. Whichever, it had been one of Janice's favorite smells ever since she was a little girl, so evocative that it immediately whisked her back to her grandmother's lake house, summer camp, and a canoe trip all at once, all at the same time. Now, of course, all of those jewellike memories would be wiped out. If she somehow survived this afternoon, a small, wise part of Janice presumed the smell of impending rain would flash her back to here and now, terror on the prairie.

Her nose told her the rain was coming even before her ears, even before she heard it, the deep churning. Now listening, at first she thought the deep roar was that of a jet, a huge one, perhaps a 747, blasting and thrusting its way into the sky, one of the summer tourist junks heading toward Thunder Bay, taking the northern shortcut over polar lands to Amsterdam. But the grumbling continued like the beat of great drums. And that, Janice realized, wasn't a plane soaring into the heavens, that was the heavens about to beat down on them.

Lying there on the floor of the van next to the open door, she heard then felt him reach in and grab her by the ankles. With one quick movement—a knife?—he popped the tape off her legs. And she was free, at least somewhat so.

"Come on, your other pal back here isn't going anywhere," he said.

What did that mean, silently begged Janice, that Kris was in fact dead?

"Out—now!"

Janice felt herself pulled sideways. Then she herself swung her legs around until they dropped out the door. She sat up, perched there for a second, her hands achingly bound behind her back, her mouth stuffed with silence, her eyes wrapped tight like a package bound for a long, bumpy journey in the U.S. post. And then she stood. She thought for a second that she might fall, not because she was faint, not because of the oppressive humidity that seemed to bear down on everything, but because her feet, which had been bound so tightly just above the ankles, had gone to sleep. Hobbling, she took one shaky step, another.

"You know why you don't want to do anything stupid?" he asked. " 'Cause I got a gun. Just don't make me use it sooner than later."

She of course couldn't say anything, and with her fingertips she felt the side of the van behind her, then leaned against the vehicle. If this was it, if the end of this journey—and her life— were near, she just wanted one thing: to get rid of the fucking gag. The heat wasn't so bad. It was the humidity, the dew point, whatever. Here in the countryside that spread so wide and far, it was as if she needed gills because everything was so close, so clammy. And all she wanted was a few good, deep breaths.

Janice felt tears come to her eyes. No, you can't lose it now. Somehow, someway, there might be a chance. You gotta stay sharp. You gotta butch it up, babe. You gotta search real hard and find the bull dyke in you. Don't give up, don't let the bastard do this to you!

At first Janice didn't know what he was doing. Above the beat of approaching thunder she couldn't really tell. But she could hear him moving. She could hear the sound of material shifting this way and that. A zipper. He was, she realized, changing clothes.

And then he laughed and said, "And now for a totally new look."

Listening to him approach, Janice's body went rigid, every muscle tightening, every limb locking. Whether he was going to shove her to the ground or merely punch her again, she didn't know, but perhaps this was it. Perhaps he was simply going to execute her right up against the side of the van, gangland style.

"Oh, baby, baby," he said, sounding like the devil—and knowing and loving it too. "This is going to hurt!"

Expecting a blast of a gun or a slash of a knife, Janice bit down on the gag, her teeth clenching the folds of material as hard as if she were birthing a baby. He grabbed her by the head. She screamed, but of course next to no sound emerged. She tugged with her neck, tried to pull away, but couldn't. He grabbed at her hair. And ripped. Dear God! Her body blistered with sweat and pain. Her eyes blistered with light and tears. She stopped biting on the gag, opened her mouth in some impossible way, and emptied her lungs.

Yes, light . . .

He'd torn off the blindfold of packing tape. Torn away hair and skin, eyelash and eyebrow. But, yes, through the shrieking pain she could see light. Or more precisely, squinting, she could see black sky.

And, yes, she could see him.

Raising her sullen head, she saw some guy who was about her height. More than that, however, she couldn't really tell, for he wore not only dark old gloves, a long-sleeved plaid shirt, and blue jeans, but also a navy-blue face mask, the likes of which nearly every Minnesotan possessed for the depths of winter. Everything about him was hidden by clothing, as if it were twenty below instead of ninety-five above.

Janice took a breath, closed her eyes. Opened them again. Yes, she could see. Him. A field of corn as thick as the one she'd once gotten lost in as a child. A sagging, faded red barn with a decrepit concrete silo clinging to one end. An old farmhouse, once white, now raw with age. And sky, one half rich and blue, the other as black as a death curse. Was it, she wondered, about to start pouring any second, or was this the kind of storm that lingered for an hour or two before pouncing, a death cloud as patient as a cat caging a trapped mouse?

Telling her the answer, the thunder growled. Not one quick

rumble. No, long and deep and continuous, on and on. Janice turned, gazed past a decapitated windmill—the blades of the fan long blown away, surely by some previous storm—and saw the black sky pulsing with strobelike lightning. It would be upon them within minutes.

Janice turned and stared at the masked head, saw sweat bleeding through the wool. And thought, Die, you fucker.

He reached back into the van, picking up what he'd momentarily set aside—a gun—and said, "We're going up to the house. And nothing funny, all right?"

Janice turned, quickly glanced into the vehicle, and saw Kris's lifeless body lying on its side, her hands taped together.

"Move it!" he ordered, shoving her on.

It suddenly became clear why he'd removed her blindfold, for it would have been next to impossible to drag her through this maze of ruin. The farm was old. And long abandoned. Surely a once-thriving homestead, it had obviously been cannibalized by either hungry neighbors or corporate giants, every square inch of the prized black soil planted, and everything else—house, windmill, that leaning barn out there, silo, outbuildings too—left to die. Her feet and eyes now free but her mouth and hands still bound, Janice led the way around the van, up the rutted drive, and through a graveyard of farm life. Walking around the skeleton of an ancient combine—half collapsed in a death kneel—she passed a disc plow, a hay chopper, a seeder, all of them once mighty and hulking machinery, now all of them rusted and sinking into the fertile earth.

Surrounded by splintered and half-dead elms, the farmhouse stood on a small rise to the right, a ghostly two-story clapboard Victorian house, tall and narrow with the delicate remains of fretwork half clinging to the eaves of the steep roof. Surely once painted a proud, clean white by either the German or Scandinavian immigrants who had taken over this area like locusts, the elements had scoured it of paint. The front porch, where families had once gathered on hot summer days such as this to shell peas or drink lemonade, was a wreck of its former splendor, the vine-covered columns doing Herculean effort to hold the porch roof, which was sagging like a broken wing. Almost every window was broken, surely by neighboring farm boys. And the red-brick chimney was all but gone, truncated either by moisture or tornadoes or both.

These things end somewhere, thought Janice. And looking at the dismal house, she saw that hers was to end there. He was going to lead her in there and pose the murder as carefully as a Hollywood director. One very dead lawyer, all posed for Todd the reporter to discover. And broadcast. But why? And what did it mean, that this masked jerk was the one who'd killed Mark Forrest? That he'd been rigging things all along, even the California murder of Dave Ravell?

What Janice feared, of course, was that she would never find out.

Catching a vision of what was to come, her stomach heaved. Okay, call me vain, she thought, but I don't want to go like that, splattered all over hell. I don't want Todd to find me like that either. No, God, no! Walking through weeds, her vision became dappled with memories. Todd and her at college, struggling to date, struggling to emerge sexually. Christine, her onetime partner. And the family—Zeb, the son she had long ago given up for adoption, and his baby—she had so recently rediscovered.

"Go up to the side of the house," he ordered.

Janice looked for a path, but it was gone, long sunk beneath a sea of daylilies, all of which were now blooming orange and yellow. Certainly once a nice, cherished perennial patch, the lilies had gone mad, Janice now saw, taking over not only the path but the yard, flooding everything and encircling the house, which, like an ark, barely floated above it all. Wading through the sea of green leaves and colorful flowers, winding around a fallen elm, she glanced over, saw the remains of a bicycle, strands of green lilies poking and pushing through every spoke. And a couple of those old metal lawn chairs, the seats rusted and crumbling, shoots of yellow flowers poking through. Mosquitoes too. This was Minnesota. This was summer. It was as hot and humid as hell. And as the two of them traversed this bizarre sea, swarms of blood-hungry mosquitoes swirled up and around them. Janice ducked to the right, rubbed her cheek on her shoulder, got one off. But with her hands strapped behind her back, she could do nothing about the two or three on her forehead or the handful feasting on her neck. She squirmed and twisted, hurried her pace, realized what she was running toward, but didn't care.

A sharp noise cracked, not something dulled with distance, but something close and definitive. No question, they were going to get dumped on.

"Hurry up!" he shouted. "Go to that side door."

Emerging from the daylilies, Janice clambered up the slope and approached the house, then stopped at three wooden steps that led to the porch. Her heart thumping, she realized she was a fool to go any farther.

"Move it!"

A tornadic gust of wind whirled out of the fields and around the edge of the house, blasting them. Sweat swelling from every fiber of his wool ski mask, her captor gazed toward the death-star clouds that were descending upon them, then turned and grabbed Janice.

"Go on!" he said, jabbing her in the ribs with his gun.

Janice climbed the half-rotted steps, circled a hole in the porch floor. The screen door was half torn off, the rusty screen curled and hanging, and the main door shut.

Janice's heart gurgled into her throat and she stopped. Don't go in there. Her mind started leaping ahead, maniacally leaping from scenario to scenario. Just how was he going to do this? And how much time did she have? Was he going to kill her now, outright? Or would he wait until Todd was here?

Think!

Her hands felt numb, and she wiggled her sweaty wrists, the plastic packing tape crinkling. The noise of it flashed her back not simply to the last time she moved and had packed countless boxes of crap, but to just last month when she'd put together one very special package of gifts and silly things for Zeb and the baby in New Mexico. This shit, this tape, was stronger than hell, for sure. But it did have an Achilles' heel: As untearable and indestructible as it seemed, one little chink on the side and it ripped as easy as sandwich wrap. Sure. She hadn't been able to find her scissors when she'd fixed the package and hence had been forced to break the tape simply—and easily—with her teeth.

He shoved past her to the door, and Janice stepped back. Her bound hands collided with the rusted, torn screen, and she seized the chance, desperately trying to saw the fine metal wires against the tape. As she stood staring at him, watching as he kicked in the door, she lifted and lowered her hands behind her back. The screen, though, was much too fine and therefore much too weak, simply not strong enough to take a bite out of anything.

"Come on!"

He grabbed Janice by the arm, shoved her into the house. Stumbling across the threshold, she entered some sort of dark hall. She glanced to the left, saw a faded yellow kitchen with an old electric range—an aluminum coffeepot still perched on the back burner—then green plaid linoleum and a small wooden table with four chairs perfectly arranged around it. He pushed Janice to the right, next steered her into a living room. Her feet stirring up a lunar coating of dust, Janice quickly apprised the situation, seeing not a deserted space stripped of every and any sign of life, but a quaintly arranged—albeit grayed with dirt and spiderwebs—collection of furniture. An ancient brown davenport sat in front of one window, in front of that a coffee table replete with a large glass ashtray, then two armchairs to the side, both with tidy little doilies on the backs. But there was something even more bizarre than a well-furnished house that looked as if it hadn't been inhabited for twenty or thirty years: a tangle of vines. Her eyes quickly flashed to the broken windows, saw that the vines, like the day-lilies, had gone mad, crawling inside and climbing not only up the legs and arms of the furniture, but slithering up the walls and across the ceiling, from which they hung here and there. Even a standing lamp had been gobbled up and stood encrusted and strangled with the snakelike plant. Studying this bizarre time capsule of life on the farm, Janice surmised that someone's grandfather or grandmother—the last of a family who'd tended the land for generations—had died, and the kids, who'd surely escaped to the city, perhaps the coasts, hadn't come back for anything, not a single stick of memory, perhaps not even the funeral. They'd just put the family homestead on the market, had a lawyer handle it all, hired someone else to straighten up and dump the clothes—unless they, too, were still packed in drawers upstairs—and sold the old place. But the new owners hadn't wanted the house. No, they'd only been after the rich soil that was so capable of producing bushels and bushels and bushels of corn.

But there was nothing, Janice realized, surveying the soft, lumpy, upholstered furniture, on which to even nick the tape.

Wait.

She saw it.

Two springs.

They were poking out of the davenport, right out of the corner of it. Not a couch or a fancy city sofa, it was a true midwestern davenport, the likes of which no farm would be without, for it could be converted into a bed. After all, before the days of cars and highways, guests didn't just come for dinner and then bop on home. They stayed the night. And then there was family that came from afar for Thanksgiving. Christmas as well. And when there was a blizzard, friends and family, even strangers, stayed and stayed. Or when a barn was raised, the old auntie or widowed granny would come to help with the cooking. And this was where they slept, on this old rotting piece of furniture.

Yes, this davenport's glory days were long gone, the material around the back had long ago disintegrated, and two rusty springs had sprung out. Janice saw them and knew it was quite possibly her only chance.

"What do you think?" he snickered. "Should we get it over with now, or shall we wait some?"

Janice turned around and backed up against the davenport. Behind her she jabbed out her hands, but she missed, striking her fists against the rotted upholstery. She took blind aim again. And again missed.

"You know what? I'm hotter than hades in this fucking mask. What do you say we just get it over with? I mean, wouldn't that make you feel better too? I mean, waiting is such a pisser. Particularly waiting for death."

This time she hit it directly, piercing the plastic tape with one of the springs.

"Janice, dear, that's a pretty good place. Why don't you stay right there?"

As she stared at him, Janice went ass-crazy on the spring, jabbing her wrists on it over and over again, poking the rusty metal through the tape just as often as scraping and scratching her skin. Frantic, Janice kept at it, then worked even faster as she felt the tape weaken, as she sensed her wrists shifting loose ever so slightly. And then it happened—the tape ripped. Finding strength she never knew she had, Janice wrenched her wrists and, once and for all, ripped them apart. She shivered with hope, but stood still, holding her wrists behind her back, telling herself: not yet.

Something flashed, an atomic-white blast of light, which for a mere moment brightly lit the room. Instinctively, they turned. And the next second everything exploded.

The storm was upon them.

As if some great fan had been turned on, the wind came up, not a gust, but a solid, strong blast. The broken windows rattled, the leaves on the vines in the living room tremored. And Janice knew this was her chance.

Into her gag, she screamed.

She probably should have plotted it all out a little better. She probably should have scoped out a real weapon—the standing lamp, a chair, a piece of wood. In the moment, though, her hand formed a fist, and as he approached she swung back and walloped him as hard as she could. At first, with no idea that her hands were free, he showed no alarm. Then he realized what was transpiring.

"What the—"

Janice was a baseball dyke from the get-go. Granted, she'd never played hardball, only softball, but everyone always said it, said she had a hell of an arm, better than half the guys. And taking her best aim and using every bit of strength she could muster, she punched him as hard as she could right on the jaw.

"Fuck!" he cried out.

Janice didn't stop. As he fell back, she lunged forward, scooping up the large glass ashtray sitting on the coffee table. Bringing her arm back, she hurled it right at him, striking him square on the forehead. Blood spurted out one of the eyeholes of his mask, and Janice dove on him, grabbing him by the collar, shoving him to the side. He fell to the floor, his right hand protectively clutching the gun to his gut, his left hand groping his head.

"Christ . . ." he moaned.

Janice made a snap decision. She could probably outthrow him. But she knew she couldn't outwrestle him. If she descended on him now, he'd simply pull the gun on her and blow her apart.

Ripping the gag from her mouth, she tore out of the living room, ducking down the short hall and out the side door. She jumped over the hole in the porch floor, flew down the steps, and ran down the small ridge and into the sea of daylilies. Glancing back, she saw no sign of him. Just a minute or two, that was all she needed.

The wind came up, lightning and thunder started to pop burst after burst, and the clouds, like some great extraterrestrial creature about to blot out life, covered the sky, sucking up any sign of day. But rather than descending into blackness, a strange, terribly eerie light suffused everything, a light that was all at once both gray and green. Looking up, Janice, a native midwesterner, knew this wasn't good, not at all. Were this the city, the sirens would be blaring, screaming: Time to head to the basements.

Hoping beyond hope, Janice ran to the van and threw open the driver's door and clambered over the seat. But good fortune wasn't hers: no keys.

"Shit!" cursed Janice.

Suddenly glass shattered up at the house. Janice turned, saw a hand and a gun jab out of one of the windows.

"You won't get away!" he screamed.

There was a crack, not of lightning but of gunfire, and the next instant the van's windshield dissolved into a million spidery cracks. Ducking, she glanced back between the seats, her eyes searching for a weapon of any kind but seeing only Kris's body. There was another burst of gunfire, and the next instant a bullet tore into the far side of the van, twanging itself deep into the metal.

Now what?

Janice had no idea. The rain was starting now, fine drops whipped along by the wind. She couldn't dash down the road; he'd catch up with her. Nor could she tear to the barn; he'd pick her off, no problem. She turned around, saw the corn, lush and tall, a neon-green mass as dense as a rain forest.

Keeping low, she tore toward the field as the thunder cracked and the rain fell. She scrambled over a rusted string of barbed wire, through a weedy ditch, then dove into a narrow row of corn. Weaseling her way between the stalks, her feet scrambling over the dirt, Janice pushed and pawed her way along, no longer cursing the heat and humidity, but thanking God for the outrageously perfect growing weather that had sent the corn soaring six and seven feet tall. Using her hands and arms like machetes, she chopped her way along, slicing through the sharp fronds, a riotous vision of green stalks that blossomed and thrived all around. Janice glanced back, saw that the edge of the field, some twenty feet behind, was already invisible.

The rain was picking up, tumbling through the thick leaves, and Janice ran one hand across her face, wiping the sweaty moisture away. Something cracked. What the hell was that? Another car? The roar of rain? She heard something rustling and she froze. A deep chill ran up her spine, and she turned and focused every bit of her energy toward the farmhouse. Was he coming now? Was he diving into the cornstalks? Was he going to catch up with her so quickly?

She heard it again, and her stomach seemed to cave in. Oh, God. That was the sound of someone coming, of course. The sound of someone rushing through the corn. But it wasn't someone chasing her from the farmhouse. No, it was coming from right behind her. Scrambling in the dirt, Janice spun around. And there, squatting in the soil, was a man, his gun trained right on her.

She gasped, "Rawlins!"

His brow furrowed like the tilled soil he knelt in, Rawlins took a deep breath, lowered his gun, and asked, "Are you all right?"

She wasn't going to cry. She'd made it this far. She was going to be okay.

Taking a deep breath, Janice said, "Yeah."

Clutching her eyes shut, Janice reached to the dark soil, braced herself. Only then did she start shaking. Only then did the fear start catching up with her. Rawlins scrambled toward her, kneeling before her, wrapping his arms around her. And Janice let herself fall into him. He's a cop, he's got a gun, it's over. Turning her head to the side, she put the left side of her face against his shoulder and clutched him. Above them lightning and thunder burst and danced.

But then in the distance she heard something else—the sound of an engine. Someone was driving up the road to the farm. Oh, God, no, she thought. It can't be him.

Desperate, she pulled away from Rawlins and said, "Tell me that's not—"

"Todd," quietly said Rawlins.

Chapter 45

Just as he drove up the lane and the farmhouse came into view, Todd's phone started ringing again. Oh, no. Not another call from Kenney. Not another set of instructions. This could screw up everything Rawlins and Todd had planned.

He grabbed the slim phone from his pocket and said, "Yeah?"

"This is McNamee."

McNamee? He was the police officer they'd called to trace the rental car Russ Fugle had seen.

"Did you get something?" demanded Todd.

"Yeah, we got it."

"Who?"

"Let me speak to Rawlins."

"Rawlins isn't here."

"But—"

"Quit fucking around and tell me who rented that car! We got a kidnapping going on right now!"

McNamee hesitated another second or two, then told Todd that Enterprise did in fact have a white Toyota with the last three letters *GMF*. And the car was in fact rented on the day Mark Forrest was killed.

Hearing the name as he drove into the farmyard, Todd demanded, "What? Are you sure?"

"Of course I am."

"But . . ." Todd shook his head. "Listen, I gotta go. We need some assistance out here—now!"

He gave McNamee his location, hung up, and threw the

phone on the passenger seat. This didn't make sense, any of it, and Todd hoped just one thing—that he wasn't too late.

He pulled up behind a van, stopping just some fifteen feet behind it. He saw the shattered windshield, prayed that it had just been hailing here, prayed there'd been no bullets flying, not yet anyway. Rawlins and he had counted on one thing and one thing alone, that Todd hadn't been called to discover a murder but, like before, to witness one.

Please, prayed Todd as he slowly opened his door and got out. Please let that be the killer's signature, his modus operandi. Please let Janice still be alive.

The sky rumbled and flashed, and the rain began to increase, the drops growing to large pellets that slapped down on Todd. Surveying the scene, he took in the farmhouse, the small outbuildings, and the barn. He couldn't see Rawlins, but Todd, who'd dropped him off just before turning down the farmhouse lane, knew he was out there somewhere in the cornfields. But would their plan work? If only Todd could find them, Janice and her would-be killer, and then keep them talking long enough for Rawlins to effect all this. What other choice was there? How else could they be doing this?

Okay, he told himself, so get on with it.

He put his hands to his mouth and hollered, "Janice!"

Feeling as if he were going fishing with himself as the bait, he left the side of his Cherokee. He walked past the van, stopped when he saw a hole in the door. Running his fingers over the small but very distinct hollow, he was sure a bullet was lodged in there. He then glanced at the finely shattered windshield, which hung in place like modern art; no, that hadn't been destroyed by hail. Continuing down the rutted lane, he descended into a pool of dread. Janice was here somewhere. The question was where.

The rain started splattering down in enormous drops, and Todd wound his way through an assortment of farm machinery that looked like tanks and battle equipment abandoned after a wartime defeat. The house? Perhaps, he thought, shielding his eyes and looking up to the right. Just as easily they could be in the barn up ahead. Or one of the outbuildings? Wherever they were, though, Todd had to stay out here. Pull them out. Make them come into the open. Or so ordered Rawlins.

"I just need," Rawlins had said, "one clean shot. That's all it'll take."

A white-hot bolt shot down from the sky, spearing a nearby tree. Todd's heart seized and he leapt aside, spun around to see a towering old elm topple in front of the house. Smoking as it fell, it crashed down in near slow motion. And then the rain started gushing, falling down as hard as if some great heavenly bucket were being dumped.

Totally drenched, Todd trotted forward in the downpour, held his arms up to shield his eyes, and shouted, "Janice!"

He glanced up at the house, kept going, tromping through puddles, slopping through mud. Half jogging, he neared the barn, a medium-size structure that was no longer barn red but driftwood gray. His eyes scanned the building, ran past the silo. Could he be heading right toward some trap? Would it be better if he simply turned around and dashed back for his car?

"Janice!"

And then, quite oddly, the rain all but stopped. The wind died. A few of the clouds parted. The grayish-green light became not brighter, but greener, horribly so. Todd stopped in the farmyard, turned around. Past the barn and the silo he saw the most full and brilliant rainbow he'd ever seen, a complete arc of queerly bright and distinct colors—yellow, orange, red, blue, purple—that for just a few moments refused to be invisible. Was the storm, so fierce in threat, already over? Or was this the proverbial lull?

In one quick second Todd had his answer: the sun—and with it the rainbow—was obliterated by a black cloud. In the distance he sensed something deep and rumbling, a sound like the most enormous locomotive in the world. Shit, he thought. That wasn't any wimpy straight-line winds. Hell, no. Turning around, he stared toward the heavens and saw the anvil of a great tornadic supercell reaching out in his direction. Although he couldn't yet see the rope of any vortex probing the ground, he was fully aware of what was coming. As if to confirm it all, the wind kicked back in, not a mere gust or two, but this time a hard, definitive wind blasting from the southwest.

And then there he was.

"Don't move, asshole!" shouted the hooded man, who stood only some ten feet off to Todd's right.

Todd lowered his eyes from the heavens and was completely still. He was the bait. And the little expedition had worked perhaps a little too well, for Todd had been gobbled up quite whole.

Todd stared over, saw the gun trained on him. Think, he told himself.

"Where's Janice?" Todd shouted over the wind.

"Good fucking question," called the deep voice as the distant noise grew closer and louder.

"Is . . . is she alive?"

"Unfortunately, the lesbian lives."

Todd's mind tracked along. Of course it was him. Todd could see that now. Upon the heels of that realization came another— yes, it had been right there in one of the articles he'd read on Lexis-Nexis—and Todd clenched his eyes. Why the hell hadn't it occurred to him before? Sure, with his job he could do this, get around the country with ease.

Out of the corner of his eye he saw someone else dash behind the barn. Todd's heart jumped: Rawlins?

Concentrating on the guy in front of him, Todd asked, "You've been using me all along, haven't you?"

"Of course. Only a gay reporter would bite hold of a story like this." As the wind beat on them he ordered, "Now, do it again, call her, tell her to get her butt out of that cornfield."

"You can't prove that your brother didn't kill himself, can you, Ron?"

He hesitated in silence, then said, "I think you better shut up."

"But you can make it look like Kris Kenney's a cop killer, right?" Praying his hypothesis was right, Todd pressed on, saying, "If you can do that, then the courts are sure to rule in your favor. What do they want now, to give you a partial settlement of your brother's life-insurance policy?"

"All I know is that he's dead because of her."

"Did he have a large policy, Ron? What was it for, a million?"

"Two million, actually, and there's no way in hell I'm settling for a tenth of that." With his left hand, Ron Ravell pulled off his ski mask and said, "But you know what? You're too smart for your own good, 'cause now I'm going to have to kill you too."

Standing there as the wind gushed over and around him, Todd watched Ron level his gun on Todd's head. Okay, thought Todd, glancing ever so slightly from side to side, where the hell are you, Rawlins?

"Just tell me one thing," said Todd, desperate to stall. "Why Mark Forrest?"

"I needed a gay cop, and I read about him in some local paper."

Like some kind of angel, Kris appeared next to the silo and shouted, "Let him go!"

Twisting toward her, Ron shouted, "I didn't think you'd wake up for another week!"

"Just a continual source of amazement, aren't I? You should've done a better job of tying me up."

Looking past them both, Todd stared at the sky beyond and saw it—a towering funnel, a gray-black, twisting cone, stretching from the clouds down to earth. Less than a mile away, Todd knew one thing quite definitely: It was coming directly toward them.

Over the oncoming roar Kris said, "Ron, you've got to believe me, I didn't kill your brother! He took the gun from me and—"

With the gun trained on his chest, Kris could have killed him right then. In one single instant she could have blasted him from this world. But of course that was what she wanted least, to lose this wonderful man, and so she froze as Dave lunged at her.

"Give me that!" he shouted, ripping the weapon from her hands.

"I . . . I . . ."

He spun around, started back toward the couch, then just as quickly turned around again, now aiming the gun on Kris, and said, "I should kill you, that's what I should fucking do, just blow your head off!"

She didn't care what happened, what he did; she wanted him to understand only one thing, and she desperately said, "I love you, Dave!"

"Stop it!"

"I do, I really love—"

"Shut the fuck up!" Turning the gun on himself, he pressed the barrel to his temple and screamed, "Just shut the fuck up!"

"No!"

As she watched in terror, he clasped shut his eyes. Then his body went rigid. Dear God, she thought, he's really going to do it, he's really going to blow his brains out!

But then, just as quickly, the moment somehow miraculously passed. He took a deep breath, opened his eyes, began to lower the gun ever so slightly.

"I thought you were it, the answer, the one girl I could truly love, and—"

As he stepped backward his foot landed awkwardly on her shoes, the very ones she'd kicked off when they'd started to make love. His face flashed with surprise, he stumbled, started to fall, and then right in front of her, right as she watched, his hand tightened on the gun.

And the world exploded.

"Fuck off, you freak!" shouted Ron.

He turned the gun on Kris. Swung his arm around and pointed the pistol directly at her. But Kris, who dove back behind the silo, was quicker. And so was Rawlins, who appeared from behind a small white building, holding his pistol in both hands.

"Freeze!" shouted Rawlins. "Don't move a goddamn muscle! Just put down the gun! Do it—now!"

Ron wasn't going to be caught though, and this time he spun toward Rawlins. And fired. Frozen in horror, Todd watched Rawlins dive to the side, then roll on the muddy ground and come up on his stomach. Without hesitation, Rawlins fired twice, clipping

Ron Ravell first in the shoulder, then directly in the chest. As Ron collapsed, Rawlins leapt to his feet and charged forward.

"Rawlins!" screamed Todd over the wind.

The tornado was dancing its way through the field, swaying and sucking, a sexy, undulating tower. Todd glanced at the barn, saw shingles ripped off and blown away as easily as dry oak leaves. Something crashed beside him: corn. First one stalk, then another, a rainstorm of the Midwest's finest, sucked into the heavens and broadcast here. Rawlins and he had but one chance.

Todd rushed over and grabbed Rawlins by the arm. "Come on!"

It was right there, this enormous twisting black thing. Right there and churning directly toward them. The sound was deafening, and Todd and Rawlins grabbed onto each other and charged the other way. Todd glanced over and saw one of the small outbuildings start to disintegrate, first the shingles, then the roof, next the door and walls, all of it breaking apart and flying into the skies.

With the wind swirling all around, Todd and Rawlins practically flew to the silo. And there, leaning out of a small side steel door, were both Kris and Janice, who reached out, grabbed them. As he leapt into the base of the concrete tower, Todd looked back. The flying debris and dirt were so thick that he couldn't see the van, or his car for that matter. Instead, he stared as the old combine started to levitate, magically rising, rising, and then whirling away as easily as paper confetti. Someone shouted at him, dragged him in, and Rawlins heaved shut the door.

"Get down!" hollered Janice at the top of her lungs.

All four of them fell in a single pile against one side of the silo. With one hand Todd grabbed onto a piece of metal, some sort of winch anchored at the base, and with the other he grabbed onto someone's arm, just whose he couldn't tell. The roar of the twister dove down on them, one long deafening explosion. Todd heard wood shattering and crashing—the barn. He looked up, saw the old cap of the silo whisked away like a pop top. Rain dumped in, and there in the sky effortlessly flew beams and boards, shingles, an elm tree, the combine, and endless stalks of corn. Something long and dark whisked by—his car? Yes, that was exactly it. And as the heart of the storm barreled right down on the silo, it, too, began to break up, huge chunks of concrete breaking and flying away.

"Ah!" shrieked Kris.

Todd clutched the metal bar and clutched Kris, who clutched Rawlins, who clutched Janice, who clutched Todd. The silo went in larger and larger bits, first the top, then more and more, huge sections of the curved walls gobbled away by the hungry storm. Todd opened his mouth and screamed, hollered as loud as he could.

And then it was over.

The roar faded. The rain stopped. And they lay there, sprawled in a sloppy mess, huffing and puffing. Todd lifted his head, looked at them. Yes. Four. All four of them were there, all four of them were breathing.

"Anyone hurt?" asked Todd, pushing himself to his feet.

"I'm okay."

"Me too."

Kris nodded.

Todd clambered over to the small steel door, pushed it open, and climbed out. He could see it in the distance, the tornado plowing through field after field, dancing along. From here it appeared a thing of beauty and awe, majestic and even graceful, but Todd knew better, knew it was destined to flatten some small prairie town and squash countless lives.

Behind him he heard steps, turned and saw Janice.

"Oh, my God," he said, opening his arms. "I was so worried about you. I was so scared."

"Me too."

They embraced, clinging to each other for a long moment, and then Todd said, "If anything had happened to you . . . well, I wouldn't have been able to handle it."

"Thanks," she said, kissing him on the cheek. "But that still doesn't get you totally out of hot water. I'm still upset about you videotaping Kris in front of City Hall, you know."

"Yeah, that was dumb of me. I'm sorry."

The sun burst out, and Todd looked up. The clouds were

breaking, cracking open, revealing cottony white interiors that
rose and rose into canyons of brilliant blue sky. He turned, saw
that only about twenty-five feet of the silo was left. The barn was
completely gone, everything picked clean save for the foundation.
There was debris everywhere, boards and shingles, walls and machinery. Chunks of green stalks. The roof of the old house had
been sliced off, while the rest of the structure somehow still stood.
And the few trees that were left standing had been denuded,
picked clean of every leaf.

"Guess we're going car shopping," said Rawlins.

Todd turned. "Where is it?"

"Over there."

Rawlins pointed to the left, and there it was, Todd's Jeep
Grand Cherokee. Now only two or three feet tall, it lay on the
edge of the field, having been picked up and tumbled about, then
dropped some hundred feet from where Todd had parked it.

"Janice, I think we can consider that videotape destroyed," he
said, smiling, because, after all, he'd left it in the backseat of his
car. "Anyone see the van?"

No one did, and stepping and climbing over the debris, Todd
and Rawlins walked into the farmyard. Todd walked through a
soupy puddle, looked down the empty drive. He scanned the area,
saw the path the tornado had cut through the corn, a broad,
muddy swath sucked clean of everything and anything. So, wondered Todd, scanning the area, where was the body of Ron Ravell?

As his foot came down, he saw it—blue wool. Todd leaned
over, picked up the ski mask. For a brief, awful moment, Todd
stirred the mud with his foot. Could there be more of him down
there? No, fortunately not. He glanced toward the house. His eyes
then turned to a large tree, which had been pulled up by the roots
and pushed on its side. Next he turned his attention to a heavy old
disc plow that looked as if it, too, had been picked up and re-
arranged.

When he saw the bent limbs against the plow, Todd said,
"Over there."

Rawlins and he started jogging. They ran through the slop,
over the heavy old barn door. And there, rolled and tumbled

against the side of the plow, lay the broken body of Ron Ravell, his face turned to the side and washed clean.

Kris walked through the deep grass, then stood quite still as she stared at the dead man. "I wish Ron could have believed me. I wish he could have believed how much I cared for his brother and that I didn't hurt him."

"There's never been anything more unfair," ventured Todd, "than the judgment of others."